D1547585

Locating Woolf

Locating Woolf: The Politics of Space and Place

Edited by

Anna Snaith
King's College London

and

Michael H. Whitworth
Merton College, Oxford

First published 2007 by
PALGRAVE MACMILLAN
Houndmills, Basingstoke, Hampshire RG21 6XS and
175 Fifth Avenue, New York, N.Y. 10010
Companies and representatives throughout the world

PALGRAVE MACMILLAN is the global academic imprint of the Palgrave
Macmillan division of St. Martin's Press, LLC and of Palgrave Macmillan Ltd.
Macmillan® is a registered trademark in the United States, United Kingdom
and other countries. Palgrave is a registered trademark in the European
Union and other countries.

ISBN 13: 978–0–230–50073–0   hardback
ISBN 10: 0–230–50073–0   hardback

This book is printed on paper suitable for recycling and made from fully
managed and sustained forest sources.

A catalogue record for this book is available from the British Library.

Library of Congress Cataloging-in-Publication Data

Locating Woolf: the politics of space and place / edited by Anna Snaith and
Michael H. Whitworth.
     p. cm.
     Includes bibliographical references and index.
     ISBN-13: 978–0–230–50073–0 (hard)
     ISBN-10: 0–230–50073–0 (hard)
     1. Woolf, Virginia, 1882–1941–Settings. 2. Woolf, Virginia, 1882–1941
–Political and social views. 3. Space in literature. 4. Politics and literature
–Great Britain–History–20th century. 5. Women and literature–England
–History–20th century. 6. Feminism and literature–England–History–
20th century. 7. Modernism (Literature)–Great Britain. I. Snaith, Anna.
II. Whitworth, Michael H.

PR6045.O72Z79 2007
823'.912–dc22   2006052190

10 9   8   7   6   5   4   3   2   1
16 15 14 13 12 11 10 09 08 07

Printed and bound in Great Britain by
Antony Rowe Ltd, Chippenham and Eastbourne

Contents

List of Illustrations

Acknowledgements

Thanks are due to Paula Kennedy at Palgrave for her support of this book, and to the anonymous reader who offered invaluable comments on the manuscript. The editors would like to thank all those who offered papers for this volume. In particular, we wish to remember Ann Veronica Simon, who died in 2003 at the age of 34. Had she lived to revise it, her essay on Woolf and Baudelaire would have been a valuable contribution to the volume and to Woolf studies.

The Introduction uses parts of 'Night and Day and National Efficiency,' a paper delivered by Michael Whitworth at the Thirteenth Annual Conference on Virginia Woolf at Smith College. Michael Whitworth wishes to thank the organizers, and to acknowledge the British Academy for providing an Overseas Conference Grant. It also uses a small section of Anna Snaith's '"The Exhibition is in Ruins": Virginia Woolf and Empire' (Sixth Annual Virginia Woolf Birthday Lecture, published by the Virginia Woolf Society of Great Britain, 2005).

For permission to include in the Introduction the section from Charles Booth's Maps of London (map 6: West Central), we wish to thank the Library of the London School of Economics and Political Science. For permission to reproduce the illustrations in chapter 4, we wish to thank Gilbert White's House and the Oates Museum, Selborne, Hampshire. All reasonable attempts have been made to brace the copyright holder for Figure 1.2 (Plate 8, section III, Bartholomew's Pocket Atlas and Guide to London. Edinburgh: John Bartholomew and Son Ltd, 1922). We will be happy to rectify this at the earliest opportunity.

Notes on Contributors

Ian Blyth is an AHRC Research Fellow in the School of English, University of St Andrews, where he is working on the Cambridge University Press edition of Virginia Woolf. *Hélène Cixous: Live Theory* (with Susan Sellers) was published by Continuum in 2004. He is currently writing a book about Woolf and late eighteenth-, early nineteenth-century travel writing, as well as a sequence of poems about coastal environments and wildlife.

Kurt Koenigsberger is Associate Professor of English and Director of Composition at Case Western Reserve University in Cleveland, Ohio. His publications include *The Novel and the Menagerie: Totality, Englishness, and Empire* and essays on William Hazlitt, Henry James, Arnold Bennett, and Virginia Woolf, and he has edited a collection of essays titled *Globalization and the Image* (a special double issue of *Genre*). He currently serves as the Associate Director of the Society for Critical Exchange.

Sei Kosugi gained her MA in English Literature at the Kobe College, Japan. She is currently Associate Professor at the Graduate School of Language and Culture, Osaka University. Her research interests are postcolonial literatures, the indigenous and immigrant literature/culture/language education in the South Pacific countries, and an interdisciplinary study of British culture (psychiatry, literature, natural history, and amateur drama) from the late Victorian era to the twentieth century. She has published several articles on Woolf, indigenous literatures and language education in Oceania and contributed to *Contemporary Postcolonial Literatures* (ed. S. Kimura, 2004). She is now teaching Maori at the Graduate School at Osaka University.

Jane Lewty is currently Assistant Professor of Twentieth Century British Literature in the Department of English, University of Northern Iowa. She recently completed a postdoctoral fellowship at University College London. Her publications include articles on the social history of broadcasting, James Joyce, and electric voice phenomenon. At present, she is working on a monograph about radio and modernist literature. She is also co-editing a volume, *Broadcasting Modernism*, which will compare the artistic response to wireless in Britain and the USA.

A graduate of University College Dublin and the University of Kent, **Suzanne Lynch** has recently completed a doctoral thesis on Virginia Woolf and Englishness at the University of Cambridge under the supervision of Gillian Beer and Trudi Tate. She also works as a freelance journalist, and has written on a variety of arts topics for the *Irish Times*.

Leena Kore Schröder gained her PhD in English at the University of London, following undergraduate and Master's studies in English at the University of Toronto, Canada. She has been a lecturer in the English departments at the Universities of Newcastle and Aberdeen, and is currently Lecturer in Twentieth-Century Literature at the University of Nottingham. She has published widely on Virginia Woolf, as well as articles on John Betjeman and Herbert Read, and is completing a book on Woolf entitled *The Lamp in the Spine: Virginia Woolf and the Corporeal Subject*. Her next project is an interdisciplinary study of Betjeman.

Nobuyoshi Ota is Associate Professor in English at Tokyo Gakugei University in Japan. His main research interests are in cultural studies and postcolonial theory. He has published articles on D.H. Lawrence, Virginia Woolf and Ernest Hemingway. He is author of 'Generations, Legacies, and Imperialisms: The Greco-Turkish War and *Jacob's Room*' in *Across the Generations: Selected Papers from the Twelfth Annual Virginia Woolf Conference* (2003); and 'Empire, the Pacific, and Lawrence's Leadership Novels' in *D.H. Lawrence: Literature, History, Culture* (2005). He is at present working on cultural representations of Anglo-Saxonism in modernist writing.

Linden Peach is Professor and Dean of the School of Arts and Social Sciences at Northumbria University. He has previously held chairs in modern literature at Loughborough University and the University of Gloucestershire. His most recent publications include *Masquerade, Crime and Fiction: Criminal Deceptions* (2006), *The Contemporary Irish Novel: Critical Readings* (2003), *Virginia Woolf* (2000), *Toni Morrison* (2000) and *Angela Carter* (1998).

Tracy Seeley teaches Victorian and Twentieth Century British Literature and nonfiction creative writing at the University of San Francisco. She has published on Dinah Mulock, Joseph Conrad, Virginia Woolf, Rebecca West and Alice Meynell. She is currently writing a creative nonfiction book about Kansas, where she grew up.

Anna Snaith is a Lecturer in English at King's College London. She is the author of *Virginia Woolf: Public and Private Negotiations* (2000), and the editor of *Palgrave Advances in Virginia Woolf Studies*. She is currently working on a book entitled 'Colonial Modernism: Women Writing London 1900–1945' and editing *The Years* for the Cambridge Edition of Virginia Woolf.

Helen Southworth is Assistant Professor of Literature in the Robert D. Clark Honors College at the University of Oregon. Her articles have appeared in *Tulsa Studies in Women's Literature*, *Journal of Modern Literature* and *Woolf Studies Annual*. She is author of *The Intersecting Realities and Fictions of Virginia Woolf and Colette* (Ohio State University Press 2004) and co-editor, with Elisa Sparks, of *Woolf and the Art of Exploration: Selected Papers from the Fifteenth International Conference on Virginia Woolf* (forthcoming).

Michael Whitworth is Lecturer in the English Faculty at the University of Oxford and a Tutorial Fellow of Merton College. He taught at the University of Wales, Bangor from 1995 to 2005, where he organized 'Voyages Out, Voyages Home', the Eleventh Annual Conference on Virginia Woolf, in 2001. He is the author of *Einstein's Wake: Relativity, Metaphor, and Modernist Literature* (2001) and *Virginia Woolf* (2005), and editor of *Modernism* (2007). He is currently working on science, poetry, and intellectual specialization, and editing *Night and Day* for the Cambridge Edition of Virginia Woolf.

List of Abbreviations

BA   *Between the Acts*, ed. F. Kermode (1992)

CDB   *The Captain's Death Bed* (London: Hogarth, 1950).

CE   *Collected Essays*, ed. L. Woolf, 4 vols, (London: Hogarth, 1966–67).

CSF   *The Complete Shorter Fiction*, ed. S. Dick, revised edition, (London: Hogarth, 1989).

D   *The Diary of Virginia Woolf*, ed. A. O. Bell and A. McNeillie, 5 vols, (London: Hogarth, 1977–84).

DM   *The Death of the Moth* (London: Hogarth, 1942).

E   *Essays of Virginia Woolf*, ed. A. McNeillie, 4 vols. to date, (London: Hogarth, 1996 onwards).

F   *Flush*, ed. K. Flint (1998)

JR   *Jacob's Room*, ed. K. Flint (1992)

L   *The Letters of Virginia Woolf*, ed. N. Nicolson and J. Trautmann Banks, 6 vols (London: Hogarth, 1975–80).

LS   *The London Scene* (London: Snowbooks, 2004).

MB   *Moments of Being*. Parenthetic dates differentiate the 1st edition (London: Chatto and Windus 1976) and the 2nd edition (London: Hogarth, 1985).

MD   *Mrs Dalloway*, ed. D. Bradshaw (2000)

MW   *The Mark on the Wall and Other Short Fiction*, ed. D. Bradshaw (2001)

ND   *Night and Day*, ed. S. Raitt (1992)

O   *Orlando*, ed. R. Bowlby (1992)

PA   *A Passionate Apprentice*, ed. M. A. Leaska (London: Hogarth, 1990).

RF   *Roger Fry*. 1941 (London: Hogarth, 1991).

ROO *A Room of One's Own*, in *A Room of One's Own and Three Guineas*, ed. M. Shiach (1992)

TG   *Three Guineas* in *A Room of One's Own and Three Guineas*, ed. M. Shiach (1992)

TL   *To the Lighthouse*, ed. M. Drabble (1992)

VO   *The Voyage Out*, ed. L. Sage (1992)

W   *The Waves*, ed. G. Beer (1992)

Y   *The Years*, ed. H. Lee (1992)

1
Introduction: Approaches to Space and Place in Woolf

Anna Snaith and Michael H. Whitworth

'Locating' Woolf is not an easy task. Telling the stories of the many spaces and places she inhabited is a project that has long concerned readers and critics of her work. The biography of Woolf's homes in London and Sussex, for example, is a complex one with its own rhythms and significances. It is, however, her imaginative travels that concern us here, or rather the interrelationships she creates between real and imagined spaces. Woolf's fictional and non-fictional writing is consistently concerned with the politics of spaces: national spaces, civic spaces, private spaces, or the textual spaces of the writer/printer. The psychology of space resonates through her autobiographical writing, from the claustrophobic, Victorian rooms of Hyde Park Gate, heavy with tangled emotions, to the airy, liberating rooms of 46 Gordon Square, Bloomsbury. While private, domestic space, the woman's room, is at the hub of her feminist politics, it is from this room that she became one of the key writers of urban modernity, particularly in its feminist articulation. London spaces were endlessly fascinating to Woolf; her novels act as an encyclopedia of the city's streets and landmarks. Always attuned to the changing uses and signification of urban spaces, her writing both reveals and creates the layered histories of spaces. *Flânerie*, as a literal and a metaphorical pursuit, was an essential fuel for her writing. *Mrs Dalloway* is constituted through a series of London walks, and as Michel de Certeau writes, 'the motions of walking are spatial creations. They link sites one to another' (de Certeau, *Reader* 105). The journeys of Clarissa, Elizabeth and Richard Dalloway, and Peter Walsh, like the chimes of Big Ben, both create networks of communal urban space and emphasize the subjectivity of spatial constructions. According to de Certeau, 'traces of a journey lose what existed' (*Reader* 106); Woolf's representations of urban perambulations highlight not only the ephemerality of time, but also space.

The question of women's relationship to the city, particularly its public spaces, is central to her spatial politics. The bus journeys taken by her female characters – Elizabeth along the Strand in *Mrs Dalloway* or Eleanor along the Bayswater Road in *The Years*, for example – are complex and dense portraits of the sexual dynamics of urban movement and interaction. Furthermore, the debates in feminist cultural theory about the possibility of the *flâneuse* are anticipated in all their variety in Woolf's novels (Wolff, Elizabeth Wilson, Parsons). Indeed, the centrality of spatial politics to Woolf's feminism has not been adequately addressed; an issue this volume will begin to rectify. Tracy Seeley's innovative reading of the much-discussed *A Room of One's Own* links narrative and physical space. The narrator, meandering her way through the essay, uses, not the tropes of classical logic, but a tropics of evasion and digression. As so many of the contributors to this book argue, alternative formal aesthetics mirror Woolf's unsettling of fixed spatial formations. In *Between the Acts*, too, as Helen Southworth argues, the unity of physical spaces and the continuity of the narrative are constantly being interrupted. The space of the novel is characterized by 'thresholds' and by 'dips and hollows', its characters dither and swither, and the discursive space of the novel relocates background and foreground, reordering the conventional spaces of gender difference.

From questions of women's relationship to national space in *Three Guineas*, to intellectual space in *A Room of One's Own*, to artistic space in *To The Lighthouse*, it was through discourses of space that Woolf articulated the exclusions and boundaries that regulated women's bodies and minds. Images of exclusive spaces and the dangers of being locked in as well as out abound in Woolf's writing, as Leslie Hankins has shown in relation to the artist, the outsider and bourgeois spaces such as Bloomsbury squares (Hankins, 'Virginia Woolf and Walter Benjamin'). Political subversion is often figured, for Woolf, in spatial terms through the figure of the trespasser.

Woolf's novels open out into global space. They are full of journeys and voyages: Rachel Vinrace to South America, Orlando to Constantinople, Jacob Flanders to Greece, North Pargiter to Africa, Peter Walsh to India. These travels serve to implicate her characters in larger cultural and imperial networks and underline Woolf's relational conception of space. Woolf often uses geographical interrelations, such as Wimpole Street and Whitechapel in *Flush* or the Thames and the Amazon in *The Voyage Out*, to speak for more abstract economic or imperial relationships. The geographer Doreen Massey has more recently articulated such ideas: 'we need to conceptualize space as constructed out of interrelations, as the simultaneous coexistence of social interrelations and interactions at all spatial scales, from the most local level to the most global' (Massey *Space, Place and Gender*, 80). Kathy Phillips, in *Virginia Woolf Against Empire*, has reminded us that questions of imperial space were foremost in Woolf's mind, particularly when she was writing about the heart of empire. Two contributors to this volume, Ian Blyth and Suzanne Lynch, significantly advance work on Woolf and imperial space. Blyth traces Woolf's reading of Richard Hakluyt, arguing that his *Principal Navigations, Voyages, Traffiques and Discoveries of the English Nation* (1589) influenced not only her understanding of colonial and national space, but specifically her imaginative geography in *Orlando*. Lynch, on the other hand, considers Woolf's relationship to Ireland's post/colonial spaces; her visit in 1934 and the imagined national community represented in *The Years*.

In *Mappings: Feminism and the Cultural Geographies of Encounter*, Susan Stanford Friedman calls for 'geopolitical literacy', namely readings which are as attuned to spatial contexts as they are to historical ones, but which also think beyond the boundaries of empire, as Nobuyoshi Ota does in his essay in this volume. Woolf's interest in the spatial formations created by new technologies, such as the telephone, and their facilitation of global capitalism is exactly what Ota is concerned with in his reading of China's position in *The Waves*. Leena Kore Schröder's chapter contributes to this debate through an insightful examination of the spatial and cultural implications of motor-car travel on Woolf's life and writing. She argues that not only did the ownership of a car alter Woolf's perception of travel both in Britain and abroad, but that car travel and its cultural politics informed more generally her ideas about embodiment in time and space. Jane Lewty's essay explores the ways that the new spacetime enjoyed by Woolf as a radio listener could be both imaginatively stimulating and oppressive.

As Andrew Thacker has argued, in a period of mass migrations and new modes of transport, 'modernist writing can be located only within the movements between and across multiple sorts of space' (Thacker 8), and Woolf, in particular, constantly traversed the borders between outer and inner space, embracing a modern, dynamic self which could unsettle fixed power hierarchies. Kurt Koenigsberger, in his reading of Woolf's neglected anti-imperialist essay 'Thunder at Wembley', links the totalizing realism of the Empire Exhibition to the critique of realism in her contemporaneous essay 'Mr Bennett and Mrs Brown'. The storm at Wembley, which disrupts the exhibition and symbolizes the failure of the exhibition's imperial, spatial control, parallels the crashing explosion of realist fiction by modernist aesthetics. Linden Peach, too, focusing on the links between Woolf and the artist Walter Sickert, argues that Sickert's concern with domestic interiors, specifically as related to poverty and prostitution, influenced what he terms Woolf's 'modernist realism': particularly the socioeconomic materiality of her 1930s fiction. In *The Years*, he argues, the relationship between people and the rooms and spaces that they occupy is a means by which to explore their interior life. The relationship between the material and the psychological is a thread which links the essays collected in this volume, hardly surprising given that relationship's centrality to Woolf's conception of space.

Surprisingly, given the prevalence of spatial concerns in Woolf's work, this is the first book-length study of Woolf and place, and it emerges out of a growing critical interest in geography and modernism, in turn the result of the primacy of spatiality in emerging scholarship on modernism and empire (Booth and Rigby, Coroneos, Thacker, Parsons). While Woolf has long been placed in the context of urban modernity, we want to consider a wider range of spatial formations: broadcasting space, geopolitical space, rural space, imperial space. The ten essays in this volume, written by an international range of Woolf scholars, all connect her writing to carefully researched historical and cultural moments. Much of the work is interdisciplinary, situating Woolf in the context of natural history (Kosugi), art history (Peach) and new technologies (Lewty). Several essays (Koenigsberger, Lynch, Blyth) contribute to perhaps the fastest growing area of Woolf Studies, namely postcolonial approaches, pointing to the inseparability of Woolf's thinking on national and metropolitan space with imperial networks. The essays provide new approaches to familiar texts (Seeley, Blyth, Ota, Lynch), but they also (re-)familiarize readers with lesser-known works (Koenigsberger, Peach, Kosugi, Kore Schröder). The broad contention of this volume is that Woolf anticipates what has come to be called postmodern geography not only by combining a materialist and a discursive understanding of space, but also implying the inseparability of 'real' and imagined spaces. Just as, to quote Edward Soja, 'social space folds into mental space', Woolf's emphasis on the spaces of lived experience does not mean that those spaces are not understood in terms of changing social and political dynamics (Soja *Postmodern Geographies*, 125). The use of the terms 'space' and 'place' in the title of this volume at once evokes distinctions between abstract, conceptual space and locatable, material places, and simultaneously complicates that split. But although the term 'place' may traditionally connote belonging and rooted identity (space opens outwards while the localism of place turns inward), Woolf herself would be the first to foreground the discursive construction of, for example, the family home. As Gillian Rose has argued, the dichotomy between real and non-real space has historically been gendered, as well as highly unstable. Woolf's writings on space negotiate the complex interrelationship between the bodies that inhabit space and the symbolic meanings that govern and regulate that habitation. Space is no longer static, neutral and objectified. Like much recent cultural theory, Woolf's work is full of spatial metaphors, but she is attuned to the literal trespasses, conquests or boundaries which can be forgotten when the 'spatial is metaphorically everywhere but oft-times nowhere' (Jacobs 3).

The recovery of Woolf's interest in space has been slow. Though early reviewers and critics had many sophisticated ideas of space available to them, none were fully exploited. In mathematics and philosophy, concepts of space had developed considerably through the nineteenth century, with analytical geometry questioning the common-sense assumption that physical space must necessarily be Euclidean and continuous. W. K. Clifford's important essay on the subject was edited by Leslie Stephen as part of a posthumous collection. Henri Poincaré's 'Non-Euclidean Geometries' and 'Space and Geometry' were translated into English and widely known (Poincaré 35–50, 51–71). Henri Bergson's recognition that our conceptualization of time involved a mental spatialization further drew attention to the existence of space not as a medium, but as a conceptual construct. The interest of physicists in electromagnetic fields and radioactive phenomena, and of epistemologists in processes of perception, led to an awareness that classical ideas of location were misleading. Material objects were confluences of material causes; they were known only by their divergent effects. As Bertrand Russell put it, 'matter' is 'a convenient formula for describing what happens where it isn't' (Russell 165).

While ideas developed by the generation immediately preceding Woolf's undoubtedly laid the foundations for the interrogation of space in the humanities and social sciences, the insights of contemporary reviewers were conceptually unsophisticated. The majority were, in any case, more concerned with her experiments with the fictional medium and her depiction of character than with her attitude to the city or to space. However, as exceptions to that broad picture, some interesting remarks emerge. Several reviewers of *Jacob's Room* remarked

on Woolf's ability to capture the atmosphere of particular *places*.
Rebecca West compared Woolf's sketches of London in *Jacob's Room* to
those of an early nineteenth-century lithographer, and her point of reference makes Woolf into a realist, capturing the essence of place: she
can convey 'how Rotten Row looks on a sweet afternoon' and 'how
the leather curtain flaps at the door of St Paul's' (in Majumdar and
McLaurin 102). More interestingly, West singles out the scene of
the 'army' of commuters crossing Waterloo Bridge in the morning
(*JR* 153–4). The scene appealed to several other contemporary critics
(Gould and Bell, in Majumdar and McLaurin 106, 147). While in one
sense it concerns a place, and in West's account is praised again for
capturing the distinctive qualities of the commuters, the scene also
depicts a practice productive of space – commuting – and the production of the bridge as a space of movement; it has nothing to say about
the bridge as a physical structure. While many reviewers explicitly
praised Woolf's depiction of place, the terms of their praise drew attention to London as a space of movements.

While working on *Mrs Dalloway*, Woolf wrote to Jacques Raverat,
exploring the difficulty of capturing a sense of space in the medium of
prose (*L* 3: 135–6). Following his death, Gwen Raverat, his widow,
responded positively to the novel: 'it's like a ballet [...] All the movements in different directions both in time and in space' (Pryor 174).
Reviewers without the benefit of authorial contact also recognized the
novel's dynamism. Gerald Bullett praised the 'curious sensation' evoked
by *Mrs Dalloway*: 'the sensation of seeing and feeling the very stream of
life, the undeviating tide of time, flowing luminously by, with all the
material phenomena, streets and stars, bicycles and human bodies,
floating like straws upon its surface' (Bullett in Majumdar and
McLaurin 163–4). Bullett's view is easily assimilated to the dominant
view of Woolf as an innovator in the 'stream of consciousness'
method, but it is worth noting that the visible indices of this stream
exist in the material space of London.

Richard Hughes's remarks on her fidelity in *Mrs Dalloway* are worthy
of more detailed consideration, because they touch on some of the
paradoxes involved in the literary representation of place and space. In
Mrs Dalloway, he wrote:

> the visible world exists with a brilliance, a luminous clarity. In par-
> ticular, it is London: to the reader, London is made, for the first time
> [...] to exist. It emerges, shining like a crystal, out of the fog in
> which all the merely material universe is ordinarily enveloped in his

mind: it emerges, and stays. The present writer has 'known' London all his life: but Mrs Woolf's evocation of it is of a very different quality from his own memories [...] To Mrs Woolf London exists, and to Mrs Woolf's readers anywhere and at any time London will exist with a reality it can never have for those who merely live there. (Hughes, in Majumdar and McLaurin 158)

Though Hughes appears to be praising Woolf for her depiction of place, much as other critics had done, the terms of his praise detach her simulacrum from the real, inverting the conventional relation between lived knowledge and its literary counterpart. His comments raise questions about the knowability of place, and literature's relation to that knowledge. They also raise questions about who Woolf is writing for.

In general terms, the recovery of Woolf's interest in space was stimulated by the rediscovery of space as a category in the social sciences and cultural studies, following the work of Lefebvre, de Certeau, Harvey, Massey, and Soja, and by the parallel rise of postcolonial studies. Solomon's 1989 essay on *A Room of One's Own* and *Three Guineas* explicitly acknowledges de Certeau. An older phenomenological tradition, deriving from Gaston Bachelard's *The Poetics of Space* (1964), has continued to cross-pollinate such work, as may be seen, for example, in Seeley's 1992 essay. While Bachelard's example has provided a valuable starting point for many critics, it has led to an overemphasis on interior spaces and a corresponding neglect of public spaces; moreover, it has served to confirm some critics in an ahistorical approach. Raymond Williams's work, particularly *The Country and the City* (1973), has also been an important influence and a valuable corrective to Bachelard. Whereas Allen McLaurin's discussion of space in 1973 approached the topic in entirely aesthetic terms, by Jeremy Hawthorn's 1975 study of *Mrs Dalloway*, the terms of debate had become socio-historical (Hawthorn 64–79). The increasing centrality of Baudelaire and the idea of the *flâneur* to theorizations of modernism posed a challenge to feminist thinkers, and therefore to critics of Woolf: was the *flâneur* a gender-specific figure? Was the *flâneuse* an impossibility? The question, first posed by Janet Wolff in 1985, was taken up by a series of writers in what has been termed 'the great *flâneur* debate' (Thacker 82). In the same year, Susan M. Squier's influential work in *Virginia Woolf and London* drew further attention to Woolf's use of the urban to represent the power dynamics of gender relations. Squier also focused attention on lesser-known 'city' texts such as *Flush* and the *London Scene* essays. More recently, Thacker has discussed Woolf's representations of movement, both urban and rural, in terms of the fusion of internal and external space, and in an incisive two-part essay, Jeanette McVicker has returned to the *London Scene* essays.

One of Woolf's earliest essays, 'Literary Geography' (1905), draws attention to another distinct critical tradition, addressed to a popular audience, which seeks to retrace the author's steps or those of her characters. Underlying it is the quasi-religious idea that the author's presence has sanctified particular locations. As Woolf remarked of the 'Pilgrimage' series, the less sophisticated reader would find it imaginatively stimulating to know 'that Thackeray rang this very doorbell or that Dickens shaved behind that identical window' (*E* 1: 32). Woolf herself has been the subject of several such works, the earliest being Jean Moorcroft Wilson's 1987 book on Woolf and London; later works include pamphlets on Rodmell (McQueeney) and St Ives (Dell), a glossily illustrated book on St Ives (Dell and Whybrow), and a study of Woolf's holiday houses (Curtis). There is, as Woolf acknowledged, a more scholarly side to such endeavours, and some works have subordinated the study of places to the study of other issues: for example, in Rudikoff's case, social class. However, typically this genre, though often embodying careful scholarship, rests on flawed premises. Not only does the genre fetishize authorial presence, but it very often assumes a static conception of place, as distinct from the idea of space as something produced through social practice. It is positivistic, and gives little role to the mediating effects of representational conventions. While it is alive to historical change, it emphasizes continuities between the past and the present, rather than recovering lost systems of meaning. Some of the practices of this critical approach – even the simplest, that of visiting a place – can yield valuable and surprising results, but they need to be undertaken with circumspection.

In line with Woolf's own attention to material bodies, in the remainder of this introduction we want to offer readings of three London spaces in Woolf's writing. As each of the chapters in this volume demonstrates, the complexity of Woolf's writings on space demands specificity. The critic can only go so far before the subject requires particularity; the three spaces we have chosen to explore more closely will lead us quickly to larger questions of national, imperial and gendered space. The space of Kingsway in *Night and Day* typifies Woolf's focus on the shifting histories of places, the use of spatial metaphors in her writing, and the city's knowability. Peter Walsh's walk in *Mrs Dalloway* raises not only questions of patriarchal ownership of urban space, but also of the extent to which space can be written and rewritten by literary activity. Woolf's essay on the Docks in *The London Scene* introduces the question of capital, class, and imperial politics in the production of space. These three readings exemplify not only the approaches to Woolf's spatial politics employed by the contributors to this volume – socio-historical, aesthetic and global – but also their interaction in her writing.

A city of flows: Kingsway in *Night and Day*

At the climactic point of *Night and Day*, Katharine Hilbery goes to look for Ralph Denham at his place of work in Lincoln's Inn Fields. Failing to find him, she leaves the Fields and walks west towards Kingsway:

> The great torrent of vans and carts was sweeping down Kingsway; pedestrians were streaming in two currents along the pavements. She stood fascinated at the corner. The deep roar filled her ears; the changing tumult had the inexpressible fascination of varied life pouring ceaselessly with a purpose which, as she looked, seemed to her, somehow, the normal purpose for which life was framed; its complete indifference to the individuals, whom it swallowed up and rolled onwards, filled her with at least a temporary exaltation. The blend of daylight and of lamplight made her an invisible spectator, just as it gave the people who passed her a semi-transparent quality, and left the faces pale ivory ovals in which the eyes alone were dark. (*ND* 462)

Jean Moorcroft Wilson notes that the setting is used 'to reflect [Katharine's] feelings', and follows the text's cue in contrasting Kingsway with Chelsea (J. M. Wilson 127); however, she does not remark upon the historic depths of the location, nor explore the consequent suggestion of ambivalence in Katharine. Kingsway was a comparatively recent thoroughfare, opened in October 1905 following a major project of slum clearance; the fact is not explicit in the text, but the knowledge was available to Woolf's readership in 1919. By recovering that knowledge, one can identify resonances between the history of the location and a central theme of the novel, the individual's relation to larger social groups.

Kingsway provides a north–south connection between two busy east–west streets, Holborn to the north and the Strand to the south;

beyond its northern end, it is connected by Southampton Row to another east–west thoroughfare, the Euston Road. The need for a north–south route had long been recognized, but not until the creation of London County Council could practical advances be made. The 'Holborn–Strand project' was approved in 1899, the name 'Kingsway' devised in 1903, and the street was opened to traffic on 18 October 1905. It combined a ground-level route for road vehicles, a spur of the underground railway, and an underground tramway connecting the northern lines with those running along the Embankment.

Kingsway was 'a multi-purpose, multi-faceted scheme', and this, coupled with its 'long period of gestation', meant that different interest groups attached different justifications to it (Schubert and Sutcliffe 116). Some of the interested parties were concerned with hygiene, morality, and criminality in the slum areas, while others were concerned with traffic flows. Others still were concerned not with movement, but with the construction of buildings that would embody London's status as an imperial capital (Schneer 19–28).

The maze of streets north of the Strand and west of Lincoln's Inn Fields had been a notorious slum since at least the mid-nineteenth century. In Charles Booth's maps in *Life and Labour of the People in London*, this area is predominantly black and blue, representing the lowest, 'vicious' and 'semi-criminal' class, and the one above ('very poor', 'chronic want'). The young Virginia Stephen would have known of it, as, in the late 1890s, her step-brother George Duckworth assisted in a revision of Booth's original survey. As well as being a slum, the area had a reputation for immorality: Holywell Street, lined with stationers and bookshops, also specialized in pornographic literature (Gordon 232; Sims 334). Duckworth noted a 'second class bookseller' and 'chemists of doubtful reputation' (Duckworth 129). Some of those who wished to see the area redeveloped were concerned for the health of the local inhabitants, while others were concerned for the middle classes of neighbouring districts who might suffer the effects of their criminality and ill-health. In the aftermath of the Boer War, the discourse of 'national efficiency' meant that a concern for the health of slum-dwellers was often presented as a concern with the health of the 'Imperial race' (Masterman 25). The commonly accepted solution was to demolish and rebuild, destroying not only individual buildings but the street pattern of the district.

Those who saw the Holborn–Strand project as an opportunity to create 'imperial symbols' often took Paris and Berlin as their reference points (Schubert and Sutcliffe 116; Arnold-Forster 266). Many of the

Holborn–Strand proposals echoed the boulevards created in Paris by Georges-Eugène Haussmann. Though some commentators felt the scheme brought 'beauty and civic dignity' to London, others were opposed. On one hand, a xenophobic lobby felt there was something fundamentally alien about the boulevard as a form. Others, such as the Labour MP John Burns, objected to the priority granted to prestige projects such as 'a few swell boulevards' at the expense of providing sanitation for all (Burns qtd. Grubb 122). Nor had slum clearance projects won the trust of slum residents. Duckworth records one plaintive voice: 'Don't pull down our houses guv'nor, before building us up others to go into' (Duckworth 131).

For socialists and New Liberals, the project was symbolic not for its architectural detail, but on account of the processes which made it possible. For some commentators, the completion of Kingsway marked a triumph for the principle of 'betterment' charges. Socialist and New Liberal commentators argued that state-funded infrastructural work such as gas pipelines or drainage brought disproportionate benefits to landowners, who received an 'unearned increment' on their property values. In the case of the Holborn–Strand scheme, the London County Council had successfully argued that it be allowed to levy a betterment charge on the owners of properties in the district. While in practice the sum raised a tiny fraction of the cost of the project, the principle was an important one. In the Budget of 1909, Lloyd George proposed a taxation of land values, a topic which, in *Night and Day*, is of common interest to Ralph and Mary (*ND* 82). Lloyd George justified the tax by arguing that the increase in land values in the past decades had been due not to the efforts of the landowners, but 'to the energy and enterprise of the community'.[1] Kingsway could also be taken to represent the success of centralized planning. In 1917, one commentator in the *New Statesman* had taken the ad hoc reconstruction of London after the Great Fire of 1666 to typify a failure of planning, the effects of which were felt in present-day congestion and imperfect street-widening schemes; that failure held broader lessons for the postwar reconstruction of other institutions ('Rebuilding'). Kingsway was a screen onto which sometimes contradictory ideals of planning and efficiency, of socialist utopia and imperial grandeur, could be projected.

In the period of its construction, however, it was also a building site. Though the street was open to traffic in 1905, the buildings were slowly developed, being completed mostly between 1913 and 1916. The buildings on the Aldwych which contributed most explicitly to the project's imperial character were among the last to be built: Australia

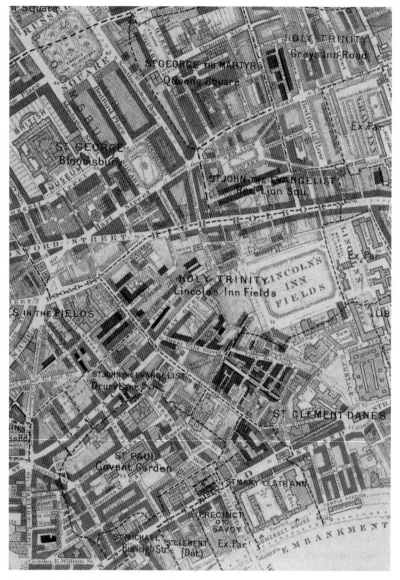

Figure 1.1 Strand-Holborn area, from Charles Booth's Map of London 1898–99

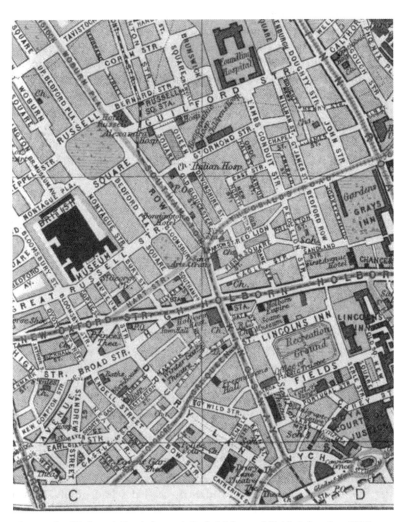

Figure 1.2   'Holborn', *Bartholomew's Pocket Atlas and Guide to London*, 1922

House from 1912 to 1918, Bush House and India House in the 1920s and 1930s (Clunn 100; Schubert and Sutcliffe 137). In 1905, the road was lined not with imperial symbols, but with advertising hoardings. The relatively slow development of the site, combined with the uncertainty of the exact period in which *Night and Day* is set, makes impossible an exact visualization of the scene quoted at the start of this section. In *The Voyage Out*, Hewet refers familiarly to the 'placards' which lined the road (*VO* 350). In 'The Mark on the Wall', published in 1917 while Woolf was writing *Night and Day*, the narrator thinks of 'a flower growing on a dust heap on the site of an old house' there (*CSF* 85). However, by the time Woolf was writing the novel, the imperial character of the road was emerging.

The vividness with which Woolf presents Katharine's perception of Kingsway implies that it forms a kind of pathetic fallacy; not only in the usual sense, in that her perception is coloured by her feeling, but in a deeper sense, because her being on Kingsway is significant of her situation. We are told that, looking at the current of commuters, she glories openly in 'the rapture that had run subterraneously all day' (*ND* 463); later, as she writes to Ralph, she feels as if 'the whole torrent' of the street had to run down her pencil (464). In this context, the metaphor of the subterranean momentarily unites the discursive fields of urban planning and psychology. The square from which Katharine has emerged, Lincoln's Inn Fields, has quite explicitly become the personification of Ralph: 'stern of aspect', serious in intent, concerned with earning a living. What Kingsway represents to her is a space that is distinctly not domestic, and she explicitly contrasts Lincoln's Inn Fields with Chelsea on this basis. The representation of Kingsway rests on the knowledge that home, for these commuters, is in the suburbs. Moreover, contemporary readers would have known that, before its redevelopment, the district was itself domestic in scale, though dubious in character.

Katharine exults in the sight of the torrent, but she is also threatened by it. She faces a choice between maintaining her independence and submerging her identity in that of some other person or larger force. At the opening of the novel her identity as a descendent of Richard Alardyce mutes other aspects of her individuality; at the culminating moment on Kingsway, the possibility of becoming merely Mrs Ralph Denham is something she must weigh against the independence that the Ralph will apparently preserve. Moreover, her identity risks becoming merged in that of the state. Many eugenicists argued that marriage and child-bearing were not private choices, but ones that had implications for the 'imperial race'. The 'complete indifference' of Kingsway is not the indifference of families, be they Alardyce or Denham, but the indifference of the state to individuals. The power of the state to relocate individuals and families, and to obliterate all traces of their existence, weighs heavily on the scene. The continuing visibility of its past made Kingsway a palimpsestic location. The flower seen in 'The Mark on the Wall', speculates the narrator, 'must have been sown in the reign of Charles the First' (*CSF* 85). Kingsway was a space in which traces of the past were confronted by the rationalizing forces of modernity, an encounter which is paradigmatic for modernism. Although in *Night and Day* the torrent of humanity is in some ways an overwhelming life force, it is also deathly: the 'semi-transparent' quality of the office workers and the 'pale ivory ovals' of their faces suggest ghosts. The First World War forms a subtext to both references. The torrent's indifference to individuals raises Liberal concerns about the powers of the state, particularly with regard to conscription; 'currents' and similar terms could derive from the discourse of traffic planning, but equally well might derive from an apocalyptic discourse in which the war was figured as 'the deluge'.

In this regard, Kingsway may seem to represent a threat to Katharine, and to be antipathetic: a warning, perhaps, against marriage. Nevertheless, there are significant parallels between Katharine's relation to her family and Kingsway's relation to the Strand district. The context of 'national efficiency' brings them into focus. The language of 'efficiency' pervades *Night and Day*. Ralph's 'rather ostentatious efficiency' annoys others at his place of work; he appeared to be 'a hard and self-sufficient young man' (*ND* 130). In thinking of the conduct of his relationship with Katharine, he adopts political discourse, contemplating taking 'courageous measures' to avoid 'pain and waste' (*ND* 391). At Mary Datchet's suffrage organization, Mr Clacton deplores the wasted effort due to 'the ramification of organizations' (*ND* 86), a key idea in the National Efficiency movement. Mrs Seal, on the other hand, represents the countervailing tendency, acting without forethought (often 'bursting' into speech), and lighting a stove 'with inefficient haste' (*ND* 84).

Mrs Hilbery is also characterized in terms drawn from contemporary political discourse. Her approach to writing the biography of Richard Alardyce is unsystematic: she has written a whole collection of brilliant paragraphs, and a whole selection of possible openings; she excels in scene-setting sketches and essays on her father's taste in hats. The fragments resemble the ad hoc, unco-ordinated institutions of the inefficient state, and the twisting streets of an unplanned town. The political parallel is suggested most directly when we are told that Katharine is 'resolved on reform'; she has, as her mother says, 'a wonderful head for business' (*ND* 38). Moreover, Katharine feels threatened: if she and her mother cannot complete the biography, they have no right to their 'privileged position'. In a submerged and marvellously condensed metaphor, it seems to her that 'Their increment became yearly more and more unearned' (*ND* 37). The work of Alardyce is the equivalent of the family estate, which has appreciated in value due to, in Lloyd George's phrase, 'the energy and enterprise of the community'. Katharine has benefited from the infrastructure of annotation, interpretation, and allusion built by poets and critics. Unpacking these metaphors, we find that Katharine is two things at once. As a member of the Alardyce family, she is a property owner, passively benefiting from the work of others; but as an individual, she is a civil engineer, planning to demolish her mother's outdated and confused structures, and to replace them with an efficient modern thoroughfare. Seeing Kingsway, she also sees a version of herself cut free from the Alardyce inheritance. The 'current of desire' that flows through her resembles the current of commuters, controlled and channelled. If for Cassandra and William, love and the city are both mazes (Squier 84), for Katharine, they are open to rebuilding. If this is, as Squier suggests, a novel which turns on the word 'prospect' (Squier 80), then the literal prospect afforded by Kingsway is an appropriate location for its pivotal moment.

It is notable that Katharine's response to the urban torrent is to stand and stare. Her reaction poses an interesting problem for those theorists, such as de Certeau, who see space as something produced by movement. De Certeau develops an analogy between linguistic practices and spatial ones: the places of the city provide a *langue*, within which individual movements are speech acts; while in a broad sense movements are constrained by the system, they are not rigidly determined by it. He also compares the act of walking to rhetoric, so that the appropriation of places can be seen as a kind of troping; the official stories about movement in the city, the recommended routes, constitute the literal norm against which such figurative language is contrasted (de Certeau, *Practice* 97–100). The analogy is suggestive, but Katherine's response serves to remind that standing still is also a spatial practice. It is analogous to a silence that disobeys the rules of discourse: Lily Briscoe's refusal to come to the assistance of Charles Tansley in *To the Lighthouse* is a case in point. Immobility is perhaps too easily associated with place, and so seen as a conservative and unproductive practice; indeed, scarcely a practice at all. However, as a response to a city that had been newly streamlined to facilitate the flow of commuters, one in which the official story was about the flow of people and goods, standing still is a form of appropriation, and a subtly subversive one at that.

Kingsway and unknowable London

The construction of Kingsway could be seen as a concrete response to a cognitive problem: modern London was becoming unknowable. In late nineteenth-century accounts of urban poverty, it was a common trope that the poor districts were as *unknown* to the rich as the heart of Africa, and this is, as we will see, an important trope for Woolf. However, the new condition of *unknowability* was distinct and systemic. The diversity of social classes contained within the city correlates to a diversity of ways of producing the space of the city, and a diversity of ways of knowing it. The city in the early twentieth century contained an unprecedented diversity of modes of transport – footpaths, tramways, underground railways, overground railways, and roads containing public buses and private motor vehicles – each of them producing the space of the city differently. To transport we may add telecommunications: having access to a telephone allows one to experience the city differently, making it less often a city of wasted journeys.

Ford Madox Ford's *The Soul of London* provides one of the earliest accounts of the newly unknowable London. He recognizes from the outset that transport produces space. To those Londoners who commute from the suburbs or commuter towns, 'London will remain a matter of a central highway, a central tunnel or a central conduit, more or less long; a daily route whose two extremities are a more or less permanent sleeping place, and a more or less permanent workshop – a thing, figured on a map, like the bolas of certain South Americans, a long cord with balls at the extremities' (Ford 11). Dickens may have been able to take a bird's-eye view of London, but the great increase in its size, and the 'change in our habits of locomotion', make such a perspective unattainable. The only bird's-eye view which Ford will allow is that of a bird 'seeking for minute fragments of seed', so close to the object that it cannot see the whole (Ford 15, 17).

Woolf too recognized the way that the railways, and particularly the Underground, reconstruct space. In *Jacob's Room* she defamiliarizes the process of commuting:

the little figures, split apart into trousers or moulded into a single thickness, jerked rapidly with angular forward motion along the pavement; then dropped into darkness. Beneath the pavement, sunk in the earth, hollow drains lined with yellow light for ever conveyed them this way and that, and large letters upon enamel plates represented in the underworld the parks, squares, and circuses of the upper. 'Marble Arch–Shepherd's Bush' – to the majority the Arch and the Bush are eternally white letters upon a blue ground. Only at one point – it may be Acton, Holloway, Kensal Rise, Caledonian Road – does the name mean shops where you buy things, and houses, in one of which, down to the right, where the pollard trees grow out of the paving stones, there is a square curtained window, and a bedroom. (*JR* 88–9)

The jerking motion was one that Woolf associated with movement in the city. Reading in the country, at Asheham House, she felt that her faculties had been 'oddly clarified', that she could see the meaning of what she was reading 'whole & truly', and 'not in jerks & spasms as so often in London' (*D* 1: 94–5). In *Jacob's Room*, the attempt to read tombstones on a mason's van is interrupted as the car in front 'jerks forward' (*JR* 154).

Though the foregoing account suggests a nostalgia for lost cognitive unity, the full picture is more complex, as the example of Kingsway shows. The Kingsway project's reshaping of city space restores unity to the transport map, albeit across a very limited area: the passenger on the Holborn to Aldwych spur of the underground knew that his or her route corresponded to the overground road and to the underground tram. For Woolf, however, such a rigid correspondence deprived the city of its emotional and narrative truth. She distrusted linearity. In her correspondence with Jacques Raverat in 1924, discussing the problem imposed by linearity in writing, she criticized 'Bennett, Galsworthy and so on' for having adhered to 'a formal railway line of sentence [...] never reflecting that people don't and never did feel or think or dream for a second in that way' (*L* 3: 135–6). Twists and turns, in syntax and in street-maps, held more interest. In *Jacob's Room* the narrator reflects that although the nature of life 'must have been apparent to every one for hundreds of years, no one has left any adequate account of it': 'The streets of London have their map; but our passions are uncharted. What are you going to meet if you turn this corner?' The question opens out into a strange digressive narrative, itself beginning as a question to the reader, though we never reach a question mark. If, rather than following the policeman's directions ('Holborn straight ahead of you'), you accept an invitation from a white-bearded egg collector, you may – 'skipping the intermediate stages' – find yourself far from civilization, on the edge of a marsh, 'drinking rum-punch', 'infected with yellow fever as likely as not.' The narrator concludes laconically: 'As frequent as street corners in Holborn are these chasms in the continuity of our ways. Yet we keep straight on' (*JR* 130). Nostalgia for lost cognitive unity must compete with nostalgia for a twisted and authentically human literal and psychological topography.

This narrative digression literalizes the metaphors that underpinned nineteenth-century urban investigative writing. It accepts their association of the dark corners of the city with the 'dark heart' of Africa (implied by 'yellow fever'); in consequence, a turn from the respectable high-road into the side streets becomes equivalent to a journey to an 'uncivilized' place where alcoholism and insanitary conditions prevail. However, it also makes this newly literal scenario into a metaphor of its own, for the nature of narrative. In this light, Katharine Hilbery's contemplation of the most pre-eminently straight road that London could offer implies that she is considering the consequences of joining a traditional and linear narrative, a marriage plot: it is a turn that is both exulting and disturbing.

Woolf was to recapitulate the scenario from *Jacob's Room*, in miniature, in 'Street Haunting', in a passage discussed also by Seeley in the present volume. '[W]hat greater delight and wonder can there be', Woolf asks, 'than to leave the straight lines of personality and deviate into those footpaths that lead beneath brambles and thick tree trunks into the heart of the forest where live those wild beasts, our fellow men?' (*E* 4: 490–1). The comparison, as Bowlby suggests, covertly displaces 'the usual opposition between the artificial city and primitive country', the 'urban landscape' becoming 'a natural wilderness' (Bowlby, 'Walking' 45). However, the displacement is not altogether Woolf's work, but draws firstly on the existing trope of 'darkest London', and secondly on the later association of linearity with imperialist triumphalism and social control.

The reconstruction of space in *Mrs Dalloway*

As the foregoing investigation of Kingsway shows, the contextual investigation of actual places can illuminate the representation of space in the literary text. However, if they are not to fall into a reductively mimetic view of the text, such investigations need to be coupled with an awareness of tropes, both literary and non-literary, and, more generally, an awareness of how texts have already reconstructed urban space. A central scene in *Mrs Dalloway* demonstrates how intertextuality can complicate the construction of space in a literary text. Peter Walsh's pursuit of a young woman from Trafalgar Square to somewhere north of Oxford Street has attracted a great deal of critical attention (Bowlby, 'Walking' 32–3; Parsons 73–4). Critical annotation has recovered many hidden connotations in particular places mentioned in the text, but such activity tends to tie the text monologically to a historically specific reality. Critical discussion has focused on Peter's relation to the Baudelairean and Benjaminian *flâneur*, but there are other literary precedents which have gone unnoticed.

When Peter first finds himself in Trafalgar Square, having followed a group of young soldiers or cadets, the location is identified indirectly, by reference to 'all the exalted images, Nelson, Gordon, Havelock, the black, the spectacular images of great soldiers' (*MD* 44); the description assumes a reader familiar with the location. Only when Peter is struck by the fact of his invisibility and anonymity is the place named. He is overcome by 'the strangeness of standing alone, alive, unknown, at half-past eleven in Trafalgar Square' (*MD* 44). Here the explicit naming could be taken as a psychologically naturalistic device, a register of Peter's sudden self-estrangement. Peter has split into intradiegetic and extradiegetic parts, and the latter looks down at the former from a great height. However, the next reference to specific street names is harder to account for: 'she's extraordinarily attractive, he thought, as, walking across Trafalgar Square in the direction of the Haymarket, came a young woman [...]' (*MD* 45). Why, one might ask, 'Trafalgar Square' and not simply 'the square', as its identity can no longer be in doubt? What we have is an interpolation of a narratorial perspective into Peter's, the return to Peter's perspective being marked by 'Peter Walsh thought'; the surname does not serve to distinguish him from any other Peter. The later reference to the young woman walking past 'Dent's shop in Cockspur Street' seems also to interpolate impersonal knowledge into Peter's perspective. This mixing of perspectives is one of the formal features of Woolf's fiction that is most relevant to the production of space.

De Certeau's distinction of the map and the tour, adopted from Linde and Labov, is relevant here. Asked to describe their apartments, New York residents resorted to two distinct kinds of discourse. The map-type discourse consisted of statements such as 'The girls' room is next to the kitchen'. The tour-type discourse described the apartments in terms of *operations* needed to get from one to the other: 'You turn right and come into the living room'. In de Certeau's summary, 'description oscillates between the terms of an alternative: either *seeing* [...] or *going* [...]. Either it presents a tableau ("there are ..."), or it organizes movements ("you enter, you go across, you turn ...")' (de Certeau, *Practice* 119). What works in apartments cannot be translated directly to city streets, but the distinction between an impersonal form of knowledge and one which assumes a situated subject is a useful one.

Discussions of Peter Walsh as *flâneur* run the risk of treating him as if he were a real person, and the text as if it were a transparent medium. Rachel Bowlby's account escapes the pitfall at the last minute, by noting the respects in which Woolf 'knowingly' fictionalizes the Baudelairean narrative of *flâneur* and *passante* (Bowlby, 'Walking' 34). Peter Walsh himself acknowledges that the escapade was 'half made up' (*MD* 46); for him, it is a matter of self-conscious role-playing. The problem is to decide *what* is known in this knowing fictionalization, and what form the knowledge takes: is it literary knowledge? Sociological knowledge? Or knowledge filtered through ideological constructs? The status of the *flâneur* has been problematic for many critics: is it a simple label for a real social practice, or an ideological construct which brings imaginary unity to an incoherent cluster of practices? (E. Wilson 99–100; Parsons 4–6). From a more biographical critical perspective, we might ask whether Woolf was actually aware of Baudelaire's poem. The centrality of Baudelaire to recent British and American accounts of modernism has led critics to assume that she was, in spite of the complete absence of his name from her writings.

If not Baudelaire, then who? Certainly Woolf was aware of T.S. Eliot's poetic versions of Baudelairean *flâneurs*. She may also have been aware of another figure in H. G. Wells's *Ann Veronica* (1909), one who moves the emphasis from passive observation of women to active pursuit; one who is as much stalker as *flâneur*. In Wells's novel, Ann Veronica Stanley runs away from her repressive home in the suburbs to make her way independently in central London. On arriving she finds a room in a hotel near the Embankment, and sets about exploring London. Wells narrates her movements twice, once in brief summary, and then again in more detail, from her perspective. In summary she makes her way 'along the Strand and across Trafalgar Square, and by the Haymarket to Piccadilly, and so through dignified square and palatial alleys to Oxford Street' (Wells 84). What we learn in the more detailed narration is that on Piccadilly Ann Veronica becomes aware of the peculiar behaviour of a middle-aged gentleman, who sidles up to her, and addresses her, in a 'curiously wheedling voice': 'Whither away?' (Wells 85). She walks westwards along Piccadilly, then north-wards, probably through Berkeley Square and certainly through Grosvenor Square, before emerging at 'the circus': Oxford Circus, that is. During this walk she realizes that the same man is still following her. She goes into a tea room, and finds that the man has followed her inside. Eventually, as twilight falls, she manages to lose him some-where between Oxford Circus and the northern end of Tottenham Court Road. The whole narrative makes clear the inhibiting effects of such encounters on the would-be independent Edwardian woman: when he has gone, she realizes that 'She had lost her nerve, and there was no more freedom in London for her that night' (Wells 88).

While the young woman in *Mrs Dalloway* does not take an identical route to Ann Veronica, the broad direction is similar enough to suggest that Woolf's intertext is Wells and not Baudelaire. Other local details are worth noting. Ann Veronica, wondering how to find work and where, 'hesitated at the window of a shipping office in Cockspur Street' (Wells 84). The young woman in *Mrs Dalloway* also goes along Cockspur Street, and Peter Walsh admires her long cloak stirring in the wind as she passes Dent's clockmakers at no. 28. Cockspur Street is simply the most direct path from Trafalgar Square to Haymarket, so the coincidence in route is not in itself noteworthy; what is important is that first Wells and then Woolf interpolate map-like detail into the tour-like discourse. Many readers of *Mrs Dalloway* have registered the street name as intrusive, and have interpreted it as a reference to Peter's libidinal motivation. However, it may also be a reminder of the broad parallel between Peter's route and Ann Veronica's.

Walking westwards along Piccadilly, Ann Veronica sees a woman approaching her from the opposite direction: 'a tall woman who at the first glance seemed altogether beautiful and fine. She came along with the fluttering assurance of some tall ship' (Wells 86). As she draws nearer, however, Ann Veronica notes the 'paint' on her face and her air of 'harsh purpose', and becomes half-conscious that she is a prostitute. She also notes that the woman is herself being followed by a smartly dressed man, an echo of her own stalker. Ann Veronica's comparison of the prostitute to a tall ship gives a different and more menacing weight to Peter Walsh's image of himself as a 'romantic buccaneer'. So too do Ann Veronica's speculations about her pursuer's perspective: 'Heaven knows what dim and tawdry conceptions of passion and desire were in that blond cranium, what romance-begotten dreams of adventure and intrigue!' (Wells 87).

Woolf's account of Peter Walsh's self-conscious *flâneuring* re-writes not Baudelaire, but Wells. The rewrite most obviously involves a change of perspective from that of female to male. It obscures the human consequences of this particular spatial practice: Woolf's text has none of the anger of Wells's. However, presenting the situation from the stalker's point of view allows Woolf to look inside the cranium, and show how and why men construct city space in this way. '[T]awdry conceptions of passion and desire' form part of it, but so do other factors. One is the city as a place of consumption: while Ann Veronica looks in the shop windows with a view to finding a job, Peter Walsh sees only commodities, and (as Bowlby notes) makes no clear distinction between them and his quarry. Another factor consists of the spatial metaphors we use to conceptualize life narratives. Shortly before Peter sees the young woman, he is overcome by a sensation of 'irrepressible, exquisite delight' as he realizes a sense of freedom, and feels as if he were standing 'at the opening of endless avenues down which if he chose he might wander'. The stalking which follows immediately afterwards appears to be the unconscious realization of this metaphor. A further factor is Peter's feeling of isolation and anonymity in the city. At the start of his pursuit, he feels that the woman, or the excitement he feels on seeing her, has 'singled him out'. It seems to him 'as if the random uproar of the traffic had whispered through hollowed hands his name, not Peter, but his private name which he called himself in his own thoughts. '"You," she said, only "you," saying it with her white gloves and her shoulders' (*MD* 45).

Woolf's text reveals the psychological motivation behind the construction of space. Her form of interior monologue is particularly well suited to this purpose, as it allows a movement between interior and exterior perspectives, between the map and the tour. Most obviously, it exposes the incompleteness of the supposedly totalizing and objective map perspective, but the hybrid discourse of the novel also exposes the limitations of the subjective tour discourse. Through various forms of intertextuality, her works are also able to present reality in an ambiguous form, sometimes trying to conjure the illusion of a world unmediated by language, and at other times forcing the reader to realize that reality is always refracted.

The London Docks and imperial space

From the environs of central London, we move now to the East End and Woolf's essay 'The Docks of London', the first piece in her much-overlooked *London Scene* essays published in 1931 and 1932 for *Good Housekeeping* magazine. Woolf took her readers on a London tour, from the Docks to Oxford Street to the House of Commons to the 'great' houses and churches of London. Ostensibly examples of literary tourism written for a popular women's magazine, the essays are concerned throughout with the materialist construction of space and, as Jeanette McVicker has pointed out, need to be seen in the context of her other writing from the early 1930s: 'Professions for Women', the beginnings of *The Pargiters*, and *Flush*, often overlooked but in fact one of her most important London novels. At a time of economic upheaval and uncertainty in Britain, questions of economics, trade and systems of government were uppermost in Woolf's mind. The essays come at London space from a variety of angles – panoramic, microcosmic – and address spaces of religion, government and commerce. London exists 'in layers, in strata' (*LS* 46) and just as the city has changed architecturally, so too the spatial configurations of modernity have replaced the 'spacious days' (51) with the 'perpetual race and disorder' (28) of modern, urban experience. Anticipating David Harvey, Woolf depicts the compression of time and space: 'space has shrivelled' as she puts it (50).

In the first essay, 'The Docks of London' (though not *only* in this essay), Woolf is writing about the spatial dimension of capitalism, or the economics of space. As with her description in a later essay of Carlyle's house as a 'scene of labour, effort and perpetual struggle' (40), she is concerned with the labour that creates and maintains space. Woolf visited the Docks twice in 1931 with Harold Nicolson, and, as one history notes: 'Few people were given the opportunity to visit the dock warehouses... [they] were one of London's best kept secrets. Those that did penetrate their security may well have been offered the ultimate geography lesson, but were as likely as not to be blinded by the sheer scale and statistics of it all' (Ellmers and Werner 89). Woolf did not need that geography lesson, and her essay does not provide the reader with one, but it was for their importance to the workings of imperial capital that the docks served as an entry point to her essay series, as of course they do for London itself. A more potent symbol of global trade networks and London's position within the empire could hardly be found. In 1931, London had eight million inhabitants, six times larger than Calcutta, the next largest city in the British empire (King 34). The Port of London, established in 1908, was the edge of empire, a space of transformation and dispersal. Often called the 'warehouse of the world', the Docks were a symbolic microcosm, compressing imperial space in a similar manner to the display of colonial commodities and raw materials in the imperial exhibitions held in the metropolis. The 'irresistible call' (*LS* 11) which lures the ships up the Thames laden with tea, coffee, tobacco, ivory, wool, jute, spices or cocoa, is the economic corollary of the political and ideological power exerted by the heart of empire, mirroring those spatial and cartographic configurations of empire which revolve around the imperial metropolis. Colonial spaces are represented by their raw materials: the profit they can supply the heart of empire. The ships from India, South America, Australia come from 'silence' (13), the *terra incognita* of colonial space, only existing in the imperial imagination when they reach the London Docks.

Influenced by Leonard's economic critique of imperialism, particularly *Empire and Commerce in Africa* (1920), Woolf's anti-imperialism often focused on the trade of commodities, as Kurt Koenigsberger and Nobuyoshi Ota's essays demonstrate. While Woolf can certainly be accused of overlooking colonial space on its own terms, she cannot be charged with ignoring the effects of imperialism on Britain, or more specifically the imperial traces found in the architecture and geography of the metropolis. She refused to see imperial space as 'out there' in more ways than one. Consistently attuned to her own locatedness, she chose rather to limit her anti-imperialist critique to the circumference of the colonizer's experience. As Bernard says in *The Waves*: 'I see India [...] I see the gilt and crenellated buildings which have an air of fragility and decay as if they were temporarily run up buildings in some Oriental exhibition' (*W* 111). By focusing on the Docks, Woolf is not only underlining the economic inequities of imperial relations, but reminding her readers of the extent of metropolitan ignorance about Britain's colonies.

'The Docks of London' references contemporary Thames writing (*Heart of Darkness, Tono-Bungay, The Waste Land*) as well as representations of the East End. While Woolf moves in her essays to Westminster, it is significant that she enters the city via the East End. As in the Whitechapel scenes in *Flush*, Woolf is alluding to nineteenth- and early twentieth-century writers, such as General Booth, who linked the East End and Africa, using the discourse of race to describe class distinctions. The Indian, West Indian and West African sailors who lived and worked in the docks made it one of the more cosmopolitan areas of late imperial London. Arthur Conan Doyle's description of the Docks uses the same images of racial contamination as, for example, Jack London or George Gissing's portrayal of working-class communities in the East End. Slum areas were seen as jungles and 'social classes or groups were described with telling frequency as "races", "foreign groups", or "nonindigenous bodies," and could thus be cordoned off as biological and "contagious," rather than as social groups' (McClintock 48). In *Flush*, Whitechapel is a jungle inhabited by violent drunken 'demons' who leer and curse (*F* 56). In 'The Docks of London', the warehouses are 'dingy' and 'decrepit' (*LS* 13), the dockworkers' houses form a 'sinister dwarf city' (14). Rat- and refuse-infested, the 'malodorous' mud-flats are derelict and desolate.

Woolf's main focus in the essay is not humans but capital: the movement, categorizing, processing, and distribution of goods. Dockland space is determined and regulated by economics. Consumer desire, as created by the seductive spectacle of Oxford Street discussed in the second essay, in turn drives those economic forces and the movement of goods. While Woolf depicts trade dictated by bodies – 'it is we – our tastes, our fashions, our needs – that make the cranes dip and swing, that call the ships from the sea' (22) – that 'we' is a mass defined by its powers of consumption. The trade in tortoise shell, used for making toys, combs, cases and boxes, for example, fell away in the 1930s, and the pre-First World War demand for ostrich feathers did not regain its momentum as fashions changed (Ellmers and Werner 96, 93). Consuming bodies exist for their part in the circulation and accumulation of capital, just as the goods exist for their exchange rather than their use value. They must, therefore, be uniform, equivalent, and categorized so as to conform to the system of exchange. Woolf would have watched wines and spirits being blended and bottled during her tour of the Docks, and sugar, tea, coffee and cocoa being 'baulked' or mixed to uniform grades. To quote David Harvey, 'money [...] functions as a concrete abstraction, imposing external and homogenous measures of value on all aspects of human life, reducing infinite diversity to a single comparable dimension, and masking subjective human relations by objective market exchanges' (Harvey 232). The final essay in the collection, 'Portrait of a Londoner', suggests that people returning to London from the reaches of the empire require the same treatment. They are raw products refined and civilized in the metropolis at Mrs Crowe's tea table. 'Timber, iron, grain, wine, sugar, paper, tallow, fruit – whatever the ship has gathered from the plains, from the forests, from the pastures of the whole world is here lifted from its hold and set in its right place' (*LS* 17–18), crucially alienated from the labour which has harvested, grown, packaged and shipped them. 'Every commodity in the world has been examined and graded according to its use and value' (19). David Harvey has emphasized the importance of space in Marx's theory of the accumulation of capital: capitalism relies on the conquest of space through the expansion of foreign trade for raw products and markets for overproduction. Woolf highlights the ways in which capitalism collapses and compresses space, what Marx described as the annihilation of space by time (Harvey 179). The essay traces the spaces created and traversed by the 'machinery of production and distribution' (*LS* 22), the flows of capital which centre around the docks. Woolf's final image of wool being distributed over England foregrounds the spatial networks so crucial to the production process.

'The Docks of London' is a case study in capitalist imperialism; the Docks are a space created by the needs of capitalism, and the needs of the commodities that sustain a capitalist economy. Everything, even language, 'has adapted itself to the needs of commerce' (*LS* 22), just as on Oxford Street the spaces required are temporary, adaptable to the whims of consumer desire: 'built to pass' (31). Her essay contains reminders of the riverscape before the factories and warehouses dominated, but the systems of trade appear naturalized. She explores the hidden spaces of production and distribution; the Docks are the unseen double of Oxford Street. This in turn, however, reveals those colonial spaces and individuals erased by capitalism. The ships come from 'silence and danger and loneliness' (13). But Woolf's Docks are a similarly depopulated, dehumanized place. By the early 1930s,100,000 people relied on the Docks for their living, working as dockers, stevedores, seamen (Ellmers and Werner 111). Apart from a few brief references to the 'lascars [who] tumble and scurry below' (*LS* 12) or 'the unconscious, vigorous movements of men lifting and unloading' (20), Woolf's representation erases labour from the picture. While revising the essay, Woolf cut a section out which included the following: 'this vast patient skillful & [unremitting] labour is full of sweat & agony & squalor & horror' (Woolf, qtd. Squier 53). Susan Squier argues that by excising the section which includes this quotation, Woolf erases acknowledgement of the working-class suffering involved in producing commodities for middle-class consumption. Squier complains that 'the workers have become invisible' (Squier 57), but it seems that this is just Woolf's point. Her dehumanized portrayal emulates the erasure of place, labour and individualism created by capitalism, particularly pertinent in an imperial context. By including Mrs Crowe, Woolf points out that women too are implicated and that issues of social conformity are as dehumanizing as economic exchange. As Henri Lefebvre puts it:

when it turns into merchandise, the object becomes detached from itself, so to speak. It enters a system of relationships that are expressed through it, so that in the end it seems to be the subject of these relationships, their causal agent. Relationships between men are masked by relationships between objects, human social existence is realized only by the abstract existence of their products. Objects seem to take on a life of their own. (Lefebvre, *Key Writings* 82)

Woolf uses the Docks to illustrate Marx's ideas on the fetishism of commodities: 'we put out of sight both the useful character of the various kinds of labour embodied in them, and the concrete forms of that labour; there is nothing left but what is common to them all; all are reduced to one and the same sort of labour, human labour in the abstract' (Marx, *Capital* 441). Marx discusses the religious analogies used to describe commodities, just as Woolf's narrator says of the Docks' wine vaults: 'we might be priests worshipping in the temple of some silent religion' (*LS* 21).

As we have seen here, and as we will see in the essays that follow, Woolf's frequent focus on particular known, locatable urban spaces allows her to open out into global and hence imagined spaces. But in the particularity of those spaces (Kingsway, the Docks) resonate their layered histories, the hidden traces available only through narrative. Locating Woolf is a task which not only permits, but requires a multiplicity of diverse approaches. For some texts, the focus naturally falls on the social production of a space represented in the text; for others, the focus falls on the literary or textual production of space. Some critics begin with a wider cultural theme, such as the motor car or radio, and trace its implications to Woolf's works; others begin with a particular passage or text, and explore its own productive activity. Some texts require the detailed investigation of the represented space; others reveal more when repressed spaces are uncovered. The essays collected in this volume demonstrate that the investigation of space and place in Virginia Woolf's works is a fertile critical activity, just as city space – 'building it round one, tumbling it, creating it every moment afresh' (*MD* 4) – fuelled Woolf's imaginative activities. The spaces of her imagination both emerged from and took her back to the urban environment.

Note

1   *Parliamentary Debates*, 29 April 1909, iv. 532.

Part I
Gendered Spaces

2
Flights of Fancy: Spatial Digression and Storytelling in *A Room of One's Own*

Tracy Seeley

> For truth... those dots mark the spot where, in search of truth, I missed the turning up to Fernham. (*ROO* 19)

> ...truth is only to be had by laying together many varieties of error. (*ROO* 137)

I begin with two epigraphs which suggest my central lines of inquiry: the idea that in pursuit of one kind of truth, one might lose one's way; and that 'many varieties of error' might give us a better sense of direction. Woolf's meandering navigation in *A Room of One's Own* begins by giving up the first pursuit, of handing over a 'nugget of pure truth' (4). Instead, she will show how she arrived at her opinion (and it's just an opinion) 'about the room and the money' (4). To show 'how she arrived' is to trace an itinerary, and that itinerary, the trajectory of an argument and a map of 'errors,' is the focus of this essay. Woolf travels over some hundred plus pages, spinning out a digressive, meandering, anecdotal, interrupted, fiction-entangled thread of what may be the least straightforward argument ever in English about women's need for money and space. Woolf's strategy, which I argue is purposefully evasive, depends not on the logical structures of classical argument, but on the illogic of tropes.

Conventionally, we think of tropes as metaphors or other figures of speech. However, embedded in the etymologies of the word are other, multiple meanings: a 'way' or a 'turning' among them. Trope-as-movement and trope-as-direction are useful for reading Woolf, once we revise Harold Bloom's claim about tropes in *A Map of Misreading*. There he argues that tropes are akin to the psyche's defence mechanisms – in this case, a defence against literal meaning. If we broaden Bloom's model of psychological defence to consider the political and social factors which might necessitate a variety of defences, we make his sense of tropes useful. Revising him further, as Hayden White does in *Tropics of Discourse*, we can argue that the trope's swerving away 'from literal, conventional or "proper" language use' (White 2) can also be a swerving towards something else. In this sense, tropes constitute not just a defensive sidewise move, but a positive, alternative trajectory to both literality and logic.[1] In *A Room*, Woolf uses both digressions and fictions for both kinds of tropic evasion: both away from and toward. They are a form of going astray, wandering off the path, a kind of errantry or erring[2] which accomplishes two ends: by turning away from the linearity of logical argument, she traces an alternative space for women, much as a literal meandering off the path inscribes a different space within which the subject acts; by eschewing the universal abstractions of logical argument, she redefines women's subjectivity as multiple and relational, establishing a collective notion of women based in the body and the material specificity of real lives.

Within the frame narrative of an ostensible talk to women, Chapter 1 launches a digressive fiction which ends over a hundred pages later with a declaration of what the talk's first sentence *would* be. The pages are still blank and the book has nearly ended. Clearly, getting directly to the point is not this journey's goal. In that first digression, the story of two days before the lecture, and in the digressive stops and starts that interrupt it, Woolf articulates both kinds of troping moves – non-literal and non-linear – she swerves both away from and toward. On the river bank, across the lawns at Oxbridge, at the closed library door, the analogy between physical movement and meandering thought underscores the need for and desirability of troping. Stopped abruptly in the track of both movement and thought by the beadle and the library door, she must change direction; the 'fish' that Thought has pulled up from the depths goes 'into hiding' (7). This forced digression, a movement caused by obstacles, brings to the fore the social and political meanings of space, and the power of spatial practice.

The idea of spatial practice comes through a line of thought beginning with Henri Lefebvre.[3] Positing that space is never 'empty,' an *a priori* blankness to be filled with social practice, Lefebvre argues that society's spaces are 'secreted' by spatial practice, and that the space thus produced 'serves as a tool of thought and action' (26). According to Lefebvre's Marxist analysis, both the 'social relations of reproduction... [and] the relations of production' are articulated through spatial configurations and practice (32). Thus, family structure, sexual relations and reproduction, divisions of labour, class hierarchy, for example, are all productive of, encoded by, and enforced by space. Think, for example, of the private home with both its internal and external boundaries, the relation of suburbs to city centre, class boundaries between neighborhoods. Ideology and practice produce the spaces which reinforce them. We might derive the same theory, in fact, from *A Room of One's Own*, for Woolf's central concern is with patriarchy, which, as a system of beliefs and practices, enacts its power spatially. It creates Oxbridge as an expression of its power and privilege, and then perpetuates both power and privilege through rules of turf protection and exclusion (stay off the grass and out of the library). Thus, space reinforces patriarchy's dominance.

Woolf's work is rife with awareness of spatial practices, and of women's relation to privilege in terms of space: the division of rooms and roles in Hyde Park Gate; the chapel at Cambridge where Jacob fumes against the distracting presence of women; a woman's 'sudden splitting off of consciousness... in walking down Whitehall'; the 'kind of glory' Woolf ironically details as she walks through Admiralty Arch (*ROO* 127, 50). These and countless others suggest her heightened awareness of patriarchy's spatial rule. As she contemplates the relative amenities of Oxbridge and Fernham, she considers 'the urbanity, the geniality, the dignity which are the offspring of luxury and privacy and space' (30). Because Woolf recognizes that space is ideological, mental and physical movement become analogous in *A Room*; the little thought-fish which later disappears first rouses her from meditative stasis and urges her first act of trespass.[4] When she first catches the fish and then puts it back in her mind, it becomes so active, 'set[s] up such a wash and tumult of ideas that it was impossible to sit still. It was thus that I found myself walking with extreme rapidity across a grass plot' (6). Physical and mental motion together enact Woolf's relation to those spatial practices which both physically and ideologically limit her movement. When the beadle herds her onto the path and the guardian angel in a black robe bars her from the library, she not only changes physical direction, but loses her train of thought.

Digression of the forced kind is relatively rare in this work. Woolf's tropes far more often suggest alternative spatial practices, both in the space suggested by 'a room of one's own,' and what we might call her spatial aesthetics,[5] used here for argumentative ends. This practice conflates thought, text, and physical movement as her 'mind wander[s]' (35) through a variety of patriarchal and other, preferred, spaces. There may be, after all, more desirable goals than getting inside the walls at Oxbridge. By the time she reaches the chapel, she 'had no wish to enter, had [she] the right' (10), and so she turns, digresses, errs.

In one frequent kind of digression, Woolf swerves aside at the last minute to avoid a conclusion or emphatic declaration. She repeatedly lands a 'fish', in other words, but 'will not trouble you with that thought now' (6). One such fish lands at the end of the digression in which she imagines the bags of gold that have poured for centuries into Oxbridge, funding buildings, laboratories, libraries, and wine; she then signals rhetorically that a conclusion has been reached: 'It was impossible not to reflect.' But the conclusion doesn't come: 'the reflection whatever it may have been was cut short. The clock struck. It was time to find one's way to luncheon' (12). The coy 'whatever it might have been' and the saved-by-the-bell strategy defer the logical end of one train of thought. She swerves off the path. Another such moment occurs at the end of Chapter 1, when she catalogues the day's thought. Returning from Fernham, she 'walked through the dark streets', pondering the effect of wealth and poverty on the mind, the 'queer old gentlemen... with tufts of fur on their shoulders', the organ in chapel, the library doors... and yet, there is no argumentative summing up. Instead she 'roll[s] up the crumpled skin of the day' and 'cast[s] it into the hedge' (30–1). In part, this troping avoids the expected criticism of her conclusions by deferring them; as Woolf writes in the opening pages, 'when a subject is highly controversial... one cannot hope to tell the truth' (4). One has to tell it slant. By swerving around the obstacle of a potentially hostile audience, she avoids a collision with controversy. This strategy, though, has created other controversy among Woolf's critics.

The rhetorical evasions of *A Room*, its lack of confrontation and anger,[6] as well as what seem to be vacillating and even contradictory positions, have all led some critics to argue that Woolf's method weakens her ideological effect. Julie Solomon, for example, argues that a 'metaphorics of trespass' are, in fact, absent from *A Room of One's Own*. Unlike *Three Guineas*, which advocates an 'outsider's' space of non-ownership, *A Room* advocates gaining power as patriarchy defines it: through acquiring property and capital. The room of one's own, Solomon suggests, 'visually concretizes the aspirations of Woolf's new political woman of 1929, a woman who like "Shakespeare's sister" longs to follow in the footsteps of her brother' (335). Thus Solomon reads Woolf's obedience to the gesticulating beadle as a 'metaphor for her willingness to acquiesce, at least publicly, in the institutional strictures of patriarchy' (336). Solomon contrasts this with Woolf's advice to 'trespass at once' in the far less deferential 'Leaning Tower' and *Three Guineas*. Solomon also finds Woolf's storytelling in *A Room*, which I am considering a second kind of troping, 'folklorish', and 'a ruse' which makes the essay less forthright and less grounded in 'contemporary political and historical reality' than *Three Guineas* (337).

Certainly, Woolf's methods in *A Room* are oblique. But the rhetorical savvy of the text is often under-appreciated, its rhetorical situation undervalued. Woolf's original lectures were straightforward; they contained no narrator or narrative frame, no Shakespeare's sister or Mary Carmichael, no 'scenes' or mention of anger (Rosenbaum xxi–xxii). It was only when Woolf revised 'Women and Fiction' for publication as *A Room* that she added many of the features which constitute her troping and which trouble critics. At least in part, we must look to her audience to explain such changes and additions. In *A Room*, Woolf was hardly preaching to the choir. She had to anticipate a non-believer's response, even a hostile one, and write persuasively without losing a chance to convert them. The fictions and digressions of *A Room* are, in part, the result. Using the most effective rhetorical strategy for persuading an audience with particular assumptions and prejudices could hardly be faulted as mere capitulation. Like Carlyle in *Sartor Resartus*, she distributes the authority of argumentative claims across layers of personae, embedded narratives, and fictional imaginings to say something daring. Without such strategies, how far would either Carlyle or Woolf have got in the face of hostile readers?

Still, where polemical ends seem to call for polemical means, *A Room's* ellipses, fragments, disruptions, and ruminations – the recognized merits of Woolf's fiction – may still cause critical unease when they appear in *A Room*. If we think of these narrative strategies, however, as part of *A Room's* argumentative aim, the tropes and digressions appear in a different light. Rachel Bowlby's wonderful reading of 'Mr Bennett and Mrs Brown' provides a place to start. For Bowlby, the linearity of the railroad line, like all its analogs (history as teleological, narration and time as linear, biography as continuous and coherent), is countered by the digressive ruminations of the novelist and the rapidly changing contexts within which Mrs Brown appears as the train moves (*Virginia Woolf* 3–15). The novelist's will to variety and incompletion ultimately gives a richer and more compelling portrait of Mrs Brown than conventional narrative could. As Bowlby suggests, she forces the train 'off the rails' (164), in favour of the non-teleological, the disjunctive, and the incoherent. *A Room* is not a novel, of course. It does seem, though, that in using fiction Woolf dismantles the usual generic boundary between argument and fiction. Her tropes, her turning aside, can also be viewed as a kind of derailment, a refusal to engage in 'truth-telling' as patriarchy and conventional argument define it. Shari Benstock makes a similar argument in her analysis of the ellipses in *Three Guineas*. For Benstock, Woolf's ellipses 'signal a falling back or turning away from the socially constructed opposition of truth and illusion... Those dots... displace narrative alignments... [and] confound representational orders' (124). Like the novelist in the train compartment, Woolf's elisions in *A Room*, marked by both figurative and textual ellipses, then also constitute a turning away, a refusal to engage in conventional rhetorical argument in which 'truth' as an absolute category must be defended and separated from fiction. In these terms, refusing to 'hit back'[7] is more than acquiescence to a 'No Trespassing' sign. She turns away not from truth, but from the absolute category 'truth', through a strategy of digression which leads elsewhere. As Elena Gualtieri persuasively argues, Woolf's refusal to 'resolve thought into either a logical argument or a storyline' (8) places Woolf's essays in the modernist European essay tradition of Lukacs, Musil, and Adorno (and we might add Benjamin). This tradition resists the 'hegemony of the scientific model of knowledge' through discontinuity and 'digressive logic' (17), a mode of thought known as 'essayism'. Essayism carries with it a 'critique of modernity as the triumph of rationalism and the culmination of a linear, progressive vision of history' (146).[8] As it does on her walk from Oxbridge to Fernham, the linear search for rational 'truth' can make one miss the turning, and so she continues to turn, in search of something else.

Still it is not 'Woolf' herself who searches in *A Room*, but a dispersed subject whose name 'is not a matter of importance' (*ROO* 5). The fictional narrator's rejection of 'I' and Woolf's assumption of impersonality have been perhaps even more troubling to many critics than other aspects of *A Room*. In part, this strategy can again be defended by considering the rhetorical situation. As Woolf wrote to Ethel Smyth,

> I forced myself to keep my own figure fictitious; legendary. If I had said, Look here am I uneducated, because my brothers used all the family funds which is the fact – Well, theyd have said; she has an axe to grind; and no one would have taken me seriously... [I should have had readers] who will read you and go away and rejoice in the personalities, not because they are lively and easy reading; but because they prove once more how vain, how personal... women always are; I can hear them as I write. (*L 5*: 194–5)

The bedrock desire to 'be taken seriously', then, underlies the assumption of impersonality, and knowing her audience, Woolf writes to give herself the best chance.[9] Still, at the edges of critical objection remains a claim that the refusal of 'I' not only pulls the argument's punches, but amounts to 'the modernist transmutation of the writerly self into an amorphous collective', something akin to T. S. Eliot's 'dissociation of sensibility' (Allan 133). Herbert Marder also argues about *A Room*'s impersonality that Woolf is divided into two: the reform-minded controversialist, and the artist who implies 'that there is a higher reality, a realm which practical politics cannot enter' (qtd. Low 266). This position essentially derives from identity-feminism, Lisa Low points out, a feminist politics that associates all impersonality in women's art with women's decorous invisibility under patriarchy. Contrarily, postmodernist feminism claims that this view reinforces 'the very ideals of a masculine culture it strives to overthrow' (Low 258), for it adheres to stable gender categories. Low argues that Woolf is writing to undermine such dualistic thinking, and that for her, impersonal writing is 'empathic and democratic' – a far cry from Eliot's impersonal authoritarianism (259). As Low suggests, even for Woolf, there is no 'higher ground to which we can go to get past the... personal details of our lives, past the bodies we inhabit...' (266). I will argue, in fact, that *A Room*, with its impersonality and praise for the 'incandescent mind', is ultimately grounded in the body. We head in that direction by considering the nature of Woolf's 'legendary' narrator, which seems not at all an evacuation of personality, or the 'total erasure of the "I", the uncontested marker of subjectivity' (Allan 135–6). It may be the erasure of 'I,' but not of subjectivity.[10] Woolf's narrator should be considered alongside her other fictional figures and pictorial asides which function as tropes in *A Room*. These tropes together create an alternative space for women's subjectivity quite unlike that of the patriarchal subject. Mary Beton/Seton/Carmichael or 'any name you please' becomes, like Shakespeare's sister, a trope or turning which leads us elsewhere.

Woolf's fictions in *A Room* differ from the tropes that involve her swerving from conclusions by elliptically omitting them, ringing a bell or throwing topics into the hedge. Here, where another rhetorician would argue to conclusion or resort to abstraction, Woolf invents. For example, rather than concluding a point about the relative conditions of Oxbridge and Fernham, she juxtaposes images of money bags with lean cows and muddy markets. Rather than presenting a generalized historical account of what our foremothers had been doing with their time, she offers Mrs Seton and her 13 children. Or, instead of reasoning to a conclusion about Professor von X, author of *The Mental, Moral and Physical Inferiority of Women*, she draws a picture of him. And of flames, which consume him in the library in effigy. Substituting a picture or fiction for a logical rhetorical move constitutes the single most powerful strategy of Woolf's argument. In key moments, she moves neither deductively, from a general accepted premise to particular instance; nor inductively, from a particular to a general abstract principle. Instead, she argues tropically, using stories to create argument-by-synecdoche; she thus calls into question the hierarchy of genres which privileges linear rationality over story. Shakespeare's sister and Mary Carmichael and her book become her most persuasive synecdoches.

By Chapter 3, Woolf has digressed, mused, walked, doodled, immolated Professor von X, looked out the window, walked and thought, looked at empty spaces on the shelf, and still not come to the point. 'Women are poorer than men because – this or that' (53). This begins the chapter in which she looks to history, and finding little, invents it. 'Let me imagine, since facts are so hard to come by, what would have happened had Shakespeare had a wonderfully gifted sister...' (60). We know this story well. What interests me here is how Woolf uses it. Based on general but scant information about women's lives in the sixteenth century, Woolf creates a fictional example, an imagined woman with a poet's gift. In the rest of the book, this fiction acts not as an example from which we should conclude an abstract 'truth' or pure nugget, however. Instead, Shakespeare's sister is a synecdoche, a particular woman who stands for all women writers who try or have tried to negotiate the material conditions of their own time in order to create.

Here I want to distinguish between example as it would be used in a logical argument, and a synecdoche as Woolf uses it here. In logic, an example can work as part of a deductive enthymeme or as an inductive example. An enthymeme begins from a universal statement like 'all men are mortal' and deduces particular cases from it (Socrates *et al.*). Woolf avoids this logic, for an enthymeme far too often begins, 'all women are' – this and that. As the narrator says, she leaves aside the problem of 'the true nature of woman and the true nature of fiction' (4). In an inductive argument, by contrast, an example like Shakespeare's sister would be added to other examples from observation, until enough examples had gathered to warrant a general conclusion. Woolf does reason this way up to a point, adding real women to her fictional one, and by the accumulation of similar cases, concluding that no woman battling conditions inimical to her creativity will write as

Shakespeare did. But inductive argument works by analogy, each example somehow like the others until the collective resemblance forces a conclusion (Gelley 3). The logic of induction, though, can only take her so far, and she goes well beyond it. By also using Shakespeare's sister as a synecdoche, Woolf leads away from absolute truth claims as either the beginning or ending of a linear argument, and away from absolutizing altogether. For by introducing this trope, Woolf begins to develop more fully the idea of a multiple female subjectivity, as women together enable Shakespeare's sister to 'walk among us in the flesh' (148). In this way, Shakespeare's sister is not simply 'like' other women by analogy; she stands for them in their collectivity. She is a part which represents the whole. Together, women are to move toward the conditions in which 'she' embodies a woman writer's mind free of obstacles: those barriers, assumptions, and internalized rules of chastity and much else which hinder them now. Like the 'incandescent' mind of Shakespeare, 'there must be no obstacle in it' if the artist's mind is to free 'whole and entire the work that is in' her (73).

For some critics, the impersonality suggested by 'incandescence' and the move toward an androgynous mind seem to contradict Woolf's materialist argument and her claim that women think back through their mothers.[11] Yet Woolf's use of 'obstacle' here is critical. Obstacles like the beadle and the library door force digression by confronting women with patriarchy's insistence on defining female subjectivity. By this logic, women are continually reminded of their place in a universal class 'woman' as conceived by men; in response, women write in anger and protest, distracted from thinking as they otherwise might. How wonderful to imagine a time, Woolf seems to argue, when women define their own subjectivity and wander freely where they will – rather than having to bang on closed library doors and argue with beadles.[12] When that time comes, Shakespeare's sister can return, her presence created in relation to other women and made possible by collective effort and will. Such incandescence does not mean that women will stop thinking as women, though they will no longer think of themselves as patriarchy does. Nor will they leave the female body with all its materiality behind; for only when Shakespeare's sister takes on flesh will the idealized future arrive. As Woolf clearly reminds us, Shakespeare's sister is not only forbidden the life of the mind, but 'severely beaten by her father.' She is not only turned away from the stage door, but is seduced and dies, her body buried in a secret grave. All this has been the cost of society's 'fetish' for chastity (64), one which makes chastity's sacrifice 'the greatest of human disasters' (139).

Is it too much to think that Woolf's argument also proposes an end to this fetish, one of women's greatest obstacles, and proposes not only aesthetic but sexual autonomy? I don't think so, particularly when considered in the light of feminist thought that views the body as space, the primary space of subjectivity.[13] Laura Mulvey, for example, analyses the body as a sign in terms of space, particularly in relation to film. There, she argues, 'the body as topography, [is] a phantasmagoric projection which attempts to conceal, but in fact reproduces, the relation of signifier "the female body" to psychic structures' (57). In other words, patriarchy constructs the space that is the female body, and by projecting it on the screen, reproduces the myths and misogyny which give 'meaning' to the body. We can easily make the analogy to other spatial practices, in which the 'projected' or created space reconfirms the power and practice that 'created' it. The body's 'meaning', in Mulvey's terms, is constructed spatially, projecting the image of 'female beauty as... an exterior, alluring, and seductive surface that conceals an interior space containing danger and deception' (58, 59). This spatial representation of the female body with its alluring outside and dangerously concealed inside, like Pandora's box, has critical implications for the relegation of women to particular social places, and spaces. As Ludmilla Jordanova argues, 'in presenting something as inaccessible and dangerous, an invitation to know and to possess is extended. The secrecy associated with female bodies is sexual and linked to the multiple associations between women and privacy' (qtd. Mulvey 61). What Woolf has done in the example of Shakespeare's sister then, is to reveal patriarchy's spatial practice in relation to women's bodies; rules of chastity enforce both the secrecy and danger of women's sexuality, as much as that 'privacy' seems an invitation to discovery and even violation. In perfect freedom, the space of the body can be rewritten by women, she seems to suggest, beginning with Shakespeare's sister. Her revival, body and spirit, depends on the spatial practices of women.

Some of the effort which will revive the dead poet is now being undertaken, Woolf suggests, by the equally fictional and synecdochic Mary Carmichael, whose imagined novel opens new paths for women's fiction. But when Woolf stops her digressive speculation on what Mary Carmichael might write, and continues reading what she has written (which is also imagined), she concludes that she's not yet there. 'Give her another hundred years... She will be a poet... in another hundred years' time' (123). Clearly, Mary Carmichael is not one 'she', but many, the women-writers-to-come. That multiplicity is also the charge Woolf lays on Mary Carmichael's fictional shoulders. She will go out 'in the spirit of fellow-ship' to re-dress and gather in 'the courtesan, the harlot and the lady with the pug dog' and record the countless lives of obscure women: the 'very ancient lady crossing the street', who remembers 'the streets lit for the battle of Balaclava', but not the details of her daily life at any given moment. Mary Carmichael in her multiplicity will write about 'the women at the street corners with their arms akimbo, and the rings embedded in their fat swollen fingers... the violet-sellers and match-sellers and old crones... [and the] drifting girls whose faces... signal the coming of men and women and the flickering lights of shop windows' (115, 116, 117). Woolf imagines this host of women as her mind wanders London streets, handing over to Mary Carmichael the freedom to wander, too.

Mary Carmichael is one of *A Room*'s last tropes, one of Woolf's many 'errors', digressions, and refusals of 'essential oil'. Like Shakespeare's sister, Woolf's third Mary creates by circuitous route a space within which women can gather, women whose commonality does not elide their specific and varied identities. For Woolf, there is no monolithic 'woman'. Even two sexes, Woolf suggests, are not enough, 'considering the vastness and variety of the world' (114). Imagine what the news of many other sexes would mean: 'we should have the immense pleasure... of watching Professor X rush for his measuring-rods to prove himself "superior"' (115). Apparently, there's more than one way to burn a professor. In other words, through her tropes of Judith Shakespeare and Mary Carmichael, Woolf gathers in all women, but rejects the universalized 'woman' which makes so easy a target for professors and patriarchs. To what can they compare themselves now if 'woman' is many women mapping spaces and tracing itineraries of their own?

This multiple subjectivity based in difference seems to have been one truth toward which Woolf's meanderings have been heading. The fictional 'I' which she replaces with the three Marys and 'any name you please' thus also becomes a synecdoche. Woolf clearly seems to intend as much, as she recites her resumé in collective historical terms: Before coming into her £500, 'I had made my living by cadging odd jobs from newspapers, by reporting a donkey show here or a wedding there;... by addressing envelopes, reading to old ladies, making artificial flowers, teaching the alphabet to small children in a kindergarten. Such were the chief occupations that were open to women before 1918' (48). Here, the Woolf made of Marys is also the many women who worked at what they could before the war. Because her class of 'women' is multiple and non-absolute, that self-confidence she imagines for the future will not come from the 'I' whose 'straight, dark bar' casts a shadow across the page, and in whose shadow 'nothing will grow'. And what is hidden behind the 'I'? 'Is it a tree? No, it is a woman. But... she has not a bone in her body... for Alan had views and Phoebe was quenched in the flood of his views' (130–1). Again, it is not merely women's views and words which concern Woolf, but women's bodies, and the freedom to give them flesh and life. The liberty of both body and thought, in a space which is not patriarchy's, may eliminate the need for certain kinds of digression, the diversion of energy into battle. But Woolf is not promoting an end to wandering. In fact wandering for her is always a spatial practice of both body and mind, one which sheds further light on her spatial practice in *A Room of One's Own*.

We know Woolf's own wandering best in relation to London, a space of both freedom and threat. To think about the meaning of walking in cities, we can turn again to spatial theory, this time the work of Michel de Certeau. In his chapter 'Walking in the City' from *The Practice of Everyday Life*, de Certeau contrasts the panoptic view of New York from atop the World Trade Center with the 'ordinary practitioners of the city' walking below (90–1). While the eye from above takes in a totalizing view of the city, the walkers 'follow the thicks and thins of an urban "text" they write' with their bodies (93). Their paths are 'intertwining, unrecognized poems in which each body is an element signed by many others,' signs de Certeau calls 'surreptitious creativities' (93, 96). These everyday practices and creativities reappropriate city space, rewrite it, and subvert the panoptic view from the tower which is analogous to the disciplinary mechanisms of city planners and 'ministers of knowledge' (95). These walking bodies create a different city, many cities, through the enunciations of their 'walking rhetorics' (100).[14] Nothing exemplifies de Certeau's ideas better than Woolf's many scenes of street haunting, among them the essay which takes that name. In 'Street Haunting', Woolf's experience of the city has virtually nothing to do with a path that can be traced on a map. For such a tracing cannot recover the experience as it happens. The multiple paths and poetries which she crosses in her ramble, with their derelicts and deformed characters, quarreling stationers, office workers bound for home, lovers on the Embankment, an overheard conversation, and a dwarf buying shoes, remind Woolf of the city's multiplicity, and the many spaces that wandering creates. 'What greater delight and wonder can there be than to leave the straight lines of personality and deviate into those footpaths that lead beneath brambles and thick tree trunks into the heart of the forest where live those wild beasts, our fellow men?' (*DM* 28). Encounters, scenes, and the projections of fiction take her off the straight path into the non-linear and multiple, even into the multiplicity of herself. When the walker imagines herself on a Mayfair balcony in pearls, she blames Nature for it. 'When she set about her chief masterpiece... she should have thought of one thing only. Instead,... into each one of us she let creep instincts and desires which are utterly at variance with his main being, so that we are streaked, variegated, all of a mixture' (*DM* 24). As she asks what the true self is, she answers by recourse to the language of space and wandering: 'Or is the true self neither this nor that, neither here nor there, but something so varied and wandering that it is only when we give the rein to its wishes and let it take its way unimpeded that we are indeed ourselves?' (*DM* 24).

In *A Room of One's Own*, Woolf, for once, is not always walking in the city.[15] But she thinks through the issues of her talk there and walks through the city to do her research. She determines, somewhat facetiously, that the British Library will surely be the place to find truth about women; for there, truths are produced by 'the learned and the unprejudiced, who have removed themselves above the strife of tongue and the confusion of the body' (32). Immediately, however, in order to get to this truth, she passes through London streets, with their dismal weather, open coal-holes, cabs with Swiss or Italian fortune-seekers or refugees and their luggage, 'hoarse-voiced men' on streets with 'plants on barrows', shouting or singing their wares (33). This is the world of the body, of de Certeau's 'intertwining, unrecognized poems', and of her own body rewriting the city and inscribing its own subjectivity, her individual gaze creating space as it moves through a world of continually-shifting perspectives and scenes. Contrast that with her entrance into the British Library, where she becomes like 'a thought in the huge bald forehead' encircled by male writers' names. As she faces the amassed material on women, she is a 'single but by now somewhat harassed thought' inside the dome (33, 37).

A Room of One's Own creates spaces within which women are not merely thoughts in a patriarchal brain. Her tropes, like those city walks, and like her walk through and away from Oxbridge to Fernham, might bring us back to consider the many spaces in her work.[16] As she suggests in *A Room*, space is written by the mind and body in motion, assertions of subjectivity. It is also created by the mobile gaze, the countless individual points of view which rewrite and challenge the spaces of the panoptic or objectivizing eye. Those multiple, singular points of view, and the 'many varieties of error' through which space is written, lead to truth. And along the way, there are countless stories to tell.

Notes

1 Travelling is even embedded in the etymology of 'metaphor,' to transfer. Even more so in contemporary usage apparently. In modern Athens, Michel de Certeau notes, mass transit vehicles are *metaphorai*. Thus one rides a metaphor to work (115).

2 While the two words originally derive from different roots, 'errant' from the Latin 'to journey,' and 'error' from the Latin 'to wander', as in wander off the 'correct' path, Woolf uses 'error' in both senses at once as she wends her way through the unfixed itinerary of *A Room of One's Own*.

3 This line has continued, importantly, in the work of Michel de Certeau and Edward Soja. Foucault's writing on the Panopticon in *Discipline and Punish* and 'Space, Knowledge, Power' articulate similar ideas. Working in a different area rooted in Dolores Hayden's work in urbanism and architecture, Daphne Spain examines how space reinforces gender relations.

4 Jane Marcus points out that Woolf's notion of trespass on patriarchal privilege and control is often conceived in spatial terms ('Thinking Back Through Our Mothers').

5 Elsewhere I develop an argument on Woolf's spatial aesthetics ('Virginia Woolf's Poetics of Space'); see also Leslie Hankins, 'Virginia Woolf's Spatial Art and Critique.'

6 For example, see Jane Marcus, 'Art and Anger', and Elaine Showalter.

7 See Lisa Low, 'Refusing the Hit Back: Virginia Woolf and the Impersonality Question'.

8 Gualtieri's reading of Woolf's essays, including *A Room*, rejects the usual distinction in essay studies between the traditions derived from Montaigne and Bacon. The first constitutes the discursiveness of the individual bourgeois subject whose non-conclusive observations claim no transcendent authority; the second leads to a distilled, aphoristic certainty. Reading Woolf in terms of this opposition eliminates the possibility of intervening in history or ideology in any meaningful way. Critics who have read Woolf's essays in the tradition of Montaigne include Catherine Sandbach-Dahlström; co-authors Ruth-Ellen Boetcher Joeres and Elizabeth Mittman; and Juliet Dusinberre.

9 In this, Woolf faced the same dilemma as her Victorian predecessors. Caught in a double-bind, women essayists in the mid-nineteenth century began publishing journalism to promote change. For these writers, personal experience provided the fuel for argument about women's need for education and work. And yet, the 'evidence' was tainted as both an inappropriate assertion of ego, and a further confirmation that women belonged in the sphere of the personal and private (Seeley, 'Victorian Women's Essays').

10 Peggy Kamuf reads Woolf's rejection of 'I' in light of her identifying that subject marker with the male author whose personality overwhelms the

text she pulls off the shelf. Kamuf's Foucauldian analysis suggests that 'I' 'is not a power derived from the masculine subject to which the 'I' simply refers. Rather the identification of subjects is already *an effect of power's articulating itself in bodies*, differentiating and ordering their intercourse' (11).

11 In response to critics who find that the modernist aesthetics of *A Room* overwhelm its effectiveness as materialist argument, Kathleen Wall argues that the fictional apparatus of the frame narrative 'create[s] a dialogue about the relationship of aesthetics to material conditions' (187) while resisting linearity and monologism.

12 For representative arguments on this question, see Tuzyline Allan and Lisa Low. Allan argues that Woolf's refusal of 'I' is a form of capitulation; Low defends Woolf's strategy.

13 Elizabeth Grosz, for example, argues that the body 'stripped' of traditional notions and oppositions ('mind and body, inside and outside, experience and social context, subject and object, self and other... male and female') is the material condition of subjectivity (241).

14 Edward Soja articulates a similar idea of one space as many spaces in his theory of 'thirdspace.' For Soja, thirdspace is experiential space or 'lived space'.

15 Rachel Bowlby briefly traces Woolf's trajectory in *A Room of One's Own* in 'Walking, Women and Writing' and points out the frequency with which Woolf links writing, women and walking. See also Susan Squier's *Virginia Woolf and London: The Sexual Politics of the City*; and Deborah Parsons.

16 Elsewhere, I develop an argument on Woolf's spatial aesthetics. See my 'Virginia Woolf's Poetics of Space,' as well as Leslie Hankins' 'Virginia Woolf's Spatial Art and Critique'.

3
Women and Interruption in *Between the Acts*

Helen Southworth

In the work of Virginia Woolf space and gender are concepts that are inextricably bound together. Space provides a vehicle for questions about gender, about the inclusion of one sex and the exclusion of the other, and about the access of each to power. Spatial configurations, represented spaces, such as houses and libraries, and textual spaces, such as parentheses and ellipses, suggest the capacity of space to divide along gender lines. They also constitute the means to overcome that same division.

Feminist scholars in the fields of geography, architecture, and anthropology have focused on the divisiveness of space in the realm of gender. In *Gendered Spaces*, Daphne Spain asserts that 'architectural and geographical spatial arrangements have reinforced status differences between women and men' and further that '"[g]endered spaces" separate women from knowledge used by men to produce and reproduce power and privilege' (3). Claudine Herrmann, speaking from a literary and legal perspective, echoes Spain: 'for man, the disposition of space is primarily an image of power, maximum power having being achieved when he can dispose of the space of others' (114).[1]

The study of space and gender in Woolf's work has ranged across her fictional and non-fictional texts, covering such topics as the split between public and private or domestic space, the work's engagement with metropolitan and imperial spaces, and its relationship to painting.[2] Building on the work of Peggy Kamuf, Rachel Bowlby, and Shari Benstock among others, and focusing specifically on the figure of interruption, I want to suggest here that Woolf manipulates space as a means to empower the women in her work and that that manipulation of space extends beyond representations of physical space to linguistic space. Thus, the following questions shape this study: How and to what effect are questions of gender filtered through a network of spatial imagery and rhetorical figures? How does a retention, rather than a resolution of the problem of space, a movement towards rather than an arrival at a destination, enable Woolf to reopen questions of sexual difference?[3]

In *A Room of One's Own*, Woolf calls for the writing of 'a supplement' to history, a body of scholarship from which women have been for the most part excluded:

> It would be ambitious beyond my daring, I thought, looking about the shelves for books that were not there, to suggest to the students of those famous colleges that they should re-write history, though I own that it often seems a little queer as it is, unreal, lopsided; but why should they not add a supplement to history? calling it, of course, by some inconspicuous name so that women might figure there without impropriety? For one often catches a glimpse of them in lives of the great, whisking away into the background, conceal-ing, I sometimes think, a wink, a laugh, perhaps a tear. (*ROO* 58)

This call for a supplement, rather than a re-writing, demands some-thing synchronous. It calls for a filling out of gaps that seeks not to erase but rather to mark those omissions as it bridges them. An inter-ruption and interpolation of this sort, a simultaneous and continual opening and closing of the text, I will argue, forces a rethinking of the parameters of an established body of scholarship, here 'history'. It does not, however, necessitate a forfeiting of difference, a coming together and a closing down of the text. Instead it enables the retention of a certain differential. Thus just as Lily Briscoe celebrates the retention of the problem of space as she completes her painting at the close of *To the Lighthouse*, '*Heaven be praised for it, the problem of space remained*, she thought, taking up her brush again' (my emphasis 231), so does Woolf. Like the hollow in Lily's painting ('And she began to lay on a red, a grey, and she began to model her way into the hollow there' [231]), the laugh, the wink, the tear, rifts in the smooth texture of the literary landscape, signal that this difference is there, and, furthermore, that it is there to be made.

Throughout Woolf's work characters, more often than not women, are found on thresholds and at the margins of the text. In *A Room of One's Own*, Woolf describes what happens as a woman enters a room, as she negotiates the threshold (of the English language/of a room), here figured at the level of the sentence by the semi-colon and the dash.

> One goes into the room – but the resources of the English language
> would be much put to the stretch, and whole flights of words would
> need to wing their way illegitimately into existence before a woman
> could say what happens when she goes into a room. The rooms
> differ so completely; they are calm or thunderous; open on to the
> sea, or, on the contrary, give on to a prison yard; are hung with
> washing; or alive with opals and silks; are hard as horsehair or soft
> as feathers – one has only to go into any room in any street for the
> whole of that extremely complex force of femininity to fly in one's
> face (113–14).[4]

The making of difference (what happens when a woman goes into a
room?), for Woolf, is thus an ongoing question, perhaps beyond the
power of the English language, in its legitimate form, to resolve. It
entails a continual renegotiation of space. Breaking the threshold over
and over again, Woolf's woman marks the line separating inside and
outside only to explode it moments later. Possibilities are layered one
on top of the other, spaces transformed one into the other, illustrating
a refusal to answer (for certain, in one word) the question of what difference it makes that it is a woman, not a man, at the door. What is
suggested, however, is that it does indeed make a difference. The flights
of words cannot comprehend the 'complex force of femininity,' that is
already current to the text. Coming in she must be prepared to go out
again. Admission of difference entails a recognition that the (textual)
space divides and separates, interrupts itself, functioning perhaps as
much as a reminder of distance and of difference as a promise of the
possibility of resolution.

In a short section of *The Infinite Conversation*, entitled 'Interruption
(as on a Riemann surface)', Maurice Blanchot points to the centrality of
interruption to what he calls 'dis-course': 'Interruption is necessary to
any succession of words; intermittence makes their becoming possible,
discontinuity ensures the continuity of understanding' (77). In the
pages that follow he distinguishes between two different kinds of interruption. These are 'the pause that permits exchange [and] the wait that
measures infinite distance' (79). One type of interruption seeks to
unify, the other serves to measure distance, to mark difference. In the
latter case, 'I no longer want to recognize one whom a still common
measure – the belonging to a common space – holds in a relation of
continuity or unity with me. What is in play now is the foreignness
between us, [...] everything that separates me from the other [...]' (77).
This second type of interruption, I suggest, informs Woolf's spatial

practice. One detects in neither the spaces represented nor the representational space in her work a desire to create a common space in which difference is left at the door. Woolf does not necessarily seek to bridge the gap separating the one from the other, but instead she aims to re-mark, to emphasize the centrality of difference to the work. 'For,' as she insists in *A Room of One's Own* when discussing the physical conditions which affect the shape of women's books, 'interruptions there will always be' (101). Rather than positing two separate spaces, permitting distinctions such as inside/outside, yes/no to persist, Woolf focuses on intersections. These spaces are fraught with possibility.

The recurrence of the spatial configuration of a woman entering a room across the length of Woolf's opus resonates with Blanchot's description of writing. For Woolf, the question of difference is indeed an ongoing one. At another point in *A Room of One's Own*, Woolf's narrator, reading the work of her own creation, fiction writer Mary Carmichael, detects or, rather, creates, an upsetting of the order of things, a deviation (a dis-course of sorts). Here Woolf in fact practices what she describes, breaking the sequence of her own sentence. Mary, she suggests, had 'broken up Jane Austen's sentence [...] Then she had gone further and broken the sequence – the expected order' (119). Mary, unshaken by the chorus of chiding voices, of bishops, deans, professors, and patriarchs, characterized as hurdles to be crossed, defies limitation, entering without hesitation.

> [S]he will not need to limit herself any longer to the respectable houses of the upper middle classes. She will go without kindness or condescension, but in the spirit of fellowship into those small, scented rooms where sit the courtesan, the harlot and the lady with the pug dog. There they will sit in the rough and ready-made clothes that the male writer has had perforce to clap upon their shoulders. But Mary Carmichael will have out her scissors and fit them close to every hollow and angle. (115)

Mary Carmichael's strength, then, is conceived as an interruption, a crossing of a different threshold. She enters a room 'without kindness or condescension', refashioning material encountered therein. Mary's/Woolf's innovation does not lie so much in a complete rejection of conventional narrative structures as in a cutting out and redressing of a line of thinking that does not account for difference, for 'every hollow and angle'. Like Lily Briscoe, Mary works in the angle and the hollow, at a turning point in the text where the line dips, wavers, doubles.

Herein lies difference. Woolf's use of the future tense throughout this passage reinforces the fact that this project is in process.

In *Mrs Dalloway*, Clarissa stands unseen at a window on the staircase observing her elderly neighbour moving from room to room. From this (liminal) standpoint, Clarissa temporarily foregoes her centrality to the major narrative and instead takes on a role peripheral to that of another. From this insecure site or intersection (neither upstairs nor downstairs, inside nor outside) she is able to contemplate her own world and that of the other, and to gain an understanding of the relationship between the two. This sighting, this re-siting, forces Clarissa to a revelation of sorts: '[A]nd the supreme mystery [...] was simply this: here was one room, there another' (108). She understands that the problem of space remains. Reading inside out, from the outside in, she understands what she terms an 'ordinary [thing]', that is, that her life runs concurrently to that of others and, most importantly, that her life is defined in relation to these other lives (108). This spatial configuration opens Clarissa's eyes to questions of difference, of otherness. Her epiphany is expressed in spatial terms: 'she came in from the little room' (158).

Woolf's last novel, *Between the Acts*, is a border text of sorts. Woolf wrote *Between the Acts* as a second world war appeared imminent and then became a reality. As critics have noted, questions of difference and sameness are central to this text.[5] While this last novel marks an ending, it also constitutes a beginning. As suggested by its title, this novel treats that which usually remains unrepresented, that which occurs in the interval, between the acts, behind the scenes. Written and set, indeed, between the wars, the destination of this novel, perhaps more than any other, is subject to question. The imminent outbreak of war threatens the calm of the English village, Englishness, tradition.

Woolf began writing *Between the Acts* as she struggled to finish her biography of Roger Fry and awaited responses to her recently published *Three Guineas*. It is clear that, while anxious over the fate of these two other works, *Between the Acts* opens up an entirely new space to her. In her diaries, she suggests she has reached a turning point in her career as a writer: 'I shall never write to "please" to convert; now am entirely & for ever my own mistress' (*D* 5: 275).

In *Between the Acts* those thresholds where the central narrative strain overlaps or intersects with a second admit difference into the novel, forcing an upsetting of the uni-directionality of the prose. They constitute outlets or, conversely, inroads; they function as signposts that guide the reader through, and often out of, the novel. They at once underscore the limitations of the novel and point to alternative possibilities, to other ways through. Women are more often than not found at these turning points in the text; they are behind these interruptions.

Early in *Between the Acts* Isa, entering the library unexpectedly, finds her father-in-law engrossed in memories of his exploits as a young soldier in the Colonies:

The door opened.
'Am I,' Isa apologized, 'interrupting?'
Of course she was – destroying youth and India. It was his fault, since she had persisted in stretching his thread of life so fine, so far. Indeed he was grateful to her, as she strolled about the room, for continuing.
Many old men had only their India – old men in clubs, old men in rooms off Jermyn Street. She in her striped dress continued him, murmuring, in front of the book cases: 'The moor is dark beneath the moon, rapid clouds have drunk the last pale beams of even ... I have ordered the fish,' she said aloud, turning, 'though whether or it'll be fresh or not I can't promise. But veal is dear, and everybody in the house is sick of beef and mutton ... Sohrab,' she said, coming to a standstill in front of them, 'What's *he* been doing?' (*BA* 16–17)

This moment, I argue, is central to the novel as a whole. Isa's physical infraction, entering the library, is matched by a verbal one: her question interrupts the nostalgic reminiscences of the patriarch. This interruption of the mental, verbal, and physical spaces occupied by Bart Oliver constitutes a disruption of her father-in-law's nationalistic sentiment, an explosion of the spatial configurations, the straight lines, drawn by patriarchy and imperialism. The threat posed by the admission of Isa, of difference, to the integrity of the library is representative of that to which the house, the family, the nation and its history, all bastions of patriarchy, are subject at this moment of temporary reprieve, between the wars.

While Isa's intrusion disrupts the nostalgia of her father-in-law, dreaming of India, her presence in the house, for the Oliver family, and her production of an heir is essential to the continuation of the name of the patriarch. This tension is paralleled at the level of the sentence. Having suspended the narrative with her intrusion she revives it only moments later, reopening it with a question. Isa remarks the gaps and at once fills them, making connections, continuing the sentence, and continuing, in both senses, his line. While Isa supplements her father-in-law, his India, her complicity is at once accommodating and disruptive. Bart Oliver's heir, Isa's son, George, is not well, he lags behind (13), and according to Isa's father-in-law he is '"a cry-baby"' (17). Isa, herself, is described as 'abortive' (14): 'she loathed the domestic, the possessive; the maternal' (17). Neither mother nor child conforms to their familial role.

This scene recalls another earlier in the novel. In a fashion characteristic of the text as a whole the reader is led from one fragment to another, each of which appears to be without any apparent connection. In this instance a discussion of Isa's heritage is followed by the observations of 'a foolish, flattering lady' (15) regarding the status of the library and its position and function in relation to the other rooms of the house, which raises questions of privilege, and of literary value. The library, the unidentified lady repeats (this is later cited by Isa [17]), 'pausing on the threshold,' is the heart of the house, and after the kitchen it is the nicest room in the house (15). Her clichéd comments are at once affirmed and denied by the narrator: 'In this case a tarnished, a spotted soul. [...] Nobody could pretend, as they looked at the shuffle of shilling shockers that week-enders had dropped, that the looking-glass always reflected the anguish of a Queen or the heroism of King Harry' (15).

This earlier intrusion into the library, like the second, opens up questions of space and gender. From the threshold the unidentified woman foolishly celebrates the opposition with which she is met, mimicking the patriarchal imperative to tell the truth; an imperative which bars her admission as a woman, as an element of difference, as a question, into this sacred space. The narrator's interjection that follows, however, pushes the door open from the inside, puncturing holes in the walls of the airtight cliché. The library, while it remains at the centre of the house, is no longer accorded the status of a singular, pure originary space; instead, it is characterized as transitional, as flawed. Its contents do not reflect 'the anguish of a Queen or the heroism of a King Harry', the books on its shelves do not perpetuate patriarchal notions of the superiority of one gender or one class over another. This library is a locus made up of the 'shilling shockers', of discursive fragments discarded by people passing through, books bought 'in order to stave off possible mind hunger' resulting from the three-hour train journey from London to 'this *remote* village in the very *heart* of England' (my emphasis 15).

The problematization of centrality and peripherality that topples the library from its place of privilege (echoed in this last quotation) is borne out across the length of the novel in terms of the architecture of Pointz Hall and the other spaces represented in the novel. The chapel has become the larder (29), the barn resembles a Greek Temple (24). The principal staircase, decorated with 'an ancestress of sorts' (7) (in fact not an ancestress at all, merely 'a picture' (33), she is an intruder), is flanked by another lesser one 'a mere ladder at the back for the servants' (6). The drama occurs on the terrace, the space that skirts the house, rather than within its walls. The trees that sit at the edge of the terrace 'suggest columns in a church; [...] a church without a roof; [...] an open-air cathedral' (59). The very house itself, Pointz Hall (hall, passageway), rests in a hollow, submerged ('Nature had provided a site for a house; man had built the house in a hollow' [9–10]). An emptiness lies at the centre of the house: 'A vase stood in the heart of the house, alabaster, smooth, cold, holding the still, distilled essence of emptiness, silence' (33–4).

Like the house, those that reside within its walls, the Olivers, despite pretensions to the contrary, are not well established (6). The authenticity of their ancestry is somewhat tenuous. They have 'no connection with [...] the old families who had all intermarried, and lay in their deaths intertwisted, like the ivy roots, beneath the churchyard wall' (6). A watch, which had stopped a bullet on the field of Waterloo, is preserved under glass, but it did not go down at the side of an Oliver, but at that of a nameless butler. The 'ancestress of sorts' (7) is accompanied by a real ancestor: '[h]e had a name. He held the rein in his hand' (33), but the ancestor's concern seems to be with whom and what has been omitted from his portrait, namely his 'famous hound', Colin (33). In this way the reader's attention is again forced to stray beyond the frame, to the 'secondary', to the outline or frame and beyond, to the omissions or gaps in the text, which, in this case, are the result of social convention. For, just as the painter had not found room for the hound in the picture, the 'Reverend Whatshisname' had refused to bury the dog at the feet of his master, in the same grave, as was his request (33). Thus, that which lies beyond the perimeters of a space dictated by social convention begins to take precedence over that which falls within its boundaries.

This is also true of the boundaries of the text itself. *Between the Acts* closes where it opens. In the opening scene a number of people sit discussing the cesspool 'in the big room with the windows open to the garden' (3); in the closing scenes of *Between the Acts* we return to the

very same room: 'Isa let her sewing drop. The great hooded chairs had
become enormous. And Giles too. And Isa too against the window. The
window was all sky without colour. The house had lost its shelter'
(197). Despite the closure suggested by a return to the same room, the
circularity is undermined by the shaking up of its contents. Isa, initially outside the room, now stands by the window, now 'all sky
without colour', its limitlessness opening the house to attack. Old
Oliver and Mrs Swithin retire, leaving Giles and Isa in their place. The
unfinished quality of the work suggested by the succession of a
younger upon an older generation is reinforced by the words with
which it ends: 'Then the curtain rose. They spoke' (197). This final
affirmation momentarily closes, only to then re-open, the novel. Like a
ledge to the novel, it is at once a part of and apart from the work.

Between the Acts flouts teleology and, like the play at its centre, is not
exclusively plot driven: 'Don't bother about the plot: the plot's
nothing' (82). The use of the term 'plot' here with its spatial connotations, that is, plot as a measure of land, suggests the resistance of
Woolf's novel to an enclosure of any kind. Like *Mrs Dalloway*, *Between
the Acts* juxtaposes two major narrative lines: in the former work the
worlds of Septimus (he is described as 'a border case' [71]) and Clarissa
exist side by side, in the latter the domestic drama being played out
within the walls of Pointz Hall runs concurrent to the pageant, Miss La
Trobe's dramatic reconstruction of the (literary) history of England,
taking place on its doorstep, on the terrace of Pointz Hall. However in
this double drama, the very title of which prefigures its slipperiness,
immediately directing the reader's attention away from the central narrative strain to a space in between, which discursive thread, whose
history, should be privileged in order to be disregarded? Do we read the
historical as privileged over the lesser domestic (the historical drama
over the domestic scene)? Or alternatively, do we understand the
domestic drama as the official history, and Miss La Trobe's as the lesser
unofficial, the 'supplement to history,' called for by Woolf in *A Room of
One's Own* (58)? The play is a parody of sorts, its author a woman, an
outsider, reputedly of Russian origin, of 'suspect' sexual orientation.

The fact that the novel is, in many respects, typically English, as
J. Hillis Miller has noted, does not downplay Woolf's innovation, but
on the contrary makes all the more striking those moments at which
she breaks with a conventional element. Woolf combines conventional
features from different places, rendering the resulting whole anom-
alous. This can be seen, for example, in her reversal of certain generic
conventions, disregarding the unities of classical and neo-classical

drama, to produce a historical drama that plots the history of England from Chaucer's time to the present day, within a novel structure that takes place over a single day. She embeds a play within the narrative, only to then go on to question its relationship to, its difference from, the novel structure within which it appears: 'Then the play began. Was it, or was it not, the play?' (70), and later 'So it was the play then. Or was it the prologue?' (70). The stage directions which accompany Miss La Trobe's play also pose problems of place in that they are at once part of the novel and part of the play. Further examples of the deconstruction of textual boundaries, of the problematization of the generic boundaries include the interpretation of the play that is attempted within the text.

Bart Oliver, like Richard Dalloway of both *The Voyage Out* and *Mrs Dalloway*, and Mr Ramsay of *To the Lighthouse*, is represented as the guardian and purveyor of a certain truth. His conception of history and of its telling is at odds with that of his sister. Bart Oliver, bolstered by his well-respected credentials, recounts with confidence the history of the land.

> The old man in the arm-chair – Mr Oliver, of the Indian Civil Service, retired – said that the site they had chosen for the cesspool was, if he had heard aright, on the Roman road. From an aeroplane, he said, you could still see, plainly marked, the scars made by the Britons; by the Romans; by the Elizabethan manor house; and by the plough, when they ploughed the hill to grow wheat in the Napoleonic wars. (3–4)

Similarly, when his sister asks him about the decision to build Pointz Hall in such an unfavourable position, in a hollow, facing north, Bart again responds with absolute conviction: '"Obviously to escape from nature [...]" Then he told her the famous story of the great eighteenth-century winter' (7). In both cases, however, the weight of Bart's assertion is undercut: like the lay of the novel itself, its surface scarred by stylistic and textual innovations of different historical moments, the lay of the land manifests at one single moment, 'the present moment', the historical transformations it has undergone; the decision to locate the house in a hollow in order to 'escape from nature,' as Bart asserts, was the wrong one.

Meanwhile Lucy, whose last name, Swithin, suggests hesitation (to swither is to hesitate), occupies murkier realms at the edges of the text. Her favorite reading is an 'Outline of History', a creative reconstruction

of the history of the world that tells of a time when 'the entire continent [...] was all one' (8). She cannot decide where to spend her
summers, Kensington or Kew, so she stays put (7). She exults in her
own 'imaginative reconstruction of the past'; 'she was given to increasing the bounds of the moment by flights into past and future; or sidelong down corridors and alleys' (8–9). She moves laterally: 'She
advanced, sidling, as if the floor were fluid under her shabby garden
shoes, and, advancing, pursed her lips and smiled, sidelong, at her
brother' (19); '[S]he left the sentence unfinished, as if she were of two
minds [...]' (68); her glance is divided (8). Lucy is 'so volatile, so
vagrant', despite the fact that she is weighted down by religious commitment (68); she believes that 'we have other lives [...] We live in
others [...] We live in things' (64); she stands 'between two fluidities,
caressing her cross' (184).

In another section that opens and closes appropriately with the
phrase '[t]hat's the problem' (26, 28), signalling its centrality to the
novel, discussion of a domestic issue – the availability of fresh fish –
leads to a question of space. In this passage questions of space and
measure are articulated with terms of gender.

> 'Are we really,' she said, turning round, 'a hundred miles from the
> sea?'
> 'Thirty-five only,' her father-in-law said, as if he had whipped a
> tape measure from his pocket and measured it exactly.
> 'It seems more,' said Isa. 'It seems from the terrace as if the land
> went on for ever and ever.'
> 'Once there was no sea,' said Mrs Swithin. 'No sea at all be-
> tween us and the continent. I was reading that in a book this
> morning. There were rhododendrons in the Strand; and mammoths
> in Piccadilly'. (27)

While Bart Oliver, Isa's father-in-law, responds without hesitation, his
accuracy and certitude intending to lay to rest, with one swift stroke
(note the somewhat comical speed suggested by the verb 'whipped'),
Isa's questioning of the border, his sister and daughter-in-law move in
different directions. The realism of Bart's concise retort, in response
to a question that appears almost rhetorical (Isa's turning movement
suggests a mulling over of the idea, rather than an effort to seek
clarification), is set in sharp contrast to the poetic, expressionistic
quality of the responses of Isa and Mrs Swithin.[6] Their answers do not
set out to refute his accuracy, but instead they move in a lateral, thick-

ening perspective. The women's use of repetition, Mrs Swithin's reference to a second text, her reconstruction of the landscape of a different
moment (juxtaposing in a single space a now and a then), the remembering, and the free association which marks the fragment from which
this quotation is lifted – 'The Pharaohs. Dentists. Fish ...' (28) – extend
the boundaries of the text on a verbal and a visual plane, to use
Geoffrey Hartman's terms.[7] Their different words cut across the limit-
line implemented by Bart. Both women promote a retention of the
problem of space, a continual getting there ('it seems'/'I read'), rather
than a resolution, an arrival at or the establishment of a fixed boundary. Isa and Mrs Swithin cannot make out a shoreline, a sure line. The
tide rises and falls, water laps, covering and uncovering the land, each
time re-marking (in a different place) the line that joins and separates.

In the same way, Isa is cut by a line that divides two spaces.
Standing at her dressing table she contemplates her own framed image
in a three-folded mirror. The image in the mirror is static, while that
beyond the frame is active.

> She lifted [her silver brush] and stood in front of the three-folded
> mirror, so that she could see three separate versions of her rather
> heavy, yet handsome, face; and also, outside the glass, a slip of
> terrace, lawn and tree tops.
> Inside the glass, in her eyes, she saw what she had felt overnight
> for the ravaged, the silent, the romantic gentleman farmer. 'In love,'
> was in her eyes. But outside, on the washstand, on the dressing-
> table, among the silver boxes and tooth-brushes, was the other love
> [...] Inner love was in the eyes; outer love on the dressing-table. But
> what feeling was it that stirred in her now when above the looking-
> glass, out of doors, she saw coming across the lawn the perambula-
> tor; two nurses; and her little boy George, lagging behind? (12–13)

Here Isa mediates, physically speaking, between inside and outside.
This scene mirrors her role, the place she occupies in the text as a
whole. Isa has married into the Oliver family. Her first appearance in
the opening pages of the novel, taking the form of an interruption,
underlines the fact that she is an outsider, that she is not really one of
them. Entering unexpectedly, she arrests the living room discussion of
the cesspool and of the history and geography of the county:

> 'But you don't remember ...' Mrs. Haines began. No, not that. Still
> he did remember – and he was about to tell them what, when there

was a sound outside, and Isa, his son's wife, came in with her hair in
pigtails; she was wearing a dressing-gown with faded peacocks on it.
She came in like a swan swimming its way; then was checked and
stopped; was surprised to find people there; and lights burning. [...]
What had they been saying? (4)

Isa interrupts and then continues the narrative: 'What had they been
saying?' (4).

Isa's patching over parallels her use of her domestic work as a front
for her creative production. She writes her poetry in a 'book bound like
an account book in case Giles suspected' (14). Disguising her creative
work as domestic work, she blurs the boundaries between the two
spheres, undoing the conventional deprivileging of the latter. This covering up is paralleled at the level of the sentence. Isa fills in the gaps,
she supplies silences. She addresses 'Mrs Manresa silently and thereby
[makes] silence add its unmistakable contribution to talk' (36). The
pairing of the full terms, such as 'contribution' and 'supply,' with the
emptiness connoted by 'silence,' endows the second term with an
unusual degree of fullness or affirmation. Isa hums her poetry; she discusses domestic matters aloud.

These citations or disjunctive asides, Isa's secret passages out of the
domestic plot, interrupt or puncture the borders of the text as they
undo the limits of the domestic space. That which Isa recites, both her
own work and that of others, questions the primacy of the central narrative strain. The difficulty encountered in attempting to untangle Isa's
discourse, to determine exactly what is hers and what is not, once
again implies a deprivileging, this time of the cited authority.

Unlike her husband Giles who is inarticulate ('[h]e had no command
of metaphor' [49] and bound by convention he is 'pressed [...] flat;
held [...] fast, like a fish in water' [43]), Isa is articulate, her language
flexible, creative. She shifts with ease from one register to another,
negotiating the spaces in the work, effecting transitions, handling
metaphor in her poetry. Isa's poetry charts a contrary impulse, that is,
to collapse oppositions and at once to refigure them elsewhere. Thus
she retains rather than resolves difference: '"What do I ask? To fly
away, from night and day, and issue where – no partings are – but eye
meets eye – and ... O ..."' (76); '"To what dark antre of the unvisited
earth, or wind-brushed forest, shall we go now? Or spin from star to
star and dance in the maze of the moon? Or ..."' (47).

In the first of these citations the opposition of night to day is erased
in an elsewhere. There it is replaced by a reciprocal, balanced con-

frontation ('eye meets eye') the affirmative outcome of which is figured in the exclamation, 'O,' and the ellipsis with which the fragment closes. In the second fragment a movement, as in the last case, a flight, elsewhere (from here to there) once again entails a confusion and rethinking of opposition. One loses there what binds one here, one gains freedom but this prize is attained at a cost. Again in the last fragment Isa raises the question of destination. The multiplication or layering of question upon question, the repetition of the conjunction 'Or,' marks a joining and parting over the terrain of the text. The other places to which the lines of Isa's poetry point are fraught with danger, 'the dark antre of the unvisited earth, the wind-brushed forest [...] the maze of the moon.' In all three moments a desire for escape is articulated, but that other place is put into question. It is conceived in terms of indeterminacy, openness.

> 'Did you feel,' she asked, 'what he said: we act different parts but are the same?'
> 'Yes,' Isa answered. 'No,' she added. It was Yes, No. Yes, yes, yes, the tide rushed out embracing. No, no, no, it contracted. The old boot appeared on the shingle.
> 'Orts, scraps and fragments,' she quoted what she remembered of the vanishing play. (193–4)

Thus that which is not voiced, is not said aloud for all to hear, takes on a singular importance to the narrative. It is marked as unsaid, denied a space in the text, at the very moment at which it is included (by an omniscient narrator). A textual undercurrent or undertow enters into a relation with the central text, arresting and undermining the unidirectionality of the narrative, entangling and complicating its multiple strains. The sub-plot (the unheard, the unsaid, the barely heard, the murmur, the hum, the whisper) unwrites, puts into question, deviates, as Woolf put it herself in a 1925 letter to French painter Jacques Raverat, from the 'formal railway line of sentence' (*L* 3: 135). In this way, marginalia become central to the text, background becomes foreground, or rather actively modifies it.

Hence Miss La Trobe's place in the text.[8] Miss La Trobe adds yet another dimension to the text, as the true outsider, marginalized further by her sexuality and her putative foreignness, she continues Isa. Entering late she remains to some degree a silent presence in the text (57). She constitutes, and is in fact in the process of writing, the subplot. Miss La Trobe writes in the margins, she stands in the wings, in the trees. Her text is split, she overturns the primacy of the main text, uncovering 'the roots beneath water' (59); 'for another play always lay behind the play she had just written' (58); 'Was it an old play? Was it a new play?' (98). '[S]he had gashed the scene here. Just as she had brewed emotion, she spilt it' (85). 'What is her game? To disrupt? Jog and trot? Jerk and smirk? Put the finger to the nose? Squint and pry? Peek and spy?' (164).

The text reaches a pitch at the moment when the two texts (play and novel) converge in the Present Moment: 'The hands of the clock had stopped at the present moment. It was now. Ourselves' (167). We find Miss La Trobe here, bringing together and at once holding apart.

> Like quicksilver sliding, filings magnetized, the distracted united. The tune began; the first note meant a second; the second a third. Then down beneath a force was born in opposition; then another. *On different levels they diverged. On different levels ourselves went forward;* flower gathering some on the surface; others descending to wrestle with the meaning; but all comprehending; all enlisted. (169–70; my emphasis)

Her 'voyage away' constitutes an entrance, her resolution, a retention, a decision to remain apart. 'She took her voyage away from the shore, and, raising her hand, fumbled for the latch of the iron entrance gate' (190). Her last words create another ledge to the text: 'she heard the first words' (191).

Like the chimes of St Margaret's that follow on those of Big Ben in *Mrs Dalloway*, in Woolf's *Between the Acts* a second voice, issuing from another place, a feminine voice, follows on the first, momentarily coinciding with it, and then takes off from it, marking an omission, forcing a gap, but refusing to fill it, except with 'orts, scraps and fragments,' other things besides (*BA* 194). Interruption, physical and textual, proves a powerful tool in reconceiving power relations between the sexes in *Between the Acts*. Retaining rather than resolving questions of space and questions of gender, Woolf's last novel moves beyond the established, solid mean or limit, established by the patriarchal law, into a new space, a space of difference.

Notes

1   See also Massey (1994).
2   Studies of space and gender in Woolf's work include: Abel, Beer (*Common Ground* 149–78), Benstock, Bowlby (*Virginia Woolf*), Kamuf, Smith, Solomon, Seeley, Friedman, Snaith, and Sarker.

3　In my 'Rooms of Their Own: How Colette Uses Physical and Textual Space to Question a Gendered Literary Tradition' (2001) I ask a similar set of questions of the work of Woolf's contemporary Colette.

4　See Peggy Kamuf's analysis of this same quotation in terms of identity and self-interruption (17–18).

5　See, for example, Miller (1982).

6　Bart's claim to clear-sightedness recalls the linear thinking of other Woolfian males, including that of Mr Ramsay in *To the Lighthouse* (he has gone from A to Q, but can go no further) and of Richard Dalloway in *The Voyage Out*, whose ideal is '[u]nity of aim, of dominion, of progress' (67).

7　In 'Virginia's Web', Hartman suggests that Woolf's combination of realistic plot and expressionistic prose enables her most effectively to counter problems of (dis)continuity within and between the different layers of the text.

8　'Her name suggests *trope*, perhaps: those liturgical phrases whose frequent repetition makes it possible to embellish and re-order them without erasing communal meaning' (Beer, *Common Ground* 146).

Part II
Urban and Rural Spaces

4
'Re-reading Sickert's Interiors': Woolf, English Art and the Representation of Domestic Space

Linden Peach

A much-discussed topic in Virginia Woolf scholarship is the extent to which she was influenced by those artists who, from the 1960s onwards, became known as the Bloomsbury Group, by the European art, especially the Post-Impressionists, to which the Bloomsbury Group introduced her, and by the organizations whose origins were within Bloomsbury – the Friday Club, the Grafton Club, and the Omega Workshops.[1] But surprisingly the influence of Walter Sickert (1860–1942), whom Woolf and many of her friends, including Roger Fry, knew personally, has received little attention. This is especially surprising since Vanessa Bell and Duncan Grant were such strong admirers of Sickert's work, and, with Paul Nash, eventually took over Sickert's Fitzroy Street studio (*W.R. Sickert* 15). Woolf's own views of Sickert's art are well documented in her essay, 'Walter Sickert: A Conversation', which developed out of an after dinner conversation with him in 1933 and her visit in November to the major loan exhibition of his work at Agnews. However, her admiration for him dates from the first decade of the new century and, although he was less of a London presence during and after the First World War, she has left on record that at a party in January 1923, he was one of the old friends with whom she talked with especial pleasure (Lee 466–7).

Walter Sickert, as David Peters Corbett argues, was 'an important figure in the development after 1850 of an art in Britain which took the circumstances of modern life for its subject matter' (Peters Corbett 150). Like Virginia Woolf, and most of the Bloomsbury artists, he was concerned with the way that the medium itself, in his case paint and in Woolf's prose, could investigate as well as reflect modern experience. In this chapter, I want to suggest that there are comparisons to be made between aspects of Woolf's fiction and Sickert's paintings, mainly figures in interiors, completed in London in the period 1910–1914. Woolf was undoubt-

65

edly familiar with these works at the time they were painted, and they largely constituted the 1933 exhibition on which she based her essay. The most obvious similarity between her earlier fiction – *The Voyage Out*, *Jacob's Room* and *Orlando* – and these paintings is their shared concern, albeit much more muted in Woolf's work, with prostitution (Marshik 853–86). However, while it is difficult to be very precise about how Sickert may have influenced this aspect of her earlier novels, her essay on Sickert suggests that in the 1930s she had a focused interest in Sickert's ideas about space which provides us with useful insights into *The Years* (1937). Sometimes seen as an anachronism in Woolf's oeuvre because of its apparent return to a realism which she rejected after *Night and Day*, *The Years* shares with Sickert's paintings an interest in the way in which space is invested with meaning through relations between objects and the human subject. Although Woolf wrote the novel at a time when she was reacquainting herself with his work, this renewed interest in Sickert, and the 'realism' of *The Years*, is a development of her concern with the fusion of the material and the psychological which may be found in all her novels, but is especially pronounced in the 1930s. Woolf's concern in *The Years* with meaning generated in a Sickert-like relation between people and objects within their shared spatial context undoes the traditional distinction between 'realism' and 'modernism' and between the 'material' and the 'psychological'.

Jane Goldman has pointed out that 'Sickert and his fellow painters were interested in portraying the everyday life of ordinary, working people' and argues that 'this portraiture of ordinary people mimics Van Gogh's taste in subject matter' (Goldman *Feminist Aesthetics*, 142). However, whilst Goldman maintains that Woolf 'in keeping with the Post-Impressionists under Sickert's influence, records social change in terms of colours' (Goldman *Feminist Aesthetics*, 142), she does not discuss their shared interest in the link between people and objects. Desmond MacCarthy pointed out in the catalogue of the 1910 exhibition that the Post-Impressionists 'were interested in the discourses of the Impressionists only so far as these... helped them to express emotions which the objects themselves evoked' (MacCarthy 8). Whilst there are parallels between Sickert's interest in ordinary working-class people and the work of Van Gogh and Cézanne, there are other important influences on his work as far as the representation of objects is concerned. Indeed, integrating human subjects and objects was a technique which Sickert undoubtedly borrowed from Lautrec – in *Femme du devant sa glace* (1897) Lautrec famously includes a tousled bed and clothes thrown over a chair – and from Degas whom he met when he visited Manet's studio. But less noted influences on this aspect of his work included Vuillard and Bonnard, whose absence from Roger Fry's 'Manet and the Post-Impressionists' exhibition at the Grafton Gallery prompted the retort from Sickert, 'Since "post" is the Latin for "after" where are Vuillard and Bonnard?' (Sickert 108). Their work was extremely influential for Sickert and others in his circle such as Spencer Gore, Harold Gilman and Charles Ginner. There are very obvious similarities between Sickert's nudes and, for example, Gilman's *A Nude in an Interior* (1911) and Vuillard's *Interior with a Screen* (1909–10). Sickert's *Le Lit de Fer* (1905), painted in one of the rooms at Fitzroy Street, achieves an effect whereby the female nude, lying on a bed aligned diagonally to the picture frame, seems identifiable with the bed and the hoop-backed chair set behind its headrail. The viewer is made to feel that this is the woman's room. As Woolf herself observed over twenty years later in her essay on Sickert, what is impressive about these early paintings is the level of intimacy between the models and the spaces which they occupy.

The emphasis upon human subjects in relation to the spaces that they occupy characterizes his studies of clothed figures together in rooms as well as his nude paintings including studies of two women together – *Les Vénitiennes* (painted in Venice, 1903–04) and *Les Petites Belges* (1906) – and, eventually, of the tension between a married couple, *The Little Tea Party: Nina Hamnett and Roald Kristian* (1915–1916). It distinguishes Sickert's domestic interiors painted over the ten-year period after *Le Lit de Fer* (1905) and *Nude on a Bed* (1905–6) from those of his Bloomsbury contemporaries. For example, Duncan Grant's *Interior, 46 Gordon Square* (1914) is a near abstract interior. The painting contains only elements recognizable as objects: a sofa, chair, and canvasses. Unlike in Sickert's work, the physical presence of the room is schematically realized through elements of the door frames and windows. There are no human subjects present.

At the time when Sickert was developing the project begun in his 1905 nudes, about the way relations between people and objects invested space with meaning, he and Woolf were virtually neighbours. Sickert had chosen to settle in London and have his studios there on his return from Dieppe in 1905. Although he continued to return each summer to France, he committed himself to Camden Town, North London, until the outbreak of the First World War. Woolf moved into Gordon Square, central London, in December 1904; the following year Sickert, who had taken rooms in a house on the corner of Mornington Crescent and Granby Street, acquired Constable's Studios in Charlotte Street, and a studio at 8 Fitzroy Street into which it runs, about ten minutes from Gordon Square across the Tottenham Court Road. In 1907, the Fitzroy Street Group was formed, consisting of William and Albert Rothenstein, Walter Russell, Spencer Gore, and, later, Ethel Sands, Nan Hudson and Lucien Pissarro. They formed the basis of the Camden Town Group which Sickert established in 1911. In the same year as Sickert moved to Fitzroy Street, Virginia and Adrian moved into 29 Fitzroy Square, where they lived until 1911. The distinction between Fitzroy Street and Fitzroy Square became so blurred that a hand-written inscription on the back of one of Sickert's paintings reads: 'Cocotte de Soho/ Sickert. Constable's Studio/76 Charlotte Street/Fitzroy Square/ Londres' (Baron and Shone 162).

These biographical details reinforce the fact that Woolf's essay on Sickert was based on paintings with which she was undoubtedly familiar years earlier – at the time Sickert worked on them. But they also suggest how she and Sickert had personal knowledge of the way that urban life in the metropolis was becoming oriented around rooms within houses, and of the way in which the material parameters of people's lives and their individual psychologies are peculiarly concentrated and interleaved in the spaces in which they live. As Woolf depicts in *The Years*, London streets and squares formerly occupied by large Victorian families gradually acquired a different social ethos in the late Victorian and Edwardian periods. In 1870, Camden Town was a wealthy and fashionable area of London, but by the time Sickert moved there, when the railways began to take the middle classes from inner London to the outer suburbs, it had become a place of boarding houses, warehouses and businesses – very similar to the London which Woolf describes in *The Years*. Fitzroy Square and Fitzroy Street themselves underwent similar changes. Many of the houses in Fitzroy Square had become nursing homes and studios; Sargent had his workshop there and in 1913 Roger Fry established his Omega workshop at which Sickert exhibited in 1915 (Lee 237).

Given the socioeconomic changes reflected in the very existence of the rooms in which he lived and worked, it is hardly surprising that Sickert's early paintings are characterized by an attempt to encapsulate the essence of modern life in the interiors of rooms. Although it was not until the 1930s that Woolf explicitly discussed Sickert's paintings in this way, there is some evidence to suggest that Sickert's work, including his infamous depiction of North London prostitutes, encouraged Woolf to think of rooms in terms of their spatial identities and their material presence in people's lives. Hermione Lee implies that Sickert's paintings may have influenced the way in which Woolf saw London on the other side of Oxford Street and the Tottenham Court

Road from Fitzroy Square. In a letter to Violet, written in November 1910, Woolf says she is dining out, 'in a little restaurant off Soho, where prostitutes lure young men. The wickedness of London on a day like this is inconceivable; one imagines vice smelling in stuffy rooms.' Lee rightly remarks that '[i]t sounds like a Sickert Camden Town painting' (290–1). Marsha Meskimmon has pointed out that 'Walter Sickert's series of works on the Camden Town murders explored the distressing theme of murdered, working-class women defined in contemporary discourse as "prostitutes" at the same time as it introduced modernist continental formal traditions into British art' (Meskimmon 10). The two-figure paintings, which Sickert began to paint around 1908, are among some of his more infamous work, including the paintings based on the murder of the prostitute Emily Dimmock in September 1907 and christened by the Press, 'The Camden Town Murder'. These include *The Camden Town Murder, or What shall we do for the Rent?* (1908); *Summer Afternoon* (1908), exhibited at the Carfax, Gallery, London, June 1911; *L'Affaire de Camden Town* (1909); and *Dawn Camden Town* (1909), exhibited at the Carfax Gallery, December 1912.[2] Woolf's phrase 'vice smelling in stuffy rooms' marks a shift in focus in her sentence from the immediate context of the restaurant, where she imagines prostitutes luring young men, to the prostitute's rented rooms which is the context in which Sickert painted them. Given that Woolf and Sickert had previously been, in effect, neighbours in Fitzrovia, and the notoriety which his paintings of prostitutes acquired, it is hard to disagree with Hermione Lee that Woolf was probably thinking of Sickert's work. However, what is more significant is that Woolf is thinking of an interior space, associated with women, in terms of the material reality and the oppression it represents.

The impact of Sickert's Camden Town nudes and his two-figure paintings, which combine Impressionist-influenced nudes and interiors with North London subject matter, lies in their social and material depth. This is achieved in the Fitzrovian nude paintings through techniques such as placing the bed at a diagonal to the plane of the picture so as to give the location greater depth and space, and by the tonal contrasts; for example, in *La Hollandaise*, the dark bedrail is picked up in the tonal caesura between the model's cheek and ear (Baron and Shone 168). In the Camden Town paintings the modernist realism Sickert sought to achieve is most obvious. For example, *The Camden Town Murder* depicts a clothed, middle-aged man in waistcoat and shirt sleeves sitting on the edge of an iron bedstead. Behind but close to him, with her hand on his knee, lies a nude companion visible from

Figure 4.1   Walter Sickert, *The Camden Town Murder*

the abdomen upwards. Her face is turned away from us; he wrings his hands and his head is bowed. The intimacy between them is mirrored in the way they are integrated with the room, the blankets and the pillow that supports her head. The despair evident in his agonized posture is underlined by the contrast between her hand on his leg and her turned head. The proximity of the bed to the wallpaper, which gives the crisis a specific material moment, is echoed in the way the two lives are physically, sexually, and psychologically entwined with each other. The constraints that render them vulnerable and lost are signified in the way the picture is contained between the boundary of his arm and the bedrail. His upper arm is thickened by the loose cut of his sleeve, suggesting the manly power made futile by the circumstances in which they find themselves; the bedrail indicates the imprisonment of the only option left to them: prostitution.

Although there is no evidence that Woolf was specifically influenced in her writing by Sickert's imaginary representation of prostitutes in their rooms, his work, like Woolf's novels, encourages us to think about prostitutes in terms of the cultural materialism that affects all women's lives. The subtitle of *The Camden Town Murder* – 'What shall we do for the rent?' – acts as a commentary on the title, directing us to think about the economic circumstances of the prostitute's life and how this has impacted on her not only materially but psychologically. The absent present in Sickert's paintings is the middle class who fail to appreciate the socio-psychic space that women such as Emily Dimmock occupy, and the economic circumstances that drive them to prostitution. In *The Voyage Out*, Woolf does not give a voice to the prostitute. The South American prostitute remains a silent presence, visiting the various hotel rooms. But she does give a voice to ill-informed, middle-class indignation through Evelyn Murgatroyd who argues for an interventionist group that will purge Piccadilly of these 'poor wretches' who are doing what they 'know to be beastly' (*VO* 289), and through Thornbury and Elliott who get the prostitute thrown out of the hotel. In doing so, Woolf interleaves different levels of ignorance of the cultural material circumstances surrounding prostitution.

Woolf's prostitutes – Mendoza in *The Voyage Out*, Florinda in *Jacob's Room* and Nell in *Orlando* – are independent characters. But the shift from Mendoza to Florinda demonstrates Woolf's increasingly explicit interest in the link between class, lack of education, economic circumstances, and prostitution. The Camden Town murder emphasized the vulnerability of prostitutes. This is exemplified in what happens to Mendoza, but is made much more potentially violent in *Jacob's Room*. After Jacob has rejected her, retreating to his privileged class and background, we hear that Florinda is pregnant. The possibilities for her now include abortion, and the risks that entails. But one wonders if Emily Dimmock's ghost haunts these pages. At this point in the novel, Florinda's facial expression is described as that of an animal, as Celia Marshik observes; it is an image that brings to mind, amongst many things, abuse and slaughter (Marshik 870). The words with which she disappears from the novel, 'she [stops] laughing', taken in context with the Camden Town murders are even more sinister than Marshik suggests. *The Voyage Out*, *Jacob's Room* and *Orlando* share Sickert's concern with suppressed emotional and physical violence, an aspect of Woolf's work which has only just begun to be addressed, as part of the material reality of domestic life.

Sickert's interest in suppressed violence as part of domestic life in his two-figure paintings is in part indebted to two Victorian genres, the social realist painting and the problem painting. These frequently depicted men and women who had fallen on hard times. James Kestner has pointed out:

> While the iconography of women in these canvasses conforms to gendered notions of female helplessness, passivity or abandonment,

males often appear feminized according to patriarchal conceptions because they were impoverished, destitute, unemployed, improvident or resourceless. (Kestner 143)

In *The Camden Town Murder*, the patriarchal paradigm, in the figure of the clothed man, is exposed as vulnerable and ineffective in the face of the economic and class constraints that impact upon their domestic lives. This painting recalls the problem picture, whose prototype was Arthur Egg's triptych *Past and Present* (1858), which depicts the fall of a wife and the consequences for herself, her unborn child, and her two daughters. Not only do we not know why Sickert's couple cannot pay the rent nor the nature of the conflict in which the two figures are embroiled, but the canvas signifies, like many Victorian problem paintings, male disempowerment as well as the vulnerability of the woman. It may be that they are discussing the only option open to them, which turns out to be an option into which she is coerced, or that he is with her after she has met with a punter.

The Victorian problem picture encourages us to look at individuals through the specific materiality of their lives. Woolf's well-known essay 'Mr Bennett and Mrs Brown' (1924) suggests that in 1923–4, despite her earlier rejection of Edwardian realism, Woolf was thinking of character in socioeconomic contexts. She started work on this essay in 1923, the year in which she coincidentally renewed her acquaintance with Sickert, and he may have influenced her developing concern to bring the material and the psychological together within one spatial frame. Sickert encouraged Woolf to rethink her criticism of the material detail in the work of Wells, Bennett, and Galsworthy. Despite their emphasis upon the material, Woolf now began to see it as insufficiently rooted in the kind of socioeconomic specificity that she had come to admire in Sickert's paintings. Sickert's work provided the materialist reading of people and society which Woolf now failed to find in writers such as Bennett. Woolf herself offers what we might describe as a 'materialist' reading of Mrs Brown, drawing attention to her neat, threadbare clothes, her anxious, harassed look, and her pinched features.

The approach that Woolf is recommending in her essay 'Mr Bennett and Mrs Brown' is much closer to Sickert's Camden Town Group and that of the Victorian problem picture, than that of Wells, Bennett, and Galsworthy. I say the Camden Town Group because Woolf's explication of Mrs Brown, and her supposition that she is a sea-side landlady, brings to mind several portraits by Sickert and his associates of female subjects which draw the viewer in, through their costumes and expressions, to the socioeconomic circumstances of their lives. These include Sickert's *The Objection* (1917), based on pen and ink drawings made in 1911; Sylvia Grosse's *The Sempstress* (1914), even though Grosse's gender disqualified her as a member of the Camden Town Group; and, albeit to a lesser extent, some of Vanessa Bell's portraits such as *Helen Dudley* (1915) and *Mrs St John Hutchinson* (1915). But the work of Harold Gilman is especially relevant. Living in a bedsit himself, he painted subjects in interiors which revelled in the kind of socio-economic context in which Woolf places Mrs Brown. Harold Gilman's *Mrs Mounter* (1917) shows an elderly lady, with pinched features and buttoned up, well-worn clothes, sat upright behind a table set with tea things. Her face looks out from a life-time of making ends meet. She is also the subject of another painting, *Interior with Mrs Mounter* (1916–1917), in which the interiority of the rooms, their dated but tidy furnishings, and their adequate but not luxurious comfort, reflects the interiority of the elderly lady herself.

Goldman argues that there are parallels between the Post-Impressionists and 'Woolf's interest in the rise of the lower classes from darkness into light' (Goldman *Feminist Aesthetics*, 142). However, their most profound influence is actually upon the rise of the lower middle class in Woolf's work from darkness into life, or a more specific realization of their cultural and material circumstances. When Woolf revisited Sickert's work in the 1930s, she was especially interested in his depiction of the way the material circumstances of people's lives impacted on their personalities and psychologies through their relation with objects in domestic interiors. In her essay on Sickert, Woolf noted the way in which he composed his paintings down to even small, precise objects such as castors on chairs and fire-irons. The point is illustrated in the essay with reference to *Ennui* (1914), the painting of a publican and his wife in their private room (see Figure 4.2), rather than to the Camden Town pictures. Yet there are elements of the relation-ship between the two figures, the tiredness and possible despair felt by the wife, which recall the Camden Town paintings. *Ennui* is a close-up view of a seated man smoking what looks like a cigar with a section of a woman behind emphasizing her head and bent shoulders. The effect of the painting is achieved by the way the figures, and the atmosphere between them, is integrated with the room, the plain wall-paper and the cheap chest of drawers. Thinking of *Ennui*, Sickert's friend Helen Lessore remembered 'the whole magic of the thing depended on the absolutely precise relation of the placing of these things' (Sickert 23).

How far Woolf in the 1930s shared, if indeed she were not directly influenced by, Sickert's investigation of the relations between spatial orientation and identity and/or gender is evident in *The Years* in the luncheon in Maggie's rooms at Hyams Place, attended by Sara and

Figure 4.2   Walter Sickert, *Ennui*

Rose. This belongs to the 1910 section of the novel which places it, perhaps not entirely coincidentally, in the period when Sickert was working on many of the paintings on which the 1933 exhibition was based. An indication of the importance which Woolf attached to this episode in the novel is that it is echoed later in the 'Present Day' section, when North is invited to lunch with Sara in her rooms at Milton Street. The interiority, and ultimately the intimacy between the people and their rooms, is pronounced because there is no attractive prospect from the windows; Maggie's rooms look out on a depressing street, dingy houses, and a large, glass-built factory.

As is the case with Sickert's Camden Town paintings, the nature of the rooms in *The Years* and the atmosphere within them are determined by very real socioeconomic forces, in society as a whole and within the lives of the inhabitants. But the emphasis is upon how the impact of these socioeconomic forces may be made evident to the reader by the individual's spatial orientation to others and the spaces which they occupy. Although, or perhaps because, previously she had lived round the corner from Hyams Place, Sara is uncomfortable in Maggie's lodgings. This aspect of the luncheon echoes Sickert's painting *The New Home* (1908) which seems to revel in the faded splendours of a dingy lodging house. A critic in the *Pall Mall Gazette*, 3 June 1908, described the painting thus: 'Here is a young woman ill at ease, apparently her hat not yet removed – her head and bust seen large against the mantelshelf – and she taking very unkindly to the second-rate, sordid lodging, to which she is condemned by an unkindly Fate' (Baron and Shone 205). Sara is as uncomfortable as Sickert's young woman. She notices that Maggie's rooms are 'poverty-stricken'; the carpet does not entirely cover the room. The space in which she sits, like that occupied by Sickert's young woman, is one upon which she has projected her own anxieties about poverty and one which she has introjected. In other words, neither Sara nor Sickert's young woman is simply placed within a relatively economically austere setting. In each case there is a dialectical relationship between the physical, material reality of the room and the psychology of the individual.

The account of the luncheon eschews the kind of detailed description that Woolf associated with Arnold Bennett's writing. Like Sickert's paintings, it is constructed around key objects: a sewing machine, to which a single sentence is devoted; an armchair by a fireplace with springs like hoops; an old Italian glass blurred with spots that used to hang in their mother's bedroom; and a crimson and gilt chair from the hall in Abercorn Terrace. As in Sickert's paintings, the dialectic between the inner subjectivity of the individual and the material reality of the room is in the detail: the silk cotton in the sewing machine, the little carvings on the doorposts, and the visible chair springs.

At one level in *The Years*, there is a sense of the upper middle class having fallen on harder, if not hard, times in that Maggie now cooks her own food, and makes her own clothes. At another, Sara and Maggie, like, maybe, Sickert's young woman, have moved from one kind of life into a new socioeconomic space in which they are forced to redefine themselves and their values.

The in-between space that Sara and Maggie occupy in terms of their past and present is analogous to the position of Maggie's rooms. The interior is never fully the 'inside' because of its proximity to the street. It is not set back from the road like the suburban Victorian villas. The street outside Maggie's room intrudes to the extent that it becomes part of the interiority. It is noisy: children are screaming, an 'iron man' bawls up to the windows, and there is a pub on the corner. In the later episode at Milton Place, the equivalent of Sara's reaction is provided by North's more uncompromising condemnation of what he sees as a sordid, low-down place. Woolf's observation of the importance of never straying outside the sound of the human voice, which was one of the things she professed to admire in Sickert's work in the 1930s, is everywhere apparent in *The Years*, where she seems especially interested to ground voices in particular material contexts. The conversation between the three women and their shared reminiscences of Abercorn Terrace are never allowed to take us very far from the reality of living in Hyams Place, through, for example, the sudden appearance of the dray or Rose's categorization of the children she taught as 'little thieves', or the man selling iron. Throughout the luncheon scene, Woolf appears anxious not to lose the 'tangible quality' that she found in Sickert's painting; the social context 'is made not of air and star-dust but of oil and earth' (*Y* 180). The 'iron man' at Hyams Place, the man selling vegetables at Milton Street, and the screaming children at both are the equivalent of Sickert's 'man selling cabbages in the shadow of the arch' (*Y* 181). The Hyams Place luncheon, like Sickert's paintings of women in rooms, pushes at the boundaries of what we mean by 'interiority' – in rooms, families, memories, individual consciousness – and its intimacy with the external in the form of material financial circumstances, physical surroundings, and social status, and their manifestation in physical objects.

Interiors such as Maggie's rooms in *The Years* are different from the utopian space, associated with the intellectual liberation for women, which Woolf envisaged in *A Room of One's Own*. But at another level, *A Room of One's Own* anticipates the ostensibly different directions in which Woolf's work was to pull her in the 1930s: between an interest in the material circumstances of women's lives on the one hand and an exploration of human consciousness, exemplified in *The Waves* (1931), on the other. Woolf comments on women's writing in *A Room of One's Own*: 'one remembers that these webs are not spun in mid-air by incorporeal creatures, but are the work of suffering human beings, and are attached to grossly material things, like health and money and the houses we live in' (*ROO* 53–4). This suggests that the emphasis upon the way space is invested with meaning through the relation between human subjects and objects in *The Years* is not the radical departure from her earlier writings that critics have presumed it to be. Instead, it should be seen as an extension of the kind of thinking about women's 'corporeality' evident in *A Room of One's Own*, which is taken to include not only the human body *per se* but the rooms in which women are forced to spend much of their time.

Thus Woolf's essay on Sickert may be seen as an extension of the ways in which she was already thinking about domestic interiors when, in the 1930s, she began to revisit works of his which she had known when she was younger. Her renewed interest in Sickert's domestic interiors, and the development of her ideas concerning subjectivity in its cultural material context in *A Room of One's Own*, was also in accord with Vanessa Bell's new-found enthusiasm for interiors. Bell's series of paintings of people in rooms began in 1934 with Duncan Grant and included *Virginia Woolf at 52 Tavistock Square* painted in the same year and *Interior with the Artist's Daughter* (1935–6). In the latter, the absorbed concentration of the female figure in the background, seated reading near a large, well-filled bookcase, is blurred with the intimacy of the room. In the foreground a large vase holding four narcissi and some artichoke leaves is positioned on a round table together with scissors, cotton and an open book. The table itself echoes the one next to the reader and the book is echoed in the one she is reading. The colours of the cloths on the table are picked up elsewhere in the room, including in the spines of the books on the shelves. But the colour of the cloth in the foreground specifically matches the dress that the woman is wearing. All these echoes serve to reinforce the relation between herself and the objects in her room while the room itself is virtually a metaphor for the self-absorbed, intimate, intellectual space which she occupies. Her position in the background, physically and mentally located in an interior within an interior, is between a bookcase which defines one limit of the painting and elements in the foreground conventionally associated with female domesticity: the vase, flowers, scissors and cotton.

There is a more pronounced interest in using the relation of human subjects to objects within interiors to explore the gendered, material context of women's lives in Bell's earlier works of the 1930s such as *The Nursery* (1930–32) and *Interior with Two Women* (1932). If we compare the former with *Nursery Tea* (1912), the cultural materialism embraced by the naturalistic style becomes evident. The social meanings in the relation of the two women, a mother and nurse, are generated not simply by their respective clothes but the poses that they adopt towards each other and towards the children. The nurse is busy and more intimately involved with the children. The mother is more distant, the child in the foreground looks away from her, and she holds one of the toys uneasily. The nurse, one suspects, appreciates more than the mother that the toys are play things; for the mother they are more likely objects. Class and economics determine individual women's experience of their subjectivity, as foregrounded in *Interior with Two Women* where the differences between two women in the painting, an artist and her naked model, belie the homogeneity of the title. The two women sit opposite each other. The relaxed, slouching model unselfconsciously confronts the viewer with her candid sexuality. The clothed artist, seated in an upright chair, is preoccupied with a bowl of fruit on a small round table beside her, perhaps lost in thought. Yet the way their feet almost touch and the way the naked flesh of the model is echoed in the bare flesh at the artist's neck and ankles suggest that there are points where the boundaries between them are blurred.

These paintings share with the luncheon in Maggie's rooms an attempt to use a domestic interior to explore female subjectivity at the interface of the inner self and the socioeconomic. This concentrated focus enabled Bell, as it did Woolf, to push back the boundaries of what we mean by 'interiority' and to investigate relations between spatial orientation and social identity. But, in appropriating techniques from Sickert's paintings and possibly even Vanessa Bell in *The Years*, the challenge for Woolf, as it so obviously was for Vanessa Bell in *The Nursery* and *Interior with the Artist's Daughter*, was how to depict an object so that it lost its 'separateness' and actually became a part of the composition of a scene without overwhelming it. Rose recognizes the chair from Abercorn Terrace with relief; it becomes part of her adjustment to Hyams Place, providing some sense of continuity with the past. Taking her cue from Sickert, as is evidenced in her essay on

Sickert, Woolf understates the combination of the psychological and the material. Rose's reaction is conveyed in no more than five words: 'she recognized it with relief' (*Y* 158). Some of the conversation in this scene, for example, when Rose talks of having lived in the district and having taught 'little thieves' (*Y* 162), is stilted, almost enigmatic, minimally interleaved with physical reminders of the materiality of the present, in this case the whirring of the sewing machine.

The force of the interconnection between the material and the psychological in Sickert's interiors caused Woolf, on the evidence of her essay on his work, to think of his paintings as 'stories' in which the material space in which the subjects are momentarily captured is inseparable from the psychological moment conveyed through a single brush stroke or colour. In writing of *Nuit d'Amour*, she imagines the young woman on the edge of the bed seeing her entire life, including her death, in a single moment and she appears to incorporate this notion into the luncheon scene where Rose, remembering details from her life at Abercorn Terrace that she had not thought about for years, thinks of herself as 'living at two different times at the same moment' (*Y* 159). Like the figures in Sickert's interiors, Rose is caught in what appeared to Woolf, in her reflections on Sickert's figures, to be a special moment. The same is true of Maggie, a few minutes later, arranging the flowers, 'not listening ... thinking her own thoughts' (*Y* 160). For Woolf, this special moment, as she explains in her Sickert essay, is one in which the individual is acutely aware of the burden that has been imposed on them by the materiality of successive, innumerable days. Rose, as Woolf envisages in discussing Sickert's figures-in-interiors, is shaken from such a moment by the materiality of the present – 'there was a great rattle under the windows. A dray went roaring past. The glasses jingled on the table' (*Y* 159–60) – into the demands of the current situation. Although Woolf's Sickert essay suggests that she developed this concept of special moments of material awareness, which she calls misleadingly a 'moment of crisis', through contemplating his works in the 1933 exhibition, it is not difficult to see the artist in Bell's *Interior with Two Women* and the mother in *The Nursery* as similarly caught motionless, as 'living at two different times at the same moment', and burdened by the materiality of their life histories.

Reading scenes such as the luncheon at Maggie's lodgings from *The Years* through Sickert's and Vanessa Bell's concern with interior spaces, and Woolf's own essay on Sickert, furthers our appreciation that the novel is a development of her long-standing interests and an exploration of spatial dynamics. Focusing upon how meaning is generated

in the relation between the psychological and the material in a concentrated space such as the interior of a room enabled Woolf to pursue
ideas which she first began to explore in her fiction years earlier in the
fusion of the private and the public. Such concentration suited her
conviction that political meaning is encapsulated, often subtly, in the
material environment, in private and personal interaction, spatial
proximity and social discourse. Attentiveness to detail in her interiors,
and the various forms of social reaction and interaction that occurred
within them, served her predilection for close, often cryptographic,
readings of social environments. Ultimately, in their imaginative rendering and analysis of how social meaning is generated in the relation
between individuals and between human subjects and objects within
domestic interiors, Sickert and Woolf are concerned, as Peters Corbett
says of Sickert, 'to enact the modernist imperative to depict the true
nature of the contemporary world'. But as 'the articulation of a meditation on the difficulty of doing so' (Peters Corbett 151), their works
constitute modernist rather than social realism.

Notes

1   See, for example, Diane Filby Gillespie, *The Sisters' Arts: The Writings and
Paintings of Virginia Woolf and Vanessa Bell* (Syracuse: Syracuse University
Press, 1988). For the Bloomsbury artists themselves, see Richard Shone,
The Art of Bloomsbury: Roger Fry, Vanessa Bell and Duncan Grant (London:
Tate Gallery Publishing, 1999). On The Camden Town Group, see Wendy
Baron, *The Camden Town Group* (London: Scolar Press, 1977).

2   On 12 September 1907, Emily Dimmock, a twenty-two year-old prostitute
well known in North London as Phylis, was found lying naked, with her
throat cut, in her bed at her lodgings at 29 St Paul's Road, Camden Town.
Sickert adopted the title 'Camden Town Murder' to encompass a series of
etchings, paintings and drawings featuring a naked woman and a clothed
man. It may be more than coincidental that Woolf changed the name of the
central character Cynthia in drafts of the text that became *The Voyage Out* to
Rachel, the name of the young model whom Sickert frequently painted in
his house at Mornington Crescent and who was the subject of *Little Rachel*
(1907). This painting is interesting when read alongside Woolf's novel in
which Rachel's voyage is a journey of sexual discovery and a journey into
herself as much as to South America. The painting is a half-length portrait of
a young girl in an interior, facing, and almost challenging, the spectator.
What particularly brings Woolf's Rachel to mind is the way she seems to be
looking out from her psychical as well as her physical location. The face
itself seems to encompass both innocence and experience.

5
Representing Nation and Nature: Woolf, Kelly, White*

Sei Kosugi

In a chapter titled 'Three around Farnham' in *The Country and the City* (1973), Raymond Williams draws an exquisite map of three versions of rural society represented in the works of William Cobbett, Jane Austen, and Gilbert White, who lived near Farnham almost in the same era. The present essay focuses on the interrelation or figurative encounter of three writers, beyond time and genre, in a particular local space of the Hampshire village of Selborne: Gilbert White (a clergyman-naturalist of the eighteenth century), Mary Kelly (an amateur pageant writer of the interwar period) and Virginia Woolf.

In 1938, Mary Kelly directed a local historical pageant in the village of Selborne.[1] The pageant was her adaptation of the famous book, *The Natural History and Antiquities of Selborne* (1789), by Gilbert White, who loved his native village throughout his life and wrote the local natural history of the region. Mary Kelly, who was born and lived in a village in Devon, was at that time very active in producing local historical pageants in several places in Britain. The pageant of 1938 was the revival of a 1926 version. In the village of Selborne in July 1938, a century and a half after the publication of *The Natural History of Selborne*, Mary Kelly launched the second production of her pageant titled *The Antiquities of Selborne*.[2] Meanwhile, in March 1937, Virginia Woolf had re-read *The Natural History of Selborne*, which had been one of her favourite books in her girlhood. Moreover, in September 1939, one year and two months after Mary Kelly's production, Woolf was writing an essay, 'White's Selborne', in the Sussex village of Rodmell, not far away, just across the South Downs from Selborne, Hampshire. How should we interpret this coincidence that two artists, Virginia Woolf and Mary Kelly, who had no personal contact, were both inspired by the eighteenth-century naturalist almost simultaneously? This question is the starting point of my discussion.

Though modernist literature is often associated with the city or urban space, the country or rural space is also an important topos in Woolf's writings. Woolf was interested in naturalist writing by Richard Jefferies and W. H. Hudson as well as Gilbert White. Woolf was a great lover of rambling in the country and was an ardent bug-hunter and butterfly collector.[3] Virginia and the Stephen family often stayed at manor houses or rectories in the countryside. In her early diaries, Woolf describes several villages such as Blo'Norton (Norfolk), Hopton (West Suffolk), and a fenland village in Huntingdonshire. There is no doubt that her early experience of nature – crab-catching in St Ives, moth-hunting or butterfly-collecting on the South Downs or on a Gloucestershire hill (*PA* 117) – provides direct sources for novels such as *Jacob's Room* (1922) and *To the Lighthouse* (1927). Furthermore, in her posthumously published novel, *Between the Acts* (1941), nature evolves into something more than a direct description. The last years of Woolf's career were a period when romantic perceptions of nature were sublimated into a representation of England itself, as Alun Howkins argues in his cultural geographical study of the English countryside. Although Woolf's perception of nature and nation is generally Darwinistic rather than 'romantic', such a cultural context still forms part of her novel. By analyzing the evolution of Woolf's nature writing in her essays, diaries, and novels, I would like to locate Woolf at the crossing point of two different, but interrelated, trends of culture in Britain: the amateur drama movements in the twentieth century and the amateur fashion for natural history, which had been popular since the Victorian era.

The Victorian fashion for natural history

According to Lynn Barber, the Victorian era was the heyday of natural history. Barber tells us (possibly with some exaggeration) that 'every Victorian lady could reel off the names of twenty different kinds of ferns or fungus' (13). It is certainly the case that fern gathering was in great vogue and books of natural history sold almost as well as Dickens' novels. A lady's chamber would be decorated with collections of shells, stuffed birds, and paintings of seaweeds. In drawing rooms where 'Wardian Cases' (fern-cases) and 'Warrington Cases' (parlour aquariums) were displayed, people discussed whether swallows migrate or hibernate. Correspondence columns in newspapers were also full of such debates. There were many female artists like Beatrix Potter, Anne Pratt, Marianne North, and Mrs John Gould who made illustrations of mushrooms, ferns, flowers, and birds (Barber 13, 14, 116, 126; see also works by David Elliston Allen).

In *Between the Acts*, we can see the residue of this upper-middle-class Victorian fashion for natural history. A variety of butterflies are named in the novel. The library of Pointz Hall holds books on local (natural) history such as *The Antiquities of Durham* and *The Proceedings of the Archaeological Society of Nottingham* (*BA* 18). Mrs Swithin, who is always thinking of swallows, is a person born and brought up in this atmosphere of the Victorian middle class. The nursery rhyme which Mrs Swithin sings – 'Come and see my sea weeds, come and see my sea shells, come and see my dicky bird hop upon its perch' (65) – is reminiscent of a Victorian upper-middle-class boudoir filled with shell collections, stuffed (or sometimes living) birds, and parlour aquariums.

It is possible to classify natural history into two groups. One can be named the colonial natural history of the adventurer or explorer, who voyages out and describes the rare animals, plants, and natives of new-found territories, of whom Alfred Russel Wallace, Henry Walter Bates, and Joseph Dalton Hooker are examples. They brought back considerable numbers of zoological and botanical specimens, which led to the foundation of Kew Gardens and other museums in Britain. This type of naturalist enterprise is closely related to the colonial expansion of the Empire. The other type might be called the domestic natural history of a hermit-like figure. The father of the latter type is Gilbert White. Quite indifferent to the political upheaval both within and outside Britain, White stayed and lived in his native village as a curate for most of his life, devoting himself to observing and describing the small creatures around him.

The Natural History of Selborne, which has been reprinted more than a hundred times, was a very influential book in the Victorian era and remained so in the twentieth century. According to Mark Daniel, it is 'the fourth most published book in English language' (Daniel p.x). W. H. Hudson remarks in his memoirs, *Far Away and Long Ago* (1918), that he read and re-read *The Natural History of Selborne* when he was 16 years old. Darwin, as a child, had a dream of becoming a country clergyman and naturalist like Gilbert White, and, in his last years, kept a diary in a rural village in Kent to write *Down Story* (Worster 183). Lynn Barber points out that White's famous book was 'an important source of inspiration for every Victorian amateur naturalist' (Barber 15). Leslie Stephen refers to Gilbert White in his eighteenth-century studies (Stephen, *English* 205). His daughter Virginia read White's *The Natural History of Selborne* in her teens and found in it an inspiration for her own creative writings.

Woolf's diary, essays, and natural history

Woolf mentions Gilbert White for the first time in her diary of 1899, written during her summer holiday in the Huntingdonshire village of Warboys. The diary opens with the record of her arrival in the village and her elation as she plunged into the fresh country air, catching a glimpse of a church spire flashing far away. In this diary 17-year-old Virginia imitates White's narration of natural history: recording the geology and altitude of the village, describing clouds at sunset, the potato harvest, and how the view of fields changes from summer to autumn. In this country writing, like the authors of the local historical pageants of the interwar years, Virginia also records some pieces of local history such as Queen Isabella's visit in the fourteenth century and the spread of an epidemic in the seventeenth. In her passionate record of moth-hunting (*PA* 145), for example, we can find a self-portrait of Virginia as a young amateur naturalist.

A brief survey of two other documents will serve further to illustrate Woolf's interest in natural history. Woolf contributed an anonymous article to the reader's column in *The Times* on 14 September 1916. The article was titled 'Butterflies and Moths: Insects in September' (Kirkpatrick and Clarke 251). In this essay, Woolf reveals the presence of small creatures which live their lives unnoticed by people: a little butterfly attached to a grass stem, swaying in the breeze like a 'highly decorated sail,' dragonflies circling over 'a patch of clover... as if they were at worship about a shrine of sun-baked turf,' a Crimson Under-wing tasting delight on a sugared tree, 'spiders and beetles and a great green grasshopper' attracted by a lantern, and 'grotesque insects, who come with angular and crab-like movements through the grass blades'. Unlike the somewhat immature Warboys Diary, this essay anticipates the clear-cut transparency and sharpness that we find in Woolf's later works, from 'Kew Gardens' (1919) to *Between the Acts*.

It is important to note that this article in *The Times* was written during the war and also during Woolf's long silent period just after her nervous breakdown. When Woolf restarts her diary during her three months' stay in Asheham House in 1917, she concentrates on recording small details of nature around her: 'mushrooms & blackberries' she gathered for food (*D* 1: 42), '[b]ees in attic chim[n]ey' (39), 'a large green caterpillar' becoming a Chrysalis (42, 43), '3 peacock butterflies' and 'innumerable blues feeding on dung' (40), '[t]he thistledown beginning to blow' (44), and the dead body of a pigeon slain and devoured by a hawk. The human world appears only rarely in this wartime diary except for a few references to a raid in Ramsgate and '[t]he great many aeroplanes' (44) passing over the house. The brief and factual descriptions of nature in the Asheham Diary are the fore-runners of those passages from 'Time Passes' in *To the Lighthouse* which depict nature without any human presence. The act of observing and describing nature, during the war and during the period of recovery from a mental breakdown, is for Woolf a means of maintaining mental stability amid chaos both external and internal.

Woolf's novels and natural history: *The Natural History of Selborne* and *Between the Acts*

It was almost forty years after Woolf had made the first entry in her diary about Gilbert White that she again grew interested in *The Natural History of Selborne*. It was just before the outbreak of the Second World War. Woolf was in the Sussex village of Rodmell, writing her final novel, *Between the Acts*. She re-read *The Natural History of Selborne* in March 1937 (*D* 5: 73) and in September 1939 she published an essay titled 'White's Selborne'. Woolf's comment on Gilbert White in her diary of September 1937 (*D* 5: 74) exactly envisions this essay of 1939. These dates are significant because the idea of her novel, *Between the Acts* (or *Pointz Hall*), was conceived during the period between them. She started her first draft on 2 April 1938 and, ten days later, made the first clear allusion to the novel in her diary as follows: 'Poyntzet Hall: a centre... composed of many different things... English country; & a scenic old house' (*D* 5: 135).

We can observe a certain interrelation between White's text and Woolf's. When she describes in the essay the opening part of *The Natural History of Selborne*, Woolf draws attention to the fact that White's narration is quite similar to that of a novelist.

> There it is before us, the village of Selborne, lying in the extreme eastern corner of the county of Hampshire, with its hanger and its sheep walks and those deep lanes 'that affright the ladies and make timid horsemen shudder.' The soil is part clay, part malm; the cottages are of stone or brick; the men work in the hop garden and in the spring and summer the women weed the corn. *No novelist could have opened better.* (emphasis added)

There are similarities between White's England, in Woolf's account, and the setting of *Between the Acts*, as the following italicized phrases particularly suggest:

just as the vicarage garden seemed to Aunt Snookes [*sic*] tortoise a whole world, so as we look through the eyes of Gilbert White England becomes immense. *The South Downs,* across which he rides year after year, turn to 'a vast range of mountains.' ... though London and Bath exist, ... *rumours from those capitals come very slowly across wild moors and roads which the snow has made impassable. In this quiet air sounds are magnified ... We hear the whisper of the grasshopper lark;* the caw of rooks is like a pack of hounds 'in hollow, echoing woods'; and on a still summer evening the Portsmouth gun booms out just as the goat-sucker begins its song ... *There is a continuity in his happiness; the same thoughts recur on the same occasions ... Year after year he was thinking of the swallows.* ... His 'days passed with scarcely any other vicissitudes than those of the seasons.' (emphasis added) (Woolf, 'White's Selborne')

When Woolf set *Between the Acts* in a small obscure village in 'the very heart of England' (15), she may have been thinking of Gilbert White and his representation of the English countryside. The general atmosphere of Selborne described by Woolf in the essay is exactly what she tries to recreate in her own novel. Incidents in the novel echo White: for example, the episode of 'the great eighteenth-century winter' when 'for a whole month the house had been blocked by snow' (7) echoes White's record of the winter of 1783. What is accentuated in *Between the Acts* is the repetition or continuity of human history and the natural circle of life: the annual enactment of village pageant, migration of swallows (they have come across Africa every year since prehistoric times) (*BA* 93), and the landscape unchanged through the centuries (the narrator says that Figgis's Guide Book of 1833 'still told the truth' in 1939) (*BA* 48). If we note Woolf's above-cited remarks that 'there is a continuity in his happiness; the same thoughts recur on the same occasions. Year after year, he was thinking of the swallows,' we can see that, at the moment of 1939 when the continuity of history is threatened by the outbreak of war, Woolf longed for the simple sense of 'continuity' that White managed to maintain in the eighteenth century.

White's Selborne and Woolf's Rodmell are both villages in the south of England. White often visited his aunt who lived near Lewes (which is close to Rodmell), and both White and Woolf used to stroll around the South Downs. It seems natural that Woolf, in her last years when she spent much time in Rodmell, felt a stronger affinity with White and saw nature in Sussex through the naturalist's eyes. White's

England is quite local, but it is universal as well, in that the eighteenth-century landscape he describes in his piece – a flock of rooks flying to their nests, wind martins circling around the church tower, and a barn owl – is something familiar in any other place in rural England as well as in the Sussex village of Rodmell in the early twentieth century.

White's natural history is, as the author himself calls it, a record of 'the life and conversation of animals' (White 67). Woolf says in the review, 'the story of Selborne is a vegetable and animal story. The gossip is about the habits of vipers and the love interest is supplied chiefly by frogs.' If we reread Woolf's *Between the Acts* from this view-point, we notice how the novel, too, is indeed filled with insects, small animals, birds, and plants: butterflies behind the stage of the pageant, dragonflies shooting through the trembling grass, spiders on the lily pond, a barn owl, mice and beetles in the barn, a flock of starlings, swallows, violets, orchids, and the cornfields and the heath moor in the background. We can hear sounds of insects, 'the swish of the trees, the gulp of a cow, and even the skim of the swallows over the grass' (175). The human beings living in Pointz Hall are also compared to different species of fowls (a duck, a swan, a canary, a swallow, an owl) and even to a pre-historic mastodon; their behaviour is narrated by analogy with that of grasshoppers, ants, and beetles. Woolf removes the boundary between humans and animals, reducing them to what White calls 'the life and conversation of animals'. John Glashan's frontispiece to *Cultures of Natural History* (1996) humorously illustrates 'History' as 'people killing each other' and 'Natural History' as 'things eating each other' (Jardine *et al.*, p.[iv]). This Darwinian view, reducing human desires to animal instincts, is also present in *Between the Acts*.

Moreover, some of the descriptions and comparisons of animals and plants in this novel are quite similar to visual illustrations in natural history books. Comparisons such as 'as a thrush pecks the wings off a butterfly' (5), similes such as 'ripe like the apricot into which the wasps were burrowing' (52), and images such as a thrush with 'a coil of pinkish rubber twisted in its beak' (8) and 'humming birds quivered at the mouths of scarlet trumpets' (98) are all akin to the vivid and colourful pictures of birds and small animals feeding. Such images recur in the minds of female characters: Mrs Haines, Mrs Manresa, and Mrs Swithin. The last example is from Lucy Swithin's meditation. Reading *Outline of History* by H.G. Wells, Lucy imagines the prehistoric landscape of Piccadilly as a swamp with 'a riot of rhododendrons, and humming birds quivered at the mouths of scarlet trumpets' (98). It is curious that there were actually neither humming birds nor rhododendrons in prehistoric Britain: humming birds are native to North and South America and rhododendrons are originally from the Himalayas.[4] It was only in the mid-nineteenth century that the rhododendron was brought into the British Isles, though it became the most popular flower in English middle-class gardens of wealthy suburbia in the early twentieth century with the rhododendron craze called 'rhododendro-mania'.[5] Old Lucy's confusion suggests the fantastic nature of Woolf's very 'English' imagination.

An essential characteristic of Woolf's representation of nature is the anti-anthropocentric point of view. Between the acts of La Trobe's historical pageant and the human drama of the people in Pointz Hall, there is another drama, what might be called 'a silent drama of nature' of birds, insects, and small animals.[6] The silent drama of small creatures such as swallows 'dancing to the unheard rhythm of their own wild hearts' (60), 'cabbage whites drink[ing] icy coolness from silver paper' (58), and mice making their nests in the barn is evolving unobserved by the human characters. Giles's discovery of a snake swallowing a toad is a rare moment when such hidden dramas are revealed to the eyes of human beings.

The vision of the silent drama of nature, which has been going on since ancient times and will go on even after humans disappear from the earth, is also present in her earlier works such as 'Time Passes' in *To the Lighthouse*, the interludes in *The Waves* (1931), or a scene in *Jacob's Room* which describes '[a] fritillary bask[ing] on a white stone in the Roman camp' (25–6). This vision of nature looms up again in Woolf's mind at the outbreak of the war when human civilization might be reduced to ashes at any moment.

At the intersection between the twentieth-century amateur drama movement and amateur natural history

In July 1938, one year earlier than Woolf's publication of 'White's Selborne', Mary Kelly had produced a historical pageant, *The Antiquities of Selborne* (Figures 5.1 and 5.2). During the period between the First World War and the Second World War, local historical pageants were popular in Britain. Amateur drama movements such as village plays developed in local communities, aided by the nationwide institutions of the British Drama League, the Village Drama Society, and The Arts League of Service, which were all established just after the First World War.[7] Mary Kelly, who wrote the pageant of Selborne, was the secretary of the Village Drama Society. Along with Louis N. Parker, she is an

Figure 5.1 'William of Wykeham finds the Canons of the Priory Maying', from Mary Kelly's Selborne Pageant of 1938

important figure in the history of amateur drama in twentieth-century Britain, especially in connection with the blossoming of local historical pageants. She contributed much to the development of amateur drama in local towns and villages in Britain. Kelly's enthusiasm for amateur theatre arose from her production of two little religious plays in the fifteenth-century barn attached to the manor house in her native village, Kelly, in North Devonshire. She wrote and directed several historical pageants: Rillington in Yorkshire (1927), Bradstone (1929) and Launceston (1931) in Cornwall, and Exeter in Devon (1932).[8] Though there is no knowing whether Woolf knew about these productions, we can find there an interesting intersection between two different cultural currents: the Victorian upper-middle-class fashion for natural history and the twentieth century grassroots amateur drama movements which developed in local communities. How did these two currents intersect? Why did this symbolic encounter between Mary Kelly and Virginia Woolf occur at a specific moment of history (the late 1930s) and at the Hampshire village of Selborne?

David Matless points out, in *Landscape and Englishness* (1998), that the landscape is 'both natural and cultural' (Matless 12). In other words, the landscape is a cultural construction; it includes the antiquities of human history as well as natural scenery. Local historical pageant and local natural history cross each other on this definition of landscape. These two cultural trends of reading nature and culture in a local landscape amalgamate in Mary Kelly's pageant, *The Antiquities of Selborne*.

Figure 5.2 'Gilbert White,' from Mary Kelly's Selborne Pageant of 1938

A new type of historical pageant comes on stage in the twentieth century. It is quite different from the official Victorian pageantry of Empire which has a grand finale with Britannia on stage and the chorus of 'God Save the Queen'. The official pageantry in a patriotic or nationalistic vein still survived on such occasions as Empire Day or coronations even in the twentieth century.[9] Alongside the old type of pageantry, however, in the interwar period a new type of historical pageant gradually became popular in small local towns and villages in Britain. It is a chronicle of ordinary life in a small community in a rural area.[10] This new type of local historical pageant shares a common structure of feeling with local natural history, which describes the colonies and communities of familiar birds, insects, and plants found in a local village.

The urge to describe ordinary, vernacular things by focusing on the hidden history of the obscure, which is one of the characteristics shared by both local natural history and the local historical pageant, also accords with Woolf's own creative urge in her later career when she wrote *The Years* (1937) and *Between the Acts*. Woolf refers to *The*

Years as 'Ordinary People' (*D* 4: 266). *Between the Acts* describes small odds and ends of local history: 'the building of a car factory and of an aerodrome', which 'attracted a number of unattached floating residents' (68–9), Cobbet of Cobbs Corner, retired on a pension from a tea plantation, tractors replacing ploughs, preservationist admiration for the old tithe barn, the building of a new village hall and so on. These fragments, if synthesized, will outline the formation of the modern countryside in Britain.

For a local community to produce a historical pageant was to confirm its sense of community by sharing the common history of the inhabitants, recreating and re-experiencing it with their own hands. People's desire to share and reinvent their history grows in the latter half of the 1930s with the rise of nationalistic sentiment. Several pageants of national history, such as *Song of England* (1937) and *Making of England* (1938), were enacted in the late 1930s.[11] *Song of England* is a nationalistic pageant with a profusion of patriotic feelings. England, however, is not represented here by the figure of Britannia as it had been in Victorian official pageantry, but by the characters such as EARTH (a woman dressed as Ceres) and her ATTENDANTS (children dressed as flowers), SEA (a woman in silver-green dress) and her ATTENDANTS (children dressed in seaweed and fins). HUSBANDRY also appears on the stage as 'a strong, fair countryman, in a waistcoat' (15). Such a representation of nation with nature is peculiar to the historical pageants of 1930s. Though different from both Victorian official pageantry and these modern pageants of national history, the village pageants or local historical pageants on a much smaller scale are nonetheless an expression of 'local patriotism' in that they tend to connect peripheral local history to some important moments of national history. We can assume that the village of Selborne attracted Mary Kelly because it was well known through White's *The Natural History of Selborne* and it seemed most appropriate to make it possible for many people in Britain to share its history by producing a pageant there.

Many English people going to the colonies in the nineteenth century took with them a copy of White's *The Natural History of Selborne*. This fact shows that Selborne was a representation of 'the country of England' or the image of 'home' which people wished to keep in their minds as 'a memory and an ideal' (Williams 281). It was also a place to retire to at the end of a long journey after the strain of years in the colonies. Darwin, for example, visited Selborne when coming back from his long voyage on the Beagle. In *The Country and the City*,

Raymond Williams explains how the idea of rural England as 'home' comes into being in the late nineteenth century during the process of industrialization and colonization. According to Williams, 'its green peace, its sense of belonging, of community' (281) comes to be idealized and contrasted with the colonial world of tension.[12] It is precisely through this process that in Victorian times White's Selborne became a representation of rural England as 'home', and we can find, in the twentieth century, certain remnants of this idea, for example, in Woolf's representation of the English countryside in *Between the Acts*. Woolf's representation of rural England in the novel is, in some parts, quite nostalgic, for example, when we see the final scene of evening – a rhapsody of starlings at the tree, the last glow of light in the fading sky, Hogben's Folly and Bolney Minster sinking into the dusk – though, at the same time, Woolf is also making fun of the sentimental idealization of 'Home' in the Victorian scene of La Trobe's pageant.

The Natural History of Selborne had once seized people's imaginations in the late nineteenth century when forests and meadows were disappearing at the outskirts of the encroaching 'Wen' and the city was undergoing rapid change with the development of an industrial society. It regained its influence in the mid-twentieth century. New editions of White's book were produced during this period: the Oxford edition of 1937, H. J. Massingham's edition of 1938, and James Fisher's editions of 1941 (Penguin) and 1947 (Cresset). H. J. Massingham, an advocate of the organic way of living, considers Selborne to be an ideal form of 'ecological and social organism' (Matless 259).

English pastoral regained its influence during the decade leading up to the Second World War. It was in the late 1930s that the magazine *Country Life* issued a series of full-page advertisements of Worthington Ale, which presented the landscapes and local histories of the English countryside with the caption of 'This England ...' Numerous books of 'country writing' were published during this period: for example, *Country Notes in Wartime* (1940) by Vita Sackville-West, *Britain and the Beast* (1937), edited by Clough Williams-Ellis, *The Countryman's Year* (1936) by Ray Stannard Baker, and *The Pageant of the Year: Birds and Their Ways and Musing by the Way* (1936) by Catherine Morison. Massingham wrote and edited a series of voluminous works such as *English Downland* (1936), *Genius of England* (1937), *Shepherd's Country* (1938) and *The English Countryside* (1939), the photographs in which helped to define ideas of the typically 'English' landscape.[13] In the late 1930s, when people envisioned that the empire was diminishing and both civilization and nature were threatened with destruction by the war, a keen sense of aspiration for the rural landscape was awakened in people's minds. We find there a structure of feeling which gives birth to a human desire to describe and preserve the minute details of reality which are condemned to perish.

Several historical pageants on the theme of English country life were produced in the 1930s: *English Country Life through the Ages* enacted in East Suffolk in 1935, *The Passing of the Seasons* produced by the National Sunday School Union in 1938, E. M. Forster's *The Abinger Pageant* in 1934 and his *England's Pleasant Land* in 1938.[14] These pageants were among the projects of the environmental and preservationist movements of the interwar years. They were also meant to revitalize the local communities. *English Country Life through the Ages*, which is a chronological medley of rural scenes from literary works and folk songs, is somewhat similar in construction to La Trobe's pageant in *Between the Acts*, which also includes several scenes from what seem to be plays. In these pageants of the late 1930s, there is a nostalgic representation of the vanishing countryside or 'England, green and eternal' (Forster, *Abinger* 349). Rural settings predominate in *The Abinger Pageant*, which the reviewer in the British Drama League magazine describes as: 'No Kings and Queens, no battles or pomp, but the Woodman, the Smith, the Lords of the Manor and the people of Abinger woven together …' ('Abinger Pageant'). Mary Kelly's pageant of Selborne in 1938 was produced in this historical context. The history of England is represented here not by Kings, Queens, and battles alone, but by rural scenes with country girls, the Squire, forests, and meadows.

While it is true that the vision of rural England presented in this period is often a nostalgic one with the image of an eternally green island, both Kelly and Woolf note the changing reality and the shift of time under the surface of its timelessness. In Kelly's pageant, White says, 'peaceful and secluded as it may appear – a vale of Arcady – stirring scenes have been enacted in past days beneath the shadow of this wood' (5). In both texts, there is a strong urge to catch a fleeting moment by describing it.

In Kelly's pageant Gilbert White remarks that the 'names and transactions' of the ancestor have been 'forgotten from century to century and sunk into oblivion' (31). Kelly lets White speak of the priority of nature over human civilization and antiquities and this sentiment is also shared by Woolf, who describes the vision of the silent drama of nature which survives human civilization. Kelly characterizes Gilbert White as an old man nearly in his dotage, who is neglectful of his duty as a historical guide to the audience, and is much happier to talk about fern owls and cuckoos. He obviously prefers 'natural' history to 'national' history. As is also true of La Trobe's pageant in *Between the Acts*, there is no grand finale or chorus of patriotic song at the end. Kelly's pageant simply closes when White and his friend Mulso walk away from the audience while talking about 'Timothy the Tortoise'. White's beloved tortoise becomes a more cherished subject of their conversation than historic figures like Edward the Confessor. What Kelly shares with Woolf is a ring of irony in her way of representing human (or national) history.[15] At the closing of the pageant, White comments on the longevity of the tortoise, which spends more than two-thirds of his existence in stuporous slumber. This reptile's life offers an effective contrast to human's toil and efforts in building up civilization to leave their own names in history. The pageant in *Between the Acts* also presents an ironic view of modern civilization in the last scene where 'the present time' is represented by people reflected on a broken mirror. Such a presentation of history makes a sharp contrast to the modern historical pageants, which conventionally end in a highly prosperous moment in history.

While keeping a distance from patriotic discourse, Woolf presents a conventionally 'English' landscape in *Between the Acts*: a church spire, swallows, cows, a manor house and its old tithe barn. Woolf's novel anticipates a post-Second World War tendency to see a symbolic vital force of regeneration in 'nature-in-ruins' (Matless 233). Richard Fitter's *London's Natural History* (1945) lists 126 species of 'flowering plants and ferns from bombed sites' (Matless 233) and reveals the presence of small birds and creatures which survive in the postwar London (Fitter plate VI). 'Nature-in-ruins' motif is also seen in the works of neo-romantic artists such as C. Eliot Hodgkin and Edwin Smith (Mellor 106, 107).[16] Likewise, we can recognize some hope of regeneration in Woolf's representation of nature in *Between the Acts*. At the closing of the novel, after the antiquities of Bolney Minster and Hogben's Folly disappear in the dusk, the landscape reduces itself into 'mere land' as it was in prehistoric time: 'It was land merely, no land in particular' (189). In such a land without borderline, which is no longer even 'English', Woolf envisions a new start to human and natural history.

Conclusion

We have seen that Woolf's interest in natural history and local history continues throughout her career – from her early diary to her posthumously published novel. The discourse of local historical pageants and that of local natural history share a common structure of feeling with Woolf's *Between the Acts*, a pageant-novel which describes the nature and the community of a local village, presenting a changing and vanishing, but still continuing reality of rural England in the twentieth century. In the late 1930s Woolf develops her own view of an 'Englishness' which is both vernacular and universal, keeping a balance between nostalgia for something 'English' and a vision which goes beyond the boundary of 'Englishness'. Just as pageant writers such as Mary Kelly tried to establish a community with common people by sharing the local history, amateur naturalists, like White, found joy in forming a community among themselves by sharing their discoveries through correspondence. While the community of Victorian amateur naturalists consists exclusively of people from the leisured classes, Woolf tried to have a larger sense of community by presenting an apparently 'timeless' vision of the English countryside, a vision to be shared by people of all classes in Britain.

Notes

* This essay is mainly based on my paper read at the 11th Annual International Conference on Virginia Woolf in Bangor, Wales on 14 June 2001 and partly on my presentation at Symposium 'Globalization, Nationalism, Englishness: Looking through Woolf's Works' at the 22nd Annual Conference of the Virginia Woolf Society of Japan on 19 October 2002. I gratefully acknowledge here several comments from members of the International Virginia Woolf Society and those of the VWSJ. I thank Gilbert White's House and The Oates Museum in Selborne for permission to reproduce a photograph of Mary Kelly's pageant. I also thank Derek Edwards, Mavis Coulson, Alastair Langlands, and Natalie Mees in Selborne for interviews and cooperation in my research. My gratitude also goes to my colleagues at Osaka University, especially Prof. Stephen Boyd, who helped me with advice on English expressions in my earlier draft and to Waltraud Ernst at University of Southampton, who told me about David Elliston Allen's works on natural history. Above all, my special thanks are due to the editors of this book, Anna Snaith and Michael Whitworth, who read my draft with care and gave me comments and advice that helped me greatly.

1 For a contemporary photograph and review, see 'Selborne Pageant, 1938' and 'Selborne Pageant.'

2 The script and photographs of the pageant are in Mary Kelly's hand-written scrapbook held in Gilbert White's House and The Oates Museum. A new pageant entitled *Selborne Story* was enacted in Selborne in 2000 as a millennium celebration. The writer (Lady Mavis Coulson), the director (Alastair Langlands, a schoolmaster) and the narrator (Derek Edwards, the president

of the Selborne Association) have been residents of Selborne for more than thirty years.

3   See Anne Olivier Bell's note on the diary of August 1917 (*D* 1: 40).

4   Lucy says her vision comes from *The Outline of History*. There is, however, no reference to, nor picture of, humming birds and rhododendrons in the prehistoric chapter of the book.

5   The Rhododendron Society was founded in 1915 and the annual Rhododendron Shows, which started in 1926, were reported in its periodicals. John Charles Williams (1861–1939) produced 267 hybrid types of rhododendron by 1917. See *A History of British Gardening* by Miles Hadfield (Harmondsworth: Penguin, 1985). We can also find many articles on the rhododendron in *Country Life* issued in 1930s. See also *The Plant Hunters: Two Hundred Years of Adventure and Discovery Around the World* by T. Musgrave, C. Gardner, and W. Musgrave (London: Cassell, 1999).

6   H. G. Wells's *The Drama of Life* (London: Cassell, 1935) has a similar vision.

7   I have given a detailed account of the amateur drama movements during the interwar period, and the intertextual relations between those pageants and *Between the Acts*, in an article (in Japanese) in Sei Kosugi, 'Woolf and Drama'. Articles by Wallis, Esty, and Yoshino are also relevant here.

8   See Kelly's *Village Theatre* (1939), and also Bottomley, and Wallis (201–03).

9   Mark Starr criticizes this type of patriotic pageant in 'Dangerous Ceremony at School' in *Lies and Hate in Education* (London: Hogarth, 1929). Starr's pacifist arguments against patriotic education are closely linked to *Three Guineas* (1938).

10 The village Drama society encouraged a village pageant to become 'a species of local chronicle play, with ... a minimizing of the circus element that was prominent in the larger pageants in the past' (Bottomley).

11 T.B. Morris, *Song of England* (London: Play Rights & Publications, 1937). *Making of England*, produced in July 1938 at Allington Castle, Kent, was written by L. G. Redmond-Howard in collaboration with Alva Delbert-Evans and published by Selwyn and Blount.

12 H.J. Massingham (ed.), *The English Countryside* (1939) frequently refers to the image of England seen through the eyes of those who went to or came back from foreign countries.

13 Massingham's *English Downland* (1936) explores the chalk country of Hampshire and Sussex, the region intimately known by White and Woolf. The chapters include photographs of the village of Selborne, a Sussex farmyard, churches, ploughing, and the downs near Lewes.

14 *English Country Life through the Ages* was produced by the East Suffolk County Federation of Women's Institutes from 19 to 20 March 1935. *The Passing of the Seasons* was written by Irene L. Johnson (London: The National Sunday School Union, 1938). *England's Pleasant Land* was performed in the grounds of Milton Court, between Dorking and Westcott.

15 Yoshino, '*Between the Acts*', gives a derailed discussion of the satirical vein in Woolf's representation of British history in La Trobe's pageant.

16 Woolf's relation to neo-romanticism is also discussed by Ito, 'Production of the South Country'.

Part III
Postcolonial Spaces

6
Virginia Woolf and the Empire Exhibition of 1924: Modernism, Excess, and the Verandahs of Realism[1]

Kurt Koenigsberger

Unlike her husband Leonard, her friend E. M. Forster, or the protagonist of her first novel Rachel Vinrace, Virginia Woolf never made the voyage out to distant quarters of the British Empire. On 29 May 1924, however, she travelled to the British Empire Exhibition, which promised to bring home and into view of the daytripper a realistic picture of imperial lands, fetching up out of the margins of empire a simultaneously fabricated and faithful representation of British holdings across the globe. Within the walled bounds of Wembley, the British Empire Exhibition sought to round out a view of the world as a whole, laying before the British people the spectacle of an entire empire in miniature. In Woolf's novel *The Waves*, published seven years later, Rhoda performs a similar feat of imagination, illuminating and drawing into almost cinematic perspective the dim margins of empire:

> [L]ook – the outermost parts of the earth – pale shadows on the utmost horizon, India for instance, rise into our purview. The world that had been shrivelled, rounds itself; remote provinces are fetched up out of darkness; we see muddy roads, twisted jungle, swarms of men, and the vulture that feeds on some bloated carcass as within our scope, part of our proud and splendid province ... (112)

Rhoda gathers 'the outermost parts of the earth' under possessive and totalizing rubrics ('our purview', 'our scope', 'our proud and splendid province') as the Empire Exhibition also did, but instead of conjuring images of integrated wholeness as Wembley's exhibits sought to do, Rhoda's vision lights upon a bloated corpse being dismembered. Rhoda gestures towards a 'round' world, one of plenitude; yet that round world also appears morbidly excessive, harbouring within it counter-vailing impulses towards dismemberment, dissolution and decomposition. In an earlier figuration of Rhoda's rounded yet disconcerting vision, Woolf cast such alienating spaces of excess in the form of circles that expand and dissolve throughout *Mrs Dalloway*, completed during the first year of the Wembley Exhibitions (1924–25).

It is in the space between visions of empire as integrated or 'rounded' totality and of its attenuation or dissolution that I seek to locate Woolf's modernist challenges to 'Edwardian' realism in 1924, the year of the Exhibition, of Woolf's expansion of her famous essay 'Mr. Bennett and Mrs. Brown' (1923) as 'Character in Fiction', and of the composition of *Mrs Dalloway*. Working within the imaginative arenas of the Wembley exhibition and of the periodical press, Woolf exposes what we might call 'exhibitionary realism' as a kind of praxis that is complicit with the totalizing aims of imperialism. Her assault on such realist practices in 'Character in Fiction' figures also as a critique of imperialism, while her essay on the Empire Exhibition titled 'Thunder at Wembley' is predicated upon a critique of the Exhibition's economy of realism. This economy posits the world as a sociospatial totality that can be observed by a disengaged spectator without entailing a loss of meaning or entangling the subject with the world as object. Woolf acknowledges that emergent modernisms appear as incomplete projects, but also that they expose the way the 'rounding' of the world – representing it as a coherent, spectacular whole – always leaves in the margins a remainder that undermines realist restricted economies. Modernism's exposure of this excess enmeshes the subject with 'life itself' ('Character', *E* 3: 436) and gestures towards the impossibility of a singular totality that might be rendered as a spectacle; instead, its 'solidity disappears', 'features crumble', and frameworks 'topple to the ground' ('Mrs. Brown', *E* 3: 387). This is a dynamic that also unfolds in 'Thunder at Wembley', though with the empire rather than the novel as its primary field of reference.

The texts upon which my attention centres here are essays that Woolf published in *The Nation and the Athenaeum* in December 1923 and in June 1924. In May 1924, Woolf expanded her December essay, 'Mr. Bennett and Mrs. Brown', as 'Character in Fiction', which was published in T. S. Eliot's *The Criterion* in July; in June she saw into print 'Thunder at Wembley' in *The Nation and the Athenaeum*. The first two of these essays – 'Mr. Bennett and Mrs. Brown' and 'Character in Fiction' – taken together constitute a sort of modernist manifesto, pro-claiming Georgian literature's break from its Victorian and Edwardian pasts with the memorable claim that 'on or about December 1910 human character changed' ('Character', *E* 3: 421). Woolf's attack upon Bennett's work as representative of the Edwardian novel reflects the fact that he explicitly theorized the objectivity of realism and claimed for the novel all the world as its domain. Three years before 'Mr. Bennett and Mrs. Brown', Arnold Bennett, though never an ardent imperialist, celebrated the novel's increasing cultural authority by comparing it to the British colonization of the globe: '[T]he novelist has poached, colonized, and annexed with a success that is not denied... [The novel] has conquered enormous territories even since *Germinal*. Within the last fifteen years it has gained. Were it to adopt the hue of the British Empire, the entire map of the universe would soon be coloured red' (39–40).

Bennett sets up the paths of a developing realism as a kind of fictional all-red route, in which the novel's methods enable it to claim all of the observed world under its banner. Woolf sought to dismantle this imaginative circuit when she published 'Thunder at Wembley' in *The Nation and the Athenaeum* in June 1924, which concludes with a vision of the British Empire dissolving in a tempest. I will direct most of my attention in the pages that follow towards this latter essay and its engagement with dominant realist practices, since Woolf makes explicit in 'Character and Fiction' that the business of the novel is not to promote the empire. Nevertheless, the larger complex of texts from 1924 – *Mrs Dalloway*, 'Character in Fiction', and 'Thunder at Wembley' – ought to be considered together, since Woolf's notebooks for *Mrs Dalloway* are interleaved with fragments of the expanded version of 'Mr. Bennett and Mrs. Brown' and the complete draft of 'Thunder at Wembley', each of which explores the spaces of empire and the modes of representing the real.

* * *

In the British Empire Exhibition at Wembley the English nation both asserted its technological modernity and openly revived the clichés of Victorian and Edwardian imperialism, hoping to allay nagging suspicions, raised in *The Nation and the Athenaeum*, that 'our fortunes have passed their zenith, and that the aspirations for a new social order [in the post-War era]... will sap the springs of enterprise and precipitate our decay' ('The Outlook for Great Britain' 38). The Exhibition celebrated the empire as an integrated whole, as a synchronic totality, to the end of persuading domestic subjects of the empire's continued significance. These subjects – including Leonard and Virginia Woolf in

May 1924 – encountered pavilions in which more than 25 of the lands under British rule offered characteristic examples of their flora, fauna, architecture, labour, leisure, and arts. In addition to these individual displays, there were a Palace of Youth, a Palace of Engineering, a Palace of Horticulture, a Civic Hall, an Aquarium, a Palace of Industry, and a Palace of Arts, all of which featured typical aspects of the far-flung reaches of empire presented in the perspective the British organizers thought most appropriate to offering spectators a representative general picture of the empire.

The realism of the exhibition implicitly acknowledged its selectivity in offering portrayals of the empire as a harmonious and profitable unit, and to this extent the interests of a commercial economy converged with the aims of a symbolic economy. The logic that the Exhibition followed appeared resolutely synecdochic, representing the whole empire through its parts. Wembley's planners emphasized the characteristic and the typical in its exhibits, hoping they would, as George V proclaimed during the opening ceremonies, 'reveal to us the whole Empire in little, containing within its 220 acres of ground a vivid model of the architecture, art and industry of all the races which come under the British flag' ('Wembley and Its Millions' 106). The popular press in the spring of 1924 filled its pages with appreciations, reading the Exhibition as a spectacularly faithful representation of the empire. The *Illustrated London News* for instance, described the Hong Kong exhibit in these terms: 'There is no "fake" about Hong Kong at Wembley. Every detail was made in the Colony and shipped to England. The result is most picturesque and attractive – a real view of the real China that salutes the British flag' ('A Wanderer at Wembley', 21 May 1924, 942).

In their relentless pursuit of 'the real' and 'the whole', the press particularly celebrated the representational strategies of the Exhibition that fostered imaginative travel. A Swedish visitor to Wembley noted that 'Exotica is a large and rich country. Trips to it are both troublesome and expensive, and only a few can hope to see its wonderlands. But this summer a person can make a little tour of the world and have his fill of exoticism at Wembley. ... [W]e have the whole world to look at if we like' (Centerwall 221–2). The Exhibition's global extension of synecdochic logic served to render accessible 'the whole world' through the 'little tour', at the end of which, declared the *Official Guide* to the Exhibition, 'You may not have put a girdle round the earth in forty minutes, but you will have done something like it' (30). The Wembley Exhibition adhered to the practices established by nine-

teenth-century exhibition organizers, whose 'ambition towards a spec-
ular dominance over a totality' expressed a desire 'to make the whole
world, past and present, metonymically available in the assemblages of
objects and peoples they brought together and ... to lay before [the
spectator] a controlling vision' (Tony Bennett 66).

The will to totalize and its concomitant emphases upon scale and
intensity of vision did not, however, make a uniformly positive impression. In *The Nation and the Athenaeum*, Roger Fry lamented the tasteless
bombast of the Exhibition's architecture: 'An area equal to that of
central London has been enclosed, and most of the buildings within it
are of abnormal size. ... In general, one may say that everything is five
times as large as the most exorbitant could demand' (242). Though the
tour of Wembley was 'little' and manageable, the representations
themselves were designed to engross and impress, in an apparent contradiction 'between the need to separate oneself from the world and to
render it up as an object of representation, and the desire to lose
oneself within this object-world and to experience it directly' (Mitchell
231). In part, the 'exorbitant', 'abnormal' scale of Wembley served to
distinguish further the exhibition from the reality it claimed to reproduce: as a French visitor pointed out, 'all this splendor is after all
nothing but a stage-setting, the representation of the moment in
which one pushes to its extreme the Empire's dignity and splendor'
(Naudeau 30). Wembley's 'extreme' but selective realism sought to
produce an 'allegory of power and wealth, a significant summing-up of
infinite resources on a world-wide scale' (28), and the engulfing scale
was important to this allegorical function.

The Exhibition's hyperbolic but selective realism appeared as a kind of
restricted economy of precise observation bounded in such a way as to
conserve and convey meaning for the ends of empire, to the exclusion of
all competing representations or entanglements. Official advertisements
for the Exhibition also touted the realistic character of the displays, as in
the promotion that appeared in *The Graphic* and announced that

> The British Empire Exhibition derives its absorbing interest from its
> intense realism. Stately and picturesque pavilions are constructed of
> materials brought from the countries they represent; trees and
> shrubs and flowers are growing around as they grow thousands of
> miles away... When one has watched the making of Indian carpets
> by native experts, he may witness an Indian play performed by
> Indian actors in an Indian theatre, or, spellbound, gaze upon an
> Indian snake charmer compelling a huge cobra to do his bidding.

Not only are there displayed the products of the vast agricultural and mineral resources of the empire; the visitor will see for himself how they are won and treated and brought to finished perfection for millions to use. (Advertisement)

English visitors, ostensibly held 'spellbound' by the 'intense realism' of the spectacle, are nevertheless rhetorically removed from the more 'picturesque' aspects of the Exhibition and expected to apprehend the pavilions and 'native experts' as though they were pictures at another sort of exhibition.

Indeed, Timothy Mitchell observes, 'the effect of such spectacles was to set the world up as a picture' (220). In this sense, the Wembley Exhibition represents a culmination of 'what one might call, echoing a phrase from Heidegger, the age of the world exhibition, or rather, the age of the world-as-exhibition. *World exhibition* here refers not to an exhibition of the world, but to the world conceived and grasped as though it were an exhibition' (222). Bror Centerwall's claim that we 'have the whole world to look at' becomes, then, characteristic of modernity's exhibitionary epistemology. The representation of the world as spectacle is related to the view of the 'real' world outside – and if the spectacle inside the exhibition faltered in its realism, it could mean that indeed 'one more doubt [was] cast upon the reality of the external world' (Naudeau). The foundation of this modern economy of realism upon the trope of the 'world-as-exhibition' is not peculiar to the colonial and imperial exhibitions, but directs literary formulae of the era as well: only a few years earlier Arnold Bennett had suggested that the obligation of the novelist is 'really to see the spectacle of the world (a spectacle surpassing circuses and even street accidents in sustained dramatic interest)' (11). The realist's world-as-spectacle thus becomes the established way of treating or looking at the world; concomitantly, looking at the world through the lenses of 'intense realism' comes to be established as an imperial way of treating it.

If the British Empire Exhibition actively aimed to cement a sense of the Empire as unitary and uniform, it also presumed that a global empire could be so described. The notion that the Empire Exhibition depended upon a view of the whole world as itself an exhibition can seem like a circular logic, but the idea becomes plainer in Bennett's theory of the realist novel:

All physical phenomena are interrelated, ... there is nothing which does not bear on everything else. The whole spectacular and sensual show – what the eye sees, the ear hears, the nose scents, the tongue tastes and the skin touches – is a cause or an effect of human conduct. ... [The novelist] can, by obtaining a broad notion of the whole, determine with some accuracy the position and relative importance of the particular series of phenomena to which his instinct draws him. (19)

The realist novel itself becomes something like an exhibition, offering up to its audience a 'whole spectacular and sensual show', appealing to each of the faculties. Likewise appealing to the senses, the strategies of the Exhibition sought in presenting the world's spectacle 'to create a distance between oneself and the world, and thus to constitute it as something picture-like – as an object on exhibit. This required what was now called a "point of view": a position set apart and outside' that show (Mitchell 229). The culmination of exhibitionary logic in 'point of view', or 'perspective', finally drives narrative prescriptions as well: 'Good observation consists not in multiplicity of detail', writes Bennett, 'but in co-ordination of detail according to a true perspective of relative importance, so that a finally just general impression may be reached in the shortest possible time' (14). The exhibitor's or novelist's perspective must approximate the 'true' in order to resolve the problem of 'co-ordination of detail' and to offer an efficient picture of the whole world.

Bennett's realist prescriptions for the novel developed during the heyday of colonial and imperial exhibitions, and it is perhaps not coincidental that his conceptions of the novel resemble those strategies of exhibitions designed to foster an intense and engrossing realism, since both the novel and the exhibition share a worldview in which 'The so-called real world outside is something experienced and grasped only as a series of further representations, an extended exhibition' (Mitchell 233). Virginia Woolf ironically reverses this perspective as it pertains to the novel, reducing Bennett's work itself to a kind of picture: 'we must do as painters do when they wish to reduce the innumerable details of a crowded landscape to simplicity – step back, half shut the eyes, gesticulate a little vaguely with the fingers, and reduce Edwardian fiction to a view' ('Mrs. Brown', *E* 3: 385). In 'Character in Fiction' and 'Thunder at Wembley', Woolf engages in even more robust challenges to the singularity of the totality represented in the Exhibition and in the vision of world-as-exhibition, stressing the way in which the excesses of the real threaten the restricted economies of realism and entangle spectators with 'life itself'.

*　*　*

In April 1924, in the pages of the same publication that printed 'Mr. Bennett and Mrs. Brown' in December, and in which 'Thunder at Wembley' was soon to appear, E. M. Forster predicted of Wembley that 'Millions will spend money there, hundreds will make money, and a few highbrows will make fun', noting that he himself 'belong[ed] to the latter class' (Forster, 'Birth' 111). Despite her early visit to the Exhibition, Woolf also took her place among the 'highbrows': in her *Diary* she compared Wembley with 'the enameled Lady Colefax' who appeared like 'a cheap bunch of artificial cherries ... on a burnished plate of facts', and who, while she could not 'sink to the depths', was nevertheless 'a superb skimmer of the surface' (*D* 2: 305). Woolf was not alone in perceiving a conventional and insubstantial realism surrounding the Exhibition: another visitor compared Wembley's displays to 'those painted pasteboard hams which give a fraudulent fillip to appetite in the show windows of certain delicatessen stores' (Naudeau 32). In a review of the Exhibition's architecture, Roger Fry dismissed 'the triviality, the niggling pedantry, and want of invention which... every one of these buildings displays' (242), and in her essay on the Empire Exhibition Woolf too complains of the lack of imagination in the Exhibition. At previous colonial exhibitions, such as the one she attended in July 1903 at Earls Court (*PA* 179–81), she recalls, 'Everything was intoxicated and transformed. But at Wembley nothing is changed and nobody is drunk' (*E* 3: 411). The 'mediocrity' of the Wembley exhibition according to Woolf is owed to its attempted realism ('Thunder', *E* 3: 411): its presentation (like Lady Colefax) as 'a burnished plate of facts' and its patent factitiousness ('a cheap bunch of artificial cherries') fail to charm. By contrast with the calculated and ordered realism of the Exhibition, Woolf relishes the display of what she calls 'Nature' in the Exhibition grounds, an uncoordinated, unpredictable, and excessive 'Nature' that she claims 'is the ruin of Wembley' (*E* 3: 410).

'Nature' for Woolf exposes the limits of the Exhibition's machinery of representation, its carefully circumscribed economy of realism. By 'Nature' Woolf means not just the world of birds and trees and sky, but also 'our contemporaries' – the English 'clergymen, schoolchildren, girls, young men, invalids in bath-chairs' who visit Wembley and use the space to their own ends, not necessarily those of the Empire: 'they reveal themselves simply as human beings, creatures of leisure, civilization, and dignity; a little languid, perhaps, a little attenuated, but a product to be proud of. Indeed they are the ruin of the Exhibition' (*E* 3: 412). They destroy the illusion of 'intense realism' the Exhibition works so hard to establish because they are the observers on whom the illusion depends – to read them as central to the Exhibition is to dissolve the limits of that realism: 'As you watch them trailing and flowing, dreaming and speculating ... the rest of the show becomes insignificant'. The boundaries of realism's economy are transgressed by the very spectators that realism was designed to dazzle, and Woolf's vision of the Exhibition encompasses the spectator, refusing to acknowledge the comforting distance exhibitionary rhetorics typically fostered. 'Nature' for Woolf signals a 'dreaming and speculating' excess characteristic of something like what she calls 'life itself' in 'Character in Fiction', an excess that is incompatible with the 'plate of facts' and 'niggling pedantry' served up at the exhibition.

Woolf seems to have understood the Exhibition primarily to reflect the English character rather than that of 'a larger world'; 'Nature' to signal the human experience in the world, instead of simple matter amenable to representation in the age of the world-as-exhibition; and the Exhibition's spatial strategies not as genuinely modern, 'Georgian' modes of representation but as testaments to the persistence of Victorian conventions. The Wembley Exhibition revived the old imperial themes – the 'crystal palaces' and 'globes, maps, [and] elephants' that typify the Victorian age in *Orlando* (1928) – and for Woolf its brand of realism appears as outmoded as 'other excrescences' of the nineteenth century (222). Woolf champions 'Nature' because it exposes the contingency of the 'real view of the real China' that the *Illustrated London News* celebrated, for example; and because it exceeds the boundaries of the restricted economy of representation that underpins the vision of empire at Wembley. In Woolf's essay, nature's excessive and disordering tendencies – particularly in the guise of the torrential rains that ruined the first days of the 'Pageant of Empire' – overwhelm the bounds of the Exhibition's realism, reduce the coherence of the concrete displays to ruins, and herald an imperial apocalypse. As 'the Massed Bands of empire are assembling and marching to the Stadium' for the 'Pageant of Empire', a wind sweeps in and the sky darkens:

some appalling catastrophe is impending. The sky is livid, lurid, sulphurine. It is in violent commotion. It is whirling water-spouts of cloud into the air; of dust in the Exhibition. Dust swirls down the avenues, hisses and hurries like erected cobras round the corners. Pagodas are dissolving in dust. Ferro-concrete is fallible. Colonies are perishing and dispersing in spray of inconceivable beauty and terror which some malignant power illuminates. Ash and violet are the colours of its decay... Cracks like the white roots of trees spread themselves across the firmament. The Empire is perishing; ... the Exhibition is in ruins. (*E* 3: 413)

If, as the Exhibition organizers maintained, the Exhibition was to be understood as a 'replica' of the empire in its entirety, then reading the deluge through Wembley's own logic of synecdochic realism undermines both the commercial and the symbolic aims of the Exhibition – and, Woolf points out, '*that* is what comes of letting in the sky' (*E* 3: 413, emphasis added).

Woolf's critique appears deliberately difficult, impressionistic, and fragmentary in style: she offers what we might term a *modernist* explosion of Wembley's logic of realism and its restricted economy of correspondences and exactitudes. The extravagances and difficulties of Woolf's essay match 'Nature's' own excess in the storms that washed over the Exhibition. It is in these stylistic and symbolic senses – the seemingly irremediable losses of the idea of empire as totality, and of the coherence of exhibitionary rhetorics of realism – that Woolf's imaginative responses to empire open up possibilities of a *general* (as opposed to *restricted*) economy of realism, a system of representation in which excess, unaccountable expenditure, and loss are the operative principles.[2] Here that excess figures as the outside of the Exhibition that cannot be excluded – human nature, the sky, the weather.

A week before she attended the Wembley Exhibition, Woolf had redrafted 'Mr. Bennett and Mrs. Brown' as 'Character in Fiction', another essay on expenditure, on 'smashing and crashing', and on the question of realism. Against the Wembley organizers' assertion that the modern element was apparent in the Exhibition's grandeur and enormity and in its 'intense realism', in 'Character in Fiction' and in 'Thunder at Wembley' Woolf insists that the Georgian notion of the real is visible in 'the spasmodic, the obscure, the fragmentary, the failure' (*E* 3: 436). This position represents a marked break both with the Exhibition's emphasis upon 'avoiding formlessness... and unrestricted individual effort' and with Bennett's admonition against 'trivial and unco-ordinated details' and his concomitant emphasis upon the coherence of a 'broad notion of the whole' (Weaver 'Note' n.p.; Bennett 14). The mutual point of interrogation in Woolf's essays, then, is the status of realism's relation to the flux and excess of the real. 'What is reality?', Woolf wonders in 'Character in Fiction' (*E* 3: 426), and despite the impossibility of settling the question, she concludes that the business of the novel that would approach the problem cannot be 'to preach doctrines, sing songs, or celebrate the glories of the British Empire' – precisely those things that Wembley's 'intense realism' did seek to do (*E* 3: 425). Woolf's interest in the way in which people live out their lives in spaces such as the suburban train on which Mrs Brown travels and the grounds of the Empire Exhibition – the way in which they turn physical places, 'the fabric of things', into special and personal spaces in which narrative unfolds – brings her to concentrate her attention on the question of character.[3]

The distinction between physical place as catalogued by the Edwardians and what Woolf casts as lived space in her essays is perhaps key to understanding her treatment of realism as it appears in Bennett's fiction and in the Wembley Exhibition. Woolf concludes that Bennett's fiction – and that of the Victorians and Edwardians more generally – concerns itself too much with ordering and recording the material trappings and environments of people (placing 'an enormous stress on the fabric of things'), and too little with the ways in which people 'reveal themselves' within the spaces they construct (*E* 3: 432). 'If you hold that novels are in the first place about people', Woolf writes, 'and only in the second about the houses they live in', then the Edwardians, and Bennett in particular, have missed the mark in giving their readers 'a house in the hope that [they] may be able to deduce the human beings who live there' (*E* 3: 432). In the manuscript of 'Thunder at Wembley', Woolf celebrates the Exhibition's travellers because 'what has happened is simply that they have been lifted out of streets and houses and set down against an enormous background which reveals *them* for the first time' ('Nature at Wembley' 35, emphasis added).

The incompatibility of human nature with 'the fabric of things' in 'Character in Fiction' is much the same difficulty that Woolf finds arising within the British Empire Exhibition, which gives the English people replicas of colonial buildings but without a concomitant sense of the ways in which real life might unfold in that space – a result of the resolute separation of the spectator from spectacle. For Woolf, 'against the enormous background of ferro-concrete Britain, of rosy Burma' it becomes clear that the presence of real people living their real lives in the spaces of Wembley must mark 'the ruin of the Exhibition' – or at least of its conception of the entire world as an exhibition disengaged from English human nature ('Thunder at Wembley', *E* 3: 412). Timothy Mitchell understands the exhibition not to divide spectators directly from the real, but rather as threading an impression of alienation through the channels of realism: 'it creates an effect *called* the real world, in terms of which we can experience what is called alienation' (225). For her part, Woolf remakes this aspect of exhibitionary rhetoric so that Wembley becomes not a place with alien pictures of the world on show, but the space in which spectators 'reveal themselves' in the world. In the process, Woolf relegates Bennett's 'whole spectacular and sensual show' to the middle ground, where it becomes just one show among several.

Unlike the exhibitionary rhetorics that sought to remove the spectator from the enframed totality of the world, Woolf's figures become part of several possible worlds, and in place of Wembley's 'summing-up' in an imposing allegory, Woolf offers us at best partial summings-up. In the same way, Woolf makes plain in 'Character in Fiction' that human nature 'will strike you very differently according to the age and country in which you happen to be born', posing human nature itself as something that cannot be summed up in a single, 'true perspective' (*E* 3: 425). As the famous figure Mrs Brown appears to reveal the Edwardian novelists as having produced merely hollow men rather than characters in 'Character in Fiction', so also she appears in Woolf's essay on the Exhibition, in the guise of 'some woman in the row of red-brick villas outside the grounds [who] comes out and wrings a dish-cloth in the backyard' ('Thunder at Wembley', *E* 3: 412), in a display of everyday waste on the verge of the Exhibition. This woman, like Mrs Brown, shows what the economy of realism must thrust aside in order to establish itself, thereby exposing the Exhibition's illusion of realism by contact with what Woolf calls in 'Character in Fiction' 'the spirit we live by, life itself' (*E* 3: 436).

In the latter essay, Woolf foregrounds the sound of conventional boundaries such as those the bounds of the Exhibition represent dissolving, particularly through her description of James Joyce's 'indecency' and 'overflowing of superabundant energy' as 'smashing and crashing' (*E* 3: 434). Woolf notes that *Ulysses* (1922) 'seems to me the conscious and calculated indecency of a desperate man who feels that in order to breathe he must break the windows'; and the 'sound of breaking and falling, crashing and destruction' that Woolf remarks as characteristic of modernism more generally heralds the collapse of the edifices of Edwardian literature, in much the way that the storm's ominous thunder reduces the empire to dust and fragments (*E* 3: 434). The destruction of Edwardian literary convention is not effected by crude 'Nature', as in 'Thunder at Wembley', but rather by a different sort of excess: Joyce's 'savagery' and T. S. Eliot's 'obscurity', which approximate 'the sound of axes' (*E* 3: 434, 435). These, Woolf suggests, have led the avant-garde charge 'to outrage [and] to destroy the very foundations and rules of literary society', a destruction visible wherever 'grammar is violated' or 'syntax disintegrated' (*E* 3: 434).

The woman who wrings her washcloth in 'Thunder at Wembley' occupies a liminal position at the edges of the Exhibition, while Mrs Brown is situated in the transitional space of the moving suburban train. These mediate, transitory positions mark what has escaped Edwardian realism and exhibitionary representation – that which Woolf codes as Georgian or modernist. The liminal positions that 'change ... the shape, shift ... the accent, of every scene' ('Mrs. Brown', *E* 3: 387) also bear a striking resemblance to what Bill Ashcroft in a remarkable essay calls 'the verandahs of meaning':

> In post-colonial discourse the body, place, language, the house of being itself are all 'verandahs'. That is, they are a process in which the marginal, the excess, is becoming the actual. The verandah is not the surplus of the building but the excess which redefines the building itself. The verandah is that penumbral space in which artic-ulation takes form, where representation is contested. (42)

James Joyce's 'savagery' and English filth sluicing to the ground at the edge of Wembley's manicured grounds signal the kind of shadowy excess that Ashcroft identifies with the postcolonial when he notes that 'The hegemony of the absolute always falls short of the continual supplement, the excess, which is the real' (35). Where Bennett's and the Empire Exhibition's representations claim to be absolute, 'true', each of Woolf's exemplars of the real appears as a supplement or *donnée* that grounds a particular symbolic economy but exists in a space properly outside it. Inscribing them within a general economy in her essays, Woolf reveals the way in which conventional realisms fall short, and in which life on the verandah reduces to 'ruins and splin-ters... this tumbled mansion' ('Mrs. Brown', *E* 3: 388). What Ashcroft calls 'the hegemony of the absolute' fails in Woolf's readings of the Empire Exhibition and of Edwardian realism not only in the face of colonial subjects such as the nameless Indian 'native experts' or Ireland's Joyce, but also in the persistence of the British 'real', a 'product to be proud of' – even as it reveals itself in prosaic 'invalids in bath chairs', 'clergymen, and children'.

In short, while 'the excess which is the real' is most apparent in the sublime vision of 'beauty and terror' that the empire's tempestuous destruction evokes, it also emerges in the quiet activities of human nature unfolding in the avenues and margins of Wembley. Ashcroft suggests that 'Post-colonial excess is quintessentially the exuberance of life which is destined to revolt. But the most effective revolt is the one which denies the system its power over representation' (38). This is what 'nature' – especially human nature in Woolf's essay – accomplishes: 'the most solemn sights she turns to ridicule; the most ordinary she invests with beauty' ('Mrs. Brown', *E* 3: 387). At stake for Woolf in denying the Empire Exhibition an unqualified power over representation – even if only in the 'highbrow' printed space of *The Nation and the Athenaeum* – is the dominance of a world picture, an epistemological outlook that apprehends the world as exhibition, and that expresses its force both in imperial sociospatial representation and in the realist novel whose all-red routes cement 'the whole spectacular and sensual show' of the world. In this way, Woolf links the excesses of modernist style – the uncoordinated detail eschewed by Bennett – to the potential devolution of the imperial whole that undergirded the British Empire's exhibitionary cultures and aspirations in the new century.

* * *

The apocalyptic vision of empire's dissolution Woolf presents in 'Thunder at Wembley' unfolded chiefly in the realm of fancy, given that the stormy summer of 1924 in reality only dampened the Exhibition, rather than bringing it to ruin, and indeed the Exhibition reopened in 1925. The provisionality of Woolf's fantastic allegory finds an analogue not only in the metaphor of the verandah but in the form of modernist style which, as Woolf suggests in 'Character in Fiction', cannot 'just at present [offer] a complete and satisfactory presentment' of reality, and Woolf rests at the end of this essay with a view of modernism as 'the spasmodic, the fragmentary, the obscure, the failure' (*E* 3: 436), between Edwardian and fully realized new conventions. In 'Mr. Bennett and Mrs. Brown', 'Character in Fiction', and 'Thunder at Wembley', though, modernism's force emerges precisely from its 'failure' in conventional terms – because it compromises extant representational economies and practices. I wish to conclude here by suggesting that Woolf's location between a 'rounded', totalized world and its dissolution in the face of the real's excess also produces an apposite figuration of imperial space in her fiction. In Woolf's work in general, and in *Mrs Dalloway* in particular, symbols of dissolving circles tend to mark this position between imperial totality and fragmentation, realism and its excess.

The manuscript of *Mrs Dalloway* (still called *The Hours* in the note-books) is itself broken up by fragments of 'Character in Fiction' and by the draft of 'Thunder at Wembley', called 'Nature at Wembley'. It seems only appropriate that in the completed novel Peter Walsh also feels disjointed after his voyage in from India. Like Rhoda's 'proud and splendid province' in *The Waves*, and like the 'native experts' on display at the Empire Exhibition, Peter too seems to be conjured up out of one of the 'dark', penumbral spaces of the world. Over the London to which Peter returns, Big Ben's 'leaden circles' sound and then 'dis-solve in the air', binding his experience of the city to his place in the imperial scheme of *Mrs Dalloway*. As Peter rushes out of the Dalloways' home, having compromised himself to Clarissa in a moment of vulner-ability, he 'step[s] down the street, speaking to himself rhythmically, in time with the flow of the sound, the direct downright sound of Big Ben striking the half-hour. (The leaden circles dissolved in the air.)' (*MD* 41). The content of Peter's speech, synchronized with the leaden rings, has to do with his self-aggrandizing imperial work: 'All India lay behind him; plains, mountains, epidemics of cholera; a district twice as big as Ireland; decisions he had come to alone – he, Peter Walsh' (*MD* 41). In this way, London too becomes an imperial space for Peter, behind which distant India stands.

Though these leaden circles appear to draw Peter's thoughts back to India, experiencing the space marked out as the centre of the rings – Big Ben, Westminster, and London – becomes an estranging encounter for the Anglo-Indian. 'Those five years – 1918 to 1923 – had been', Peter observes, 'somehow very important. People looked different. Newspapers seemed different', and Peter finds that London begins to seem incompatible with his Indian experience (*MD* 61). As in the instance of Big Ben's 'leaden circles', Woolf's spreading circles encom-pass that which they push across, but as they widen they simultane-ously diminish in power, receding from the 'pale shadows on the utmost horizon' that Rhoda seeks to illuminate in *The Waves*. As images of containment, the 'leaden circles' seem to promise the possi-bility that imperial relations might be bound within a totalizing figure, and yet as they dissolve in the air they announce the radical contin-gency of such totalizations. In 1941, beyond the bounds of Virginia Woolf's writing career, Carl Sandburg noted that Woolf had remade the places of Empire in her work as a kind of festival space: 'The British Empire – her special and personal Empire – floats and sways as a bundle of toy balloons' (54). As I hope to have shown in these pages, if Woolf's 'personal British Empire' in any way seems a 'bundle of toy balloons', these are balloons that round themselves only to burst, like the leaden skies over Wembley in the summer of 1924.

Notes

1 A fully elaborated version of this argument appears in Kurt Koenigsberger, *The Novel and the Menagerie: Totality, Englishness, and Empire* (Columbus: Ohio State University Press, 2007).
2 Georges Bataille outlines key theoretical distinctions between 'restricted' and 'general' economies in *The Accursed Share Vol. I*, 9–23.
3 Character in Fiction' *E* 3: 432. I invoke here Michel de Certeau's distinction between place and space: 'In short, *space is a practiced place*. Thus the street geometrically defined by urban planning is transformed into a space by walkers' (117).

7
Virginia Woolf and Ireland: The Significance of Patrick in *The Years*

Suzanne Lynch

The complex modification of Virginia Woolf's draft novel-essay 'The Pargiters' into what was to become the 1937 novel *The Years* has been well documented, and it is evident that the final edited form avoided much of the overt politics and polemic that characterized its earlier version.[1] Instead, the politics is discernible on a more implicit level in *The Years* as the portrait of the everyday lives of the Pargiter family is structured loosely around key social and political events of the years in question. Alongside allusions to social changes such as the women's suffrage movement, the First World War, and Britain's shifting class divides, the contemporary political situation in Ireland is mentioned repeatedly in the novel. The question this essay seeks to address is why, when the overt politics and polemic of 'The Pargiters' had been significantly compressed, the Irish question remained such a strong presence in *The Years*? This leads to the further question of why Woolf fails to take this opportunity, through the character of Patrick, to denounce the British imperial system she was to condemn so vehemently in *Three Guineas*. The reason, I will argue, can be traced to the Woolfs' only trip to Ireland in April 1934, where one can find a source for the most overt engagement with the Irish question in Woolf's writing. The following examination of Woolf and Ireland also hopes to generate further thinking about Woolf's relationship to the nation and to open up wider issues and debates: how the experience of living the everyday in England is conditioned by the colonial other, and the different ways in which nations are represented and constructed.

The subject of Ireland was to the forefront in British constitutional life from the 1880s, and Gladstone introduced the first Home Rule Bill to Parliament in 1886.[2] Although the bill was defeated, the Irish bid for greater political autonomy and even separation from the British

Empire was gaining political momentum, not least due to the political magnanimity of Charles Stewart Parnell who became head of the Irish representatives in the House of Commons in 1882. The fear of total devolution of one of Britain's most troublesome colonies and the notoriety of Parnell's political demise and death in 1891 following his scandalous affair with Mrs O'Shea, wife of a former colleague, ensured the continued significance of the Irish Question in British public life. Although the second Home Rule Bill of 1893 was also defeated, the abolition of the veto of the House of Lords in the referendum of 1911 promised that the major stumbling block to Home Rule for the Irish Nationalists in Parliament had been demolished. Though the 1912 bill was finally passed, growing unrest from Unionists in Parliament and Belfast ensured that its actual implementation was delayed. When war broke out in 1914, Ireland all but disappeared from the British press, and it was not until the Rising of Easter 1916 that it again began to make headline news. Violent reprisals from the British forces led to growing restlessness in Ireland as the Irish Nationalists raised the stakes to full independence. What followed was a period of violent political unrest, when British troops known as 'Black and Tans' warred with Irish republican groups. An Irish Free State, with full independence for 26 of the 32 counties, was finally declared in December 1921 but led to a period of civil war as great as the 'troubles' of the previous two years as factions split into pro- and anti-treaty pacts. With the assassination of Michael Collins in 1922, the bitter civil war finally petered out, and what emerged was the first independent Irish State after centuries of British domination.

Turning to Woolf's diaries and letters during the early years of her life one finds references to this tempestuous situation in Ireland at various points. In light of the relative dearth of references to political events in her diary – the suffrage vote, for example, is mentioned, frustratingly, only spasmodically – any mention of Ireland must be seen as significant in itself. References to Ireland are particularly prolific at the height of the Troubles and the Irish civil war. In an entry for October 1920, Woolf reveals her knowledge of contemporary events by recording the death of the Irish nationalist Lord Mayor of Cork by hunger strike alongside a reference to the miners' strike in Britain: 'no newspaper placard without its shriek of agony from some one. McSwiney this afternoon & violence in Ireland; or it'll be the strike' (*D* 2: 72–3). In March 1921 one finds a more telling allusion which illustrates Woolf's access to information about Ireland through friends and acquaintances such as Dora Sanger: 'People go on being shot & hanged in Dublin.

Dora described mass going on all day in Dublin for some wretched boy killed early on Monday morning' (*D* 2: 100). Undoubtedly the contemporary political situation in Ireland was a topic of discussion at parties and social gatherings attended by Woolf and her Bloomsbury friends. An entry for June 1921, for example, records, 'We went to Miss Royde Smith's party on Thursday to discuss Ireland' (*D* 2: 122), referring to the well-known literary hostess Naomi Royde-Smith, literary editor of the liberal publication *The Saturday Westminster Gazette*. The *Westminster Gazette* carried detailed coverage of events in Ireland during this time and its editorial stance firmly denounced the British handling of the situation.[3] That many of Woolf's closest friends had an interest in Irish affairs is also evident. In June 1919 she jokingly quotes her friend Lytton Strachey's throwaway comment at a lunch-party he attended: '"But I'm *not* interested in Ireland–"'(*D* 1: 281). Similarly, Woolf's husband Leonard was a key political player in early twentieth-century international relations. His experience as a British colonial servant in Ceylon from 1904 to 1911 helped to shape the anti-imperialist stance that was to inform his political writings. On returning from Ceylon Leonard swiftly became involved in the Fabian Society through Sidney and Beatrice Webb, leading to a lifelong commitment to socialism and participation in Labour Party politics. Though Ireland does not feature explicitly in his writing, the issue undoubtedly permeated the political environment of which he was a part.[4] Woolf and her group were regular contributors to the political and artistic journal the *Nation*, of which Leonard was literary editor from 1923 to 1930. The journal's liberal stance was, in general terms, anti-imperialist, but for all its alleged support for Ireland, in the years before the First World War it approved only Home Rule rather than full independence.[5]

The parties held by literary hostess Lady Ottoline Morrell gave Woolf an opportunity to meet the great Anglo-Irish figures of the literary establishment, such as Shaw, Yeats, and Elizabeth Bowen. But she also had access to another source of information pertaining to Ireland other than just casual discussion or media opinion, through her first cousin H.A.L. Fisher, whom she met frequently in her early years. Although the Woolfs joked about him in private and Leonard ran against him as Labour candidate in the 1922 election, in later years Woolf was to visit him intermittently in Oxford (L. Woolf, *Downhill* 34–7). Although Fisher refused the Irish secretaryship in 1918 on the grounds of his opposition to enforced conscription to Ireland, he was a member of the Coalition Cabinet's Irish Committee, and thus presented Woolf with a source close to the hub of British parliamentary policy on Ireland

(Ogg 91–2). She records at length a meeting with Fisher in a diary entry for April 1921 during the height of the troubles in Ireland, and the following quotation shows Woolf's access, through Fisher, to the government's perspective on the British army's increasingly violent role in Ireland:

> The upshot of it all was that he couldn't be blamed for his conduct about Ireland. And then he was careful to explain that the public is ridiculously in the dark about everything. Only the cabinet knows the true spring & source of things he said. That is the only solace of his work. A flood tide of business flows incessantly from all quarters of the world through Downing Street; & there are a few miserable men trying desperately to deal with it. (*D* 2: 112)

The influence of Ireland on everyday British life is hinted at in many of Woolf's novels, where Ireland, like India, lies at the fringes of the social world she describes. In *Flush*, Woolf's biography of Elizabeth Barrett-Browning's dog set in the 1840s, one of the few social references concerns the Irish famine of the time: 'But suppose Flush had been able to speak – would he not have said something sensible about the potato disease in Ireland?' (*F* 27). In her final novel, *Between the Acts*, Ireland features in Bludge's speech in which the merits of the British Empire are sardonically debunked: 'Some bother it may be in Ireland; Famine. Fenians' (*BA* 145). In the 1914 section of *The Years*, Martin, struggling to make conversation at a dinner party, declares: ' "I've thought of three subjects to talk about," he began straight off, without thinking how the sentence was to end. "Racing; the Russian ballet; and" – he hesitated for a moment – "Ireland. Which interests you?" ' (*Y* 239). Although the subject of Ireland is added as an afterthought, the passage suggests that Ireland was a common topic of conversation at dinner parties at the time. Sure enough, conversation soon turns to Ireland at the other end of the table and Martin's discomfort is quickly forgotten: 'He threw himself into their conversation. It was about politics of course, about Ireland' (*Y* 241), as one of the guests begins '"When I was in Ireland," he began, "in 1880..."' (*Y* 241).

References to Ireland pepper Woolf's portrait of First World War life in her third novel, *Jacob's Room*. Ireland is continually referred to as one of the most significant political issues of Edwardian England. While Jacob is in London, we are informed that, at his homestead in Cornwall, 'the Captain would sometimes talk, as the evening waned, about Ireland or India' (*JR* 123). Meanwhile 'Mr. Asquith's Irish policy' (*JR* 144) is one of the numerous thoughts of Miss Marchmont as she sits reading in the British Museum. Jacob himself also discusses contemporary events in Ireland such as the constitutional crisis of 1911 whose outcome paved the way for the third Home Rule Bill: ' "I say, will King George give way about the peers?" "He'll jolly well have to," said Jacob' (*JR* 178). But the pressing question of Irish Home Rule represents a threatening menace to Jacob's ideology of British national identity which has been carefully solidified throughout his upbringing: 'But then there was the British Empire which was beginning to puzzle him; nor was he altogether in favour of giving Home Rule to Ireland. What did the *Daily Mail* say about that?' (*JR* 191). In *Jacob's Room* Woolf acknowledges the prominence of current debates about Ireland on English social life and threads the Irish question into the fabric of English life and consciousness.

Information about Ireland in Woolf's fiction is disseminated primarily through the medium of public mass media, the newspaper. Like Jacob, whose knowledge of Home Rule reaches him in London through the newspaper, Woolf's access to information about Ireland depended, we must assume, on *The Times*, which she read on a daily basis. In a passage that culminates with Jacob pondering the Home Rule Bill, the narrative pauses over the phenomenon of the newspaper: 'These pinkish and greenish newspapers are thin sheets of gelatine pressed nightly over the brain and heart of the world. They take the impression of the whole. Jacob cast his eye over it. A strike, a murder, football, bodies found; vociferation from all parts of England simultaneously' (*JR* 133). But despite this vociferation, the report of the Prime Minister's Speech prompts Jacob thinking about Ireland: 'He was certainly thinking about Home Rule in Ireland – a very difficult matter' (133). The function of the newspaper in disseminating news to the British public is indicated in a letter written by Woolf to Dora Carrington a few days after the assassination of Irish nationalist figure Michael Collins: 'I open the paper and find Michael Collins dead in a ditch' (*L* 2: 552). In his seminal work, *Imagined Communities*, Benedict Anderson traces the emergence of an imagined national community to the advent of print-capitalism. He argues that in the act of reading a national newspaper, 'each communicant is well aware that the ceremony he performs is being replicated simultaneously by thousands (or millions) of others of whose existence he is confident, yet of whose identity he has not the slightest notion' (Anderson 39). The role of the newspaper in creating an imagined national community that links individuals across time and space is suggested at various points in

Woolf's novels. In her satirical sketch of Edwardian English life, *The Voyage Out*, the characters turn to the English broadsheet when away from the imperial centre in order to keep informed on events in Ireland: '"They're making a mess of it," said Mr. Thornbury. He had reached the second column of the report, a spasmodic column, for the Irish members had been brawling three weeks ago at Westminster over a question of naval efficiency' (*VO* 125). The dependence of the English holidaymakers on *The Times* is satirized throughout the novel, but ironically foreshadows Woolf's own desire for access to the newspaper when she herself was abroad. In a letter to her sister Vanessa after hearing of the death of their half-brother George Duckworth during her trip to Ireland, Woolf writes 'we only got the *Times* yesterday and read about George' and continues, 'It was mere chance we found a copy of the *Times* lying about' (*L* 5: 299).

The function of the newspaper is developed more fully in *The Years*, where characters at various points turn to the headlines in order to hear the latest news from Ireland. On returning from colonial work in India in 1914 Martin buys a paper in order to read about Britain's nearest colony: 'he turned to read the news from Ireland' (*Y* 224). News of the death of Parnell is channelled through the communal domain of the evening headlines displayed on placards in the streets:

> Then she [Eleanor] felt vaguely that something was happening. The paper boys at the gates were dealing out papers with unusual rapidity. Men were snatching them and opening them and reading them as they walked on. She looked at a placard that was crumpled across a boy's legs. 'Death' was written in very large black letters.
> Then the placard blew straight, and she read other word: 'Parnell.'
> "Dead"... she repeated. "Parnell." She was dazed for a moment. How could he be dead – Parnell? She bought a paper. They said so...
> "Parnell is dead!" she said aloud. She looked up and saw the sky again; clouds were passing; she looked down into the street. A man pointed at the news with his forefinger. Parnell is dead he was saying. He was gloating. But how could he be dead? It was like something fading in the sky. (*Y* 109)

Eleanor's disbelief in the death of a figure who she knows solely through newspaper coverage is only quelled by her trust in the veracity of the medium of the newspaper report: 'How could he be dead... They said so'. But she is also persuaded by the comforting awareness of a joint community of readership as she notices that other readers too seem to believe the headlines: 'a man pointed at the news with his forefinger'. Meanwhile the Colonel hears the news in similar fashion: 'He leant out and a paper was thrust up at him. "Parnell!" he exclaimed, as he fumbled for his glasses. "Dead by Jove!" The cab trotted on. He read the news two or three times over' (*Y* 112). Just as by reading the news from Ireland in *The Times* the characters of *The Voyage Out* are united in a common band of national solidarity, Eleanor and the Colonel are united through their reading of the same news on the same day in the imperial centre of London. The simultaneity of the reception of the news connects the characters and allows a sense of community to be imagined.

More than any British politician, the figure of Charles Stewart Parnell surfaces at various points in *The Years*. The influence of an Irish nationalist politician on the middle-class Londoners of *The Years* invokes Edward Said's argument concerning the interconnectedness between the colonies and the metropolitan centre outlined in his book *Culture and Imperialism*: 'As we look back at the cultural archive, we begin to reread it not univocally but *contrapuntally*, with a simultaneous awareness both of the metropolitan history that is narrated and of those other histories against which (and together with which) the dominating discourse acts' (Said 59). The numerous allusions to Parnell and the Irish political situation in the portrait of British life and culture in *The Years* invites the reader to bring this very notion of a contrapuntal reading to the novel, as imperial centre and colonial periphery become intertwined.

In *The Years*, the death of Parnell is set up as the most significant event of the year 1891. It is also worth noting that in her biography of Roger Fry published three years later, Ireland is mentioned in the description of the year 1892 and is one of the few political references in the book: 'The peace was so profound. Politically, the most stirring question was the fate of the Home Rule Bill' (*RF* 82). From Woolf's diary we learn that in 1933 she was reading R. Barry O'Brien's 1898 biography of Parnell (*D* 4: 143). In August 1934, while she was still working on the 'novel-essay' version of *The Years*, she even considered the life of Parnell as material for her next book: "Also, a play about the Parnells. Or a biography of Mrs. P" (*D* 4: 238). O'Brien is notably reticent on the relationship between Parnell and Kitty O'Shea.[6] But Woolf's interest in the personal life of Parnell, and his relationship with his wife for whom he sacrificed his political career, is picked up by Eugénie in *The Years*:

"Parnell," said Abel briefly. "He's dead."

"Dead?" Eugénie echoed him. She let her hand fall dramatically.

"Yes. At Brighton. Yesterday."

"Parnell is dead!" she repeated.

"So they say," said the Colonel. Her emotion always made him feel more matter-of-fact; but he liked it. She took up the paper.

"Poor thing!" she exclaimed, letting it fall.

"Poor thing?" he repeated. Her eyes were full of tears. He was puzzled. Did she mean Kitty O" Shea? He hadn't thought of her.

"She ruined his career for him," he said with a little snort.

"Ah, but how she must have loved him!" she murmured. (*Y* 115–16)

The passage conveys the impact of a public figure on the emotions of a private individual by showing how political events can impinge in very real terms on the private world, affecting different people in different ways. On hearing of Parnell's death Eleanor's thoughts turn immediately to her sister Delia: 'She must go to Delia. Delia had cared. Delia had cared passionately. What was it she used to say – flinging out of the house, leaving them all for the Cause, for this man? Justice, Liberty? She must go to her. This would be the end of all her dreams' (*Y* 109–10). Even the Colonel himself, a representative figure of British imperialism, reacts paradoxically to the news of Parnell's death:

He's dead, he said, taking off his glasses. A shock of something like relief, of something that had a tinge of triumph in it, went through him as he leant back in the corner. Well, he said to himself, he's dead – that unscrupulous adventurer – that agitator who had done all the mischief, that man... Some feeling connected with his own daughter here formed in him; he could not say exactly what, but it made him frown... One could respect him, he thought, as the cab passed the House of Commons, which was more than could be said for some of the other fellows... and there'd been a lot of nonsense talked about the divorce case. (*Y* 112)

As an ex-colonial officer, the death of the powerful Irish nationalist figure initially comes as a relief to the Colonel, but by falling sway to 'some feeling connected with his own daughter' he admits a degree of respect for Parnell. Although this suggests a possible understanding between the British subject and the nationalist leader, significantly it is only when Parnell's threat to British hegemony has been removed through his death, that the Colonel can allow himself some sympathy with him. The lengthy descriptions in *The Years* of the effect of Parnell's death on the various members of the Pargiter family might be read as an interesting footnote to cultural representations of this chapter in Irish history. By showing the affect of events in the colonies on the average Londoner, Woolf reveals how British identities are informed and influenced by events abroad. The manifold reactions to Parnell's death bring to mind Said's assertion that the cultures and histories of different nations are intertwined: 'Partly because of empire, all cultures are involved in one another; none is single and pure, all are hybrid, heterogeneous, extraordinarily differentiated and unmonolithic' (Said xxix).

The treatment of Parnell and the significance of his death in the early sections of *The Years* pave the way for the greatest exploration of the Irish Question at the end of the novel through the figure of Patrick. In light of Woolf's anti-imperialism it seems surprising that the only representation of an Irish person in her fiction is a supporter of the Empire. One explanation for the complex characterization of Patrick in *The Years*, I will argue, can be found in Woolf's own response to Ireland during her visit in 1934. Now, for the first time, Woolf's knowledge about Ireland was no longer mediated through casual conversation or newspaper reports, but rather through first-hand experience of the country. Ironically however, as we shall see, Woolf's trip to Ireland served to complicate her ambivalent relationship to Ireland – 'Ireland' for Woolf was now negotiated in the complex interchange between the imaginary and the real.

The first mention of a possible trip to Ireland can be found in a diary entry of 1932: 'I want to go to Ireland, Could that be managed' (*D* 4: 119), and in a letter of August 1932 she writes to Hugh Walpole: 'I'm contemplating a voyage to Ireland – where I've never been – in September: but that's all; and no doubt that wont come off' (*L* 5: 92). Her visit to Ireland at this time coincided with the early stages of her friendship with the Anglo-Irish novelist Elizabeth Bowen whom she had briefly met at a party given by Lady Ottoline Morrell. Although the two did not become friends until later in the 1930s, Woolf's trip to Ireland was to incorporate a visit to Bowen's country house in Cork (Lee 650–2). Woolf wrote to Bowen in early April 1934: 'In fact I can hardly write sense, owing to the fact that it is the first hot day and I have been walking on the downs, and found a whole bank of violets – will there be violets in Ireland? I am very much excited to think of going there at last, and seeing your house' (*L* V 287). Leonard and Virginia planned to begin the itinerary in Bowen's Court in Cork, from there to Kerry, onto the Aran Islands in the West, and finally to finish in Dublin. At first Woolf's eager anticipation was not disappointed and she even considered buying a house there, writing to Bowen from Kerry: 'In fact, your island is too seductive, and we have already been asking about houses, whether one can get them easily, – and one can: so expect us as your neighbours in future' (*L* 5: 298). But the notion of buying a house in a foreign country was not an uncommon fad, and was an idea with which the Woolfs had toyed on previous journeys to the Continent: just a year earlier, Virginia had written to her sister from Italy: 'I'm just off to buy a farm in the hills. This is where we must live' (*L* 5: 183), but the idea never came to fruition.

As the Woolfs moved further away from the Anglo-Irish stronghold of the Big House and penetrated the world of the Irish peasant, Woolf was shocked by the 'extreme poverty' which greeted them: 'one can see, after Bowen's Court, how ramshackle & half squalid the Irish life is, how empty & poverty stricken' (*D* 4: 210). By the end of her trip she writes: 'No, it wouldn't do living in Ireland, in spite of the rocks & the desolate bays. It would lower the pulse of the heart: & all one's mind wd. run out in talk' (*D* 4: 216). Her perception of Ireland, where even 'the Irish loudspeaker is inferior like everything else in this down trodden land' (*D* 4: 214), becomes more and more characterized by comparison with England. Her first impressions of the country are: 'A mixture of Greece, Italy & Cornwall; great loneliness; poverty & dreary villages like squares cut out of West Kensington' (*D* 4: 209). Similarly her description of Dublin is based on comparison to its superior original in London: 'The scene is St Stephen's Green, an Irish attempt at Lincoln's Inn Fields, just as Merrion Square attempts Bedford Sqre & so on' (*D* 4: 215). Later she complains: 'Grafton Street is not on the level of Sloane Street' (*D* 4: 216). This process of negative comparison, and her exposure to what she sees as the utter depravity of Irish life, results in her declaring the very sentiment that Patrick is to echo in *The Years*: 'At last I gather why, if I were Irish, I should wish to belong to the Empire: no luxury, no creation, no stir, only the dregs of London, rather wish-washy as if suburbanised' (*D* 4: 215). In fact, an anecdote recorded by Woolf in her diary perhaps suggests a direct source for her Irishman in *The Years*. She writes at length of 'an extremely interesting encounter' (*D* 4: 211) with a Mr and Mrs Rowlands whom they met on first leaving Bowen Court:

> They began directly, & so we talked,—they accepted us as their sort, & were gentry, Irish gentry, very much so, he with a house 500

years old, & no land left. "But I love my King & Country. Whatever they ask me to do I'd do it"—this with great emotion. Oh yes, we believe in the British Empire; we hate the madman de Valera." There they live, 14 miles from Cork, hunting, with an old retriever dog, & go to bazaars miles & miles away. "That's the way we live— no nonsense about us—not like the English people. Now I'll give you my name, & I'll write to my friend & she'll tell you of a — & I hope you'll live in Ireland. We want people like ourselves. But wait, till the budget." This she said, with all the airs of the Irish gentry: something very foreign about her, like old Lady Young, & yet in slave to London; of course everyone wants to be English... But I'd do anything for my King & Country, though you've always treated us very badly... These are the ways they live... & all the sons going away to make their livings & the old people sitting there hating the Irish Free State & recalling Dublin & the Viceroy. (*D* 4: 211–12)

Like Mr Rowlands, it is evident in *The Years* that Patrick's family is of old Anglo-Irish stock: ' "I come of a family," he said to North, "that has served its king and country for three hundred—" "English settlers," said Delia, rather shortly, returning to her soup' (*Y* 381). The parody of Delia's youthful idealism is given much weight in *The Years*: 'For the thousandth time he had dashed her dream. Thinking to marry a wild rebel, she had married the most King-respecting, Empire-admiring of country gentlemen' (*Y* 378). But even in the opening section of the novel Delia's naïvety is already implied. Though she fervently believes in the ideals of the Irish nationalist movement embodied by Parnell, she is enraptured by the romance of her father's own colonial past and ignorant of the real political situation that lies beneath its ideology: 'Delia liked listening to her father's stories about India. They were crisp, and at the same time romantic. They conveyed an atmosphere of officers dining together in mess jackets on a very hot night with a huge silver trophy in the middle of the table' (*Y* 35). She herself fantasizes about a future working for the 'cause of liberty': 'She was on the platform; there was a huge audience; everybody was shouting, waving handkerchiefs, hissing and whistling. Then she stood up. She rose all in white in the middle of the platform; Mr Parnell was by her side' (*Y* 22). The outcome of her marriage discloses her earlier fantasies as absurd. After the novel's description of her early dedication to Parnell, Delia is absent from the intervening years and it is mentioned only that 'she married an Irishman' (*Y* 160). With the reader having been led to believe that Delia's dream has been fulfilled through a suitable marriage, the juxtaposition of Delia with Patrick's views at the end serves to heighten the irony of her choice of partner. Unlike Parnell, Patrick is a stalwart supporter of the Empire ' "What I'm always telling you," said Patrick, wiping his mouth. "The only civilized country in the whole world," he added... "Ah, but it's true," he sighed, going on with his own thoughts, "I'm sorry to say it – but we're savages compared with you"' (*Y* 379). Patrick's status as an Anglo-Irish subject is significant and can probably be explained by Woolf's own acquaintance with a primarily Anglo-Irish social set both during her visit to Ireland and in her London circle. As an anglicized Irishman, Patrick presents an ideologically complicated and marginal perspective on Irish national identity: he is both English and Irish, occupying a paradoxical midpoint in the imperial dialectic. Patrick's nostalgic allegiance to England in *The Years* can perhaps be explained as a defiant but futile gesture against the demise of the Anglo-Irish ascendancy that was an outcome of Irish independence.[7] But how far we are to take Patrick and his views seriously remains ambiguous in the novel. Though Woolf seems to be aware of the complex identity of the Anglo-Irish – 'that hyphenated people – forever English in Ireland, forever Irish in England', as Declan Kiberd describes them (Kiberd 367), the character of Patrick is subtly satirized in the novel. There is a sense that his views are outmoded and outdated. In contrast to Eleanor who has tried to adjust to modernity, he remains rooted in a bygone era of Empire that has lost its relevance to the younger generation of a changing England.

The ambiguity surrounding the representation of Patrick in *The Years* can be seen to reflect Woolf's own contradictory feelings towards Ireland. As we have seen from her diary entries and letters written during her trip to Ireland, Woolf shared, albeit in private, some of the views on Ireland held by her character, Patrick, most notably her assertion that 'if I were Irish, I should wish to belong to the Empire' (*D* 4: 215). However, Woolf's views on Ireland were by no means purely negative. She delighted in what she described as the garrulousness of Irish people, writing to Vanessa: 'We never stop talking. The Irish are the most gifted people in that line' (*L* 5: 299). This 'notion of the flowing, yet formed sentences, the richness & ease of the language' fascinates Woolf who wonders 'Why arent these people the greatest novelists in the world?' (*D* 4: 213). Ultimately, however, Woolf's trip to Ireland served to bring to the surface her own sense of Englishness. Significantly, it was when returning from Ireland that Woolf experienced what she was to describe later in a letter of 1941 to Ethel Smyth as one of her rare moments of 'patriotism': 'in Warwickshire, one Spring [May 1934] when we were driving back from Ireland and I saw a stallion being led, under the may and the beeches, along a grass ride; and I thought that is England' (*L* 6: 460). Gillian Beer reads this disclosure as the 'invocation of Ireland as the necessary other island' (Beer, *Common Ground* 168), and it seems that this sense of a dialectical relationship between imperial centre and its colonial sibling is what essentially emerges from Woolf's experience in Ireland.

Thus, Woolf's relationship to Ireland provides a fascinating insight into the relationship between a middle-class intellectual in London and the political situation in Ireland in the early twentieth century. At this time, it is most likely that Woolf, like many of her contemporaries, would have been more familiar with continental Europe than her nearest colonial neighbour. That Woolf chose to include Ireland as one of the most significant aspects of British social life between 1880 and the 1930s in *The Years* is thus important in itself, and can be traced to her own interest in the Irish question during her life.

By tracing the history of the Pargiter family over a period of fifty years, *The Years* explores how nations are lived and experienced in the everyday as much as through their reification in key social and political events. Like India and Africa, Ireland exists as an imaginary space on the periphery of the text but, as I have shown, the novel shows how events in the colonies can impinge on the formation of the British subject at home. By highlighting the numerous ways in which information about Ireland can be channelled – the youthful fantasies of the young, newspaper reports, the perspective of an elderly Anglo-Irish man – the novel explores the different ways in which nations are imagined, constructed, and represented. Similarly, the changing aspects of Woolf's own relationship to Ireland – her access to information through the newspaper, an acquaintance with the Anglo-Irish literary set in London, the trip in 1934 – enriches the portrayal of the Irish Question in *The Years*. In her lifetime Woolf witnessed the declaration of the Irish Republic and its emergence as a postcolonial state. Because of her trip Woolf felt at once qualified and compelled to include Ireland as an important facet of British social history represented in *The Years*. But the benefits of travel that Woolf enjoyed through her visit to Ireland served, paradoxically, to intensify the complex interchange between the imaginary and the actual that contributed to her ideas about England and its relationship to the imperial other. Despite her ambivalent attitude to Ireland which finds its fullest expression in *The Years*, I have shown that Virginia Woolf's relationship to Ireland is significant in numerous ways; ultimately, it shows that it is in the complex politics of space and place that national identities can be negotiated.

Notes

1 For an examination of the influence of 'The Pargiters' on *The Years*, see Snaith 88–112; Squier; and Jane Marcus, 'Pargetting'.

2 For a general analysis of this period of Irish history, see Beckett 376–461; Clarke 62–70; and Foster 400–535.

3 An example of this viewpoint can be found in the response to the sacking of towns in Ireland by British forces voiced in an editorial for 28 September 1920: 'The raising and despatching to Ireland of the force known as "Black and Tans" has been a disastrous mistake, and, before anything else is done, that force should be disbanded at once and withdrawn from Ireland.'

4 In a letter to Virginia in March 1914 when Leonard was staying with Strachey in Wiltshire he writes, 'I'll keep all gossip till we meet principally because I'm engaged in an argument against Lytton & [Harry] Norton on the Ulster Question – which prevents my writing this' (*Letters*, ed. Spotts 200).

5 The following excerpt from *The Nation* in January 1913 encapsulates the circumscribed sympathy for Ireland that characterized the editorial stance of the journal at this time. Rather than viewing Home Rule as a stepping-stone to Irish independence, paradoxically the editorial sees it as a way of securing Ireland's presence in the British Empire: 'The passing of the Home Rule Bill through the House of Commons restores the internal government of Ireland to the most brilliant political race in the British Empire, perhaps to the most naturally gifted people in the world [...] this wonderful race, half-estranged and half-enslaved, is now ours; that is to say, *it has become a vital part of the Imperial system*, instead of an alien and highly inflammable body in it' ('The Acceptance of Home Rule' 688, emphasis added).

6 O'Brien writes: 'I do not think that it is any part of my duty as Parnell's biographer to enter into the details of his *liaison* with Mrs O'Shea. I have only to deal with the subject as it affects his public career, and when I have stated that he lived maritally with Mrs O'Shea I feel that I have done all that may reasonably be expected of me' (O' Brien 163).

7 The decline of the Anglo-Irish ascendancy was one of the emerging factors in a radically changing Ireland. For an excellent account see Bence-Jones who suggests at one point: 'According to a list drawn up by Colonel O'Callaghan-Westropp, the number of Ascendancy families in County Clare went down from about eighty in 1919 to a mere ten in the early 1930's. The exodus was worse in Clare that in most parts of Ireland; nevertheless, it went on all over the country during the years following the ending of the Civil War' (Bence-Jones 262). For a recent examination of the demise of the ascendancy in terms of the Big House see Dooley.

Part IV
New Technologies

8
'Reflections in a Motor Car': Virginia Woolf's Phenomenological Relations of Time and Space

Leena Kore Schröder

Modes of transport feature regularly in the work of Virginia Woolf. Aeroplanes, as Gillian Beer has noted, are central images in *Mrs Dalloway*, *Orlando*, *The Years*, and *Between the Acts* (Beer, *Common Ground* 149–50). Urban traffic is also a familiar feature, and provides Woolf with key metaphors through which to consider larger issues of identity and narrative, such as the London omnibuses in sketches like 'Monday or Tuesday' or 'Kew Gardens', or in *Mrs Dalloway* where they offer both Elizabeth and Clarissa Dalloway an exhilarating escape from what Woolf elsewhere terms the 'damned egotistical self' (*D* 2: 14). Taxis are also locations in which the possibilities for a plural and communal self can be explored: 'Where does she begin, and where do I end?' Peggy asks herself in *The Years* as she drives across London in a cab with Eleanor (317), while in *A Room of One's Own* the sight of a man and woman driving off in a taxi triggers a more general speculation on such destructive polarities as male and female, mind and body, self and other (126). The Tube, too, is a familiar trope by which the narrow confines of self are capable of extension, as in the essay 'Craftsmanship', where the Underground becomes a working metaphor for the vagaries of language itself (*DM* 125–32), or in 'The Mark on the Wall', where 'being blown through the Tube at fifty miles an hour' conveys the real fluidity and fleetingness of individual experience (*MW* 4). Indeed, as Woolf observes in that story, 'As we face each other in omnibuses and underground railways we are looking into the mirror... And the novelists in future will realize more and more the importance of these reflections, for of course there is not one reflection but an almost infinite number' (*MW* 6). Trains are Woolf's most well-known examples of locomotive placement, with their solitary female passengers (Mrs Brown, Millie Masters, Minnie Marsh) – those archetypal Woolfian figures of dis-location who are her founding mothers of narrative: 'I believe that all novels begin with an old lady in the corner opposite'.[1]

Of modern forms of transport available to Woolf, by the turn of the century the train (both railway and London Underground) had already revolutionized travel; with rapidly developing technology, motor omnibuses, taxis, aeroplanes and private cars all became accessible in her lifetime. As Laura Marcus points out, these new forms of travel in the early decades of the twentieth century introduce new relations between space, time and self that are expressive of those explorations of subjectivity which we have come to associate with the Modernist age (122 ff.). It is the car, however, that expresses this new experience of subjectivity most fully of all these new modes of transport, by offering the most immediately available knowledge of the body-in-the-world. Foucault's throwaway observation in 'Of Other Spaces', therefore, need not apply to trains alone: 'a train is an extraordinary bundle of relations because it is something through which one goes, it is also something by means of which one can go from one point to another, and then it is also something that goes by' (23–4). This 'bundle of relations' is surely true of all forms of modern transportation: to travel in any moving vehicle is already to be introduced to altered complexities of time, space and perception. To travel in one's own car, however, is to embody these complexities at the most intimate and private level of self.

The car is thus my metaphor for understanding the nature of embodiment in time and space, but, more importantly, from the early twentieth century onwards it became one of the key modes for comprehending the very nature of corporeal experience, revealing to us at the most mundane and subliminal level of the daily business of getting to work, going shopping and running errands, that human embodiment is at the centre of the subjective world. As technology changes, so do the ways in which we conceive of, and explain, our corporeal reality: X-rays, telephones and radios, for instance, have all subtly altered our conception of the body in time and space, and it is entirely significant that so much of the technological revolution that affected the day-to-day life of ordinary people in the West in the twentieth century – in domestic arrangements, transport, entertainment, medical treatment – took place during Virginia Woolf's lifetime. 'We opened one little window when we bought the gramophone', she observes in her diary; 'now another opens with the motor' (*D* 3: 151). Car ownership in Britain shot from 100,000 after the First World War to 2,000,000 just before the Second (Stevenson 130), and the Woolfs form part of these statistics, together buying three cars: a second-hand Singer ('The Umbrella') in 1927, replaced by another (with 'sunshine roof') in 1929, and finally a new and much grander Lanchester ('The Deluge') in 1933. Technology has a real effect on how we experience and understand our bodies, and of all such change, perhaps the car carries the most far-reaching effects. At least, so thinks Leonard Woolf, who unequivocally declares in his autobiography that 'Nothing ever changed so profoundly my material existence, the mechanism and range of my every-day life, as the possession of a motor-car' (*Downhill* 178).

The car has a profound effect upon body-image for the essential reason that it throws the body into movement. But the body both does and does not partake of this motion: in itself sitting passively in an intimate space (here I am referring to both driver and passenger) the body is nevertheless actively responsible for directing its movement. Constantly propelled forward in time and space, the body is passive in so far as it cannot do anything but sit, yet it exists in a state of pure mobility. In the way that active and passive as discrete subject positions are collapsed by the experience of the automotive self, so does the very language for describing speed twist space into time: *miles per hour*. In a car, movement is as much in terms of time as it is of space, without being exclusively assigned to either. Moreover, we have become accustomed to the artificial figure/ground distinction between our perceiving selves and the surrounding world, as if space and time were a backdrop for our existence. It is in a moving car (as Orlando's drive out of London demonstrates) that the erroneousness of this distinction is revealed. Rather, space and time are settings in constant interrelation with the perceiving self, a mutuality which movement lays bare. Kurt Goldstein's observations of 1923, quoted by Merleau-Ponty, describe this bond: 'We perform our movements in a space which is not "empty" or unrelated to them, but which on the contrary, bears a highly determinate relation to them: movement and background are, in fact, only artificially separated stages of a unique totality' (Merleau-Ponty 138).

It is through movement, therefore, that the nature of our embodiment is revealed more tellingly than in stasis, even though there is no essential difference between the two states. Because the mobile body no longer *seems* passively subjected to the effects of time and space, it becomes accordingly easier to realize that we do not inhabit the world in the way that inanimate objects are located in space and time, but rather, that there is an *interactive* relation between us and the world. Regardless of whether the body is or is not in movement, our perception of the world cannot be separated from our active participation in the world: a realization that is enabled by the car because its motility actively places the body into a dynamic relation with time and space. Contrary to the idea that we sit passively in cars, surveying an external world, cars grant us a view from within that world that is neither detached nor disinterested, but has meaning because of its spatio-temporal relation to us. The experience of travelling by car permits a better understanding of an observation like Merleau-Ponty's on body, space and time relations:

> We must avoid. ... saying that our body is *in* space, or *in* time. It *inhabits* space and time. ... In so far as I have a body through which I act in the world, space and time are not, for me, a collection of adjacent points nor are they a limitless number of relations synthesized by my consciousness, and into which it draws my body. I am not in space and time, nor do I conceive space and time; belong to them, my body combines with them and includes them. (Merleau-Ponty 139–40).

Merleau-Ponty conceives of the body's relations to time and space in ways which fundamentally refute such dualist, essentially Cartesian, constructions such as self and world, consciousness and body, intellect and instinct, active and passive. In his analysis the body is never a privileged origin of the first-person point of view, but is simultaneously the perceiving subject and perceived object available to other points of view. Again, movement is the process which breaks down such ossifying dualisms, and in order to chart the way in which the subject is embodied through movement, Merleau-Ponty pays considerable attention to the pathology of cognitive disorders such as apraxia: a disorder of motor skills, whereby an otherwise physically healthy person who is capable of recognizing, naming and describing a movement or an implement, is completely unable to execute that movement for themselves or put that implement to its proper use. Apraxia and other phenomena which straddle the psychological and physiological self, such as the phantom limb or the even more puzzling condition of anosagnosia, whereby the individual is utterly convinced that a limb is alien and must be amputated, reveal the inadequacy of the Cartesian explanation of self in terms of consciousness alone. When motor skills are thus interrupted in their normal functioning, it becomes evident that there is a physical as well as an intellectual knowledge of the world. It is in the research of such psycho-physiological disorders that Merleau-

Ponty looks to understand what he calls the 'magical process' by which the body and mind can move together unproblematically: 'The problem can be solved', he urges, 'only provided that we cease to draw a distinction between the body as a mechanism in itself and consciousness as being for itself' (Merleau-Ponty 139n). The experience of the self in the moving car is truly one of these 'magical processes' by which the distinction between the passively mechanical and the actively conscious is overthrown. In the sense that sitting in a moving car is at once to be passive in, and actively propellent of, space and time, it is an experience that is itself a kind of apraxia: in other words, a physiological and psychological interruption of habitual motor skills which suddenly exposes the illusion of consciousness as the controlling origin of self.

Intriguingly, one of Merleau-Ponty's most frequently cited sources for his discussion of the way in which motor-skill disorders lay bare the nature of a normally integrated body-subject is the published research of Henry Head, a pioneer of modern neuropsychology and Woolf's own personal choice of doctor when faced with the necessity of medical consultation during her severe mental breakdown in 1913 (she may have been influenced in her decision by Roger Fry's high regard for Head). It is research such as the famous experiment conducted upon his own body (performed in 1903; results published 1908), in which Head had the nerves in his hand severed and stitched back together, which throws the mental and sensory functions out of their normal synchronization and informs Merleau-Ponty's observation, that 'for us to be able to conceive space [and time], it is in the first place necessary that we should have been thrust into it by our body' (Merleau-Ponty 142).[2] Head was only to be involved in Woolf's case for the brief but acute twenty-four hours during which he first saw her, was called to her bedside after her serious suicide attempt and, together with Geoffrey Keynes, worked to save her life. Unfortunately, we can only speculate what benefit Woolf might have had from a doctor who endorsed an essentially ambiguous explanation of the embodied subject (the concept of 'body-image' is his term).[3] Head addresses that same chiasmatic conception of relations between identity, consciousness, body, space and time which Woolf herself never ceased to explore in and through her writing, and if he remains tantalizingly on the fringes of her life, nonetheless, like Woolf herself, he is part of the larger twentieth-century cultural, philosophical and pathological revisioning of the body as the centre of the cognitive world.

The complexity of such an understanding of the body-subject was registered in a dramatically new way for Woolf once she had access to a car. Travelling that used to be restricted to timetables and fixed stations was now suddenly 'all as light & easy as a hawk in the air' (so Virginia rhapsodizes in her diary, a few weeks after the arrival of the Singer: *D* 3: 151). Leonard too appreciates the new-found freedom: 'In the old way of travel one was tied to the railway; as one moved through a country, one followed the straight steel parallel lines, one had no contact with the life of the road, the village, and the town' (*Downhill* 181). Virginia took driving lessons, but she was not to become a confident or accomplished driver. Without confirming the cliché of the inept lady driver, she could ironically play the part, triumphantly writing, for example, to Ethel Sands after having had the Singer for only a week, that 'I have driven from the Embankment to the Marble Arch and only knocked one boy very gently off his bicycle', but then adding more warmly, 'I would rather have a gift for motoring than anything' (*L* 3: 400). Leonard became the regular chauffeur, and for the rest of her life Virginia appears to have sat happily in the passenger seat.

Whether driving or being driven, both Virginia and Leonard appreciate that what sets the car apart from other modes of mechanized transport is freedom. All other forms (save the bicycle) require the traveller to submit to routes, tickets, schedules or, at least, as in the case of taxis, to identify and be acknowledged as a traveller. The urge to wander at will is fulfilled by the motor car, a kind of *flânerie* on wheels. Automobile travel also encourages motility enjoyed for its own sake, a phatic movement with no fixed goal. The impetuosity of Elizabeth Dalloway's decision to board a bus and the gay spontaneity of her ride mark her out as a 'free spirit', but such impulse for movement was satisfied by motoring in ways that regulated public transport could never quite equal. Contemporary advertising of motor oil and petrol plays upon precisely these aspects of driving, with emphasis upon speed, modernity and freedom of access to the countryside. The Shell posters of the 1920s exhort the motorist to 'see Britain First' or 'See Ireland First', with accompanying romantic images of vast (and usually empty) landscapes of mountains, rivers and glens.[4] The kind of leisure that these images assume is, quite rightly, pointed out by Lord Montagu of Beaulieu as alluding to

> a motoring public drawn from the upper middle classes and upper classes who typified the private motorists of the 1920s. This was a social class attuned to the sophistication and wit of much of Shell's press advertising at the time. It was also a class that celebrated the

exciting possibilities afforded by the relatively new pastime of motoring. (Montagu of Beaulieu, np)

Leonard and Virginia Woolf fit this image precisely. As if following the directions of the Shell command, from 1928 onwards, with very few exceptions, they undertook an annual motoring holiday, roughly alternating between Britain and the Continent: France, Germany, Italy, Holland, Ireland, Cornwall, Scotland and the Western Isles were all tackled, in many cases more than once. When one remembers that such journeys were undertaken in the 1920s and 1930s without AA Five-Star insurance and the infrastructure of motorways and petrol stations that serve today's motoring tourists, one realizes that the 'easy flight of the hawk' was in reality somewhat trammelled, particularly by tyres which wore out very quickly on back roads and punctured regularly. By Leonard's calculations, on the return leg of their first journey to the south of France, they had to stop to mend a puncture on average every twenty-five miles: 'It seemed to me that there was hardly any road in France on which I had not grovelled in the mud changing wheels' (*Downhill* 184). There was nothing passive about driving a car through the Massif Central in 1928. But this too afforded fresh experiences. Both Leonard and Virginia individually and appreciatively record breaking down in a remote mountain village in the Auvergne and being invited into a cottage where the daughter of the house happened to be writing to a penfriend who lived in Brighton (*D* 3: 179; *Downhill* 184). Virginia, typically, greatly welcomed these fragmented and fleeting glimpses into other lives which travelling by car offered her. At the end of her first summer with a car, she observes that:

> What I like, or one of the things I like, about motoring is the sense it gives one of lighting accidentally, like a voyager who touches another planet with the tip of his toe, upon scenes which would have gone on, have always gone on, will go on, unrecorded, save for this chance glimpse. Then it seems to me I am allowed to see the heart of the world uncovered for a moment. (*D* 3: 153)

Leonard corroborates the pleasure Virginia took from these motoring holidays:

> The most important change and the greatest pleasure came ... from a holiday 'touring' on the Continent – I do not think that anything gave Virginia more pleasure than this. She had a passion for

travelling, and travel had a curious and deep effect upon her. When she was abroad, she fell into a strange state of passive alertness. She allowed all these foreign sounds and sights to stream through her mind; I used to say rather like a whale lets the seawater stream through its mouth, straining from it for its use the edible flora and fauna of the seas. Virginia strained off and stored in her mind those sounds and sights, echoes and visions, which months afterwards would become food for her imagination and her art. This and the mere mechanism and kaleidoscope of travel gave her intense pleasure, a mixture of exhilaration and relaxation. (*Downhill* 178–9)

Leonard remains our only eyewitness to those long automobile journeys: what did they do for days on end, husband and wife, squeezed side-by-side into a narrow and uncomfortable car? Some idea of the experience, for Virginia at least, is conveyed in her motoring sketch, 'Evening Over Sussex: Reflections in a Motor Car', written in the 1927–28 period after the purchase of the Singer. We do not have access to the hours that she spent staring out of her car window, but her experiences are reconfigured in the writing which emerges out of these years when motoring was still a novelty for her. Her pleasurable exclamation in her diary, 'We spin off to Falmer, ride over the Downs, drop into Rottingdean, then sweep over to Seaford' (*D* 3: 151), reveals that she rewrote her drives into fiction, for 'Evening Over Sussex' covers the same coastal territory, naming the county and specifically identifying its towns of Eastbourne, Bexhill and St Leonards (*DM* 11). A peremptory reading of this sketch would assign it the usual figure–ground relation of perceiving self (sitting in the car) surveying the passing Sussex landscape. But such a relationship quickly breaks up, as the 'I' begins to splinter into various selves, not only responding to the world outside the car, but also in dialogue with each other: one self is 'eager and dissatisfied', another 'stern and philosophical', a third is melancholy, a fourth, 'erratic and impulsive' (*DM* 12–13). As the car drives along, the narrative voice admits a polyphony of selves that range as fluidly over the Sussex landscape as they do through time, spanning its reference from the arrival of William the Conqueror 'ten centuries ago', through the present moment, to what Sussex will be 'in five hundred years to come' (*DM* 11, 13). The self here is positioned as much in a fluid temporal interrelation with past, present and future, as it is in the spatial interstices that forever open before, and close behind, the moving car. Each voice attempts to capture the moment, but the very fact that it is ever-passing in time and space ensures the futility of a single and final order. The sliding relations between space, time and self in the car play out Merleau-Ponty's meaning of the body as not passively inserted into time and space, but actively combining with and including them. The figure proposed at the end of the sketch, therefore, as the culmination of the day's experiences, necessarily remains but a lifeless mannequin on the speaker's knee:

> We sat and looked at the figure we had made that day. Great sheer slabs of rock, tree tufted, surrounded him. He was for a second very, very solemn. Indeed it seemed as if the reality of things were displayed there on the rug. A violent thrill ran through us; as if a charge of electricity had entered into us. We cried out together: 'Yes, yes,' as if affirming something in a moment of recognition. (*DM* 13–14)

This puppet figure, needing that electric charge in order to be kick-started into life, fails helplessly at the sound of the real, living body whose voice brings the sketch to its close. The final admission of the body, with its emphasis upon food, eating, tastes and sensations, is particularly striking. The narrative voice becomes simultaneously expressive of both body and car, combining physical needs and pleasures with the rhythm of the engine and wheels. Effectively, the body and car become one, the car not an active tool by which the passive body can propel itself through time and space, but an extension of the body itself that incorporates space and time into a self that at every moment is created anew.

> And then the body who had been silent up to now began its song, almost at first as low as the rush of the wheels: "Eggs and bacon; toast and tea; fire and a bath; fire and a bath; jugged hare," it went on, "and red currant jelly; a glass of wine; with coffee to follow; with coffee to follow – and then to bed; and then to bed."
>
> "Off with you," I said to my assembled selves. "Your work is done. I dismiss you. Good-night."
>
> And the rest of the journey was performed in the delicious society of my own body. (*DM* 14)

Even as the sketch concludes with this marked admission of corporeality, at the same time it implies that if the body is known by the extent to which it incorporates time and space, then its corporeal boundaries can never be all-embracing and all-defining. This point is made yet more emphatically in the famous extended description of Orlando driving out of London, where the proliferation of the subject through driving this time stretches to over 2,000 selves. It is entirely significant that this piece, too, written during that first heady period after acquiring a car and learning to drive, uses the device of the car in movement to render the horizon indeterminate and ever-changing, ensuring a relativity of self whose synthesis of time and space must be forever re-calculated rather than fixed:

> Nothing could be seen whole or read from start to finish. What was seen begun – like two friends starting to meet each other across the street – was never seen ended. After twenty minutes [of driving] the body and mind were like scraps of torn paper tumbling from a sack and, indeed, the process of motoring fast out of London so much resembles the chopping up small of identity which precedes unconsciousness and perhaps death itself that it is an open question in what sense Orlando can be said to have existed at the present moment. (*O* 293)

While the car loses its dominance as an image in Woolf's writing throughout the 1930s, she never ceased that inquiry into space–time relations which in 'Evening Over Sussex' and *Orlando* were worked out in terms of the self in movement. Nevertheless, motoring references resurface from time to time, such as Peggy and Eleanor's taxi ride in *The Years* (315–20), or the parade of branded luxury cars in *Between the Acts* (Woolf herself took great delight in their expensive new Lanchester, bought in 1933):[5] 'Dear me, the parking arrangements are not what you might call adequate ... I shouldn't have expected either so many Hispano-Suizas ... That's a Rolls ... That's a Bentley ... That's the new type of Ford' (*BA* 180–1). It is in *Between the Acts* that the car is once again integrated with Woolf's writing practice. Whereas in 'Evening Over Sussex', the stylistic difficulties of finding a language for each of the different selves is part of the overtly declared intention, in *Between the Acts*, the multiplicity of register is absorbed into the narrative itself. Significantly, the following passage is once again achieved by means of the motor car:

> Pointz Hall was seen in the light of an early summer morning to be a middle-sized house. It did not rank among the houses that are mentioned in guide books. It was too homely. But this whitish house with the grey roof, and the wing thrown out at right angles,

lying unfortunately low on the meadow with a fringe of trees on the bank above it so that smoke curled up to the nests of the rooks, was a desirable house to live in. Driving past, people said to each other: 'I wonder if that'll ever come into the market?' And to the chauffeur: 'Who lives there?'

The chauffeur didn't know. The Olivers, who had bought the place something over a century ago, had no connection with the Warings, the Elveys, the Mannerings or the Burnets; the old families who had all inter-married, and lay in their deaths intertwisted, like the ivy roots, beneath the churchyard wall.

Only something over a hundred and twenty years the Olivers had been there. Still, on going up the principal staircase—there was another, a mere ladder at the back for the servants—there was a portrait. A length of yellow brocade was visible half-way up; and, as one reached the top, a small powdered face, a great head-dress slung with pearls, came into view; an ancestress of sorts. Six or seven bedrooms opened out of the corridor. The butler had been a soldier; had married a lady's maid; and, under a glass case, there was a watch that had stopped a bullet on the field of Waterloo. (*BA* 6–7)

This passage is given in its entirety in order to convey a fuller sense of how curiously Woolf manages a conventional requirement of fiction-writing: to describe setting. Essentially, Pointz Hall is a medium-sized house, yet already the objective certainty of this opening statement is bent to the qualified perspective of 'was seen' and 'in the light of an early summer morning'. The fact that it is not mentioned in guidebooks immediately alludes to the contemporary proliferation of volumes such as those in the *Shell Guides* (appearing regularly from 1933 onwards) or in Batsford's *English Life*, *British Heritage*, and *Face of Britain* series (initiated 1932, 1933 and 1936 respectively): publications whose readership was created entirely by the massive expansion in leisure motoring throughout the 1930s. The bias of such subsequent tags as 'homely', 'unfortunately' and 'desirable', therefore, all derive from a particular point of view: that of passing motorists (and also, it should be added, motorists with chauffeurs). Thus, the entire descriptive piece is managed in these specifically situated terms. More interestingly still, even though the chauffeur is *unable* to provide the information about Pointz Hall, we learn about who lives there. An omniscient narrator (who of, course, is present in the text) would have no difficulty in establishing how long the Olivers had lived at Pointz Hall. Whoever it is who hazards the vague 'something over a century ago', it is someone who thinks in terms of county class-connections. That voice, too, is suddenly dropped, for no social snob could aspire to the poetry of the intertwisted ivy roots, but it returns full force with the fine discrimination of '*Only* something over a hundred and twenty years'. The passage follows through with an account of the main features of the interior which maintain Woolf's typical interest in the incongruous with the inclusion of the Waterloo watch (compare it, for example, to the 'piece of a policeman's trousers lying cheek by jowl with Queen Alexandra's wedding veil' in *Orlando*, 75), yet manage to retain its gossipy social prejudices with such off-hand provisos as 'an ancestress *of sorts*', 'six *or* seven bedrooms', and the nosy detail of the butler who 'had married a lady's maid'. What in 'Evening Over Sussex' is stage-managed perhaps rather clumsily, here becomes both form and content, sliding its narrative seamlessly over multiple discourses of class and register which are at once individually specific, yet defy any fixed identity.

Pointz Hall is very definitely *not* included in contemporary motoring guidebooks, but it *is* featured in the fictional gazetteer of a previous age, Figgis's Guide Book of 1833. This information is given on occasion of yet another description of the setting of Pointz Hall, again requiring extensive quotation:

> Giles went back to the house and brought more chairs and placed them in a semi-circle, so that the view might be shared, and the shelter of the old wall. For by some lucky chance a wall had been built continuing the house, it might be with the intention of adding another wing, on the raised ground in the sun. But funds were lacking; the plan was abandoned, and the wall remained, nothing but a wall. Later, another generation had planted fruit trees, which in time had spread their arms widely across the red-orange weathered brick. Mrs Sands called it a good year if she could make six pots of apricot jam from them — the fruit was never sweet enough for dessert. Perhaps three apricots were worth enclosing in muslin bags. But they were so beautiful, naked, with one flushed cheek, one green, that Mrs Swithin left them naked, and the wasps burrowed holes.
>
> The ground sloped up, so that to quote Figgis's Guide Book (1833), 'it commanded a fine view of the surrounding country ... The spire of Bolney Minster, Rough Norton woods, so called because ...'
>
> The Guide Book still told the truth. 1833 was true in 1939. No house had been built; no town had sprung up. Hogben's Folly was still eminent; the very flat, field-parcelled land had changed only in

this—the tractor had to some extent superseded the plough. The horse had gone; but the cow remained. If Figgis were here now, Figgis would have said the same. So they always said when in summer they sat there to drink coffee, if they had guests. When they were alone, they said nothing. They looked at the view; they looked at what they knew, to see if what they knew might perhaps be different today. Most days it was the same. (*BA* 47–8)

This second account of the Pointz Hall setting, like the first example, hovers over multiple points of view, from the specific markers of Giles (whose awareness admits the presence of previous owners of Pointz Hall, with their half-realized plans), Mrs Sands (who also alludes to the insufficiencies of the place, but from a servant's point of view), and Mrs Swithin (who sees its beauty despite the shortcomings), to the more generalized opinions of the omniscient narrator, the Pointz Hall community and Figgis. This time, the Hall is not described externally in terms of passers-by, but from within, with the inhabitants looking out upon their estate. But while the location of the gaze is thus switched, nevertheless its class origins are the same: both chauffeured motorists and landed gentry are of equal status. Class is an issue here, and Woolf is aware of the implications of her setting. This is no simple celebration of Englishness. What a character like Lucy Swithin so appreciatively surveys is an unchanged, idyllic English pastoral scene, but the specific identifications of 1833 and 1939 do not simply signify the 'timelessness' of the unchanged landscape. If little has changed since Figgis described it, then that in itself means something different in 1939 than it did in 1833. This land, like the house itself, is 'desirable', and the fact that 'no house had been built; no town had sprung up' upon it means that the owners of Pointz Hall have been able to resist the financial temptations of development, for all that the improvements upon their own estate may not have been easily funded (but then, shabbiness is itself part of the 'country house' image). Giles, in passages immediately following, is irritated by the complacency of this very English scene in contrast with the arming of Europe ('At any moment guns would rake that land into furrows; planes splinter Bolney Minster into smithereens and blast the Folly', *BA* 49), but the moment is threatened by more than the war. The tractor that has taken over the horse-drawn plough is but one motor on this landscape, which is also traversed by Hispano-Suizas, Rolls-Royces, Bentleys and Fords. Significantly, what has been noted by Figgis in 1833 is no longer there in the contemporary motoring guide.

The narrative complexity of these examples from 'Evening Over Sussex', *Orlando* and *Between the Acts* should therefore also be read in terms of the larger socio-historical moment. A little over three decades span the composition and temporal setting of 'The Journal of Mistress Joan Martyn' (1906) and that of *Between the Acts* (1939). These years witnessed the founding and popularization of movements whose concerns with the conservation of rural Britain and its architectural heritage continue to fire public opinion to this day. After the establishment of the National Trust (1895) came the Council for the Preservation (now Protection) of Rural England (1926) and the Ramblers' Association (1935): it is not to overstate the case that these movements gained impetus in direct proportion to the rise of private motor-car ownership that facilitated the very invasion of the countryside which they fought to oppose. In 1906 Rosamond Merridew, travelling 'the Thetford road from Norwich to East Harling' (almost certainly by horse-drawn carriage), suddenly spies an ancient manor house:

> one eye, my archeological eye, kept itself awake to the landscape through which we passed. And it was in obedience to a telegram from this that I leapt up in the carriage, at a certain point and directed the driver to turn sharply to the left. We passed down a regular avenue of ancient elm trees; but the bait which drew me was a little square picture, framed delicately between green boughs at the far end, in which an ancient doorway was drawn distinctly in lines of carved white stone. (*CSF* 35)

In 1939 the eyes of discerning passers-by (now in motor cars) are similarly caught by a glimpse of Pointz Hall. Between these two poles – one at the beginning of her writing career, the other at its end – Woolf herself partakes of such architectural voyeurism. Returning from a visit to Vita in September 1927, she records in her diary: 'We motored to Long Barn & back yesterday, through suburbs for the most part. ... Now & again one comes on something consciously preserved like the Wren house at Groombridge. One stops the motor & looks. So do other motorists' (*D* 3: 157).

The ownership of a motor car and the leisure pastime of motoring, therefore, include Woolf as part of the very problem she deplores. 'This is a great opening up in our lives', she acknowledges to herself, 'One may go to Bodiam, to Arundel, explore the Chichester downs, expand that curious thing, the map of the world in ones mind' (*D* 3: 147). Yet this mental expansion necessarily bears material consequences.

'Evening Over Sussex' is, after all, a literary 'going for a spin' ('We spin off to Falmer', as the diary puts it, *D* 3: 151). It is notable, for example, that Woolf takes her bearings in the sketch from the very chain of towns – Eastbourne, Bexhill, St Leonards – where the speculative building and ribbon development that was to disfigure the south coast between the wars had already started. Leonard and Virginia passionately regretted the development of their beloved Sussex coastline, but it should be remembered that their adoption of Sussex as second home was itself part of a much larger social phenomenon, as H.V. Morton would have cause to observe in his travels through England in 1939: 'Sussex has suffered an invasion almost as complete and overwhelming as that which transformed the northern towns during the first stages of the Industrial Revolution. But the Sussex invasion was not of workers, but of retired people and wealthy week-enders' (Morton 96–7). Indeed, in spite of its bohemian and intellectual reputation, Bloomsbury's settling in Sussex is consonant with the social pattern of its time. And just as the Sussex 'invasion' went hand-in-hand with the rise in private motor-car ownership, so did Bloomsbury acquire its various cars: 'We talk of nothing but cars', Virginia records again in July 1927; 'word is brought that Mrs Bell is at the door in her car. I rush out, & find her, rather nervously in control of a roomy shabby Renault. ... The Keynes's have one too – a cheap one' (*D* 3: 146–7). If, therefore, the car opens up for Virginia a new experience of time and space that becomes expressive of a new sense of the subject, it nevertheless also implicates her in the world of the middlebrow, with the suburban gardens and red-brick villas that she loathes. 'Evening Over Sussex' begins by *erasing* the signs of middlebrow habitation as twilight falls over the view from the car – 'All Eastbourne, all Bexhill, all St. Leonards, their parades and their lodging houses, their bead shops and their sweet shops and their placards and their invalids and their chars-à-bancs, are all obliterated' (*DM* 11) – even as the point of view is in itself already 'middlebrow' for being automotively oriented, therefore establishing the sketch as part of the very middlebrow world it seeks to denigrate.

This condenses the contradiction found elsewhere in Woolf's writing if we set the excited diary entries of the summer of 1927 beside her 'reader's letter' to the *Nation and Athenaeum* just three years earlier:

The English road, moreover, is rapidly losing its old character – its colour, here tawny-red, here pearl-white; its flowery and untidy hedges; its quiet; its ancient and irregular charm. It is becoming, instead, black as cinders, smooth as oilcloth, shaven of wild flowers, straightened of corners, a mere racing-track for the convenience of a population seemingly in perpetual and frantic haste not to be late for dinner. (*E* 3: 440)

The route of the drive in 'Evening Over Sussex' takes precisely these black, smooth, race-track roads, made all the clearer by the telling identification of Bexhill: a town almost entirely created by and for the motor car, it was the site of the first motor race-track in England, built in 1902. Moreover, for all its aesthetic appreciation of the Sussex evening, the sketch nevertheless hurries to its close with the same greed as the common motorist's anticipation of a good dinner. The splintering of the unified self through the action of driving, as the different selves multiply and the single narrative voice becomes a chorus, is therefore carried through even into its writing, in the way that the sketch admits the very position which it ostensibly seeks to write against.

From the evidence in 'Evening Over Sussex' it cannot be ascertained beyond doubt whether its narrator is the driver, or is being driven. Indeed, with the increasing proliferation of narrative selves in the sketch, the very communality and plurality of its voice directly counteract the single-mindedness required for safe and effective driving. But the sketch is not a parody of absent-minded women drivers, any more than its multiple voices are of the conventional first-person narrator. Indeed, though similarly dispersed over a range of potential selves, Orlando is a crack driver, manoeuvring her automobile deftly through the West End traffic, haranguing cars in her way, adroitly changing gear, for all that she forgot to buy the sardines, bath salts and boots on her shopping list. Significantly, only when Orlando is at the wheel is she able to expose the illusion of 'the Captain self, the Key self', skittering in time and space, 'changing her selves as quickly as she drove – there was a new one at every corner' (*O* 295–6).

These selected readings of 'Evening Over Sussex', *Orlando* and *Between the Acts* reveal that Woolf not only writes out of the great and genuine enjoyment of the contemporary motoring enthusiast (with all the contradictions that activity entails), but also that she is a contemplative writer responsive to these new sensations of speed and space. As Henry Head discovered through neuropsychological research, and Merleau-Ponty in phenomenological speculation, the experience of driving offered Woolf an *embodied* knowledge of time and space. In the way that apraxia suddenly reveals the body to itself, and 'makes strange' what is otherwise so automatic that it is never brought to consciousness, so does driving defamiliarize the habitual identity which ordinarily assumes its coincidence with time and space. Not for nothing does Woolf point out in another essay, 'On Being Ill' (1926), that it is only when one is subjected to pain or illness that suddenly the mind's tactics of erasure are exposed for what they are: 'literature does its best to maintain that its concern is with the mind; that the body is a sheet of plain glass through which the soul looks straight and clear, and, save for one or two passions such as desire and greed, is null, and negligible and non-existent' (*E* 4: 317). Sickness, pain and disease, like apraxia, reveal the indivisibility of corporeal and intellectual experience by foregrounding what is usually *sous rature*: the body. Without doubt Woolf wrote 'On Being Ill' out of her own personal knowledge of bodily illness, but neither should the exploration of the nature of selfhood that preoccupied her throughout her writing career be limited to the insights of suffering alone. Woolf's achievements as a writer were wrought more through empowerment and enjoyment, than they were through handicap: it is this power of re-accessing the body that was granted to her by the motor car.

Notes

1 'Character in Fiction', *E* 3: 425. See, for example, Rachel Bowlby's reading of 'Mr Bennett and Mrs Brown' (Bowlby, *Virginia Woolf* 3–15). The other 'railway women' are found in 'The Shooting Party' and 'An Unwritten Novel', *MW* 69–76 and 18–29.
2 Head's experiment (with photographs) is described in Miller 318–21.
3 A valuable account of the research and practice of Henry Head, together with Woolf's other doctors (Savage, Craig and Hyslop – but not Octavia Wilberforce) is given in Trombley, esp. 159–82.
4 See examples in *The Shell Poster Book*, esp. nos. 8, 9 and 13.
5 'We have bought a brand new and very expensive car. ... It is the apple of L's eye. It is on the fluid flywheel system. It will cruise – how I love technical words – at 50 miles an hour' (to Ethel Smyth, *L* 5: 146). Virginia was quite right about Leonard's pride in the new car: decades later he still recalled the specifics of the 'Lanchester 18 car with a Tickford hood' (*Downhill* 188).

9
Virginia Woolf and the Synapses of Radio

Jane Lewty

It is probable that Virginia Woolf would have endorsed the 1993 Penguin edition of *The Years*, whose cover depicts a painting by C.R.W. Nevinson, 'Amongst the Nerves of the World' (*c*.1930). The scene is one of muted energy, where the observer is positioned over a drab, shaded street filled with automobiles and countless hurrying stick figures, ink-black, tiny and sexless. From concealed points above, and within, the buildings, a tensile web of lines glitters darkly against the pale blocks of granite, cross-connecting all disparate elements in the field of view. Although these charged lines, or filaments, clearly form an internal network, the suggestion is that they hover invisibly, stretching beyond the limits of the painting. It is a mere segment, representing the new era where noise and time flow incessantly through electric capillaries, where human systems are reordered even at street level.

Essentially, the painting records a cultural shift occurring between 1920 and 1940, where the dimensions of personal and societal experience were significantly altered. Even inveterate technologies, such as writing, became subsumed by 'the omnipotence of integrated circuits', one of the many descriptions offered by media theorist Friedrich Kittler (Kittler 19). By this, he implies that a gradual, nevertheless dramatic, revolution of electronic media permeated every facet of the early twentieth century, whose citizens were forced to consider the wiring, or absence of wiring, in the very nature of communication itself. The Futurist Filippo Marinetti, initially envying those to be born into electric utopia (where 'men can write in books of nickel no thicker than three centimetres [...] and still containing one hundred thousand pages'), admitted in 'Destruction of Syntax' (1913) that all recipients of telephone, phonograph, 'dirigible or airplane' were vulnerable, as intervention by machines had seemingly exerted 'a decisive influence on their psyches' (Marinetti 45). Furthermore, certain orders of sense experience became gradually polarized by electric media, which seemed to replace the functions of the central nervous system with wires; for example, the trained cinema eye swivels alone, requiring none of the effort of multi-sense hallucination demanded by the printed page. The quiet interior space of the brain, where words might flow unimpeded was challenged by other narrative strategies.

In Stephen Kern's classic text, *The Culture of Time and Space*, the focus is on the restructuring of time among individual, and mass, consciousness, and how 'any number of perspectives' was opened up by a film story or wireless signal, which collapsed space to an instant. He notes that:

> Simultaneity also had the broader cultural impact. One response was a growing sense of unity among people formerly isolated by distance [...]. This was not, however, unambiguous, because proximity also generated anxiety – apprehension that the neighbours were seen as getting a bit too close. (Kern 88)

John Durham Peters similarly charts the dyadic element of communication; how large-scale message systems inevitably generate personal anxiety. The isolated soul in the crowd has, he writes, 'resonated through the art and social thought of the twentieth century' (Peters 15). This is found in the microdramas of modernist literature, where the lament is often for a missed understanding – 'not what I meant at all' – implying that one-to-one dialogue is actually a disjunction between speaker and hearer. A similar problem is enacted in distortions of mass media, where, in the case of radio, electromagnetic signals are scattered among those attuned to a particular wavelength, regardless of destination or intended recipient. The notion that 'Especially for you' means 'all of you' was the concern of many early commentators (Lowenthal 507).

Research in the separate, and often integrated, fields of literature and media studies has latterly recognized how the advent of radio produced reactions in the culture of the written word. However, most studies incorporate the relationship into a wider analysis of philosophy and the arts under scientific progress, or prefer to concentrate on one aspect of wireless – namely, its social function. This essay seeks to expand upon ideas raised by Gillian Beer and Keith Williams; it argues that aspects of radio broadcasting were a formal influence on interwar literature, both explicitly and subliminally. Despite this, Williams asserts that a type of 'radio-novel' was never defined in the 1930s, whereas '[f]ilm technique came into its own as a new principle of poesis' (Williams 128). Although claiming that 'radiogenic' notions were present in literary texts 'long before the medium itself', Williams only fleetingly refers to the parallel development of radio and the Modernist novel, citing Ibsen's *Peer Gynt*, the 'Circe' chapter in *Ulysses* and George Orwell's linguistic experiment, the Trafalgar Square section of *A Clergyman's Daughter*. Traditionally, critics have placed Woolf in the field of cinematic influence, and Williams continues to do so, noting how the multiple consciousness of her narrative often evokes a film, where the single viewpoint is scattered into 'mobile images' (Williams 129).

Woolf herself considered cinema to be unrefined, 'born fully clothed', and only capable of artistry once 'some new symbol for expressing thought is found' (*CE* 2: 272 and 271). Only then could 'the exactitude of reality' be attained without excess verbiage or clunking props, where a 'broken cup is jealousy' (*CE* 2: 271 and 270). Woolf adds that the dislocation caused by reading a novel could be assuaged by this idealists' cinema where '[the] past could be unrolled, distances annihilated' (*CE* 2: 271). This comment implies that Woolf was unmoved by the actual process of picture-making, as she clearly preferred concept to actuality; a response which also informed her ambivalence towards wireless, which, I suggest, played a significant role in her work between 1929 and 1939. I would argue that the creative process of any writer during this time was affected by the surround-sound of context or, rather, the colonization of daily life by radio. Over the course of a decade, wireless had swelled from an instrument for point-to-point contact into a blanket of mass broadcasting where others were indeed 'a bit too close'.

Gillian Beer has written at length on the climate fostered by the new physics, spearheaded by James Jeans and Arthur Eddington throughout the 1930s, whose rhetoric made the infinity of space – its multiple perspective and muddle of soundwaves – seem partially accessible. Beer notes that up to 40 per cent of the articles in the *Listener* between 1920 and 1934 were concerned with science, reprints of talks enthusiastically transmitted by the BBC which, noted one employee, 'seemed cleverer than anybody, a kind of super Dr Arnold who was always right' (Black 79). A broadcast on 'The Quivering Universe' by the scientific popularizer Gerald Heard did little to threaten the security of the general public, being, as it was, a single component of Lord Reith's campaign to educate and inform. However, as Woolf appreciated, the loneliness of the knowing mind was surely intensified by 'a shift in the scale'; a barrage of unsettling information which provoked awareness of one's insignificance in the grand scheme (*CE* 2: 254).

Conceivably, the point of reference was wireless, not merely as a vehicle to popularize these theories, but as evidence for the vagaries of time. On citing Eddington, who notably used radio broadcasting to expound the diffuse components of signal, sign and location, Beer writes:

> The everyday substantial world is no longer solid but itself transmissive. Wireless makes intermittently manifest the invisible traffic passing through us and communicating by our means [...] In such a newly imagined world [it] becomes more than a metaphor for the almost ungraspable actuality of the universe. (Beer, 'Wireless' 153)

Elsewhere, Beer observes that *Orlando* and *The Waves* were indebted to Woolf's reading of Jeans, how the 'ethereal world of play and representation in physics' corresponded to her emerging rhythmic prose and boundless approach to time, crucially inferring – in an aside – that radio 'fascinated' Woolf with its separation of source and receiver (Beer, *Common Ground* 122, 118).

Wireless time

Certainly, in 'A Sketch of the Past', Woolf imagines how previous sensations might be accessed:

> Instead of remembering here a scene and there a sound, I shall fit a plug into a wall; and listen in to the past. I shall turn up August 1890. I feel that strong emotion must leave its trace; and it is only a question of discovering how we can get ourselves again attached to it, so that we shall be able to live our lives through from the start. (*MB* [1976] 67)

Although the phrase 'listen in' might refer to radio listening, with the 'plug' being an aerial, the implication of eavesdropping also suggests the lack of privacy within a non-automated telephone switchboard system. If Woolf's 'plug' is part of an exchange, the idea is reminiscent of work by scientist Karl Pearson, whose *Grammar of Science* (1892) contains a section on 'The Brain as a Central Telephone Exchange'. To operate, a 'clerk' automatically links sender B with receiver X. A sensory nerve conveys a message to the brain, thus causing 'permanent impress' from which memory and thought arises (Pearson 44–5). Here, the vocabulary of electric communication is used to highlight the layers of consciousness, implying that to retrieve past traces may be a rather mechanical act. The same analogy is used in one of Woolf's diary entries relaying a conversation with Sybil Colefax, who seems transparent, 'popping up one light after another: like the switchboard at the telephone exchange at the mention of names' (*D* 3: 116). Woolf, however, seems to desire a specific conduit into different spheres of time, and not merely an involuntary reminder by Pearson's invisible 'clerk'. In her portrait of childhood, she regrets the 'general impress', the residue left by listening to 'the roll of Meredith's voice [...] the humming and hawing of Henry James' voice'. Eavesdropping from the hallway, she remembers 'not what they said but the atmosphere surrounding them' (*MB* [1976] 136). These 'invisible presences' shape the memoir; they are referred to in 1924 as 'voices of the dead', channelled through an agitated brain for lack of a more efficient medium (*D* 2: 283). It is significant that Louis, Woolf's character in *The Waves* (1931) who inhabits all spatial expanses, claiming 'I seem already to have lived many thousand years' (*W* 52), is an advocate of modern communications. Being 'half in love with the typewriter and the telephone', he fuses his 'many lives into one' (*W* 138–9) by forging lines of contact across the globe, but, like Woolf, needs a conduit for memory, lost images and stray words: 'What is the solution, I ask myself, and the bridge? How can I reduce these dazzling, these dancing apparitions to one line capable of linking all in one?' (*W* 182–3).

Louis perceives himself as a cable running underground, weaving together all fragments of the friends' history. His exposure to, and use of, telegraphy allows for this comparison. Woolf's more playful, earlier, piece about connections – to one another, to the social world of England – *Orlando* (1928) suggests that 'we are somehow successive, & continuous, we human beings' (*D* 3: 218), like parts of an atom, subject to fluctuation and able to transgress bodily death. Once again, 'plugging' into the past is the only way to achieve perfect repetition; to alight upon a frequency where voices still exist. In *The Waves*, Woolf achieved her aim of '[doing] away with exact place and time' (*D* 3: 122) as the characters' voices stretch backwards and forwards. Rhoda's absence for two sections obfuscates her actual suicide, a barrier over which she still speaks, possibly as an echo. Things are, explains Woolf 'oddly proportioned [...]. The unreal world must be round all this – the phantom waves' (*D* 3: 145). She once alluded to *The Waves* as 'a mosaic [...] all at high pressure' (*D* 3: 156) which required immersion in its sphere. 'From some higher station', she wrote, 'I may be able to pull it together' (*D* 4: 4). James Jeans's analysis of the etheric expanse could apply to the figures in *The Waves* who amalgamate, yet 'carry [their] own ether, much as in a shower of rain each observer carries his own rainbow about with him' (Jeans 91).

Steven Connor considers that our perception of time is both ordered, and complicated, by sound.

> We hear time passing rather than seeing it, because passage is the essential condition of sound. [...] Time speaks to us, in the machines we use to mark it. [...] Our world is a world of recordings, replications and action replays [...] characterised by multiple rhythms, durations and temporalities [...] of rifts and loops and pleats in the fabric of linear time. (Connor 'Noise (2)')

In 1931, while debating the existence of *the* ether, admittedly a 'pure abstraction; at best a local habitation and a name', James Jeans had proposed a frame of reference to understand the time-dimension, a tactic 'of course ready to hand – it is the division of the day into hours, minutes and seconds' (Jeans 92–3). This material comparison is important, as it justifies 'ether behaviour' and provides an outlet for escape, as such, into the machines which 'mark it'. In the Hampton Court episode of *The Waves*, every character is 'lost in the abysses of infinite space [and] illimitable chaos' (*W* 173), to be reorientated once again by sounds of life. Bernard says: 'But now listen; tick, tick; hoot, hoot; the world has hailed us back to it. I heard for one moment the howling winds of darkness as we passed beyond life. The tick, tick (the clock); then hoot, hoot (the cars). We are landed' (*W* 188).

Woolf does not consistently favour these safer limits imposed by external markers. The 'unlimited time of the mind', fuelled and dangerously proved by the new physics, often clashes with 'that other clock': the logical route. Bernard summarizes these fluctuating perceptions, whereupon a ticking sound in the immediate environment causes one to retract from a blissful, perpetual state 'which stretches in a flash from Shakespeare to ourselves'. He describes the transition as 'painful' (*W* 228).

As the 1930s drew to a close, Woolf's diaries indicate that such acoustic markers became more prevalent than any private retreat into a boundless void. Certain modern devices, while offering the characteristics of ideal time travel, were utilized as an index of certainty which rooted the individual to the here and now. Despite being 'raddled and raked with people, noise, telephones', who all construct the temporal progress, Woolf complains that she has '[n]o time. Time wasted writing an angry letter [...] My new clock says its just on one: & *my new clock cant lie*' (*D* 5: 155). Time was literally speaking, not through the consciousness of an Orlando, but in the sound of contemporary technologies.

Radio time

After listening to the wireless throughout October 1938, Woolf noticed that the measured tone of the BBC, slashing gamely through Hitler's 'baying', had created a 'sense of preparation to the last hair' (*D* 5: 178). Her diaries often leave the impression that this heavy, suspended sentence – the lead-up to war – had been rigidly orchestrated by radio which could simultaneously transmit cold menace and factual detail. 'Bach at night. Man playing oboe fainted in the middle. War seems inevitable', she writes in 1935 (*D* 4: 336). The act of waiting, of straining to listen, is repeatedly asserted: 'Sybil threatens to dine, but may put us off – should a Cabinet Minister crop up. Politics marking time' (*D* 5: 165); and later, '[i]n fact, we are simply marking time as calmly as possible until Monday or Tuesday when the Oracle will speak' (*D* 5: 167). It is wireless which 'announces the result' of Munich; war is 'staved off', 'postponed', and even '24 hours longer' (*D* 5: 170, 174). Here, home-front trauma arises from the paradox of immediacy and separation; an electronically mediated, time-warped state where communication is vital, yet always inadequate. Substituting an invisible signal for human contact highlights the issue of 'presence', that is, the address gap in every facet of wireless contact, where the message can be waylaid, misdirected or misheard. In the late 1930s, the approach to conflict was fraught and fragmented, with only, as Louis MacNeice wrote in *Autumn Journal*, 'a howling radio for our paraclete' (MacNeice 144) through which, for Woolf, Hitler merely exists as 'a mad voice [...] lashing himself up' (*D* 5: 232). In reviewing the growth of telecommunications as 'an abuse of army equipment', Friedrich Kittler argues for 'war as acoustic experience' (Kittler 97), a phrase which, at one level, relates to the manner of British broadcasting in the 1930s. 'Yes we are in the very thick of it', Woolf complains. 'Are we at war? At one I'm going to listen in [...] One touch on the switch & we shall be at war' (*D* 5: 230). Tension is heightened the following week: '[w]ill the 9 o'clock bulletin end it all? – our lives, oh yes, & everything else for the next 50 years'(*D* 5: 231).

During the hot, static summer of 1939, evoked in *Between the Acts*, Woolf records Prufrock's lament on two separate occasions in her notebook: 'Human voices awake us and we drown' (*D* 5: 227–8). Her recollection of these lines was perhaps prompted by the deluge of intrusive bleeps and ticks which sliced up the day into newsflashes, ordering and infiltrating every layer of life. Even when the radio ceases, Woolf detects 'a kind of perceptible but anonymous friction [...] The Poles vibrating in my room' (*D* 5: 225) rather like the eminent voices which accompanied her childhood. Notably, at the end of the waiting period, described by Robert Graves as a 'war of nerves' (Graves 452), Woolf reports how she and Leonard briefly 'stood by' on 3 September for Chamberlain's declaration of war, but to no avail; the wireless lures her back at 'about 10.33 [...] I shall now go in' (*D* 5: 233). This prompts the memorable image at the close of Graves's *The Long Weekend*, where the intelligentsia ('those in the know') are 'left staring rather stupidly at the knobs of their radio sets' with the time limit expired and their fears finally pronounced (Graves and Hodge 455).

Travesty and distortionment

Though Woolf often included newspaper extracts in her diary, after the outbreak of the Second World War she rarely discussed them, noting that they merely 'boom, echoing emptily, the BBC' (*D* 5: 263), almost as though the printed word were behind schedule, failing to arrest that immediate dart of information vital to morale. 'Scarcely worth reading any papers', she writes, 'Emptiness. Inefficiency' (*D* 5: 234). The dispatching of news had always concerned Woolf; as early as 1921, she contemplated the futile search for an accurate rendition:

> But how is one to arrive at truth? I have changed the Daily News for the Morning Post. The proportions of the world at once become utterly different. The Daily News has become a vivacious scrapbag. News is cut up into agreeable scraps and written in words of one syllable. I may well ask, what is truth? (*D* 1: 127–8)

Radio, too, was by nature terminally insincere, 'a mere travesty and distortionment' as Woolf complained to Ethel Smyth (*L* 3: 146). Twisting the dial of her radio set, like any listener of the time, Woolf would have encountered shards of unconnected dialogue, the hissing of static and superheterodyne screeching, all enveloping the 'genuine' message from a disembodied voice at the opposite end of the circuit.

Woolf's denouncement of wireless is emblematic of a particular period where norms of attentiveness were deeply affected by political and national unease. Of the Munich *bierhalle* bombing in November 1939, she notes the lack of balanced reporting, as 'all the loudspeakers [contradict] each other' (*D* 5: 245). The situation resembles 'a crosseyed squint' like searchlight beams or even a jumble of wires through which there is no 'getting at truth'. One example of radio duplicity is the *Graf Spee* episode which reached a dramatic finale on 17 December 1939 during the Battle of the River Plate. The German pocket warship was scuttled by her captain, Hans Langsdorff, in the neutral port of Montevideo, Uruguay, as a more favourable alternative to bombardment. British wireless reports had been so successful in assembling mythical fleets of destroyers, that an artillery officer of the *Spee* had hallucinations of battleship *Renown* through his range-finder; a factor which cemented Langsdorff's decision. In reality, all that could bar the *Spee*'s passage was two cruisers, *Ajax* and *Achilles*, with six-sevenths of their outfit fired, and manned by sailors who, confessed one, 'laughed hollowly' when the BBC promised 'interesting developments' (Millington-Drake 337). Virginia Woolf deplored the allegiance of the BBC in what appeared to be the hijacking of naval intelligence. 'And we shall have it served up for us', she wrote, 'as we sit over our logs this bitter winter night' (*D* 5: 351). The fate of the *Spee*, lured to destruction by wireless, the twentieth-century siren whose words rebounded off the waves, certainly verifies Kittler's observation that war might be perceived sonically. William Shirer, an American journalist in Berlin, noted that Goebbels' contingency plan was to broadcast news of an alleged air victory and hide the fact of Langsdorff's suicide (Shirer 179). The captain was said to have remained on his ship until the bitter end; a single death falsely relayed to a multitude, of a man who had, for days, been harried by artful means and appliances for the benefit of mass psychology. For passive recipients, such as Woolf, this atmosphere of mutual dissembling would highlight the issue of trying to detect the one pure signal amid the noise.

In wartime, constant listening (the very *act* of tuning in) was necessary and thus like a guilty, unsatisfying addiction; however, the idea of being severed from potential truth was even more unsettling. On a brief visit to her Mecklenburgh Square flat in London, Woolf recalls keeping 'one ear pricked' as the 'sense of siege' became apparent: 'One seemed cut off. No wireless' (*D* 5: 242). A notion conceived years before, during the air raids of 1917, is sustained and brought to fruition, where, as Woolf wrote, '[h]aving trained one's ears to listen one can't get them not to for a time' (*D* 1: 84).

Behind the lines

Anna Snaith has catalogued in detail the levels of 'invasion' wreaked upon the private by the public, a 'radical intermingling' (Snaith 132) which informed Woolf's last few years, particularly in the diaries of the period, where invasion – both actual, by media, and prospective, by the enemy – is often enacted textually. Snaith notes a 'bizarre dichotomy' (138), where a concerted effort is made to separate the realms of public and private, 'as though by indicating the difference she can prevent any kind of guilty overlap' (Snaith 135). I would add that Woolf's style is resonant of soundbites, newsworthy bulletins which rapidly sketch the atmosphere: 'Pop-pop-pop as we play bowls. Probably a raider over Eastbourne way' (*D* 5: 132). For, as Beer points out, 'very little time seemed left', which made acceptable the hasty indulgence and recording of pastimes which 'suggest that there is time in abundance' (Beer, *Common Ground* 130) and, adds Snaith, any guilt is mingled with urgency; 'she needs to use what time she has' to preserve her thoughts (Snaith 138). At one point, Woolf commends herself for '[forging] ahead with PH [Pointz Hall]' while waiting for a radio bulletin, which seems to demand the hidden mental resources usually required for writing. Acoustic interference was beginning to impede words on the page. As the bombers swoop past Woolf's Sussex enclave and on to London, 'the twang of plucked strings' causes a rupture in concentration: 'I must black out. I had so much to say' (*D* 5: 320).

Additionally, her diaries and correspondence often express psychological tension through scientific terminology, such as the friends left in London 'jangling like so many strained wires' (*L* 4: 356), and her awareness that any 'feeling faculty gives out' after continual assault on the nerves: 'next day one is disembodied, in the air. Then the battery is recharged, & again – what?' (*D* 5: 285). It is as though she is scattered, like Rhoda in *The Waves*, 'without anchorage anywhere [...] incapable of composing any continuity' (*W* 100). Crucially, she feels that 'all creative power is cut off' (*D* 5: 235). Woolf's writing patterns were evidently affected, not merely by the war, which she blamed for preventing entry 'to that exciting layer so rarely lived in: where my mind works [...] like the aeroplane propellers' (*D* 5: 214), but the methods by which conflict imposed itself.

After Hitler's invasion of Denmark and Norway on 9 April 1940, Churchill broadcast a speech detailing 'the first main clinch of the war'; a phrase inaccurately heard by Woolf, who relays it in her diary as 'crunch', and cues it later when describing her effort to write: 'a crunch, after the long lapse' (*D* 5: 280). This slight degree of misinterpretation is characteristic of wireless, particularly if dialogue is reiterated or obscured. It is a technique incorporated into *Between the Acts*, where, as Beer notes, 'the ear is the arbiter of significance' and words 'spring apart and re-order themselves with kaleidoscopic comedy' (Beer, *Common Ground* 133–5). More importantly, it is the 'interrupted mind action' where a great wealth of past traces and flickering words are shaded into one spoken sentence, or gesture, only to disperse into meaningless 'random ribbons'.

Another instance of Woolf's growing alertness is an extract from June 1940, during a particularly concentrated period of radio broadcasts cited in the diaries – heavy fighting in France and Churchill's rallying calls to the country. Elizabeth Bowen's presence at Monk's House is unsettling, as Woolf believes her stammer to have 'a disintegrating effect [...] a whirr of sound that makes the word quiver and seem blurred' (*D* 5: 299). It is pertinent that Woolf considers dialogue with her guest to be smothered by vibration, an irritant which extends the act of *waiting* for a word to fall. Melba Cuddy-Keane dismisses the idea of 'a specific technological influence' on Woolf's work, yet proposes a 'new acoustical perception closely related to the experience of listening to and working with electronic media' (Cuddy-Keane 72). In analysing Woolf's textual incorporation of aural stimuli, Cuddy-Keane writes that 'with attentive hearing, there is in reality no silence'. Furthering this observation, I would assert that Woolf's sounds are often distorted and misheard; in 'training' her ears to listen, she was also vulnerable to background static. Feeling trapped in the circuit, or 'circumference' of war (*D* 5: 284), Woolf found 'the present moment [...] difficult to centre', wondering if 'I shall ever write again one of those sentences that give me intense pleasure' (*D* 5: 357).

The issue is whether Woolf was, to some degree, aware of radio becoming psychically assimilated into her work, given that she openly equated its capacities with a sense of oppression. In 'The Leaning Tower' (1940) she defines wireless as an instigator of contemporary malaise, given that writers in the nineteenth century never heard Napoleon on the air, and were thus granted a kind of 'immunity from war' (*CE* 2: 164) As early as 1927, in 'The Narrow Bridge of Art', she sees the dualism of a technology which binds the individual to 'his fellows by wires overhead' (*CE* 1: 17) yet oddly reduces the communal act of partaking. Each person exists in a separate box, lazily waiting to be connected, like the component parts of *The Waves* who tune in, listen, occasionally speak, but always fade away. Therefore, her following statement on modern poetry – that 'emotions which used to enter the mind whole are now broken up on the threshold' – would imply an early recognition of how radio might permeate every layer of creativity. Her *direct* experience occurred within a welter of auditory disruption in the late 1930s, where broadcasts merged with other '[i]ncessant company' listed in her diaries: visitors, droning wasps, unidentified chatter from a distance, and the aeroplanes overhead.

Faulty receptions

The journalist A.R. Pinci once admitted to punctuating his space bar 'as I typewrite, to whatever tempo radio sets for me' (Pinci 4), which may be comparable to Woolf's strange dilemma. The exquisite pain of composition, for her, was an internal, pulsing rhythm which punctuated all other levels. She writes of attacking *The Waves* 'at such high pressure [...] that I can only write it for about one hour, from 10 to 11.30' (*D* 4: 4), striving to synchronize the various elements. After the cathartic completion, she is silent, recalling 'the voices that used to fly ahead [...] when I was mad' (*D* 4: 10), as though the alarm calls are partially harnessed into printed lines and the emotional battle postponed. Later, the question remains, '[s]o now, what shall I work at? So many works hover over me' (*D* 4: 49). Woolf generally considered herself 'a mere target for impressions' (*L* 4: 172); here, she operates like an antenna, plucking out and intercepting invisible signals in order to complement the inner tempo. This method of composition evidently faltered under a more insistent presence: the accepted cycle of the broadcast day, where unwelcome facts crowd in, irrespective of the mental effort to be selective.

In a broadcast of 1937, Woolf attributes the complications of writing to words themselves 'being out and about on people's lips', airborne and instant. Slurred and sulky, the recording is a notoriously inaccurate rendition of her voice as she ends abruptly, enacting the title of the BBC series for which the talk was commissioned: 'Words Fail Me'. Woolf reworked the piece as 'Craftmanship', emphasizing that 'words, like ourselves [...] need privacy' (*DM*: 132). She implies that the free character and over-usage of all things 'broadcast' may have contributed to the death of mnemo-technology, a situation where the ancient power of words and their meaning was annulled in the chaotic public forum of twentieth-century media. Woolf objected to the 'high-flown tense voice' distinctive of radio commentary, likening it to 'the imposition of personality' in writing by Meredith or Carlyle, where words seem ancillary (*D* 5: 290). A letter to Edward Sackville-West accentuates this concern: 'Did [your] diary ever take shape? I wish it would. I want some fragmentary but natural voice to break into the artificial bray to which we're condemned' (*L* 4: 365).

In terms of radio, such artificiality was maintained by scheduling, patterning, and planning on the part of the BBC. It is hard not to imagine Woolf reacting with horror to the idea of mass subliminal persuasion – a nullifying blanket of sound. In general, habitual radio listening may enfeeble the refined process of finding words for oneself, as interruptions are more readily absorbed. Only occasionally is Woolf able to recede from the site of conflict and utilize it for expressive purposes. Consider the scene in *The Years*, where North reads poetry to Sara Pargiter in the shadows of her dingy apartment:

> The words going out into the room seemed like actual presences, hard and independent; yet as she was listening they were changed by their contact with her. But as he reached the end of the second verse–
>> Society is all but rude–
>> To this delicious solitude ...
> he heard a sound. Was it in the poem or outside of it, he wondered? (*Y* 322)

Here, Woolf charges poetry with another layer of meaning when recited through the darkness from one terminus to another, speaker and receiver, both invisible. The interruption, however, is not Marvell's poem resonating with implied sound; the ripe apples dropping on to the soft grass, or 'th'industrious Bee'. It is the measured thud of footsteps in the hallway. This is different to the method described in Cuddy-Keane's analysis of 'Kew Gardens', where sounds are 'integrated by the narrative ear'. Here, the steps rupture transmission. Another, more strident example of Woolf's technique can be found in the sundering of Mr Streatfield's speech in *Between The Acts* by an aeroplane formation, which begins as 'distant music': '"So that each of us who has enjoyed this pageant has still an opp..." the word was cut in two. A zoom severed it' (*BA* 173–4). This may be read as an example of correctly received speech decisively lost: Woolf 'zooms' away from her own material as if changing frequencies on a radio waveband.

The speaking self

It is tempting to visualize Woolf enclosed in the precincts of Monk's House, attempting to pick up 'impressions'. She resembles Eleanor, the grand dame of *The Years*, the 'I' at the epicentre, who sits 'at her table [...] digging little holes from which spokes radiated' (*Y* 348). This is equivalent to a successful flight from the citadel of the self; becoming an arbitrary dispatcher of 'waves', and, correlatively, a receiver of certain stimuli. By this maxim, one would assume Woolf to be a model broadcaster, sending poetry into the dark from a closed controlled space. The evidence is, however, that Woolf's direct involvement in radio plainly manifested her dread of dissociation, a widening schism felt towards the end of her life, when she concluded that 'the writing "I" [had] vanished. No audience. No echo. That's part of one's death' (*D* 5: 293). This Emersonian 'condition of infinite remoteness' (Emerson 427) is a fundamental concern over the fragile wiring of humanity, whose failure naturally begins with inscription. Writing on paper, as opposed to transliteration across the mind of another, instantly severs any mutuality, leaving words to circle abroad like a spectral radio broadcast. Although the studios of the BBC restaged the philosophical scenario of interaction through walled space, it would transpire that a microphone offered no contract of reciprocity. Gilbert Seldes summarized this experience: 'You think [...] the operator has turned off the current, that everyone has tuned out. You wonder who these people are who may be listening, in what obscurity, in what hostility' (Seldes 140).

Walking home after a session for the BBC Talks Department in 1937, Woolf also reflected that all her efforts had gone unnoticed, thinking 'that very few people had listened: the world much as usual' (*D* 5: 83). She often writes harshly with regard to her minimal radio work; talks she could never 'time' accurately (*D* 4: 80). The mechanics, the constant re-recording was something to 'get through' with huge relief in the aftermath. As aforementioned, her surviving broadcast is unusually blurred and halted; the voice of a pale shadow aired to an audience who will never know what she really *meant*. It seems likely that Woolf was unnerved by her own transition into the robotic voice-in-a-box issuing impure words like a radio propagandist, words that have failed her. In adopting the role of broadcaster, she colludes with 'the premonitory shivers and disgusts of that BBC' (*D* 5: 83) which dutifully scattered the seeds of chaos.

Acoustic effigies persist through Woolf's prose, chiefly in *Between the Acts*, where, regardless of the 'oracle' spewing its scraps and orts of mimicry, the spectators can thank nobody for their entertainment. Successful discourse in the novel is an ideal soul-to-soul exchange:

> He [Giles] said (without words) 'I'm damnably unhappy'.
> 'So am I', Dodge echoed.
> 'And I too', Isa thought. (*BA* 158)

Sound functions as a reminder of the abyss, and of the genuine signal lost in transit. Despite a chorus of intrusive surface noise, 'horns of cars [...] the swish of trees', the audience waits for an announcement which will deliver them onto the next stage: 'All their nerves were on edge. They sat exposed [...] They were suspended, without being, in limbo. Tick, tick, tick went the machine' (*BA* 159).

Mr Oliver wonders if is possible to transmit thoughts without words, a concept raised in 1950 by Britain's foremost mathematician, Alan Turing. In his essay 'Computing Machinery and Intelligence' he proposed an experiment involving three parties, where an interrogator is separated from two information sources; one human, the other machine. The objective was to define an 'intelligent' machine, through the inability of the third person to specify which of the veiled interlocutors was artificial. All signs of embodiment were removed, the dialogue proceeding through a text-only channel, which could be screened, interpreted and ignored. This was, noted Turing's biographer, 'like an ideal for his own life, in which he would be left in a space of his own, to deal with the outside world solely through rational argument' (Hodges 423).

The Turing test seeks to create the meeting of minds as if physical interaction were unimportant; it re-enacts the classic idealist image of a teleproof room or opaque sphere reflected upon by F.H. Bradley or even Karl Pearson's telephone exchange. The imperfections that constitute a mortal being are disregarded, namely, the desire for the other. In practice, though, Miss La Trobe in *Between the Acts* must concede that hiding the body in the machine is no guarantee of triumph, as the audience never grasps her meaning. Alex Zwerdling observes that Woolf's 'subsidiary theme' in her writings – that of human isolation – is given prominence in the pageant, where each spectator is 'trapped in the prison of self' with no general coherence of interpretation (Zwerdling 320). Woolf recognizes that if shared consciousness, a soul-to-soul transfer, is the criterion of success, then human communication is impossible and we therefore stick in the impasse of solipsism.

Four days prior to her suicide, Woolf fantasized that she and her sister Vanessa could 'infuse souls', a hope which anticipates Turing's noiseless rustle of intelligence, unobstructed by impure words or bodies. All other mediums seemed deficient; wireless, in theory so liberating, was in actuality the most remote of transactions. Promising the wonders of time travel, its prosaic function was to dismantle the boundaries which once preserved the individual from a troubled environment; in doing so, it accentuated the contradictions of modern life. The role of a listener was to linger ineffectively, to 'stand by' the dial, as just one of an atomized mass. Waiting for the next tick to legitimize one's situation – to be as painfully 'landed' as the characters in *The Waves* – may result in paranoia, regarded by Geoffrey Tandy in the *Criterion* as 'an infectious ether-borne disease' (Tandy 288). Similarly, the *BBC Yearbook* (1940) reported that employees of the monitoring service were subject to nervous breakdown, being so intensively wired to 'the poisonous flood emanating from the radio of the Third Reich' (Harding 87).

Woolf was to experience dissociated voices in her head, a potential relapse of an earlier breakdown when she seemed to 'stumble after some sort of speaker' (*D* 4: 10). By their resurgence, these voices were a danger signal, a personal Cassandra bell denoting a future period of internal suffering. It would be incautious to attribute any of Woolf's psychological deterioration to aspects of radio; however, I would contend that the individual often projects his/her dominant fear onto any new aspect of cultural change. Furthermore, in recalling Marinetti's comment on psychic disturbance, it should be added that fragmentation and disjunction was, and is still, a feature of radio sound in itself. This would account for a state of perceptual confusion in the listener, who could grow to be highly sensitized to the nuances of a medium which blurred the definitions of interior and exterior. It is possible, then, that Virginia Woolf was a wireless purist who felt betrayed by its tangible form. Charmed by the concept of an electric spark which might retrieve lost traces of the dead or probe the expanses of time, she also wished to access, and express in words, a fleeting order of consciousness through the void: thought transference far beyond the logic of radio. With no public to 'echo back', and her work dropping into the gigantic ear of the body politic (which was collectively affixed to its wireless set), Woolf may have felt bombarded by a medley of voices compiled not only from the deepest recesses of her mind, but from the intrusive sounds of radio.

Part V
Transcultural Spaces

10
'Our Commitments to China': Migration and the Geopolitical Unconscious of *The Waves*

Nobuyoshi Ota

(Re)locating Woolf in the geopolitical space

In *Mappings: Feminism and the Cultural Geographies of Encounter*, Susan Stanford Friedman proposes a geopolitical reading of Woolf beyond questions of the British Empire. A recent focus of Woolf studies has been debate about Woolf's critique of, or orientalist participation in, British imperialism.[1] Reviewing these readings, Friedman raises two problems:

> First, our overreliance on models of center/periphery and subject/object often denies agency to multiple others in a rush to condemn the center. Second, such binary oppositions tend to enmesh us Woolf critics in an unanswerable debate about whether to celebrate Woolf as critic of empire or to critique her as participant in and beneficiary of imperialism. (Friedman 119)

Friedman's aim is to seek the geopolitical Woolf beyond the reductionist binaries centre/periphery and subject/other, by extending the conventional notion of geopolitics to theorize the global space of complex power relations. Her reading of *To the Lighthouse*, for example, shows brilliantly how any local gender formation is informed by the transnational and how the global is always present within the local, by analysing the figures of Mr and Mrs Ramsay. Tennyson's 'Charge of the Light Brigade', spouted by Mr Ramsay, brings the geopolitical realm of the Crimean War into the heart of domestic life, while Mrs Ramsay, having nourished the domestic space, leaves home imaginatively for the Indian plains and the Roman church. Friedman's geopolitical reading traces these special interconnections as they constitute the shifting complexities of their locational movements.

To this provocative intervention, I would like to add that the site of the local can also be detected in the aesthetic space of the artist figure. While emphasizing global space and intercultural movements, Friedman does not forget to highlight the continuing importance of 'the family, the home, and domesticity' for geopolitically informed cultural studies (Friedman 114). Certainly, as Susan Meyer's *Imperialism at Home: Race and Victorian Women's Fiction* has already shown, English domestic fiction, such as Charlotte Brontë's *Jane Eyre*, is explicable through this kind of feminist analysis of power relations between home and colony. However, Woolf's modernist departure from the realist novel demands a different account of such relations.[2] It is not only Susan Gubar's feminist reading of the *Künstlerroman* that overlooks the theme of colonialism, privileging the artist as heroine in twentieth-century novels. Even Elizabeth Abel's sophisticated examination of Woolf's refigurations of the female *Bildungsroman* in relation to the discourses of psychoanalysis cannot be said to go beyond the framework of nation-state in which only the ideologically internalized and privatized space of Oedipal relations is shown to be critically deconstructed by modernist figures such as Lily Briscoe.[3] With Woolf's use of interior monologue and aesthetic thematization, *To the Lighthouse* and *The Waves* seem to replace the centrality of the domestic woman with the figure of the artist: painter or writer.

This chapter is concerned with reading migration in *The Waves* through the figure of the artist. Louis, who is 'half in love with the typewriter and the telephone' (*W* 138), is not only crucial to Bernard's construction as a writer, but he also mediates the images of migrating people and China, and therefore the novel's interest in imperialism via global communication and economic expansion.[4] I will argue that the geopolitical unconscious of this text can be detected in the contradictory relations between British imperialism and its Other as the image of the yellow men migrating around the globe.[5] The figure of Louis in *The Waves* represents the reach of western imperialism beyond the merely political control of the British Empire to the Pacific. To put it differently, the problems of migration and/or immigration both in the Pacific and in the Atlantic realms are ideologically motivated or overdetermined by Britain's commercial interest in Asia, or, 'our commitments to China' (*W* 139).

The Migrating Other and British Imperialism

It is not difficult to relate the image of migrating people or the racial other to the political themes of antifascism and feminism in Woolf's

modernist texts. This thematic connection is most salient in the monologue of Louis, the son of an Australian banker:

> It is the hour when Miss Johnson brings me my letters in a wire
> tray. Upon these white sheets I indent my name... I, now a duke,
> now Plato, companion of Socrates; the tramp of dark men and
> yellow men migrating east, west, north and south; the eternal pro-
> cession, women going with attaché cases down the Strand as they
> went once with pitchers to the Nile; all the furled and close-packed
> leaves of my many-folded life are now summed in my name; incised
> cleanly and barely on the sheet. (*W* 138)

According to Kathy J. Phillips, the 'dark men and yellow men migrating' (*W* 138) are imagined to be the target of his totalitarian, megalomaniac aggression in which the colonized people may be cut down
with a hatchet.[6] Louis is 'the one most actively involved in creating
and maintaining the Empire' (Phillips 158). And yet his aggression,
Phillips further argues, does not stem only from his imperialist ambition. *The Waves* demonstrates that Empire-making springs from the
same totalitarian impulse in fascism. 'Woolf thus exposes the totalizing
impulse of Empire as totalitarian, and, in fact, Louis resembles the fas-
cists coming to power in Europe in the decade before *The Waves*. His
calls for an "august master" reveal him as the citizen who would abdi-
cate decisions to a Führer or Duce' (Phillips 161). The portrait of Louis
in *The Waves*, then, might become one of Woolf's most frightening
analyses of imperial and other totalitarian impulses as compensation
for self-doubt, and his effort to belong to an established group only sets
other people adrift from their roots. Focusing upon the Atlantic region
and the relation between Europe and Britain, Phillips' reading differs
from other political readings which are concerned with Percival, an
active colonizer.[7]

Nevertheless, Phillips' analysis associates Louis's fascism with Britain's
colonial domination of India through the cultural image of Egypt:
'they went once with pitchers to the Nile' (*W* 138). The Empire and the
totalitarian state become for the characters in *The Waves* compensation
for their fractured and fragmentary identities. Feeling excluded from
the university paths where Bernard and Neville can walk, Louis, a
multinational businessman, fabricates an older tradition for himself,
'not unlike the Italian revival of old Rome or the Nazi appropriation of
an "Aryan" history in Germanic myth' (Phillips 162). Yet, Louis' yearn-
ing need for a past and a tradition does not merely suggest fascist

power. 'As a shipper', Phillips argues, 'Louis would know about modern Egypt and its appropriation by Britain to facilitate trade with India' (Phillips 162–3). The representation of Egypt reveals that not only Percival but also Louis is complicit with the British Empire and its colonialism, and the text seems to be conflating the totalitarian power of fascism with British colonialism over India. In other words, in spite of meticulous examinations of geopolitical allusions and factual details, Phillips' interpretation of British imperialism in *The Waves*, in fact, ends up confirming the colonial relation between Britain and India.

However, the allusion to Egypt carries an alternative meaning to British military and political control. The image of women carrying red pitchers to the Nile is associated with the image of contemporary businesswomen, 'women going with attaché cases down the Strand' (*W* 138), not with the image of primitive civilization in the exotic Orient. Moreover, the figure of working women might be construed as the mirror image of the female vagrant in *Mrs Dalloway* or 'white slavery' in a 'White Slave Traffic' Bill.[8] Since 1912 there had been renewed public interest in the social problem of 'white slavery', and, as Lucy Bland suggests,

> Immigration into Britain of foreigners, especially Jews, became the basis for another fear – that of the racial Other. In addition, the old anxiety over the dangers of urban life took simply a racial and class form, but a gendered one too, as young women moved into cities to take up new occupations, with new freedoms, away from the traditional networks of support and control. (Bland 301)

The representations of migration, metonymically juxtaposed across the categories of race and gender, are conflated with the figure of prostitutes moving around the world. In *The Waves*, too, not only Louis' mistress with a cockney accent but also a prostitute appear when he waits for Rhoda to come to the attic room: 'some slattern squinting in a cracked looking-glass as she arranges her face for the street corner' (*W* 140). Undermining Louis' imaginary and megalomaniac synthesis of the ego on which his totalitarianism is necessarily based, the juxtaposed figures of the non-white people and various working women reveal that the spatial image of Egypt is not solely related to the political and commercial interests of the British Empire.

Political readings like that of Phillips, referring to and even privileging the image of oppressive colonial relations between Britain and India, tend to evade global politics, specifically socioeconomic and military conflicts in the Pacific. We should not appropriate the representation of non-European colonies or territories; rather, we need to explore not the narrowly political, but the geopolitical relationships articulated in *The Waves*. The problems of migration and immigration, I suggest, need to be reconsidered both in the Pacific and in the Atlantic regions.

Louis, China and economic globalism in the interwar British Empire

Louis is crucial to a reading of *The Waves*, because he does not simply express the colonial status of Australia – though he is anxious to 'expunge certain stains, and erase old defilements' – but he signifies the future of the British Empire in a wider context (*W* 139). A victim of childhood abuse, he now spreads global order through networks of communication and economic expansion. He is an anti-artist of media technologies such as the typewriter and the telephone. Louis' work recovers the degeneracy of the British Empire:[9] 'Louis [...] must sit down in his office among the typewriters and the telephone and work it all...for our regeneration, and the reform of an unborn world' (*W* 164–5). Therefore, while Woolf's psychopathology of Louis may be read as the expression of that sense of inferiority of colonial origin which served as the ideological justification for his complicity with the British Empire, the representation of Louis articulates that combination of antagonistic principles, that is, 'the essence of imperialism' that made the Second World War inevitable. The location of such antagonism on a global scale is alluded to as follows:

> I like to be asked to come to Mr. Burchard's private room and report on our commitments to China. I hope to inherit an armchair and a Turkey carpet. My shoulder is to the wheel; I roll the dark before me, spreading commerce where there was chaos in the far parts of the world. If I press on, from chaos making order, I shall find myself where Chatham stood, and Pitt, Burke and Sir Robert Peel. Thus I expunge certain stains, and erase old defilements; the woman who gave me a flag from the top of the Christmas tree; my accent; beatings and other tortures; the boasting boys; my father, a banker at Brisbane. (*W* 139)

Woolf describes Louis as an outsider to the ruling class because of his Australian accent. And yet, ironically, his resentment at being bullied at school fuels his expansionist and imperialist tendencies. As Louis' report on 'our commitments to China' discloses, he represents Britain's commercial interest in Asia in the interwar years, articulating the global, geopolitical relations between Britain, America and Japan in the Pacific.

As Peter Cain's new interpretation of British imperialism shows, 'to assume that Britain's economic position in the world was uniformly undermined in the 1920s would be a mistake' (Cain 239–40).

> Despite the growth in American foreign investment, British-based international banks comfortably retained their position of leadership ahead of those of any other nation even in Latin America, and continued to hold their own in Australia, New Zealand and South Africa with ease. In trade terms, Britain's dependence on those white colonies grew while their dependence on her market lessened: but all three remained financial satellites, reliant on the London market for funds and with their money supply still controlled from London. (Cain 240)

As for India, the British presence there was not weakened but rather consolidated by Britain's gentlemanly capitalist rulers' new tactics of investment.[10] 'In India, British trade suffered badly from Japanese and indigenous competition and tariff autonomy was conceded. But part of the reason for the tariff concession was the need for fresh means of raising revenues to pay India's debts in Britain and enhance financial authority, the chief concern of the British politicians both in London and Delhi' (Cain 240). According to Cain's analysis, Britain retained her position in India by encouraging a significant flow of direct investment by new British industries. After the Great War, there was a fresh battle for global economic control between Britain and the other great powers, and the outcome was far too complex to signify the wholesale decline of British imperialism.

More interestingly, some of the intricacies of this battle can be revealed by looking at British–Chinese relations:

> China ceases to figure in studies of British imperialism after 1914 because it is usually assumed that a collapse in informal influence was the inevitable outcome of a decline in Britain's economic presence there. Britain's share of China's imports did decline in the war and in the 1920s, but she remained far and away the biggest single investor in China throughout the interwar period and fought hard to retain her position there if only because it was assumed, even, as

in the nineteenth century, that China was the most promising market in the underdeveloped world. (Cain 241)

Before 1914 the key to Britain's strategy of economic imperialism was the organization of financial consortia, centred in London, formed to lend to Chinese governments. A similar strategy was employed immediately after the war in the Second Consortium. Its aim was to rein in the increasing ambitions of Japan and the United States, and ensure the continued superior status of London in Chinese finance.

However, the battle for global expansion in the world is not only economic but also political and military: we need to examine Britain's appeasement policy towards Japan as well as Chinese monetary reform in 1935. For instance, Shigeru Akita revises Cain and Hopkins' rather Anglocentric interpretation of British imperialism in the 1930s, especially concerning China: 'From this critical review of the Cain/Hopkins thesis, it becomes clear that we should re-evaluate the struggle for British hegemony in East Asia during the 1930s in the context of an already dominating Japanese presence combined with the rising power of the 'Pax Americana'. We also need to place a greater emphasis on the UK–US economic rivalry in assessing the extent of any genuine resurgence of British global power' (Akita 156). Furthermore, the British appeasement policy can be reinterpreted by taking into consideration Britain's ambivalent attitude towards Japan. 'The adoption of an appeasement policy in itself seems to suggest the limits of British hegemony on a global scale' (Akita 156). From Akita's viewpoint, British hegemony in East Asia, especially in China, needs to be reconsidered in the geopolitical conflicts between Britain, America and Japan. Behind the appeasement policy towards Japan in the mid-1930s lay the weakness of British military and naval power in East Asia. Recognizing this, Neville Chamberlain pursued a rapprochement between Great Britain and Japan.

The Anglo-Japanese Alliance had always had an important naval dimension, and the bond between the two countries was already declining in the early 1920s.[11] The cabinet decided in June 1921 in favour of building the Singapore base, and the reason for the decision is clearly stated in Overseas Defence Committee paper 501, dated 7 June 1921:

in a war with Japan the use of Singapore as a rendezvous and fuelling and repair base for the main British battle fleet would be essential. Further, it would be obvious that, were this port to fall into the hands of the enemy, it would increase incalculably the difficulties of operating with the British fleet in the Western Pacific and of keeping open sea communication with Australia and New Zealand. (qtd. in Nish 255–6)

Some statesmen, such as Winston Churchill and Lord Lee of Fareham, strongly influenced by the view of the Commonwealth and the United States, were disapproving of Japan's expansion in the Pacific. Despite Britain's financial and monetary control over China, the military and naval strengths and expansionist policies of British, American and Japanese powers must be taken into consideration.[12]

These contradictory relations between Britain and the Pacific after the First World War, I think, constitute a socially concrete subtext for *The Waves*. My intertextual reading does not intend to explore an essentially one-to-one relationship between particular representations and their social and historical reference; rather I am interested in the traces of the contradictory, and in some senses unrepresentable, history of British imperialism. In the present age of neo-colonialism and decolonization, contemporary postcolonial theories are concerned with the relationship between First and Third World countries, disclosing the latter's economic subordination to or cultural dependency on the former. From the end of the nineteenth century to the First World War, the represented conflicts of imperialism existed between the First World powers. In the modernist period, Jameson remarks, the relationship of domination between the First and the Third World was masked and displaced by the ideological consciousness of imperialism into a relationship between the various imperial states, and this consciousness of the imperialist subject tended to repress the more fundamental axis of otherness.[13] Despite such ideological displacement and repression of the racial other, the geopolitical unconscious of Woolf's text attempts to conceive the global space of complex power relations in the representations of the yellow men's migration around the world. Such fragmentary images of Otherness are momentarily evoked in Louis' consciousness along with an allusion to China as an important market. His daily business communications, expanding over both the Atlantic and the Pacific realms, suggest financial capitalism or economic globalism as well as totalitarian domination. The relation between English modernism and transnational, global capitalism in the interwar years cannot be reduced to such narrowly political issues as the rivalry of the imperial powers (i.e. Britain's liberal imperialism and Germany's totalitarian fascism) and Britain's colonial domination over India.

Meanwhile, the rather schematic and allegorical representation of the relations between Percival and native people in India within

The Waves can be understood as a formal and aesthetic attempt to bridge 'the increasing gap between the existential data of everyday life within a given nation-state and the structural tendency of monopoly capital to develop on a worldwide, essentially transnational scale' (Jameson, *Fables* 94–5). The interwar British Empire, inextricably involved in and dependent on direct investment and military presence in the territories beyond the national situation, generates as its cultural product the colonial allegory of a novel like Forster's *A Passage to India*. The narrative of an individual character, then, cannot be expected to achieve formal completeness within English life. Similarly, in Woolf's novel the lived experience of six characters is domestic while the text's structural intelligibility is international. The highly poetic and allegorical form seeks to resolve this tension, but the representation of migration or China immediately questions any totalizing colonialist narrative. This suggests that the ideological displacement of cultural others through such 'colonial allegory' remains incomplete, and the narrative of *The Waves* cannot end without further ideological, aestheticizing operations.

Woolf's aestheticizing strategy and the haunting other

Woolf's highly poetic style in *The Waves* represents, within the national situation, the conflicts of British imperialism in the cultural difference between high art and commerce, that is, the modernist artist and capitalist modernity. Such cultural difference is represented, in this novel, through the contradictory relations between Bernard, a national artist who attempts to write the absolute book about life, and Louis, an anti-artist of global media technology. The opposition between the aesthetic creation of the book about organic society and the mechanical production of various economic commodities through information technology is embodied in this opposition. Bernard is valorized by the thematic structure of the text, and the narrative closes with him summing up the major characters' lives.[14] The monologue of this imperialist subject seems to assume the point of view of the absolute and transcendental artist, and symbolically resolve binary oppositions such as art/life, subject/object and West/East, by appropriating the repressed voice of the colonized in the interludes.[15] The ending, however, betrays Woolf's uneasiness about her own aestheticizing tactics in which her use of racial difference as a signifier involves a brutal silencing, an erasing of the reality of world politics outside the Atlantic region.

Recalling his course of life, Bernard regrets 'so much litter, so much unaccomplishment and separation, for one cannot cross London to see a friend, life being so full of engagements' (*W* 236). He compares his imperfect life with an unfinished book and phrase:

> I said life had been imperfect, an unfinished phrase. It had been impossible for me, taking snuff as I do from any bagman met in a train, to keep coherency – that sense of the generations, of women carrying red pitchers to the Nile, of the nightingale who sings among conquests and migrations. (*W* 236)

Without using violent forces of 'conquests' outside the western world, it seems to be impossible to construct a coherent and meaningful world of writing in which the fragmentary images of various social groups, such as generations, gender differences and other races, are to be subsumed. Moreover, what is internalized in Bernard's mind is not only Louis' desire for power and order; the repetition of Louis' voice, 'the nightingale' (*W* 236), here covertly discloses the subversive counterforce of 'migrations' (*W* 236) against the conqueror's colonial territorialization.

Bernard's vast artistic undertaking to connect the heterogeneous social spaces of self and the Other, like the voyage to the North Pole (*W* 236), is desperately exorbitant. In comparison, Louis is portrayed as accomplished and able to unify his life. The contrast of the failed artist with the successful man of business is shrewdly marked here. Such comparison between two different men is repeated in the eighth section of the text. Bernard cannot know 'the true story' (*W* 182) and has to keep waiting, speculating, and accumulating during his life, whereas Louis, 'wild-eyed but severe, in his attic, in his office, has formed unalterable conclusions upon the true nature of what is to be known' (*W* 182).

Nevertheless, Woolf's portrait of Bernard as an artist is inseparable from Louis, who is involved with Britain's commercial interest in Asia. Indeed, Bernard himself is thematically connected with the medium of information technology. His daily life at home, furnished with *The Times*, letters and the telephone, is open to the other location of England, so that he is able to act his part in British imperialism:

> Toast and butter, coffee and bacon, The Times and letters – suddenly the telephone rang with urgency and I rose deliberately and went to the telephone. I took up the black mouth. I marked the ease

with which my mind adjusted itself to assimilate the message – it might be (one has these fancies) to assume command of the British Empire; I [...] had created, by the time I put back the receiver, a richer, a stronger, a more complicated world in which I was called upon to act my part and had no doubt whatever that I could do it. (*W* 218)

The world of global communication and imperial control appears as a compensatory fantasy for Bernard's anxiety about writing. This anxiety, like Woolf's lingering uneasiness about British imperialism, becomes evident in the spectre of the racial other that remains to haunt the ending of the novel. Bernard experiences the meaningless-ness of life and becomes a man 'without self' (*W* 239) in a degenerat-ing world. The earth is 'a waste of shadow' (*W* 238) and 'no fin breaks the waste of this immeasurable sea' (*W* 237). This waste land is the space in which the white, male self recognizes the repressed Other, that is, the 'shadows of people' (*W* 241) he cannot help recalling. Bernard's imaginative confrontation with the hairy, ape-like savage in 'the remote verges of the desert lands' (*W* 243) disrupts the seemingly utopian vision of 'the eternal renewal' (*W* 247), indicating that national daily life, the world of inner or metropolitan space in which this Englishman lives, is still not fully dissociated from the political conflicts in the remote verges of the Oceanic regions.

The desperate vision of the degenerate water world in which Bernard confronts the hairy ape-like savage as his shadow and enemy, recalls an entirely opposite vision. In his escapist wish-fulfillment, the imagi-native journey to the utopian world reaches beyond Rome, the capital of the Roman Empire, towards the Pacific realm.

These moments of escape are not to be despised. They come too seldom. Tahiti becomes possible. Leaning over this parapet I see far out a waste of water. A fin turns. This bare visual impression is unat-tached to any line of reason, it springs up as one might see the fin of a porpoise on the horizon. (*W* 157)

In order to decipher and translate these visual impressions into verbal signs, Bernard marks this Utopian vision in the margin of his aesthetic text: 'I note under F., therefore, "Fin in a waste of waters." I, who am per-petually making notes in the margin of my mind for some final state-ment, make this mark, waiting for some winter's evening' (*W* 157).

The particular sight of Tahiti – 'Tahiti becomes possible' (*W* 157) – figuratively refers to the South Sea Islands:[16] 'We have to leap like fish, high in the air, in order to catch the train from Waterloo. And however high we leap we fall back again into the stream. I shall never now take ship for the South Sea Islands. A journey to Rome is the limit of my travelling' (*W* 180). While the artist figure in early twentieth-century Britain suddenly transfigures himself into a young man riding on a horse with his spear couched like a chivalric knight, like Percival, in the final scene of the text, Bernard's life here in these scattered fragments of representations is dislocated and transferred to a paradisal world where he is associated with 'a naked man spearing fish in blue water' (*W* 236). Bernard attempts to differentiate himself from Louis, a nascent economic imperialist. However, the figure of Louis makes a significant 'return of the repressed' in the fantasy world of Bernard. No longer simply opposed and safely confined to the margins of his mind, the voice of Louis as the haunting Other erupts from within the aestheticizing discourse of English modernism.

I have been arguing that the geopolitical unconscious of this text represents the contradictory relations between British imperialism and the Pacific as the image of the yellow men migrating around the globe. As my reading has shown, the representation of migration in *The Waves* is mediated through Louis as an anti-artist of global media technology who is involved with Britain's commercial interests in Asia. In contradistinction to Bernard, the modernist writer who attempts to totalize the national wholeness of England, the figure of Louis thus can be read as a trace of the economic globalism of British imperialism.

More generally, the thematic opposition between Louis and Bernard should be construed as figuring the difficult relationship between two different forms of imperialism in interwar Britain. Lloyd George attempted to resolve the contradictory forces of social and liberal imperialism in his political project of a grand coalition for British imperialism beyond the traditional political party system.[17] His coalition government, then, marked or prefigured the very moment in which the national and global conception of the British Empire would be redefined and rearticulated in terms of the British Commonwealth of Nations with its new structuring and coordination of the metropolis, the Dominions and the other imperial locations.[18] In these years of sociopolitical upheavals after the First World War, not only the hegemony of the British Empire but also the pre-First World War diplomatic system of nation-states seemed to be dislocated, so that the principal agents of history came to be represented by post-national ideologies of communism and fascism. Yet, neither the war nor the domestic conflicts led simply to what George Dangerfield calls 'the strange death of liberal England'. A rare instance of an achieved 'national' government in the history of the British Empire came into being under the leadership of Lloyd George, ceaselessly reproducing the liberal constitution of Britain throughout the interwar period.

These two coordinated and interconnected forces of the British Empire, social and liberal imperialism, also marked in the more global context of geopolitics the moment in which the nascent process of economic globalization began to emerge and invite various political and cultural reactions. Michael Hardt and Antonio Negri's reassessment of Empire in the context of contemporary globalization relies on a genealogical narrative of modern imperial history that presupposes a set of binary oppositions: Europe versus America, Lloyd George's war machine versus Wilson's pacifism and the League of Nations, cultures of modernism versus cultures of postmodernism. And yet, as they themselves remark, Empire and its various processes of globalization are not unified or univocal, so that the binary opposition of old European imperialism and new American Empire is deconstructed by the complex and contradictory cultural exchanges and negotiations between Britain and America over the questions of the Pacific regions. We might, therefore, contemplate the place of various discourses about the Yellow Peril and the geopolitical alliance between the British Empire and Japan in redefinitions of the British Empire. While the hegemony of British imperialism during the interwar years was dependent on, and determined by, Britain's rapprochement with the United States of America, it was also overdetermined by the questions of renewal of the Anglo-Japanese Alliance and migrant workers in the Pacific.[19]

The Waves, then, could be grasped in the properly globalized cultural history of British imperialism. Britain's geopolitical relations with Japan as well as America are not overtly representable in the writings of English modernism. Indeed, despite her persistent concern with imperialist ideology and violence, Woolf's modernist text does not depict any particular political situation in the Far East. Nevertheless, imperialism is tangible in the representations of China and the South Seas through the figures of Louis and Bernard. *The Waves* thus illustrates an instance of Woolf's geopolitically symbolic responses to the processes of globalization and restructuring within the culture of British imperialism.

Notes

1 For postcolonial readings of Jane Marcus and Patrick McGee, see Ota, '*Nami*.' These political readings are mainly concerned with the problem of

subject, presuming that the fundamental conflict in the text lies in the relations between Bernard's art and Nature, or Percival and native people in
India. Indeed, Marcus asserts that Woolf's radical politics is definitely
expressed in Bernard's final ride against death, that is, the struggle of the
white male subject against the racial or sexual other. Despite the disintegra-
tion of the modern bourgeois subject, we need to examine the possibility of
recuperation of new subjectivities in the various criss-crossed power relations of British imperialism.

2 For the aestheticizing strategy of modernism, see also Jameson 'Modernism
and Imperialism.' Taking the image of the Great North Road as infinity from
the opening pages of E. M. Forster's *Howards End*, Jameson grasps a modernist
style as conjoining spatial images with a metaphysical concept or substitution
of contingency of physical objects for aesthetic and moral meaning. Then
the representations of the country house and the maternal body (the late
Mrs Wilcox) are interpreted in terms of Forster's providential ideology which
transforms the contingent encounters between isolated persons into a
momentary utopia of achieved community. Forster's political as well as aesthetic agenda in his novel, 'this coincidence of the political (grasped in moral
terms) and aesthetic' is 'what allows other related works (such as those of
Virginia Woolf) to refocus it by way of operations which look more aestheticizing than Forster's' (Jameson 'Modernism and Imperialism' 59).

3 For a geopolitical reading of *To the Lighthouse*, see Ota, 'Lily Briscoe.'
Although this chapter is not overtly concerned with the thematics of race
and imperialism, my analysis tries to explicate the sociopolitical function of
Lily's painting, from the viewpoint of Gilles Deleuze and Felix Guattari's
'Capitalist Machine'. Lily's desire for the mother figure, I argue, is not
merely sexual; rather the image of Mrs Ramsay should be construed as the
figuration of transnational capital moving around the globe.

4 In contrast to my interpretation, postcolonial readings of *The Waves* have
been focusing upon 'the Lady at a Table Writing' who embodies British
imperialism as the figure of Britannia, although this mysterious lady is construed as serving as allegory for Bernard, the artist figure (see Marcus,
'Britannia' 140). Paying attention to 'the subtlety of Woolf's unstable irony'
or modernist style, McGee critically re-examines Marcus' analysis of the
writer figure: 'To say that Bernard is a parody of authorship is to grant
authorship an authority that Woolf's novel calls into question by insisting
on the artificiality or constructedness of the frame that gives the author
power over the text he or she writes' (McGee 640). The woman who rules
The Waves is the very figure who calls attention to the undecidability of the
text. Yet, McGee's deconstructive interpretation remains to be historicized,
and my geopolitical reading attempts to do such a task by focusing upon
the other representation of writing, that is, the figure of Louis.

5 For the distinction between political and geopolitical, I am indebted to
Jameson, 'The Geopolitical'. Jameson's reinvention of the geopolitical
unconscious can be understood as a theoretical and practical response to
the present social and cultural situation, that is, 'the cultures of globalization'. See Jameson and Miyoshi.

6 For historical studies of migration and 'yellow people', see Panayi, Roe,
Hoppenstand and Walter.

7 Marcus, 'Britannia', and McGee. See also Peach.
8 For the representation of the female vagrant in *Mrs Dalloway*, see Schröder. Exploring the historical background of Woolf's texts, especially its ideological categorizations and connections between female vagrancy, indecent behaviour and mental deficiency, Schröder interprets Woolf's 'larger, transnational desire of "peace and freedom for the whole world"' (Schröder 337–8).
9 For the discourses of degeneration/regeneration and their relationships with British imperialism, see Hackett, Greenslade, and Childs.
10 For gentlemanly capitalism and its relation to the history of British imperialism, see Cain and Hopkins.
11 Nish 255.
12 See Nish and Kibata, and McKercher.
13 Jameson 'Modernism and Imperialism,' 47–8. For a different view on the representation of imperialism and the racial Other, see also Spivak.
14 See Fleishman.
15 See Marcus, 'Britannia', and McGee.
16 For the representations of the Pacific, the South Sea Islands and Tahiti, see Edmond and Rigby.
17 For instances of such reforms to the British political system, e.g. the 'Party of National Efficiency', see Searle.
18 Lloyd George's foreign policy towards the Near East, in particular the Chanak fiasco, broke up his political career and his imperialist reform in 1922. For the relation between Lloyd George's imperialism and Woolf's modernist text, see Ota, 'Generations, Legacies, and Imperialisms'. Rhoda in *The Waves* also implicitly criticizes Lloyd George by briefly alluding to the Greco-Turkish War: 'We hear a drumming on the roofs of a fasting city when the Turks are hungry and uncertain tempered' (*W* 192).
19 For the determinant significance of the Far Eastern political situation on the cultural representations of Anglo-American relationships in the modernist period, see Ota, 'Empire, the Pacific, and Lawrence's Leadership Novels'.

11
Orlando and the Tudor Voyages

Ian Blyth

At the beginning of the fulsome and occasionally fantastical acknowl-
edgements that form the preface to *Orlando*, Woolf pays tribute to a
number of writers who 'are dead and so illustrious that I scarcely dare
name them'; 'no one', she goes on to say, 'can read or write without
being perpetually in the debt of Defoe, Sir Thomas Browne, Sterne, Sir
Walter Scott, Lord Macaulay, Emily Brontë, De Quincey, and Walter
Pater,—to name the first that come to mind' (*O* 5). Woolf's debt to the
writers she mentions has long been established and commented upon.
Other names spring to mind that may be added to this list. In terms of
Orlando in particular, there is one glaring omission from Woolf's
gallery of illustrious forebears: Richard Hakluyt, preacher, colonial
administrator, scholar, occasional spy and editor of *The Principal
Navigations Voyages Traffiques & Discoveries of the English Nation*
(published in 1589, with a considerably expanded three-volume
second edition following in the years 1598–1600). Hakluyt's *Principal
Navigations* is a source book of letters, contracts, eye-witness accounts
and reports that bear vivid and eloquent testimony to the early days of
English enterprise and maritime exploration – it is also instrumental in
setting the tone, choosing the scenery and selecting the key players for
Woolf's tongue-in-cheek romp through English literary history.

An air of rough simplicity

In a thoughtful and comprehensive discussion, Alice Fox makes a
strong case for the importance of *The Principal Navigations* to Woolf's
perception of the sixteenth century (Fox 20–50).[1] As Fox shows,
Woolf's reading in the literature of the English Renaissance was wide
and well informed – Shakespeare, Donne, Spenser, Jonson and Dekker

all had their parts to play. But it was neither the poetry nor the drama of the period that initially fired Woolf's imagination: 'It was the Elizabethan prose writers I loved first & most wildly', she writes in her diary in December 1929, significantly adding that this was 'stirred by Hakluyt' (*D* 3: 271). Reading *The Principal Navigations* in 1897, Woolf soon became 'enraptured' and 'entranced', not just by its contents, but by its language: 'I used to read it', she recalled, '& dream of those obscure adventurers, & no doubt practised their style in my copy books' (*D* 3: 271). *The Principal Navigations* was an integral part of her apprenticeship in writing: the only one of her essays she showed to her father was on the subject of 'the Elizabethan voyagers' (*MB* [1976] 118; Fox 20).[2] This interest was carried over into adult life.

Woolf writes six essays on Hakluyt in the years between 1906 and 1925.[3] Her 1918 essay, 'Trafficks and Discoveries', was meant to be a review of a reprint of J.A. Froude's 1895 *English Seamen in the Sixteenth Century*. However, the draw of Hakluyt proves to be too much. In the course of her review Woolf as good as advises her readers to put away Froude and pick up *The Principal Navigations* instead. She considers Froude to be 'among the greatest of historians', remarking that he is in possession of 'superb dramatic power' (*E* 2: 329–30), but no matter how good a re-writer Froude is, he simply cannot and will not (in her view) match up to the original documents. For Woolf, Froude's gilt-edged, finely spun, wonderfully crafted words seem to fall mysteriously flat when compared to the raw power of the writing in *The Principal Navigations* – a point of view that she had expressed in 1906:

> The charm of Hakluyt's great book [...] does not lie in any medi-tated felicity so much as in its air of rough and unsophisticated sim-plicity, so often made a matter for apology by the writers themselves. They have neither learning nor leisure to 'vary or multi-ply words'. But their laborious pens, dipping into the stately vocab-ulary which was common to seaman and poet, build up such a noble structure of words in the end that the effect is as rich and more authentic than that got by more artistic processes. (*E* 1: 121–2)

The pleasure Woolf derives from reading the accounts of these early voyagers is readily apparent. However, as is so often the case, her admi-ration does not seem to be reflected in the critical opinion of her con-temporaries. Other writers focus their comments on the quotidian, functional aspects of Hakluyt's work. W.P. Ker praises Hakluyt's own writing, but laments that there is too little of it. 'Literary fame' lay within Hakluyt's grasp, he claims, yet Hakluyt 'sacrificed this prospect for the sake of his lifelong work of research' (Ker 513, 516). Seccombe and Allen likewise comment that 'the aims of prose style in [Hakluyt's] work are necessarily subordinated to those of research' (Seccombe and Allen 1: 203), while George Saintsbury remarks that one looks to Hakluyt 'for interest of matter, if not perfection of style' (Saintsbury 220–1). But, as Woolf consistently argues, Hakluyt was much more than a mere collator of documents, and the writers he anthologizes cannot be dismissed as amateurish reporters of 'interesting matter'. *The Principal Navigations* is a treasure-trove of early-modern English prose. Comparing the early accounts with those of the later selections, Jack Beeching writes that 'there is a perceptible enrichment of language' – one can see, he adds, 'the authentic eloquence that arrives within one generation' (Hakluyt, *Voyages and Discoveries* 13). It was this that inspired the young Virginia Woolf and, as Alice Fox remarks, 'She returned to the collection throughout her life and frequently enough for its subject-matter and its style to exert a continuing influence on her creative imagination' (Fox 22).[4] While echoes and allusions may be found in any number of Woolf's novels – Fox mentions *The Voyage Out, Jacob's Room*, and *To the Lighthouse* – it is in *Orlando*, she concludes, that 'Woolf's long acquaintance with the Elizabethan voyages is most evident' (Fox 46).

A question of geographical background

The connection between Woolf's writing and the sixteenth-century accounts of voyaging and exploration was first made by Winifred Holtby in 1932. In her study of Woolf (the first of its kind, in English) Holtby draws attention to the remarkable similarities between two passages describing a South American riverbank – one from Woolf's novel *The Voyage Out*, the other from Sir Walter Raleigh's *Discovery of Guiana*, which was published in 1596 and reprinted by Hakluyt in the second edition of *The Principal Navigations* (Hakluyt, *Principal Navigations* 10: 338–431). Holtby claims that Woolf has 'consciously or unconsciously' lifted her description 'straight out of' the pages of Raleigh's account – yet she mentions this fact with no thought of censure: 'The plagiarism is as justifiable as Shakespeare's. Mrs Woolf's business is with the human spirit; she can borrow her geographical background from whom she pleases. Her rivers and cities are symbols, not natural curiosities to be described from first-hand evidence for their own sake' (Holtby 78–9).[5] Holtby's geographically disinterested argument appears to hold for *To the Lighthouse*, the novel previous to *Orlando*, in which

Woolf seemingly transports the St Ives of her childhood all the way north to what is probably Skye, despite the fact that she had not visited Scotland (nor would she until 1938).[6] One can indeed argue that the location of *To the Lighthouse* is secondary to the ideas it represents – my own suggestion would be that Woolf borrowed at least some of her background from Boswell's *Tour* and Johnson's *Journey*.[7] However, it is much more difficult to support such a reading when it comes to the question of the geography of *Orlando*. For instance, the fact that Orlando's change of sex occurs in Constantinople, as opposed to anywhere else, is highly significant.

Unlike South America, or Scotland (prior to 1938), Woolf actually visited Constantinople: once in 1906, and again in 1911. In 1906 Woolf takes the opportunity 'to rid myself of certain preconceptions' (*PA* 351). One of these concerns the supposed restrictive conventions of dress in Turkey, especially the wearing of the veil. Woolf is surprised to observe that '[m]any native women walked bare faced; & the veil when worn is worn causally, & cast aside if the wearer happens to be curious' (*PA* 352). This process of veiling and unveiling is arguably mirrored in the description of Orlando's transformation. When Orlando stands 'upright in complete nakedness', the Ladies 'Chastity, Purity, and Modesty, inspired, no doubt by Curiosity, peeped in at the door' (*O* 132–3). They throw 'a garment like a towel at the naked form', which happens, 'unfortunately', to fall 'short by several inches' (*O* 133). A great deal more is revealed in Constantinople. During Woolf's 1911 visit her sister Vanessa Bell suffered a miscarriage. Following this, Woolf writes to her friend (and sometime aunt) Violet Dickinson: 'I know most of the parts of the female inside by now, but that is useless knowledge in my trade, the british [*sic*] public being what it is' (*L* 1: 465). Orlando's real-life counterpart, Vita Sackville-West, travelled to Constantinople with Harold Nicolson in 1913, soon after their marriage and what Victoria Glendinning calls 'her sexual initiation' (Glendinning 68). Even the semantic reshuffling Orlando's transformation from male to female provokes – 'in future we must, for convention's sake, say "her" for "his", and "she" for "he"' (*O* 133) – can be said to be a sly glance at Constantinople's own crisis of identity: the city having changed its name to Istanbul only two years previously. None of these symbolic and biographical allusions would work if Woolf had set Orlando's change of sex in Alexandria, for example. A similar place-specific imperative is attached to Orlando's first encounter with the representatives of a different culture: the members of the Muscovite Embassy.

The rise and fall of the Muscovy Company

Alice Fox makes many connections between the accounts of sixteenth-century Russia found in Hakluyt and Woolf's descriptions of the Muscovites in *Orlando*. Fox claims that Woolf uses Hakluyt to give texture, shading and depth to the Muscovites. Among the items she traces back to *The Principal Navigations* are Sasha's 'unfaithfulness', the violent nature of Russian society, the eating habits of the Muscovites, their fondness for tallow, their rough and ready housing, and the wide open expanses of the Russian landscape (Fox 46–8). What is more, Fox shows that Woolf sticks fairly closely to her source. While there is the occasional questionable moment, such as Orlando's notion that 'he had heard that the women in Muscovy wear beards and the men are covered with fur from the waist down' (*O* 46), on the whole, Fox observes, 'it is remarkable that in this work of fancy Woolf uses very little licence in her entire coverage of Russia' (Fox 47). Yet the one question Alice Fox does not ask is why did Woolf choose to make Sasha a Muscovite in the first place? What was so special about Russia and the Russians?

Woolf did not visit Russia but, as Roberta Rubenstein notes, when considering Sasha's Russian lineage, she was an avid reader and reviewer of nineteenth-century Russian literature (Rubenstein 166). Woolf began studying Russian with S.S. Koteliansky in 1921 (*L* 2: 459). She also assisted Koteliansky with his translations, correcting the English text of Dostoevsky's *Stavrogin's Confession* (1922), *Tolstoi's Love Letters* (1923) and Goldenveizer's *Talks with Tolstoi* (1923). This experience of working with Koteliansky might help explain the acknowledgement in the preface to *Orlando* in which Woolf thanks the Russian dancer Lydia Lopokova for being 'at hand to correct my Russian' – despite the fact that there are no Russian words in the novel (*O* 5). Woolf's fascination with the writings of the Tudor voyagers overlaps with her interest in modern Russian language and literature. This blurring of the boundaries between the historical and the modern might account for why the Muscovites speak French – a language all but unknown in the sixteenth-century Russia visited by Hakluyt's sources, but very familiar to the twentieth-century exiles Woolf knew. The historical and the modern, Hakluyt and the present day, are linked in other ways too. When Orlando sees Sasha in the twentieth century, it is in a department store (*O* 198). In the early seventeenth century, when Orlando shows Sasha the sights of London, he 'bought her whatever took her fancy in the Royal Exchange' (*O* 42). The Royal Exchange was the forerunner of the modern department store, collecting a large number of diverse objects under the one roof, much like the manner in which *The Principal Navigations* gathered a diverse collection of documents into one publication. It could be argued that both the Royal Exchange and Hakluyt's book owed their existence to the growth in the importance of international trade.

England was a relative latecomer to the global economic stage. In the 1580s, Hakluyt was involved in the plan to establish an English colony in America. He collected for publication various travel narratives and documents about America, as well as other items of intelligence for Sir Frances Walsingham, a pro-expansionist diplomat and politician who is perhaps now best remembered for his role as the head of Elizabeth's secret service. Hakluyt's first collection, *Divers Voyages Touching the Discovery of America and the Islands Adjacent* (1582), has a distinct whiff of Walsingham's influence hanging over it. The opening sentence of its 'Epistle Dedicatorie', addressed to Sir Philip Sidney, Walsingham's son-in-law, sets the tone: 'I maruaile note a little (right worshipfull) that since the first discouerie of America (which is now full fourescore and tenne yeeres), after so great conquests and plantings of the Spaniardes and Portingales there, that wee of Englande could neuer haue the grace to set fast footing in such fertill and temperate places as are left as yet vnpossessed of them' (Hakluyt, *Divers Voyages* 8). Hakluyt goes on to present his readers with examples of earlier voyages, two sets of notes or instructions issued to voyagers, and a list of 'The Names of Certaine Commodities Growing in part of America, not presently inhabited by any Christians', including 'rivers full of incredible store of all good fishe', 'Gold, in good quantitie' and (surely erroneously) 'Silke wormes fayre and great' (Hakluyt, *Divers Voyagers* 139–40). Hakluyt's next work in this field was his 'Discourse of Western Planting', an even more explicit piece of propaganda, written in 1584 on behalf of Sir Walter Raleigh, and presented by Raleigh to the queen (as this latter work was a private state document it was not, unlike much of the material in *Divers Voyages*, reprinted in *The Principal Navigations*). Finally, in the year following the momentous and highly improbable victory over the Spanish Armada, the first edition of *The Principal Navigations* appeared – complete, perhaps inevitably so, with an 'Epistle Dedicatorie' addressed to Walsingham (Hakluyt, *Principal Navigations* 1: xvii–xxii).

In one respect, both Hakluyt's political associations and the timing of the first edition of *The Principal Navigations* were unfortunate. As Beeching laments, Hakluyt's scholarly achievement 'has too long been obscured by the glowing patriotic penumbra diffused about his work since the Armada' – a state of affairs that has led to his work being viewed 'mainly as a source of rattling good yarns' (Hakluyt, *Voyages and Discoveries* 21, 9). Typical of the reaction Beeching speaks of is John Dover Wilson's decision to include an excerpt from Hakluyt's 1589 dedication to Walsingham in an anthology of Elizabethan prose under the heading 'Hakluyt extols England's greatness at sea' (J.D. Wilson 251). As might be expected, Woolf was one of those who looked deeper into the matter. She relates her findings in her 1919 essay 'Reading':

> These are the fine stories, used effectively all through the West Country to decoy the strong men lounging by the harbour side to leave their nets and fish for gold. Less glorious but more urgent, considering the state of the country, was the summons of the more serious-minded to set on foot some intercourse between the merchants of England and the merchants of the East. (*E* 3: 147)

It was no idle thought that prompted Hakluyt to add the word 'Traffiques' to the title of the second edition in 1598. The future of the country lay in trade, and it was merchants, not privateers, who were to be its adventurers. Russia featured strongly in this respect. J.S.G. Simmonds estimates that 'between a quarter and one-third of the total text of the first edition' of *The Principal Navigations* was taken up with papers relating to 'the Muscovy trade', with 'about a third as much again' added in the 1598–1600 second edition (Simmonds 161, 163). Simmonds notes that Hakluyt gained access to these 'official and unofficial' papers through such contacts as his cousin 'Richard Hakluyt who was an early advisor to the Muscovy Company', and 'Burleigh and Walsingham' who 'facilitated his access to complementary sources of information such as the reports and conversation of returning diplomats' (Simmonds 161). 'Moreover', Simmonds adds, 'for the vast bulk of this material Hakluyt remains the only source; little of it was taken from printed books and almost the manuscript originals have perished' (Simmonds 166).

The mercantile exchanges between England and Russia happened more through chance than design. In an essay reviewed by Woolf (*E* 1: 120–4), Walter Raleigh (the critic) notes that after Magellan's pioneering voyage into the Pacific in 1520 'for many years, the aim of the European navigators was not to explore or settle America, rather to discover a passage whereby America might be avoided, and a way opened to the lands beyond' (Hakluyt, *Principal Navigations* 12: 9). It was in the east, Raleigh argues, and in the route to India and China where the great riches were to be found. However, getting there was no simple matter. The routes to the south were controlled by the Spanish and Portuguese. As early as 1527 Robert Thorne appealed to Henry VIII, pointing out that the only option left to the English was to venture 'into the North: for that of the foure partes of the worlde, it seemeth three parts are discovered by other Princes' (Hakluyt, *Principal Navigations* 2: 161). Thorne's call was taken up, and English ships set off in search of this northern route. Initial attempts were focused on the North West Passage, but, as Raleigh remarks, these expeditions 'had been but poorly rewarded; and for a time attention was turned to the possibility of reaching Cathay by way of the North East' (Hakluyt, *Principal Navigations* 12: 22). In May 1553 Sir Hugh Willoughby and Richard Chancelor, with three ships, embarked on a search for this alternate route. They were soon separated by a storm. Willoughby, with two of the ships, was forced to shelter for the winter in Lapland – both ships' companies froze to death. Chancelor, on the other hand, having waited in vain at the rendezvous point for some sign of his companions, carried on alone. Much to his surprise, he arrived in Russia and proceeded to Moscow, where he was well received by the emperor. Relations between the two countries blossomed. Ambassadors were exchanged. Patents and charters were granted. Goods began to flow. 'Strange must have been their thoughts', writes Woolf, 'strange the sense of the unknown; and of themselves, the isolated English, burning on the very rim of the dark, and the dark full of unseen splendours' (*E* 3: 147). However, all this was not to last. In the 1580s Martin Frobisher briefly reopened the search for the North West Passage. In the south, Hawkins and Drake began to harass the Spanish seriously, and returned with ships laden with gold. Other interests suffered. The North East Passage faded from view. The search for the North West Passage, as Raleigh recounts, 'passed into the hands of the Dutch, who were beginning also, before the [sixteenth] century closed, to supplant the English in the trade with Russia' (Hakluyt, *Principal Navigations* 12: 30).

Such, then, was the state of Anglo-Russian relations at the time Orlando met, fell in love, and attempted to elope with Sasha. Nostalgia is a major theme in *Orlando* – Woolf writes it, after all, at the time when her affair with Vita Sackville-West is reaching its inevitable close. There must also have been a hint of nostalgia when contemporary readers of *The Principal Navigations* read the accounts of the English merchants in Russia. It is not just Woolf who would have seen 'the glories of Moscow [...] preserved as if under shades of glass' (*E* 3: 148). The fact that, for the English, the Russians effectively disappeared back into the dark at the beginning of the seventeenth century perhaps suggested to Woolf that they would be the ideal people to represent, symbolically, the nostalgia she herself was feeling for her affair with Vita Sackville-West – or indeed, the nostalgia Vita Sackville-West may have been feeling for her affair with Violet Trefusis (*née* Keppel), the probable inspiration for the character of Sasha. Orlando's last sighting of Sasha combines both the early accounts of Russia in Hakluyt, and Raleigh's later assessment of the end of the affair (when the English were supplanted by the Dutch, just as Woolf was supplanted by Mary Campbell, and Violet Trefusis by Harold Nicolson):

> But the Russian ship was nowhere to be seen. For one moment Orlando thought it must have foundered; but, raising himself in his stirrups and shading his eyes, which had the sight of a hawk's, he could just make out the shape of a ship on the horizon. The black eagles were flying from the mast-head. The ship of the Muscovite Embassy was standing out to sea.
>
> Flinging himself from his horse, he made, in his rage, as if he would breast the flood. Standing knee-deep in water he hurled at the faithless woman all the insults that have ever been the lot of her sex [...]; and the swirling waters took his words, and tossed at his feet a broken pot and a little straw. (*O* 62)

The arrival in London of the first Russian ambassador in February 1556 had been preceded by a disastrous shipwreck off the Scottish coast; Chancelor was among those who drowned. What little of the ambassador's possessions that did make it to shore, 'the Jewels, rich apparell, presents, gold, silver, costly furres, and such like, were conveyed away, concealed and utterly embezelled' by the local Scots (Hakluyt, *Principal Navigations* 2: 353). The ambassador, like Orlando, was left with little more than flotsam and jetsam (another reason for Sasha's need to go shopping). But this passage also looks forward in time, to the departure of the Muscovites in the early seventeenth century. The unseen splendours of Russia have run through Orlando's fingers like so many grains of sand, much like the once lucrative Russian trade slipping out of the grasp of the merchants of the Muscovy Company.

It's about all a fellow can do these days

A decidedly more light-hearted kind of nostalgia is brought to bear on the characterization of Orlando's other great love, 'Marmaduke

Bonthrop Shelmerdine, Esquire' (*O* 239). In many respects, as Alice Fox observes, given her interest in Hakluyt's work, 'Woolf's choice of a sailor for Orlando's mate seems almost inevitable' (Fox 50). It is a trend that ran in the family: Woolf's father, Leslie Stephen, comments in his essay 'National Biography' that '[t]here is no class of lives which has a more distinctive character than the lives of our naval heroes, from the Elizabethan days to our own' (Stephen, *Studies* 1: 25–6). Soon after Orlando's return to court, during the time of the Great Frost, 'Admirals' can be found striding 'up and down the narrow pathways, glass in hand, sweeping the horizon and telling stories of the north-west passage and the Spanish Armada' (*O* 34). Later on, as he waits for Sasha near Blackfriars' Bridge, Orlando hears 'a few seamen [...] telling their stories of Drake, Hawkins and Grenville' (*O* 56). Later still, the slightly older (and now female) Orlando hears Shelmerdine's descriptions of his own 'desperate and splendid [...] adventures' (*O* 241).

Despite the bravado with which these tales are told, it is apparent that the life of a sixteenth-century sailor was far from easy. There are rumblings 'of hardship and cruelty on the Spanish main [*sic*]' (*O* 28). The departure of a ship, notes Woolf in the 1918 'Trafficks and Discoveries', was a time of 'solemn leave-taking' for all concerned: 'the voyage was generally a voyage to an unknown land, over seas made dangerous by hostile Spaniards, Portuguese, and French [...]. Many would come back no more' (*E* 2: 331). 'Every day', the narrator of *Orlando* remarks, 'sailed to sea some fine ship bound for the Indies; now and again another blackened and ragged with hairy unknown men on board crept painfully to anchor' (*O* 29). In her reading of Hakluyt, Woolf seems to have been particularly taken with the story of Sir William Buts's return from a voyage to Newfoundland in 1536 (see *E* 2: 332, *E* 3: 146, *E* 4: 54). The voyage had been long and fruitless. Lying at anchor in the frozen seas, 'they grew into great want of victuals' (Hakluyt, *Principal Navigations* 8: 5). Famine ensued, and some of the sailors were driven to cannibalism. In 'Reading', Woolf slightly embellishes the original, placing Buts in the role of 'the boy who went years ago to sea and is now come back to his father's house' (*E* 3: 146). William Buts's voyage actually lasted a mere six months (from the end of April to the end of October 1536), but there is no denying the dramatic change brought about by his experiences: 'M. Buts was so changed in the voyage with hunger and miserie, that sir William his father and my Lady his mother knew him not to be their sonne, untill they found a secret marke which was a wart upon one of his knees' (Hakluyt, *Principal Navigations* 8: 7). There is a certain kudos attached to having experienced and lived though such hardship as this. Shelmerdine's adventures, like those of the Tudor voyagers, were often fraught with danger: 'Masts had been snapped off; sails torn to ribbons (she had to drag the admission from him). Sometimes the ship had sunk, and he had been left the only survivor on a raft with a biscuit' (*O* 241). It is not hard to find parallels for Shelmerdine's tales in *The Principal Navigations*. Sinking ships were all too common. For instance, Woolf makes reference to the last words of Sir Humphrey Gilbert – 'We are as neere to heaven by sea as by land', he had cried out a few hours before his 'Frigat was devoured and swallowed up' (Hakluyt, *Principal Navigations* 8:74) – no less than five times (*E* 1: 123, *E* 2: 93, *E* 2: 331, *E* 3: 146, *E* 4: 54). As for Shelmerdine's meagre feast, this can be placed alongside the misfortunes suffered by the Earl of Cumberland, George Clifford, and his crew when they returned from the Azores in 1589.

Woolf refers to Clifford's voyage twice in her essays (*E* 2: 331, *E* 4: 54). The 'Earl of Cumberland' also makes an appearance in *Orlando*: it is he who discovers Orlando and Sukey in one of his ships, and mistakes them 'for a phantom sprung from the graves of drowned sailors to upbraid him' (*O* 29). The repentant earl establishes a 'row of alms houses [...] in the Sheen Road' (*O* 29) – the subject of 'a little joke' that passes between him and Orlando in the twentieth century (*O* 287). In the sixteenth century, Clifford and his crew, plagued by unfavourable winds, laboured for two weeks off the coasts of Cornwall and Ireland. When the water ran out, desperate measures were taken:

> The raine-drops were so carefully saved, that so neere as wee coulde, not one was lost in all our shippe. Some hanged up sheetes tied with cordes by the foure corners, and a weight in the midst that the water might runne downe thither, and so be received into some vessell set or hanged underneth: Some that wanted sheetes, hanged up napkins, and cloutes, and watched them till they were thorow wet, then wringing and sucking out the water. And that water which fell downe and washed away the filth and soyling of the shippe, trod under foote, as bad as running downe the kennell many times when it raineth, was not lost I warrant you, but watched and attended carefully (yea sometimes with strife and contention) at every scupper-hole, and other place where it ranne downe, with dishes, pots, cannes, and Jarres, whereof some drunke hearty draughts even as it was, mud and all, without tarrying to clense or settle it: Others clensed it first, but not often, for it was so thicke and went so slowly thorow, that they might ill endure to tary

so long, and were loth to loose too much of such precious stuffe: some licked with their tongues (like dogges) the boards under feete, the sides, railes, and Mastes of the shippe. (Hakluyt, *Principal Navigations* 7: 22–3)

One can appreciate Woolf's admiration for the sheer dramatic power contained in writing such as this. Things were rough – indeed it is not an exaggeration to say that things were extremely rough – but the author of this piece, Edward Wright, tells his tale in direct, unadorned language. His is the voice of unmediated experience, and his matter-of-factness carries the indelible ring of truth. There is no appeal to pity or compassion: it is a prosaic and brave reaction to events, displaying, one might say, a quintessentially English stiff upper lip. It is instructive to compare this account with Shelmerdine's reaction to his own misadventures: '"It's about all a fellow can do these days", he said sheepishly, helping himself to great spoonfuls of strawberry jam' (*O* 241). Woolf's writing here is pure boys' own stuff: a wonderful parody not only of Hakluyt, but also of Haggard, Henty, Buchan et al. Like so many of the nineteenth-century gentlemen imperialists, Shelmerdine is a boy who does not want to grow up. Woolf's creation of Shelmerdine, like Jane Austen's creation of Captain Frederick Wentworth (the sublimely decent yet exasperatingly fragile hero of *Persuasion*), comically satirizes some of the more absurd manifestations of masculine heroics. Orlando and Shelmerdine's consummation of their desire occurs rather more suddenly than Anne Eliot could ever have hoped to expect, but like Austen's most famous naval officer, Shelmerdine is frequently made to appear both truly magnificent and slightly ridiculous, often at the same time.

A gentleman in America

In her 1917 essay, 'Sir Walter Raleigh', comparing 'the world of Shakespeare' with 'the world of Hakluyt and Raleigh', Woolf concludes that '[t]he navigator and the explorer made their voyage by ship instead of by the mind, but over Hakluyt's pages broods the very same lustre of the imagination' (*E* 2: 91–2). She observes in her reading notes for the 1918 'Trafficks and Discoveries' that *The Principal Navigations* contains a 'great wealth of good reading' (*E* 2: 357). In the essay itself, she advises that '[t]he only possible course to take with Hakluyt's voyages [...] is to read them through; to read dedications, ambassages, letters, privileges, discourses, advertisements; for only thus will you become possessed of the unity of the whole' (*E* 2: 333). It is this reading that Woolf uses to such effect in *Orlando*. As Hermione Lee remarks, Woolf 'liked best books which fired her thoughts with hard factual information' (Lee 216). Her love of Hakluyt works its way into the style and diction of the early chapters, the nostalgia and regret of the description of the Muscovites, and the stirring tales of Shelmerdine's seafaring adventures. On the surface, *Orlando* may appear to be a whimsical flight of fancy, but it is built upon the solid granite of truth. Regrettably, this is something that would have eluded many of her readers – as Jane Goldman points out, by the late 1920s Woolf had an 'established reputation for factual inaccuracy' (Goldman, 'Metaphor' 147). The furore surrounding her description of the Western Isles in *To the Lighthouse* cannot have helped. Woolf received a number of irate letters from readers, not to mention some fairly uncomplimentary reviews pointing out her 'inaccuracies'. One letter in particular seems to have caused Woolf an undue amount of exasperation, as she reports to her sister Vanessa Bell on 22 May 1927:

> Lord Olivier writes that my horticulture and natural history is in every instance wrong: there are no rooks, elms, or dahlias in the Hebrides; my sparrows are wrong; so are my carnations: and it is impossible for women to die in childbirth in the 3rd month – He infers that Prue had a slip (which is common in the Hebrides) and was 9 months gone. This is the sort of thing that painters know nothing of. (*L* 3: 379)

Whether or not Woolf replied to this letter is not recorded. It seems likely, however, that she did not forget receiving it. Sydney Haldane Olivier, Baron Olivier (1859–1947), a Fabian politician and ex-governor of Jamaica, was known to Woolf through his four daughters – all of whom had been Neo-Pagans (*L* 3: 78n).[8] Olivier is not mentioned by name in the preface to *Orlando*, but it is tantalizing to think that he might be there nonetheless, lurking in the shadows:

> Finally, I would like to thank, had I not lost his name and address, a gentleman in America, who has generously and gratuitously corrected the punctuation, the botany, the entomology, the geography, and the chronology of previous works of mine and will, I hope, not spare his services on the present occasion. (*O* 7)

Is this fastidious and punctilious 'American' gentleman none other than a certain English lord? If he is, he appears not to have taken the bait. This was probably for the best, for if he (whoever he might be) had indeed gone ahead and tried to correct the geography of Woolf's latest work, one can't help thinking that he would have been in for quite a humbling experience.[9]

Notes

1   It must be said that not everyone agrees with Fox on the importance of Hakluyt to Woolf. In another recent study of Woolf and the Renaissance, Juliet Dusinberre chooses to give Hakluyt a mere cursory glance (Dusinberre 8, 93). Nor is there an essay on Hakluyt in Sally Greene's 1999 collection, *Virginia Woolf: Reading the Renaissance*, although his name is mentioned on four separate occasions (Greene 21, 23, 29, 246).

2   This reference is missing from the 2nd edition of *Moments of Being*, which prints 'a revision' of the relevant section of 'A Sketch of the Past' (*MB* [1985] 125n).

3   1906: 'Trafficks and Discoveries' (*E* 1: 120–4); 1917: 'Sir Walter Raleigh' (*E* 2: 91–6); 1918: 'Trafficks and Discoveries' (*E* 2: 329–36); 1919: 'Reading' (*E* 3: 141–61); 1924: 'Richard Hakluyt' (*E* 3: 450–1); 1925: 'The Elizabethan Lumber Room' (*E* 4: 53–61). Note that the 1906 and 1918 'Trafficks and Discoveries' are entirely different works; on the other hand, the section on Hakluyt in 'The Elizabethan Lumber Room' is, on the whole, a reworked version of Woolf's comments in 'Reading'.

4   A point also made by Hermione Lee, who observes (without making any mention of Fox's book) that Woolf's childhood reading of Hakluyt 'would lastingly influence her writing' (Lee 142).

5   Nancy T. Bazin sees Woolf's description of the unspoiled riverbank as a symbolic representation of Rachel Vinrace's state of sexual innocence (Bazin 52–3). Again, the actual location is unimportant, any stretch of 'virgin' rainforest will do.

6   See, for example, the Scottish critic David Daiches: 'It is clear that Virginia Woolf is here more concerned with conveying a general impression of sea, sand and rocks than with describing any particular place' (Daiches 82).

7   A suggestion that is also made by Jane Goldman, who goes on to propose that as well as Boswell and Johnson, Woolf may have drawn on the work of Sir Walter Scott, and several historical accounts of the 1745–6 Jacobite rebellion (Goldman 137–55).

8   Olivier was also the uncle of the actor Laurence Olivier.

9   Versions of this chapter were given as conference papers at the Universities of St Andrews and Dundee. I'd also like to thank Michael Whitworth, who provided invaluable comments on an early draft. This chapter was prepared for publication during an AHRC-funded research fellowship in the School of English, St Andrews.

Works Cited

Abel, Elizabeth. *Virginia Woolf and the Fictions of Psychoanalysis*. Chicago: University of Chicago Press, 1989.

'The Abinger Pageant.' *Drama* 13 (Oct. 1934): 15. [*Drama* was the journal of the British Drama League.]

'The Acceptance of Home Rule.' *The Nation* 12 (25 Jan. 1913): 688.

Advertisement. *The Graphic* (24 May 1924): 834.

Akita, Shigeru. 'British Informal Empire in East Asia, 1880–1939: A Japanese Perspective.' *Gentlemanly Capitalism and British Imperialism: The New Debate on Empire*. Ed. Raymond E. Dumett with an Afterword by P.J. Cain and A.G. Hopkins. London: Longman, 1999. 141–56.

Allan, Tuzyline Jita. 'A Voice of One's Own: Implications of Impersonality in the Essays of Virginia Woolf and Alice Walker.' *The Politics of the Essay*. Ed. Ruth-Ellen Boetcher Joeres and Elizabeth Mittman. Bloomington: Indiana University Press, 1993. 131–47.

Allen, David Elliston. *The Victorian Fern Craze*. London: Hutchinson, 1969.

Allen, David Elliston. *The Naturalist in Britain: A Social History*. London: Allen Lane, 1976.

Anderson, Benedict. *Imagined Communities: Reflections on the Origin and Spread of Nationalism*. London: Verso, 1983.

Arnold-Forster, Hugh Oakeley. *Our Great City, or, London the Heart of Empire*. London: Cassell, 1900.

Ashcroft, Bill. 'Excess: Post-colonialism and the Verandahs of Meaning.' *De-Scribing Empire: Post-colonialism and Textuality*. Ed. Chris Tiffin and Alan Lawson. London: Routledge, 1994. 33–44.

Austen, Jane. *Persuasion with A Memoir of Jane Austen by J.E. Austen-Leigh*. Ed. D.W. Harding. Harmondsworth: Penguin, 1977.

Barber, Lynn. *The Heyday of Natural History, 1820–1870*. Garden City: Doubleday, 1980.

Baron, Wendy, and Richard Shone, eds. *Sickert: Paintings*. London and New Haven: Royal Academy of Arts in association with Yale University Press, 1992.

Bataille, Georges. *The Accursed Share: An Essay on General Economy. Volume I: Consumption*. Trans. Robert Hurley. New York: Zone Books, 1991.

Bazin, Nancy Topping. *Virginia Woolf and the Androgynous Vision*. New Brunswick: Rutgers University Press, 1973.

Beckett, J.C. *The Making of Modern Ireland 1603–1923*. London: Faber and Faber, 1966.

Beer, Gillian. *Virginia Woolf: The Common Ground*. Edinburgh: Edinburgh University Press, 1996.

Beer, Gillian. 'Wireless: Popular Physics, Radio and Modernism.' *Cultural Babbage*. Ed. Francis Spufford and Jenny Uglow. London: Faber and Faber, 1997. 149–166.

Bence-Jones, Mark. *Twilight of the Ascendancy*. London: Constable, 1987.

Bennett, Arnold. *The Author's Craft*. London: Hodder and Stoughton, 1913.

Bennett, Tony. *The Birth of the Museum*. London: Routledge, 1995.

Benstock, Shari. *Textualizing the Feminine: On the Limits of Genre*. Norman: University of Oklahoma Press, 1991.

Black, Peter. *The Biggest Aspidistra in the World*. London: BBC Publications, 1972.

Blanchot, Maurice. 'Interruption (as on a Riemann surface).' *The Infinite Conversation*. Trans. Susan Hanson. Minneapolis: University of Minnesota Press, 1993.

Bland, Lucy. *Banishing the Beast: Sexuality and the Early Feminists*. New York: New Press, 1995.

Bloom, Harold. *A Map of Misreading*. New York: Oxford University Press, 1975.

Boetcher Joeres, Ruth-Ellen and Elizabeth Mittman. 'An Introductory Essay.' *The Politics of the Essay*. Ed. Ruth-Ellen Boetcher Joeres and Elizabeth Mittman. Bloomington: Indiana University Press, 1993. 12–22.

Booth, Howard, and Nigel Rigby, eds. *Modernism and Empire*. Manchester: Manchester University Press, 2000.

Bottomley, Gordon. 'The Village Drama Society 1918–1931.' *Drama* 10 (Oct. 1931): 3–5.

Bowlby, Rachel. *Virginia Woolf: Feminist Destinations*. Oxford: Blackwell, 1988.

Bowlby, Rachel. 'Walking, Women and Writing: Virginia Woolf as Flâneuse.' *New Feminist Discourses*. Ed. Isobel Armstrong. London: Routledge, 1992. 26–47.

Cain, Peter. 'British Economic Imperialism 1919–1939: Towards a New Interpretation.' *Osaka University of Foreign Studies Bulletin of Asian Studies* 4 (1994): 233–54.

Cain, P.J., and A.G. Hopkins. *British Imperialism: Crisis and Deconstruction 1914–1990*. London: Longman, 1993.

Centerwall, Bror. 'Men and Beasts at Wembley.' *The Living Age* 322 (2 August 1924): 221–4.

Certeau, Michel de. *The Certeau Reader*. Ed. Graham Ward. Oxford: Blackwell, 2000.

Certeau, Michel de. *The Practice of Everyday Life*. Trans. Steven Rendall. Berkeley: University of California Press, 1984.

Childs, Donald J. *Modernism and Eugenics: Woolf, Eliot, Yeats, and the Culture of Degeneration*. Cambridge: Cambridge University Press, 2001.

Clarke, Peter. *Hope and Glory: Britain 1900–1990*. London: Penguin, 1996.

Clifford, William Kingdon. 'The Philosophy of the Pure Sciences.' *Lectures and Essays*. Ed. Leslie Stephen and Frederick Pollock. 2 vols. London: Macmillan, 1879. 1: 301–49.

Clunn, Harold P. *The Face of London*. London: Simpkin Marshall, 1932.

Colomina, Beatriz, ed. *Sexuality & Space*. Princeton, NJ: Princeton Architectural Press, 1992.

Connor, Steven. 'Noise (2)' [BBC radio talk]. 25 May 2006. http://www.bbk.ac.uk/english/skc/noise/noise2.htm.

Coroneos, Con. *Space, Conrad, and Modernity*. Oxford: Oxford University Press, 2002.

Cuddy-Keane, Melba. 'Virginia Woolf, Sound Technology and the New Aurality.' *Virginia Woolf in the Age of Mechanical Reproduction*. Ed. Pamela L. Caughie. New York: Garland, 2000. 69–98.

Curtis, Vanessa. *The Hidden Houses of Virginia Woolf and Vanessa Bell*. London: Robert Hale, 2005.

Daiches, David. *Virginia Woolf*. London: Poetry London, 1945.

Dangerfield, George. *The Strange Death of Liberal England*. 1936. Stanford. Stanford University Press, 1997.

Daniel, Mark. Introduction. *The Essential Gilbert White of Selborne*. London: Breslich and Fross, 1983.

Dell, Marion. *Peering through the Escallonia: Virginia Woolf, Talland House and St Ives*. Bloomsbury Heritage 23. London: Cecil Woolf, 1999.

Dell, Marion and Marion Whybrow. *Virginia Woolf & Vanessa Bell: Remembering St Ives*. Padstow: Tabb House, 2003.

Dooley, Terence. *The Decline of the Big House in Ireland: A Study of Irish Landed Families 1860–1960*. Dublin: Wolfhound, 2001.

Dostoevsky, Fyodor. *Stavrogin's Confession (Three hitherto unpublished chapters of the novel 'The Possessed') and the plan of the Life of a Great Sinner*. Trans. S.S. Koteliansky and Virginia Woolf. London: Hogarth, 1922.

Duckworth, George H., et al. Notebook B354, covering District 2, Strand and St Giles (12 July–30 Sep. 1898). Booth Collection, London School of Economics. Accessed in digitized form, 17 May 2006. http://booth.lse.ac.uk

Dusinberre, Juliet. *Virginia Woolf's Renaissance: Woman Reader or Common Reader?* Basingstoke: Macmillan, 1997.

Edmond, Rod. *Representing the South Pacific: Colonial Discourse from Cook to Gauguin*. Cambridge: Cambridge University Press, 1997.

Ellmers, Chris, and Alex Werner, eds. *Dockland Life: A Pictorial History of London's Docks 1860–2000*. Edinburgh: Mainstream Publishing, 2000.

Emerson, Ralph Waldo. 'Consecration of Sleepy Hollow Cemetery.' *Miscellanies*. Boston: Houghton Mifflin, 1904. 426–7.

Esty, Joshua D. 'Amnesia in the Fields: Late Modernism, Late Imperialism, and the English Pageant-Play.' *ELH* 69 (2002): 245–76.

Fitter, R.S.R. *London's Natural History*. London: Collins, 1945.

Fleishman, Avrom. *Virginia Woolf: A Critical Reading*. Baltimore: Johns Hopkins University Press, 1975.

Ford, Ford Madox. *The Soul of London*. 1905. Ed. A.G. Hill. London: Dent, 1995.

Forster, E.M. *Abinger Harvest and England's Pleasant Land*. London: André Deutsch, 1996.

Forster, E.M. 'The Birth of an Empire.' *The Nation and the Athenaeum* 35 (26 April 1924): 110–11.

Foster, R.F. *Modern Ireland 1600–1972*. London: Penguin, 1988.

Foucault, Michel. 'Of Other Spaces.' *Diacritics* 16 (1986): 22–7.

Foucault, Michel. 'Space, Knowledge and Power.' Interview. Rizzoli Communications, March 1982. Rpt. *The Foucault Reader*. Ed. Paul Rabinow. New York: Pantheon, 1984. 239–56.

Fox, Alice. *Virginia Woolf and the Literature of the English Renaissance*. Oxford: Clarendon, 1990.

Frank, Joseph. *The Idea of Spatial Form*. New Brunswick: Rutgers University Press, 1991.

Friedman, Susan Stanford. *Mappings: Feminism and the Cultural Geographies of Encounter*. Princeton: Princeton University Press, 1998.

Froude, J.A. *English Seamen in the Sixteenth Century*. London: Longmans, 1918.

Fry, Roger. 'Architecture at Wembley.' *The Nation and the Athenaeum* 35 (24 May 1924): 242–3.

Gelley, Andrew. 'Introduction.' *Unruly Examples: On the Rhetoric of Exemplarity.* Ed. Andrew Gelley. Stanford, California: Stanford University Press, 1995. 1–24.

Glendinning, Victoria. *Vita: The Life of Vita Sackville-West.* Harmondsworth: Penguin, 1987.

Goldenveizer, A.B. *Talks with Tolstoi.* Trans. S.S. Koteliansky and Virginia Woolf. London: Hogarth, 1923.

Goldman, Jane. *The Feminist Aesthetics of Virginia Woolf: Modernism, Post-Impressionism and the Politics of the Visual.* Cambridge: Cambridge University Press, 1998.

Goldman, Jane. 'Metaphor and Place in *To the Lighthouse*: Some Hebridean Connections.' *Tea & Leg-Irons: New Feminist Readings from Scotland.* Ed. C. Gonda. London: Open Letters, 1992. 137–55.

Gordon, Charles. *Old Time Aldwych, Kingsway, and Neighbourhood.* London: T. Fisher Unwin, 1903.

Graves, Robert, and Alan Hodge. *The Long Weekend: A Social History of Great Britain 1918–1939.* New York: Norton, 1963.

Greene, Sally, ed. *Virginia Woolf: Reading the Renaissance.* Athens: Ohio University Press, 1999.

Greenslade, William. *Degeneration, Culture and the Novel 1880–1940.* Ithaca: Cornell University Press, 1983.

Grosz, Elizabeth. 'Bodies-Cities.' Colomina 241–53.

Grubb, A.P. *From Candle Factory to British Cabinet: The Life Story of J. Burns.* London: Edwin Dalton, 1908.

Gualtieri, Elena. *Virginia Woolf's Essays: Sketching the Past.* Basingstoke: Macmillan; New York: St Martin's, 2000.

Gubar, Susan. 'The Birth of the Artist as Heroine: (Re)production, the Künstler-roman Tradition, and the Fiction of Katherine Mansfield.' *The Representation of Women in Fiction* Ed. Carolyn G. Heilbrun and Margaret R. Higonnet. Baltimore: Johns Hopkins University Press, 1983. 19–59.

Hackett, Robin. 'Sapphism and Degeneracy in *The Waves.*' *Virginia Woolf and Her Influences.* Ed. Laura Davis and Jeanette McVicker. New York: Pace University Press, 1998. 44–8.

Hakluyt, R. *Divers Voyages Touching the Discovery of America and the Islands Adjacent.* Ed. J.W. Jones. Hakluyt Society, First Series, 7. London: Hakluyt Society, 1850.

Hakluyt, R. *The Principal Navigations Voyages Traffiques & Discoveries of the English Nation.* 12 vols. Hakluyt Society, Extra Series 1–12. Glasgow: MacLehose, 1903–5.

Hakluyt, R. 'Discourse of Western Planting.' *The Original Writings & Correspondence of the Two Richard Hakluyts.* Ed. E.G.R. Taylor. Vol 2. Hakluyt Society, Second Series, 77. London: Hakluyt Society, 1935. 211–326.

Hakluyt, R. *Voyages and Discoveries.* Ed. J. Beeching. Harmondsworth: Penguin, 1972.

Hankins, Leslie. 'Virginia Woolf and Walter Benjamin Selling Out(siders).' *Virginia Woolf and the Age of Mechanical Reproduction.* Ed. Pamela L. Caughie. New York: Garland, 2000. 3–35.

Hankins, Leslie. 'Virginia Woolf's Spatial Art and Critique: Trespassageways for the Twentieth Century and Beyond.' Diss. University of North Carolina at Chapel Hill, 1991.

Harding, E.A. 'Listening Post.' *BBC Yearbook 1940*. London: BBC Publications, 1940. 84–7.

Hardt, Michael, and Antonio Negri. *Empire*. Cambridge, MA: Harvard University Press, 2000.

Hartman, Geoffrey. 'Virginia's Web.' *Chicago Review* 14.4 (Spring 1961): 20–32.

Harvey, David. *The Urban Experience*. Oxford: Basil Blackwell, 1989.

Hawthorn, Jeremy. *Virginia Woolf's Mrs Dalloway*. Brighton: Sussex University Press, 1975.

Hermann, Claudine. *The Tongue Snatchers*. Trans. Nancy Kline. Lincoln: University of Nebraska Press, 1989.

Hodges, Andrew. *Alan Turing: The Enigma*. New York: Vintage, 1983.

Holtby, Winifred. *Virginia Woolf*. London: Wishart, 1932.

Hoppenstand, Gary. 'Yellow Devil Doctors and Opium Dens: A Survey of the Yellow Peril Stereotypes in Mass Media Entertainment.' *The Popular Culture Reader*. Ed. Christopher D. Geist and Jack Nachbar. 3rd ed. Bowling Green, Ohio: Bowling Green University Popular Press, 1983. 171–85.

Howkins, Alun. 'The Discovery of Rural England.' *Englishness: Politics and Culture 1880–1920*. Ed. Robert Colls and Philip Dodd. London: Croom Helm, 1986. 62–88.

Ito, Yuko. 'The Production of the South Country in the Bloomsbury Group's Writings.' *Virginia Woolf and Her Influences:Selected Papers from the Seventh Annual Conference on Virginia Woolf*. Ed. Laura Davis and Jeanette McVicker. New York: Pace University Press, 1998. 257–61.

Jacobs, Jane M. *Edge of Empire: Postcolonialism and the City*. London: Routledge, 1996.

Jameson, Fredric. *Fables of Aggression: Wyndham Lewis, the Modernist as Fascist*. Berkeley: University of California Press, 1979.

Jameson, Fredric. *The Geopolitical Aesthetic: Cinema and Space in the World System*. Bloomington: Indiana University Press, 1995.

Jameson, Fredric. 'Modernism and Imperialism.' *Nationalism, Colonialism and Literature*. Terry Eagleton, Fredric Jameson and Edward W. Said. Intro. Seamus Deane. Minneapolis: University of Minnesota Press, 1990. 43–66.

Jameson, Fredric and Masao Miyoshi. *The Cultures of Globalization*. Durham: Duke University Press, 1998.

Jardine, N., J.A. Secord and E.C. Spary, eds. *Cultures of Natural History*. Cambridge: Cambridge University Press, 1996.

Jeans, James. *The Mysterious Universe*. 2nd ed. Cambridge: Cambridge University Press, 1931.

Johnson, Samuel, and James Boswell. *A Journey to the Western Isles of Scotland and The Journal of a Tour of the Hebrides*. Ed. Peter Levi. London: Penguin, 1984.

Kamuf, Peggy. 'Penelope at Work: Interruptions in *A Room of One's Own.*' *Novel: A Forum on Fiction* 16 (1982): 5–18.

Kelly, Mary. *The Antiquities of Selborne: Shown to the World by the Rev. Gilbert White, of Selborne, in the County of Southampton*. London: Dulau, 1926.

Kelly, Mary. *Village Theatre*. London: Thomas Nelson and Sons, 1939.

Ker, W.P. 'Richard Hakluyt.' *English Prose: Selections*. Ed. Henry Craik. 5 vols. London: Macmillan, 1893. 1: 513–16.

Kern, Stephen. *The Culture of Time and Space 1800–1918*. Harvard: Harvard University Press, 2003.

Kestner, Joseph A. *Masculinities in Victorian Painting*. Aldershot, England: Scolar, 1995.

Kiberd, Declan. *Inventing Ireland*. London: Cape, 1995.

King, Anthony D. *Global Cities: Post-imperialism and the Internationalization of London*. London: Routledge, 1990.

Kirkpatrick, B.J., and Stuart N. Clarke, eds. *A Bibliography of Virginia Woolf*. 4th edn. Oxford: Clarendon, 1999.

Kittler, Friedrich. *Gramophone, Film, Typewriter*. Stanford: Stanford University Press, 1999.

Kosugi, Sei. 'Woolf and Drama: In the Context of Amateur Drama Movements in Britain.' *The Edgewood Review* 13 (1996): 1–38. [The title and the text are in Japanese.]

Lee, Hermione. *Virginia Woolf*. London: Chatto and Windus, 1996.

Lefebvre, Henri. *Key Writings*. Ed. Stuart Elden, Elizabeth Lebas and Eleonore Kofman. New York: Continuum, 2003.

Lefebvre, Henri. *The Production of Space*. Trans. Donald Nicholson-Smith. Oxford: Blackwell, 1991.

Low, Lisa. 'Refusing the Hit Back: Virginia Woolf and the Impersonality Question.' *Virginia Woolf and the Essay*. Ed. Beth Carole Rosenberg and Jeanne Dubino. New York: St. Martin's, 1997. 257–73.

Lowenthal, Leo. 'Biographies in Popular Magazines.' *Radio Research 1942–43*. Ed. Paul Lazarsfeld and Frank N. Stanton. New York: Sloan, Duell and Pearce, 1943. 507.

Luckhurst, Nicola. '"To quote my quotation from Montaigne."' Greene 41–64.

MacCarthy, Desmond. 'The Post-Impressionists.' *Manet and the Post-Impressionists*, 8 November to 15 January, 1910–1911. Grafton Galleries Exhibition Catalogue, 1910.

McClintock, Anne. *Imperial Leather: Race, Gender and Sexuality in the Colonial Conquest*. New York: Routledge, 1995.

McGee, Patrick. 'The Politics of Modernist Form; Or, Who Rules *The Waves*?' *Modern Fiction Studies* 38 (1992): 631–49.

McKercher, B.J.C. *Anglo-American Relations in the 1920s: The Struggle for Supremacy*. London: Macmillan, 1991.

MacNeice, Louis. 'Autumn Journal.' *Collected Poems of Louis MacNeice*. Ed. E.R. Dodds. London: Faber and Faber, 1966.

McVicker, Jeanette. '"Six Essays on London Life": A History of Dispersal.' *Woolf Studies Annual* 9 (2003): 143–65, and 10 (2004): 141–72.

Majumdar, Robin, and Allen McLaurin, eds. *Virginia Woolf: The Critical Heritage*. London: Routledge and Kegan Paul, 1975.

Marcus, Jane. *Art and Anger: Reading Like a Woman*. Columbus: Ohio State University Press, 1988.

Marcus, Jane. 'Britannia Rules *The Waves*.' *Decolonizing Tradition: New Views of Twentieth-Century 'British' Literary Canons*. Ed. Karen Lawrence. Urbana: University of Illinois Press, 1992. 136–62.

Marcus, Jane. 'Pargetting the Pargiters.' *Virginia Woolf and the Languages of Patriarchy*. Ed. Jane Marcus. Bloomington: Indiana University Press, 1987. 57–74.

Marcus, Jane. 'Thinking Back Through Our Mothers.' *New Feminist Essays on Virginia Woolf*. Ed. Jane Marcus. Lincoln: University of Nebraska Press, 1981. 1–30.

Marcus, Laura. *Virginia Woolf*. Plymouth: Northcote House, 1997.

Marinetti, F.T. *Let's Murder the Moonshine: Selected Writings*. Ed. R.W. Flint. Los Angeles: Sun & Moon Classics, 1991.

Marshik, Celia. 'Publication and "Public Women": Prostitution and Censorship in Three Novels by Virginia Woolf.' *Modern Fiction Studies* 45 (1999): 853–86.

Marx, Karl. *Capital*, in *The Portable Karl Marx*. Trans. Eugene Kamenka. Harmondsworth: Penguin, 1983.

Massey, Doreen. 'Politics and Space/Time.' *New Left Review* 196 (1992): 65–84.

Massey, Doreen. *Space, Place and Gender*. Minneapolis: University of Minnesota Press, 1994.

Masterman, C.F.G. 'Realities at Home.' *The Heart of the Empire*. By C.F.G. Masterman, *et al*. London: T. Fisher Unwin, 1901. 1–52.

Matless, David. *Landscape and Englishness*. London: Reaktion, 1998.

Mellor, David. *A Paradise Lost: the Neo-Romantic Imagination in Britain 1935–55*. London: Lund Humphries, 1987.

Merleau-Ponty, M. *Phenomenology of Perception*. Trans. Colin Smith. London: Routledge, 1998.

Meskimmon, Marsha. *Engendering the City: Woman Artists and Urban Space*. London: Scarlet, 1997.

Meyer, Susan. *Imperialism at Home: Race and Victorian Women's Fiction*. New York: Cornell University Press, 1996.

Miller, J. Hillis. 'Between the Acts: Repetition as Extrapolation.' *Fiction and Repetition*. Cambridge: Harvard University Press, 1982. 203–31.

Miller, Jonathan. *The Body in Question*. London: Jonathan Cape, 1978.

Millington-Drake, Eugene. *The Documentary Anthology of the Graf Spee 1914–1964*. London: Peter Davies Ltd., 1964.

Mitchell, Timothy. 'The World as Exhibition.' *Comparative Studies in Society and History* 31.2 (April 1989): 217–36.

Montagu of Beaulieu. Foreword. *Shell Poster Book*. London: Profile Books, 1998. n.p.

Morris, Meaghan. 'Great Moments in Social Climbing: King Kong and the Human Fly.' Colomina 1–51.

Morton, H.V. *I Saw Two Englands*. London: Methuen, 1942.

Mulvey, Laura. 'Pandora: Topographies of the Mask and Curiosity.' Colomina 53–71.

Naudeau, Ludovic. 'The British Empire at Wembley.' *Living Age* 322 (5 July 1924): 28–33.

Nish, Ian. 'Echoes of Alliance, 1920–30.' Nish and Kibata 1: 255–78.

Nish, Ian and Yoichi Kibata. *The History of Anglo-Japanese Relations: The Political-Diplomatic Dimension, 1600–1930*. Ed. Ian Nish and Yoichi Kibata. 2 vols. London: Macmillan, 2000.

O'Brien, R. Barry. *The Life of Charles Stewart Parnell, 1846–1891*. 2 vols. London: Smith, Elder & Co, 1898.

Official Guide: British Empire Exhibition 1925. London: Fleetway Press, 1925.

Ogg, David. *H.A.L. Fisher, 1865–1940: A Short Biography*. London: E. Arnold, 1947.

Ota, Nobuyoshi. 'Empire, the Pacific, and Lawrence's Leadership Novels.' *D.H. Lawrence: Literature, History, Culture*. Ed. Michael Bell, Keith Cushman, Takeo Iida, and Hiro Tateishi. Tokyo: Kokusho-KankoKai, 2005. 50–72.

Ota, Nobuyoshi. 'Generations, Legacies, and Imperialisms: The Greco-Turkish War and *Jacob's Room.' Across the Generations: Selected Papers from the Twelfth Annual Virginia Woolf Conference*. Ed. Merry M. Pawlowski and Eileen Barrett. Bakersfield: Center for Virginia Woolf Studies at California State University, 2003. 49–54.

Ota, Nobuyoshi. 'Lily Briscoe and the Problem of Expression: The Social Function of Her Painting in *To the Lighthouse.' Shiron: Essays in English Language and Literature* 28 (1989): 53–67.

Ota, Nobuyoshi. '*Nami*, Louis, Taiheiyo: "I am half in love with the typewriter and the telephone" (*The Waves*, Louis, and the Pacific: "I am half in love with the typewriter and the telephone").' *Shiron: Essays in English Language and Literature* 40 (2001): 35–56.

'The Outlook for Great Britain.' *The Nation and the Athenaeum* 35 (12 April 1924): 38–9.

Panayi, Panikos. *Immigration, Ethnicity and Racism in Britain, 1815–1945*. Manchester: Manchester University Press, 1994.

Parsons, Deborah. *Streetwalking the Metropolis*. Oxford: Oxford University Press, 2000.

Peach, Linden. 'No Longer a View: Virginia Woolf in the 1930s and the 1930s in Virginia Woolf.' *Women Writers of the 1930s: Gender, Politics and History*. Ed. Maroula Joannou. Edinburgh: Edinburgh University Press, 1999. 192–204.

Pearson, Karl. *The Grammar of Science*. 1892. London: Adam and Charles Black, 1911.

Peters, John Durham. *Speaking Into the Air: A History of the Idea of Communication*. Chicago: University of Chicago Press, 2001.

Peters Corbett, David. 'Seeing into Modernity: Walter Sickert's music-hall scenes, c 1887–1907.' *English Art 1860–1914*. Ed. David Peters Corbett and Lara Perry. Manchester: Manchester University Press, 2000. 150–67.

Phillips, Kathy. *Virginia Woolf Against Empire*. Knoxville: University of Tennessee Press, 1994.

Pinci, A.R. 'This is Radio-Casting Station H-O-M-E.' *Dearborn Independent* (10 September 1924): 4–17.

Poincaré, Henri. *Science and Hypothesis*. Trans. 'W.J.G.' London: Walter Scott, 1905.

Pryor, William, ed. *Virginia Woolf and the Raverats: A Different Sort of Friendship*. Bath: Clear Books, 2003.

Quinn, D.B., ed. *The Hakluyt Handbook*. 2 vols. Hakluyt Society, Second Series 144–5. London: Hakluyt Society, 1974.

'The Rebuilding of the State.' *New Statesman* 9 (14 April 1917): 32–3.

Rigby, Nigel. '"Not a Good Place for Deacons": the South Seas, Sexuality and Modernism in Sylvia Townsend Warner's *Mr Fortune's Maggot*.' Booth and Rigby 224–48.

Roe, Michael. *Australia, Britain, and Migration, 1915–1940: A Study of Desperate Hopes*. Cambridge: Cambridge University Press, 1995.

Rose, Gillian. 'As If the Mirrors Had Bled: Masculine Dwelling, Masculinist Theory and Feminist Masquerade.' *Bodyspace*. Ed. Nancy Duncan. London: Routledge, 1996. 56–74.

Rosenbaum, S.P. 'Introduction.' *Women and Fiction: The Manuscript Versions of A Room of One's Own*. Ed. S.P. Rosenbaum. Oxford: Blackwell, 1992.

Rubenstein, Roberta. '*Orlando*: Virginia Woolf's Improvisations on a Russian Theme.' *Forum for Modern Language Studies* 9 (1973): 166–9.

Rudikoff, Sonya. *Ancestral Houses: Virginia Woolf and the Aristocracy*. Palo Alto: Society for the Promotion of Science and Scholarship, 1999.

Russell, Bertrand. *An Outline of Philosophy*. London: Allen and Unwin, 1927.

Said, Edward. *Culture and Imperialism*. London: Chatto & Windus, 1993.

Saintsbury, George. *A History of Elizabethan Literature*. London: Macmillan, 1887.

Sandbach-Dahlström, Catherine. '"Que scais-je?": Virginia Woolf and the Essay as Feminist Critique.' *Virginia Woolf and the Essay*. Ed. Beth Carole Rosenberg and Jeanne Dubino. New York: St Martin's, 1997. 275–93.

Sandburg, Carl. 'Virginia Woolf's Personal Decision.' *Home Front Memo*. New York: Harcourt Brace, 1943. 53–5.

Sarker, Sonita. 'Locating a Native Englishness in Virginia Woolf's "The London Scene."' *NWSA Journal* 13.2 (Summer 2001): 1–30.

Schneer, Jonathan. *London 1900: The Imperial Metropolis*. New Haven and London: Yale University Press, 1999.

Schröder, Leena Kore. '*Mrs. Dalloway* and the Female Vagrant.' *Essays in Criticism* 45 (1995): 324–46.

Schubert, D., and A. Sutcliffe. 'The "Haussmanization" of London?: The Planning and Construction of Kingsway-Aldwych, 1889–1935.' *Planning Perspectives* 11 (1996): 115–44.

Searle, G.R. *Country Before Party: Coalition and the Idea of 'National Government' in Modern Britain, 1885–1987*. London: Longman, 1995.

Seccombe, T., and J. W. Allen, eds. *The Age of Shakespeare (1579–1631)*. 2 vols. London: G. Bell, 1903.

Seeley, Tracy. 'Victorian Women's Essays and Dinah Mulock's Thoughts: Creating an Ethos for Argument.' *Prose Studies* 19.1 (April 1996): 93–109.

Seeley, Tracy. 'Virginia Woolf's Poetics of Space.' *Woolf Studies Annual* 2 (1996): 89–116.

'Selborne Pageant.' *Drama* 17 (October 1938): 15.

'Selborne Pageant, 1938' [photograph]. *Drama* 17 (October 1938), plate, facing p.13.

Seldes, Gilbert. 'Listening In.' *New Republic* (23 March 1927): 140–1.

Shell Poster Book. London: Profile Books, 1998.

Shirer, William. *Berlin Diary*. London: Hamish Hamilton, 1941.

Showalter, Elaine. *A Literature of Their Own: British Women Novelists From Brontë to Lessing*. Princeton: Princeton University Press, 1977.

Sickert, W.R. 'Post-Impressionists.' *A Free House! or the Artist as Craftsman*. Ed. Osbert Sitwell. London: Macmillan, 1947. 97–108. [First published in *The Fortnightly Review,* January, 1911.]

Simmonds, J. S.G. 'Russia.' Quinn 1: 161–7.

Sims, G.R. *My Life: Sixty Years' Recollections of Bohemian London*. London: Eveleigh Nash, 1917.

Smith, Lenora Penna. 'Rooms and the Construction of the Feminine Self.' *Virginia Woolf's Themes and Variations: Selected Papers from the Second Conference on Virginia Woolf*. Ed. Vara Neverow-Turk and Mark Hussey. New York: Pace University Press, 1993. 216–25.

Snaith, Anna. *Virginia Woolf: Public and Private Negotiations*. Basingstoke: Macmillan, 2000.

Soja, Edward. *Postmodern Geographies*. London: Verso, 1989.

Soja, Edward. *Thirdspace: Journeys to Los Angeles and Other Real-and-Imagined Places*. Oxford: Blackwell, 1996.

Solomon, Julie R. 'Staking Ground: The Politics of Space in Virginia Woolf's *A Room of One's Own* and *Three Guineas.*' *Women's Studies* 16 (1989): 331–47.

Southworth, Helen. 'Rooms of Their Own: How Colette Uses Physical and Textual Space to Question a Gendered Literary Tradition.' *Tulsa Studies in Women's Literature* 20 (2001): 253–78.

Spain, Daphne. *Gendered Spaces*. Chapel Hill: University of North Carolina Press, 1992.

Spivak, Gayatri Chakravorty. 'Can the Subaltern Speak?' *Colonial Discourse and Post-colonial Theory: A Reader*. Ed. Patrick Williams and Laura Chrisman. New York: Columbia University Press, 1994. 66–111.

Squier, Susan M. 'A Track of Our Own: Typescript Drafts of *The Years.*' *Virginia Woolf: A Feminist Slant*. Ed. Jane Marcus. Lincoln: University of Nebraska Press, 1983. 198–211.

Squier, Susan M. *Virginia Woolf and London: The Sexual Politics of the City*. Chapel Hill: University of North Carolina Press, 1985.

Stephen, Leslie. *English Literature and Society in the Eighteenth Century*. London: Duckworth, 1904.

Stephen, Leslie. *Studies of a Biographer*. 4 vols. London: Smith, Elder, 1907.

Stevenson, John. *British Society 1914–1945*. Harmondsworth: Penguin, 1984.

Tandy, Geoffrey. 'Broadcasting Chronicle.' *Criterion* 17 (Jan. 1939): 288–96.

Thacker, Andrew. *Moving Through Modernity*. Manchester: Manchester University Press, 2003.

Tolstoy, Leo. *Tolstoi's Love Letters, with a study of the autobiographical elements in Tolstoi's work by Paul Biryukov*. Trans. S.S. Koteliansky and Virginia Woolf. London: Hogarth, 1923.

Trombley, Stephen. *'All That Summer She Was Mad': Virginia Woolf and her Doctors*. London: Junction Books, 1981.

W.R. Sickert: Drawings and Paintings 1890–1942. Liverpool: Tate Gallery Liverpool, 1989. [Exhibition, 21 March 1989–4 February 1990].

Wall, Kathleen. 'Frame Narratives and Unresolved Contradictions in Virginia Woolf's *A Room of One's Own.*' *Journal of Narrative Theory* 29 (1999): 184–207.

Wallis, Mick. 'Delving the Levels of Memory and Dressing Up in the Past.' *British Theatre between the Wars, 1918–1939*. Ed. Clive Barker and Maggie B. Gale. Cambridge: Cambridge University Press, 2000. 190–214.

Walter, P.J. 'The Chinese.' *History Today* 35 (1985): 8–15.

'A Wanderer at Wembley.' *Illustrated London News* (21 May 1924): 932–6.

Weaver, Lawrence. '"The Palace of Industry": A Note on the Arrangement of Exhibits.' *The Empire Exhibition 1924 Official Catalogue*. London: Fleetway Press, 1924.

Wells, H.G. *Ann Veronica*. 1909. Harmondsworth: Penguin, 1968.

'Wembley and its Millions of Visitors.' *Illustrated London News* (19 July 1924): 106–7.

White, Gilbert. *The Natural History of Selborne*. New York: Penguin, 1997.

White, Hayden. *Tropics of Discourse: Essays in Cultural Criticism*. Baltimore: Johns Hopkins University Press, 1978.

Whitworth, Michael. 'Woolf's Web: Telecommunications and Community.' *Virginia Woolf and Communities: Selected Papers from the Eighth Annual Conference on Virginia Woolf.* Ed. Jeanette McVicker and Laura Davis. New York: Pace University Press, 1999. 161–7.

Williams, Keith. *British Writers and the Media 1930–1945.* Basingstoke: Macmillan, 1996.

Wilson, Elizabeth. 'The Invisible Flâneur.' *New Left Review* 191(1992): 90–110.

Wilson, Jean Moorcroft. *Virginia Woolf: Life and London: A Biography of Place.* London: Cecil Woolf, 1987.

Wilson, John Dover. *Life in Shakespeare's England: A Book of Elizabethan Prose.* Cambridge: Cambridge University Press, 1911.

Wolff, Janet. 'The Invisible Flâneuse: Women and the Literature of Modernity.' *Theory, Culture and Society* 2.3 (1985): 37–46.

Woolf, Leonard. *Beginning Again: An Autobiography of the Years 1911–1918.* London: The Hogarth Press, 1962.

Woolf, Leonard. *Downhill all the Way: An Autobiography of the Years 1919–1939.* London: The Hogarth Press, 1967.

Woolf, Leonard. *The Letters of Leonard Woolf.* Ed. Frederic Spotts. London: Bloomsbury, 1992.

Woolf, Virginia. *Between the Acts.* 1941. Ed. Frank Kermode. Oxford: Oxford University Press, 1992.

Woolf, Virginia. *The Captain's Death Bed and Other Essays.* Ed. Leonard Woolf. London: The Hogarth Press, 1950.

Woolf, Virginia. *The Collected Essays of Virginia Woolf.* Ed. Leonard Woolf. 4 vols. London: The Hogarth Press, 1966–67.

Woolf, Virginia. *The Complete Shorter Fiction of Virginia Woolf.* Ed. Susan Dick. London: The Hogarth Press, 1985.

Woolf, Virginia. *The Death of the Moth and Other Essays.* London: The Hogarth Press, 1942.

Woolf, Virginia. *The Diary of Virginia Woolf.* Ed. Anne Olivier Bell and Andrew McNeillie, 5 vols. London: The Hogarth Press, 1977–84.

Woolf, Virginia. *The Essays of Virginia Woolf.* Ed. Andrew McNeillie, 4 vols. London: The Hogarth Press, 1986–94.

Woolf, Virginia. *Flush.* 1933. Ed. Kate Flint. Oxford: Oxford University Press, 1998.

Woolf, Virginia. *Jacob's Room.* 1922. Ed. Kate Flint. Oxford: Oxford University Press, 1992.

Woolf, Virginia. *The Letters of Virginia Woolf.* Ed. Nigel Nicolson and Joanne Trautmann Banks, 6 vols. London: Chatto and Windus, 1975–80.

Woolf, Virginia. *The Mark on the Wall and Other Short Fiction.* Ed. David Bradshaw. Oxford: Oxford University Press, 2001.

Woolf, Virginia. *Moments of Being: Unpublished Autobiographical Writings.* Ed. Jeanne Schulkind. London: Chatto and Windus for Sussex University Press, 1976.

Woolf, Virginia. *Moments of Being.* Ed. Jeanne Schulkind, 2nd edn. San Diego: Harcourt Brace, 1985.

Woolf, Virginia. *Mrs. Dalloway.* 1925. Ed. David Bradshaw. Oxford: Oxford University Press, 2000.

Woolf, Virginia. 'Nature at Wembley.' 1924 Notebooks Vol. 2. British Library shelfmark Add. 51044–51046. 33–8.

Woolf, Virginia. *Orlando: A Biography*. Ed. Rachel Bowlby. Oxford: Oxford University Press, 1992.

Woolf, Virginia. *A Passionate Apprentice: the Early Journals*. Ed. Mitchell A. Leaska. London: The Hogarth Press, 1992.

Woolf, Virginia. *Roger Fry*. 1940. London: The Hogarth Press, 1991.

Woolf, Virginia. *The Voyage Out*. 1915. Ed. Lorna Sage. Oxford: Oxford University Press, 1992.

Woolf, Virginia. *The Waves*. 1931. Ed. Gillian Beer. Oxford: Oxford University Press, 1992.

Woolf, Virginia. 'White's Selborne.' *New Statesman and Nation* (30 September 1939): 460.

Woolf, Virginia. *The Years*. 1937. Ed. Hermione Lee. Oxford: Oxford University Press, 1992.

Worster, Donald. *Nature's Economy: A History of Ecological Ideas*. Cambridge: Cambridge University Press, 1977.

Yoshino, Ayako. '*Between the Acts* and Louis Napoleon Parker – The Creator of the Modern English Pageant.' *Critical Survey* 15.2 (2003): 49–60.

Zwerdling, Alex. *Virginia Woolf and the Real World*. Berkeley: University of California Press, 1986.

Index